PRIZE STORIES 1964

PRIZE
STORIES
1964:

EDITED AND WITH AN INTRODUCTION BY

THE
O. HENRY
AWARDS

RICHARD POIRIER

DOUBLEDAY & COMPANY, INC., GARDEN CITY, NEW YORK, 1964

PUBLISHER'S NOTE

The present volume is the forty-fourth in the O. Henry Memorial Award series. No collections appeared in 1952 and 1953, when the continuity of the series was interrupted by the death of Herschel Brickell, who had been the editor for ten years.

In 1918 the Society of Arts and Sciences met to vote upon a monument to the American master of the short story, O. Henry. They decided that this memorial should be in the form of two prizes for the best short stories published by American authors in American magazines during the year 1919. From this beginning, the memorial developed into an annual anthology of the best American short stories, published, with the exception of the years mentioned above, by Doubleday & Company, Inc. Blanche Colton Williams, one of the founders of the awards, was editor from 1919 to 1932; Harry Hansen took over from 1933 to 1940; Herschel Brickell from 1941 to 1951; Paul Engle from 1954 to 1959; Mary Stegner in 1960; and Richard Poirier from 1961 until now.

Doubleday has also published First-Prize Stories from the O. Henry Memorial Awards 1919–1963.

The stories chosen for this volume were published in the period from the winter of 1962 to the summer of 1963. A list of the magazines consulted appears at the back of the book. The choice of stories and the selection of prize winners are exclusively the responsibility of the editor.

The editor wishes to express his gratitude to Mr. William Abrahams for his help in the preparation of this volume, and will welcome him as associate editor in the 1965 edition of O. Henry Prize Stories.

CONTENTS

INTRODUCTION: THE O. HENRY PRIZE STORIES, 1964

How do we really know that a story is "about" anything beyond the mere anecdotes that are to some extent its subject? This question will no doubt seem unnecessary to anyone whose idea of taking fiction seriously is to make it into a form of history or mythology. Most academic courses in American fiction continue to be organized around wars, depressions, social movements, and catch phrases like "the lost generation." (I remember one examination question asking what Faulkner's "The Bear," published in 1940, could tell us about the '40s!) And there have been a number of anthologies proposing that fiction be packaged by the decade. One does not need to be told that this is a convenience, but to whom?

Of course really to be serious about fiction is to be wary of turning it into anything else, and to accept a kind of limitation not customary in most journalistic or, for that matter, in much academic commentary. The limitation involves a reluctance to talk big, a refusal to expand the themes of a story. The effort is rather in the more modest but more difficult direction of seeing how and how well—if at all—the reader is made to care about extended significances.

Quite recently, the fiction of James Baldwin has been treated as if it were nearly absolved from this kind of critical attention by virtue of its relevance to racial issues. It is itself an ironic comment on the way those issues are being discussed that Mr. Baldwin apparently cannot be taken seriously (i.e. critically) as a novelist because he is also, in a brilliantly polemical way, a spokesman for his race.

Fiction is unquestionably the form of literature that, more than any other, reflects contemporary political and social problems. In this volume, for instance, Irwin Shaw's "The Inhabitants of Venus" undoubtedly appeals to predictable public interest in our possible attitudes toward German Nazis, pre- and postwar, and Lillian Ross's "Night and Day, Day and Night" directs a Swiftian wit at forms of behavior that become daily more observable even while being increasingly the object of satire. In her story, which has since become part of a novel, psychoanalytical categories and jargon are a rationalization for obtuse forms of social fakery, for the hopped-up geniality of suburban house parties, and the self-deceptions that are the price of adjusting to the "gang," or the "kids," as they are sometimes called. Kitty Lenz "could afford to stand around telling the truth," complains Spencer Fifield. "She was on the outside of everything anyway." The effectiveness of Miss Ross's indictment is inseparable from the poised inexplicitness of her satire: she lets her characters be quite happy while they are hanging themselves. Like Miss Ross, Bernard Malamud in "The Jewbird" expresses his meanings as much in his satiric manner as in his ostensible subject, which is racial bias. While there is considerable mimicry of Jewish conversational rhythms in his story, much of it is given to a rather tawdry bird who somehow speaks English and claims refuge from "Anti-Semeets": "I'm running. I'm flying, but I'm also running." The use of a speaking, sometimes *dovening* Jewbird as a central character is surprisingly convincing and creates a distance between the author and his material evidently necessary to his articulation of quite complicated attitudes about a personally painful subject.

To ask how a story makes us care, often in unanticipated ways, about issues of current importance is to involve ourselves mostly with elements of performance, with a writer's own presence in the pace, the stress, the sounds of his fiction. A story by one of the most distinguished writers in this collection, "The Scream on 57th Street" by Hortense Calisher, has been described by a reputable commentator as "perhaps the best study we have yet had of lonely widowhood." To which one must reply that a story is a story, not a study, and that what might well be said in this instance is that by being at a few points so emphatic about the theme of loneliness (the scream turns out to sound like "alone—oh") Miss Calisher does herself the disservice of wasting some of the other suggestions that emerge from her subtle fashioning of detail. A similar tendency is evident in the sadly funny story "So I'm Not Lady Chatterley So Better I Should Know It Now." Under the pseudonym "Sara," the author is apparently a woman who has developed a very sensitive eye and ear to elements of Jewish life in Boston and New York. But from a relaxed and

loving intimacy in the portraiture of the girl and her boy friend,
Moe Schlepp, the author lifts her attention now and then to
something more anxiously ambitious: "It was, in short, a summer
of war, and of girls approaching womanhood without men and a
place fast loosening an outworn restraint." No doubt these considerations of time and social change are necessary to the dis-
interested tenderness with which the narrator looks back at her
characters. What is not at all apparent, however, is the necessity
at such points for a puffy portentousness of tone momentarily
swelling the story to a size that cannot be filled, much to their
credit, by two such lovingly drab young people. I criticize these
stories because each of them seemed at times worthy of one of
the first three prizes. They are quite strong enough to bear criticism, indeed to have initiated the very kinds of discrimination
that led to a preference for the stories by John Cheever, J. C.
Oates, and Margaret Shedd.

John Cheever's fiction has never been sufficiently praised for
the extraordinary deftness with which it probes the chaos beneath
the fashions of *The New Yorker* ethos, even when his stories are
published in that magazine. These fashions include the built-in
defenses of being a bit self-critical in order not to appear callow,
of being a bit cynical in order really to lament the lost glories
of childhood at the shore, of being a bit skeptical in order to
justify an ultimate placidity about the emotional stalemates that
are thought to be a sign of maturity. Cheever adopts these fashions as the merely initial condition of his characters and of the
community of Proxmire Manor, but he goes far beyond them in
suggesting that the assemblage of his people does not constitute
a society at all but a kind of dream, itself a Cythera, not unlike
Jessica's "emotional island," a place "ruled by the absolute authority and range of her desire." It is not possible for her or for the
reader to ascertain the boundaries of the society in which she
actually lives, to put together some of its elegant pretentions with
some of the attendant evidences of poverty and simplicity encountered by Jessica in her affair with the grocery boy.

The characters in Cheever's story are motivated by visions of
opportunity caught only in accidental glimpses and about which
they can never be articulate. They feel a pulsing in the natural
world and in their veins so smothered and remote that the public

movement of individual lives can only be clumsily synchronized
with it. The story, though unruffled on its surface, is nonetheless
full of lyrical interruptions that have a loveliness never woven into
the recognizable texture of daily life: the intense, unfathomable
intimacy that a mother feels for her baby son while doing nothing
more than enjoying the "comfortable slovenliness" of eating with
him from a can of figs, the glimpse through the window of a
hospital room where a newly arrived pregnant woman unbuttons
her dress and cradles her husband's head between her breasts,
the sense given—and seldom caught in literature—of how the
physical promptings of early sex, graphically described in the character of Emile, get expressed in an energy of idealism: "Oh I
want—I want to do so well." Cheever never announces his
"significance," and his prose lets us share the naggingly painful
mysteriousness that seeps into the consciousness both of the hopeful adolescent and of the increasingly dream-ridden older woman.
That they should share unknowingly this sense of mystery while
being otherwise related only in their ridiculous assignations is
one of the great achievements of the story. It is Cheever's way of
honoring something in life which is all but invisible in the ambi-
ence he presents. In doing so he creates images that escape the
customary banalities about the mechanization of modern life and
show instead, with remarkable intelligence, the confusion of impulse and fabricated sensation with which we are all at times
strangely visited. Thus, from the Moonlite Drive-In theater where
Emile takes his girl friend, one can hear a noise, like the sea,
"of traffic on the great Northern Expressway that flows southward
from Montreal to the Shenandoah, engorging in its cloverleafs
and brilliantly engineered gradings the green playing fields, rose
gardens, barns, farms, meadows, trout streams, forests, homesteads,
and churches of the golden past." Emile sits naked with his girl
in the back seat of the car "as if the rose gardens and playing
fields buried under the expressway were enjoying a revenge." A
passage of this kind illustrates how writing can be in the best
sense seriously expressive of large propositions. The prose allows
us a very rewarding honesty of response to Emile's conduct: its
vulgarity is worthy, necessary, funny, even, within the geographi-
cally historical dimensions alluded to, noble, while being for all

that still shabby to a degree that makes us at once like and feel
sorry for him.

The seasonal and geographical details in Cheever's story give
it an amplitude apparent also in the opening of Wallace Stegner's
"Carrion Spring," placed last in this collection with the intention
of ending it strongly, and to some extent in Shirley Schoonover's
"Old and Country Tale." In both of these, in Sallie Bingham's
"The Banks of the Ohio" and in David Stacton's "The Metamorphosis of Kenko" there are discoveries of what Stacton calls "the
wonder of a recognized affinity" between people and objects of
the natural world. In proposing this affinity, however, the stories
are quite different from one another, the toughest of them, the
one least persuaded of any easy "affinity," being Mr. Stegner's
often brutal, specifically knowledgeable story. An "affinity" with
nature is recognized by his characters only after they show in
themselves a hardness of self-hood that is a match for what the
seasons have done to them. In quite another tone, Mr. Stacton,
among the most careful and talented stylists in this volume, is also
tough minded about extending the significance of his story by
analogies between nature and human activities. His central character is a fourteenth-century Buddhist recluse who has retired
from the Japanese court to escape a requirement of marriage.
Written in a prose that reflects the very world of refined courtli-
ness from which he has absented himself, the story is urbanely
gossipy, sophisticated, and literary: "and though one may, in the
very best prose, compare a woman's beauty to a young pine tree,
what do you say about a pine tree when there is no woman to
compare it to?" The suave mockery in this sentence suggests that
Kenko knows little about the uniqueness of a pine tree or of a
woman, that for him one can exist only in a metaphorical compar-
ison to the other, and that apparently he has never felt any love
for either. What is most admirable here is that Stacton never
anxiously checks, for thematic clarity, the multiple pleasures offered by such a sentence.

Other stories in this volume are, like Stacton's, relatively peculiar in their circumstances. Such stories can become of general implication because there is nothing so peculiar that it cannot—by an
effort of style—be made coherent with what the reader already
accepts as reality. Of the stories that are remote from contem-

porary life, or highly selective in the particular problems with
which they deal, none will perhaps seem more esoteric than J. C.
Oates's "Stigmata." The opening of the story carries some re-
assurance, however, that we are to be concerned less importantly
with ancient forms of stigmatism, of bearing the wounds of Christ,
than with stigmatism in a more contemporary sense. It becomes
finally a refraction of a character's capacity to see things, caused
in the old man by a failure to love and in his youngest son by
the wounds of childhood, of family rivalry, of encounters with
the demands of contemporary life expressed in economics, social
habits, even architecture. The style of the opening sentence is
remarkably calm in revealing a violent shift of feeling, ultimately
to be registered in the story as a whole, from general reverence
to specific distaste: "Though his father had been at St. Jerome's
Home for the Aged for five or six years now, Walt Turner had
never seen the home before—he had seen his father, of course, at
various Christmases, at various houses of brothers and sisters, and
the old man had journeyed down out of these saintly hills one
fall to attend a Sunday High Mass sung by his eldest son, newly
ordained a priest—but Walt had never visited him at the home
and had never imagined visiting him, since he did not like his
father particularly." The achieved modulations of this sentence are
among the signs that Mrs. Oates is a writer of major promise.
The style encourages the reader to a flexibility of attitudes and
to an ironic comprehension that will protect him from the parti-
sanship called for by the characters. Walt's final view of the evidence of his father's sainthood is that it is a punishment for the
old man's never having accepted the pains of common humanity.
This may also be the author's view, but Walt expresses it in a
much cruder version of Mrs. Oates's own polished acerbity,
sufficiently cruder to suggest that he can only look at the signs of
stigmata on his father through the stigmatisms in his own nature.

    That a character can glimpse an essential aspect of the truth and
yet give us an unsatisfactory account of the whole of it is one of
the conditions cherished by any writer of fiction. It is what allows
him to make the manner in which facts are related, the particular
slant given them by an observer, all as expressive of social, historical, and psychological significance as are the facts themselves.
George Zorn's story of a drably ordinary man bewitched by

vampires (or is he?) is one instance, its effectiveness being that the action can be explained either by supernatural or merely by accidental causes. Another, especially poignant example is Margaret Shedd's "The Everlasting Witness." Mrs. Shedd places her story in Mexico City, not merely because she knows it, having for years sustained the Center for Mexican Writers, but also because only in a foreign city can the central character exercise her necessary illusions, if such they are, about the fate of her son. We are allowed to glare, so to speak, into the workings of a desperate hope, with a view totally unencumbered by the social requirements which would force the woman, were she at home, to sift and correct her impressions. Marian yearns for the confusions of what is unfamiliar, her escape from order and security being her only way of maintaining the scraps of hope that are the benefit of uncertainty. By making compassionate allowances to this woman's view of things while nonetheless refusing wholly to authenticate it, the story moves beyond the seeming ingenuity of its initial circumstances and becomes an eloquent drama of a mind refusing to cope with the issues of life and death.

Stories need not, of course, be "about" anything so large as the issues of life and death. George Lanning in "Something Just for Me" and Philip Roth in "Novotny's Pain" actually seem to be dissuading us from any such enlargements of the pathetic and tawdry lives of their characters. Mr. Roth is particulary insistent upon the very limited consequences of Novotny's troubles, however locally terrifying. Like Saul Bellow, he shows a reluctance to make his characters available to the moral and literary metaphors that often heighten, complicate, and confuse our lives. Living is difficult enough, such a reluctance implies, without the colorings of sometimes irrelevant and self-aggrandizing metaphysics. Which is to say not that daily living has no metaphysical implications, but rather that in discovering what they are we should look at life much as we look at fiction—with an open, lively, but skeptical expectation.

—RICHARD POIRIER

PRIZE STORIES 1964

JOHN CHEEVER was born in Quincy, Massachusetts, and attended Thayer Academy. He is the author of *The Wapshot Chronicle*, which was awarded the National Book Award in 1958, *The Housebreaker of Shady Hill, Some People, Places and Things That Will Not Appear in My Next Novel*, and *The Wapshot Scandal*.

The Embarkment for Cythera

Tom and Jessica Coliver lived in Proxmire Manor, a place that was known up and down the suburban railroad line as the place where the lady got arrested. The incident had taken place five or six years before, but it had the endurance of a legend, and the lady had seemed briefly to be the genius of the pretty place. The facts are simple. With the exception of one robbery, still unsolved, the eight-man police force of Proxmire Manor had never found anything to do. Their only usefulness was to direct traffic at weddings and large cocktail parties. They listened day and night on the interstate police radio to the crimes and alarms in other communities—car thefts, mayhem, drunkenness, and murder—but the blotter in Proxmire Manor was clean. The burden of this idleness on their self-esteem was heavy as, armed with pistols and bandoleers of ammunition, they spent their days writing parking tickets for the cars left at the railroad station. It was like a child's game, ticketing commuters for the most trifling infractions of the rules the police themselves invented, and they played it enthusiastically.

The lady—Mrs. Lemuel Jameson—had similar problems. Her children were away at school, her housework was done by a maid, and though she played cards and lunched with friends, she was often made ill-tempered by abrasive boredom. Coming home from an unsuccessful shopping trip in New York one afternoon, she found her car ticketed for being a little over a white line. She tore the ticket to pieces. Later that afternoon, a policeman found the pieces in the dirt and took them to the police station, where they were pasted together.

The police were excited, of course, at this open challenge to their authority. Mrs. Jameson was served with a summons. She called her friend Judge Flint—he was a member of the Club—and asked him to fix it. He said that he would, but later that afternoon he had an attack of acute appendicitis and was taken to the hospital. When Mrs. Jameson's name was called in traffic court and there was no response, the police were alert. A warrant for her arrest was issued, the first such warrant in years. In the morning two patrolmen, heavily armed and in fresh uniforms and in the company of an old police matron, drove to Mrs. Jameson's house with the warrant. A maid opened the door and said that Mrs. Jameson was sleeping. With at least a hint of force, they entered the beautiful drawing room and told the maid to wake Mrs. Jameson. When Mrs. Jameson heard that the police were downstairs, she was indignant. She refused to move. The maid went downstairs, and in a minute or two Mrs. Jameson heard the heavy steps of the policemen. She was horrified. Would they dare enter her bedroom? The ranking officer spoke to her from the hall. "You get out of bed, lady, and come with us, or we'll get you up." Mrs. Jameson began to scream. The police matron, reaching for her shoulder holster, entered the bedroom. Mrs. Jameson went on screaming. The matron told her to get up and dress or they would take her to the station house in her night clothes. When Mrs. Jameson started for the bathroom, the matron followed her and she began to scream again. She was hysterical. She screamed at the policemen when she encountered them in the upstairs hallway, but she let herself be led out to the car and driven to the station house. Here she began to scream again. She finally paid the one-dollar fine and was sent home in a taxi.

Mrs. Jameson was determined to have the policemen fired, and the moment she walked into her house she began to organize her campaign. Counting over her neighbors for someone who would be eloquent and sympathetic, she thought of Peter Dolmetch, a freelance televison writer, who rented the Fulsoms' gatehouse. No one liked him, but Mrs. Jameson sometimes invited him to her cocktail parties, and he was indebted to her. She called and told him her story. "I can't believe it, darling," he said. She said that she was asking him, because of his natural eloquence, to defend her. "I'm against Fascism, darling," he said, "wherever it raises its ugly head." She then called the mayor and demanded a hearing. It was set for eight-thirty that night. Mr. Jameson happened to be away on business. She called a few friends, and by noon everyone in Proxmire Manor knew that she had been humiliated by a policewoman, who followed her into the bathroom and sat on the edge of the tub while she dressed, and that Mrs. Jameson had been taken to the station house at the point of a gun. Fifteen or twenty neighbors showed up for the hearing. The mayor and his councilmen numbered seven, and the two patrolmen and the matron were also there. When the meeting was called to order, Peter stood and asked, "Has Fascism come to Proxmire Manor? Is the ghost of Hitler stalking our tree-shaded streets? Must we, in the privacy of our homes, dread the tread of the Storm Troopers' boots on our sidewalks and the pounding of the mailed fist on the door?" On and on he went. He must have spent all day writing it. It was all aimed at Hitler, with only a few passing references to Mrs. Jameson. The audience began to cough, to yawn, and then to excuse themselves. When the protest was dismissed and the meeting adjourned, there was no one left but the principals, and Mrs. Jameson's case was lost, but it was not forgotten. The conductor on the train, passing the green hills, would say, "They arrested a lady there yesterday"; then, "They arrested a lady there last month"; and presently, "That's the place where the lady got arrested." That was Proxmire Manor.

The village stood on three leafy hills north of the city, and was handsome and comfortable, and seemed to have eliminated, through adroit social pressures, the thorny side of human nature. This knowledge was forced on Jessica Coliver one afternoon when a neighbor, Laura Hilliston, came in for a glass of sherry. "What I wanted to tell you," Laura said, "is that Grace Lockhart is a slut." Jessica heard the words down the length of the room as she was pouring sherry, and wondered if she had heard correctly, the remark seemed so callous. What kind of tidings were these to carry from house to house? She was never sure—how could one be, it was all so experimental—of the exact nature and intent of the society in which she lived, but did it really embrace this kind of thing?

Laura Hilliston laughed. Her laughter was healthy and her teeth were white. She sat on the sofa, a heavy woman with her feet planted squarely on the rug. Her hair was brown. So were her large, soft eyes. Her face was fleshy, but with a fine ruddiness. She was long married and had three grown sons, but she had recently stepped out of the country of love—briskly and without a backward glance, as if she had spent too much time in its steaming jungles. She was through with all *that*, she had told her wretched husband. She had put on some perfume for the visit, and she wore a thick necklace of false gold that threw a brassy light up onto her features. Her shoes had high heels, and her dress was tight, but these lures were meant to establish her social position and not to catch the eyes of a man.

"I just thought you ought to know," Laura said. "It isn't mere gossip. She has been intimate with just about everybody. I mean the milkman, and that old man who reads the gas meter. That nice fresh-faced boy who used to deliver the laundry lost his job because of her. The truck used to be parked there for hours at a time. Then she began to buy her groceries from Narobi's, and one of the delivery boys had quite a lot of trouble. Her husband's a nice-looking man, and they say he puts up with it for the sake of the children. He adores the children. But what I really wanted to say is that we're getting her out. They have a twenty-eight-thousand-dollar mortgage with a repair clause, and Charlie Peterson at the bank has just told them that they'll have to put a new roof on the house. Of course, they can't afford this, and so Bumps Trigger is going to give them what they paid for the place and they'll have to go somewhere else. I just thought you might like to know."

"Thank you," Jessica said. "Will you have some more sherry?"

"Oh, no, thank you. I must get along. We're going to the Wishings'. Aren't you?"

"Yes, we are," Jessica said.

Laura put on a short mink jacket and stepped out of the house with that grace, that circumspection, that gentle and unmistakable poise of a lady who has said farewell to love.

Then the back doorbell rang. The cook was out with the baby, and so Jessica went to the back door and let in one of Mr. Narobi's grocery boys. She wondered if he was the one Mrs. Lockhart had tried to seduce. He was a slender young man with brown hair and blue eyes that shed their light evenly, as the eyes of the young will, and were so unlike the eyes of the old—those haggard lanterns that shed no light at all. She would have liked to ask him about Mrs. Lockhart, but this, of course, was not possible. She gave him a quarter tip, and he thanked her politely, and she went upstairs to bathe and dress for the Wishings' dance.

The Wishings' dance was an annual affair. As Mrs. Wishing kept explaining, they gave it each year before the rugs were put down. There was a three-piece orchestra, a fine dinner with glazed salmon, bœuf en daube, a dark, flowery claret, and a bar for drinks. By quarter after ten, Jessica felt bored and would have asked Tom to take her home, but he was in another room. Lovely and high-spirited, she was seldom bored. Watching the dancers, she thought of poor Mrs. Lockhart, who was being forced out of this society. On the other hand, she knew how easy, how mistaken it was to assume that the exceptions—the drunkard and the lewd— penetrate, through their excesses, the carapace of immortal society. Did Mrs. Lockhart know more about mankind than she, Jessica? Who did have the power of penetration? Was it the priest who saw how their hands trembled when they reached for the chalice, the doctor who had seen them stripped of their clothing, or the psychiatrist who had seen them stripped of their obdurate pride, and who was now dancing with a fat woman in a red dress? And what was penetration worth? What did it matter that the drunken and unhappy woman in the corner dreamed frequently that she was being chased through a grove of trees by a score of naked lyric poets? Jessica was bored, and she thought her dancing neighbors were bored, too. Loneliness was one thing, and she knew herself how sweet it could make lights and company seem, but boredom was something else, and why, in this most prosperous and equitable world, should everyone seem so bored and disappointed? She asked Bumps Trigger to get her a drink, and he brought her back a glass of dark bourbon. She felt a profound nostalgia, a longing for some emotional island or peninsula that she had not even discerned in her dreams. She seemed to know something about its character—it was not a paradise, but its elevating possibilities of emotional richness and freedom stirred her. It was the stupendous feeling that one could do much better than this; that the reality was not Mrs. Wishing's dance; that the world was not divided into rigid parliaments of good and evil but was ruled by the absolute authority and range of her desire.

She began to dance then, and danced until three, when the band stopped playing. Her feelings had changed from boredom to a ruthless greed for pleasure. She did not ever want the party to stop, and stayed until dawn.

On Sunday night, Tom took a plane to Detroit, planning to be gone three weeks. On Monday night, alone in the house with her son and the cook, Jessica had a sentimental dream. The landscape was romantic. It was evening, and since there was no trace anywhere of mechanical things—automobile tracks and the noise of planes—it seemed to her to be evening in another century. The sun had set, but a polished afterglow lighted up the sky. There was a winding stream with alders, and on the farther banks the ruins of a castle. She spread a white cloth on the grass and set this with long-necked wine bottles and a loaf of new bread, whose fragrance and warmth was a part of the dream. Upstream a man was swimming naked in a pool. He spoke to her in French, and it was part of the dream's lightness that it all happened in another country, another time. She saw the man pull himself up onto the bank and dry himself with a cloth while she went on setting out the things for supper.

She was waked from this dream by the barking of a dog. It was 3 A.M. She heard the wind. It was changing its quarter and beginning to blow from the northwest. She was about to fall asleep when she heard the front door come open. Sweat started at her armpits and her young heart strained its muscles, although she knew it was only the wind that had opened the door. Not long ago, a thief had broken into a house in the neighborhood. In the garden, behind a lilac bush, a pile of cigarette ends had been found, where he must have waited patiently for hours for the lights of the house to be turned out. He had made an opening in a window with a glass cutter, rifled a wall safe of cash and jewelry, and left by the front door. In reporting the theft, the police had described his movements in detail: He had waited in the garden. He had entered by a back window. He had gone through the kitchen and pantry into the dining room. But who was he? Had he been tall or short, heavy or slender? Had his heart throbbed with terror in the dark rooms, or had he experienced the thief's supreme sense of triumph over a pretentious and gullible society? He had left traces of himself—cigarette ends, footprints, broken glass, and a rifled safe—but he had never been found, and so he remained disembodied and faceless.

It was the wind, she told herself; no thief would have left the door standing open. Now she could feel the cold air spreading through the house, rising up the stairs and moving the curtains in the hall. She got out of bed and put on a wrapper. She turned on the hall light and started down the stairs, asking herself what it was she was afraid of in the dark rooms below. She was afraid of the dark, like a primitive or a child, but why? What was there about darkness that threatened her? She was afraid of the dark as she was afraid of the unknown, and what was the unknown but the force of evil, and why should she be afraid of this? She turned on the lights one after another. The rooms were empty, and the wind was enjoying the liberty of the place, scattering the mail on the hall table and peering under the edge of the rug. The wind was cold, and she shivered as she closed and locked the front door, but now she was unafraid and very much herself. In the morning she had a cold.

The doctor came several times during that week, and when she got no better he ordered her to go to the hospital. In the middle of the morning, she went upstairs to pack. She had been to the hospital in recent years only once, to have her son, and then the drives of pregnancy had carried her unthinkingly through her preparations. This time she carried no life within her; she carried, instead, an infection. And, alone in her bedroom, choosing a nightgown and a hairbrush, she felt as if she had been singled out to make some mysterious voyage. She was not a sentimental woman, and she had no sad thoughts about parting from the pleasant room she shared with her husband. She felt weary but not sick, although there was a cutting pain in her chest. A stranger watching her would have thought she was insane. Why did she empty the carnations into the wastebasket and rinse out the vase?

Why did she count her stockings, lock her jewelry box and hide the key, glance at her bank balance, dust off the mantelpiece, and stand in the middle of the room, looking as if she was listening to distant music? The foolish impulse to dust the mantelpiece was irresistible, but she had no idea why she did it, and anyhow it was time to go.

The hospital was new, and conscientious efforts had been made to make it a cheerful place, but her loveliness—you might say her elegance—was put at a disadvantage by the undisguisable atmosphere of regimentation, and she looked terribly out of place. A wheelchair was brought for her, but she refused to use it. She would have looked crestfallen and ridiculous, she knew, with her coat bunched up around her middle and her purse in her lap. A nurse took her upstairs and led her into a pleasant room, where she was told to undress and get into bed. While she was undressing, someone brought her lunch on a tray. It was a small matter, but she found it disconcerting to be given a chop and some canned fruit while she was half naked and before the clocks had struck noon. She ate her lunch dutifully and the doctor came at two and told her she could count on being in the hospital ten days or two weeks. He would call Tom. She fell asleep, and woke at five with a fever.

The imagery of her fever was similar to the imagery of love. Her reveries were spacious, and she seemed to be promised the revelation of some truth that lay at the center of the labyrinthine and palatial structures where she wandered. The fever, as it got higher, eased the pain in her breast and made her indifferent to the heavy beating of her heart. The fever dreams seemed like a healthy employment of her imagination to distract her from the struggle that went on in her breast. She was standing at the head of a broad staircase with red walls. Many people were climbing the stairs. They had the attitudes of pilgrims. The climb was gruelling and lengthy, and when she reached the summit she found herself in a grove of lemon trees and lay down on the grass to rest. When she woke from this dream, her nightgown and the bed linen were soaked with sweat. She rang for a nurse, who changed them.

She felt much better when this was done. She felt that the fever had been a crisis and that, passing safely through it, she had triumphed over her illness. At nine the nurse gave her some medicine and said good night. Some time later she felt the lassitude of fever returning. She rang, but no one came, and she could not resist the confusion in her mind as her temperature rose. The labored beating of her heart sounded like a drum. She confused it with a drum in her mind, and saw a circle of barbaric dancers. The dance was long, rising to a climax, and at the moment of the climax, when she thought her heart would burst, she woke, shaking with a fresh chill and wet with sweat. A nurse finally came and changed her clothing and her linen again. She was relieved to be dry and warm. The two attacks of fever had weakened her but left her with a feeling of childish contentment. She felt wakeful, got out of bed, and by supporting herself on the furniture made her way to the window to see the night.

While she watched, clouds covered the moon. It must have been late, because most of the windows were dark. Then a window in the wall at her left was lighted, and she saw a nurse bring a young woman and her husband into a room identical with the one where she sat in the dark. The young woman was pregnant but not having labor pains. She undressed in the bathroom and got into bed while her husband was unpacking her bag. The window, like all the others, was hung with a Venetian blind, but no one had bothered to close the slats, and the exposure of this intimate scene, long past midnight, was startling. When the unpacking was done, he unfastened the front of her nightgown, knelt beside the bed, and laid his head on her breasts. He remained this way for several minutes without moving. Then he got up—he must have heard the nurse approach—and covered his wife. The nurse came in and snapped the blind shut.

Jessica heard a night bird calling, and wondered what bird it was, what it looked like, what it was up to, what its prey was. There was a deep octave of thunder, magnificent and homely, as if someone in heaven had moved a chest of drawers. Then there was some lightning, distant and discolored, and a moment later a shower of rain dressed the earth. The sound of the rain seemed to Jessica, with the cutting pain in her breast, like the repeated attentions of a lover. It fell on the flat roofs of the hospital, the lawns, and the leaves in the wood. The pain in her chest seemed to spread and sharpen in proportion to her stubborn love

of the night, and she felt for the first time in her life an unwilling-
ness to leave any of this; a fear as senseless and powerful as her
fear of the dark when she went down to shut the door; a horror
of death.

Tom got home the next day, and came to the hospital every
evening. Facing her in an armchair, he drank whiskey and read
the paper. One night he kissed her, locked the door, and began
to throw off his clothing. To her own astonishment, she began
to cry.

"I'm sorry," he said. "I wasn't thinking. I suppose you must
still be tired." He meant to be gentle, but he was only baffled,
and when he sat down in the chair again, with his face half in the
light, she saw the bewilderment he always suffered when he was
frustrated in expressing the importunate, cheerful, and vulgar
demands of his body.

At the end of two weeks she went home, although she still
felt unlike herself and tired easily. The drugs that cured her
depressed her. She felt, like any convalescent, unnaturally sentient,
as if there was some persistent imbalance in her appetites, her loss
of strength, giving her an illusion of spirituality—which did not,
however, overwhelm her abundant common sense. She stood, late
one afternoon, at her window watching the ring of golden light
that crowned the eastern hills at that season and time of day.
It rested also on the Babcocks' lawn, the Fillmores' ranch house,
the stone walls of the church, the Thompsons' chimney—
lambent, and as yellow and clear as strained honey, and really
a ring, because, as she watched, she saw at the base of the hill a
clear demarcation between the yellow light and the rising dark,
and watched the band of light lift past the Babcocks' lawn, the
Fillmores' ranch house, the stone walls of the church, and the
Thompsons' chimney, up into thin air. The street was empty,
or nearly so. Everyone in Proxmire Manor had two cars and no
one walked, with the exception of old Mr. Cosden, who belonged to the generation that took constitutionals. Up the street
he came, his blue eyes fixed on the last piece of yellow light that
touched the church steeple, as if exclaiming to himself, "How
wonderful, how wonderful it is!" He passed, and then a much
stranger figure took her attention—a tall man with unusually long

arms. He was a stray, she decided; he must live in the slums of Parthenia. In his right hand he carried an umbrella and a pair of rubbers. He was terribly stooped, and to see where he was going had to crane his neck forward and upward like an adder. He had not bent his back over a whetstone or a workbench or under the weight of a brick hod or at any other honest task. It was the stoop of weak-mindedness, abnegation, and bewilderment. He had never had any occasion to straighten his back in self-esteem. Stooped with shyness as a child, stooped with loneliness as a youth, stooped now under an invisible burden of social disregard, he walked with his long arms reaching nearly to his knees. His wide, thin mouth was set in a silly half grin, meaningless and sad, but the best face he had been able to hit on. As he approached the house, the beating of her heart seemed to correspond to his footsteps, the cutting pain returned to her breast, and she felt the return of her fear of darkness, evil, and death. Carrying his umbrella and rubbers, although there was not a cloud in the sky, he duck-footed out of sight.

A few nights later, Jessica was driving back from the village of Parthenia. The street was lighted erratically by the few stores that hung on at the edge of town—general stores smelling of stale bread and bitter oranges, where those in the neighborhood who were too lazy, too tired, or too infirm to go to the palatial shopping centers bought their coffee rings, beer, and hamburgers. The darkness of the street was sparsely, irregularly checkered with light, and she saw the tall man crossing one of these apertures, throwing a long, crooked shadow ahead of him on the paving. He held a heavy bag of groceries in each arm. He was no more stooped than before—the curvature of his spine seemed set—but the bags must be heavy, and she pitied him. She drove on, evoking defensively the worlds of difference that lay between them and the chance that he would have misunderstood her kindness had she offered to give him a ride. But when she had completed her defense it seemed so shallow, idle, and selfish that she turned the car around in her own driveway and drove back toward Parthenia. Her best instinct was to help him—to make some peace between his figure and her irrational fear of death—and why should she deny herself this? He would have passed the lighted stores by this time, she decided, and she drove slowly up the dark street, looking for his stooped figure. When she saw him, she turned the car around and stopped. "Can I help you?" she asked. "Can I give you a ride? You seem to have so much to carry." He turned and looked at the beautiful stranger without quite relaxing his half grin, and she wondered if he wasn't a deaf-mute as well as weak-minded. Then a look of distrust touched the grin. There was no question about what he was feeling. She was from that world that had gulled him, pelted him with snowballs, and rifled his lunch-box. His mother had told him to beware of strangers and here was a beautiful stranger, perhaps the most dangerous of all. "No!" he said. "No, no!" She drove on, wondering what was at the bottom of her impulse; wondering, in the end, why she should scrutinize a simple attempt at kindness.

On Thursday the maid was off, and Jessica took care of the baby. He slept after lunch, and she woke him at four, lifting him out of his crib and letting the blankets fall. They were alone. The house was quiet. She carried him into the kitchen, put him in his high chair, and opened a can of figs. Sleepy and docile and pale, he followed her with his eyes, and smiled sweetly when their eyes met. His shift was stained and wet, and she wore a wrapper. She sat by him at the table, with her face only a few inches from his, and they spooned the figs out of the can. He shuddered now and then with what seemed to be pleasure. The quiet house, the still kitchen, the pale and docile boy in his stained shift, her round white arms on the table, the comfortable slovenliness of eating from a can were all part of an intimacy so intense and yet so tranquil that it seemed to her as if she and the baby were the same flesh and blood, subjects of the same heart, all mingled and at ease. What a comfort, she thought, is one's skin. . . . But it was time then to change the boy, time to dress herself, time to take up cheerfully the other side of her life. Carrying the child through the living room, she saw, out of the window, the stooped figure with his rubbers and umbrella.

A wind was blowing, and he moved indifferently through a diagonal fall of yellow leaves, craning his neck like an adder, his back bent under its impossible burden. She held the baby's head against her breast, foolishly, instinctively, as if to protect his eyes from some communicable evil. She turned away from the window, and shortly afterward there was a loud pounding on the back door. How had he found where she lived, and what did he want? He might have recognized her car in the driveway; he might have asked who she was, the village was that small. He had not come to thank her for her attempted kindness. She felt sure of that. He had come—in his foolishness—to accuse her of something. Was he dangerous? Was there any danger left in Proxmire Manor? She put the boy down and went toward the back door, summoning her self-respect. When she opened it, there was Mr. Narobi's good-looking grocery boy.

He made it all seem laughable—came in beaming and with a kind of radiance that seemed to liberate her from this absurd chain of anxieties.

"You're new?" she asked.

"Yes."

"I don't know your name."

"Emile. It's a funny name. My father was French."

"Did he come from France?"

"Oh, no. Quebec. French Canadian."

"What does he do?"

"When people used to ask me that, I used to say, 'He plays the harp.' He's dead. He died when I was little. My mother works at the florist's—Barnum's—on Green Street. Maybe you know her?"

"I don't think I do. Would you like a beer?"

"Sure. Why not? It's my last stop."

She asked if he wanted something to eat, and got him some crackers and cheese.

"I'm always hungry," he said.

She brought the baby into the kitchen and they all three sat at the table while he ate and drank. Stuffing his mouth with cheese, he seemed to be a child. His gaze was clear and disarming. She couldn't meet it without a stir in her blood. And was this sluttishness? Was she worse than Mrs. Lockhart? Would she be dragged figuratively out of Proxmire Manor at the tail of a cart? She didn't care.

"Nobody ever gave me a beer before," he said. "They give me Cokes, sometimes. I guess they don't think I'm old enough. But I drink. Martinis, whiskey, everything."

"How old are you?"

"Nineteen. Now I have to go."

"Please don't go," she said.

He stood at the table, covering her with his wide gaze, and she wondered what would happen if she reached out to him. Would he run out of the kitchen? Would he shout, "Unhand me!"? He seemed ripe; he seemed ready for the picking; and yet there was something else in the corner of his eyes—reserve, wariness. He perhaps had a vision of something better, and if he had, she would encourage him with all her heart. Go and love the drum majorette, the girl next door.

"Oh, I'd like to stay," he said. "It's nice here. But it's Thursday, and I have to take my mother shopping. Thank you very much."

The Moonlite Drive-In was divided into three magnificent parts. There was the golf links, the roller rink, and the vast amphitheatre itself, where thousands of darkened cars were arranged in the form of an ancient arena, spread out beneath the tree of night. Above the deep thunder from the rink and the noise from the screen, you could hear—high in the air and so like the sea that a blind man would be deceived—the noise of traffic on the great Northern Expressway that flows southward from Montreal to the Shenandoah, engorging in its cloverleafs and brilliantly engineered gradings the green playing fields, rose gardens, barns, farms, meadows, trout streams, forests, homesteads, and churches of a golden past. The population of this highway gathered for their meals in a string of identical restaurants, where the murals, the urinals, the menus, and the machines for vending sacred medals were uniform. It was some touching part of the autumn night and the hazards of the road that so many of these travellers pleaded for the special protection of gentle St. Christopher and the blessings of the Holy Virgin.

An exit (Exit 307) curved away from the Northern Expressway down toward the Moonlite, and here was everything a man might need: the means for swift travel, food, exercise, skill (the golf links), and in the dark cars of the amphitheatre a place to perform the rites of spring—or, in this case, the rites of autumn. It was an autumn night, and the air was full of pollen and decay. Emile sat in the back seat with Louise Mecker. Charlie Putney, his best friend, was in the front seat with Doris Pluzinski. They were all drinking whiskey out of paper cups, and they were all in various stages of undress. On the screen a woman exclaimed, "I want to put on innocence, like a bright, new dress. I want to feel clean again!" Then she slammed a door.

Emile was proud of his skin, but the mention of cleanliness aroused his doubts and misgivings. He blushed. These parties were a commonplace of his generation, and if he hadn't participated in them he would have got himself a reputation as a prude and a faggot. Four boys in his high-school class had been arrested for selling pornography and heroin. They had approached him, but the thought of using narcotics and obscene pictures disgusted him. His sitting undressed in the back seat of a car might be accounted for by the fact that the music he danced to and the movies he watched dealt less and less with the heart and more and more with overt sexuality, as if the rose gardens and playing fields buried under the Expressway were enjoying a revenge. What is the grade-crossing tender standing in the autumn sun thinking of? Why has the postmaster such a dreamy look? Why does the judge presiding at General Sessions seem so restless? Why does the cabdriver frown and sigh? What is the shoeshine boy thinking of as he stares out into the rain? What darkens the mind and torments the flesh of the truck driver on the Expressway? What are the thoughts of the old gardener dusting his roses, the garage mechanic on his back under the Chevrolet, the idle lawyer, the sailor waiting for the fog to lift, the drunkard, the soldier? The times were venereal, and Emile was a child of the times.

Louise Mecker was a tomato, but her looseness seemed only to be one aspect of a cheerful disposition. She did what she was expected to do to get along, and this was part of it. And yet in her readiness she sometimes seemed to debase and ridicule the seat of desire, toward which he still preserved some vague and tender feelings. When the lilac under his bedroom window bloomed in the spring and he could smell its fragrance as he lay in bed, some feeling, as strong as ambition but without a name, moved him. Oh, I want—I want to do so well, he thought, sitting naked at the Moonlite. But what did he want to do? Be a jet pilot? Discover a waterfall in Africa? Manage a supermarket? Whatever it was, he wanted something that would correspond to his sense that life was imposing; something that would confirm his feeling that, as he stood at the window of Narobi's grocery store watching the men and women on the sidewalk and the stream of clouds in the sky, the procession he saw was a majestic one.

He thought of Jessica, who by giving him a beer had penetrated into his considerations. In the last six or eight months, he had been bewildered by the sudden interest men and women took in his company. They seemed to want something from him and to want it ardently, and although he was not an innocent or a fool, he was genuinely uncertain about what it was they wanted. His own desires were violent. While he was shaving in the morning, a seizure of sexual need doubled him up with pain and made him groan. "Cut yourself, dear?" his mother asked. And yet he was a young man who could be dissuaded from the most violent sexual excitement by the sight of a pear tree blooming in a back yard. Louise satisfied him, but Mrs. Coliver excited a much broader realm of desire. He thought of her—oddly enough—as a tragic figure, frail, lonely, and misunderstood. Her husband, whoever he was, would be obtuse, stupid, and clumsy. Weren't all men his age? She was a fair prisoner in a tower.

Halfway through the feature, they got dressed and, with the cutout open and the radio blaring "Take It Easy, Greasy," roared out of the Moonlite onto the Expressway, jeopardizing their lives and the lives in every car they passed (men, women, and children in arms), but gentle St. Christopher or the mercies of the Holy Virgin spared them and got Emile safely home. He climbed the stairs, kissed his mother good night—she was studying an article in *Reader's Digest* about the pancreas—and went to bed. Lying in bed, he decided, quite innocently, that he was tired of tomatoes, movies, and paper cups, and that he would become Mrs. Coliver's lover.

He went to the house three or four times a week. Jessica was usually alone in the late afternoon, and he timed his visits. He wondered if he should bring her a present—a box of candy or something like that. Sometimes she seemed to be waiting for him. No one had ever been so attentive. She seemed interested in all the fact of his life—that his father had been a surveyor, that Emile drove a second-hand Buick, that he had done well at school.

She usually gave him a beer and sat with him in the kitchen. Her company excited him. It made him feel that some of her worldliness, some of her finesse, would rub off on him and get him out of the grocery business. Suddenly, one afternoon, she said quite shyly, "You know, you're beautiful."

He wondered if she hadn't lost her marbles. He had heard that women sometimes did. Had he been wasting his time? He didn't want to be the lover of a woman who had lost her marbles. He knew he wasn't beautiful. If he was beautiful, someone would have said so before. . . . And if he *had* been beautiful, and had been convinced of this, he would have concealed it—not through modesty but through an instinct of self-preservation. He sensed that uncommon beauty, like any other uncommon gift, would entail responsibilities, and he would have wanted to evade them. At this level he resisted her praise flatly. But at another level, and one much more wary, appeared her right to say what she felt. Was it possible that people could love and praise one another openly without having lost their marbles? This was what he had wanted, this was what he had planned, but it was all in the wrong terms. "Oh, I'm not beautiful," he said earnestly, and finished his beer. "Now I have to get back to the store."

Jessica went shopping a few days later. She took a midmorning train and sat with her neighbor, Gertrude Bender. Gertrude had silver-gilt hair, skinned back in a chignon with such preciseness and skill that Jessica wondered how it had been accomplished. She had matching silver-gilt furs, and rattled six gold bracelets. She was a pretty, shallow woman who wielded the inarguable powers of great wealth and whose voice was shrill. She talked about her daughter Betty. "She's worried about her schoolwork, but I tell her, 'Betty,' I tell her, 'don't you worry about your schoolwork. Do you think what I learned in school got me where I am today? Develop a good figure and learn the forks. That's all that matters.'"

In the seat in front of Jessica there was an old lady whose head was bowed under the weight of a hat covered with cloth roses. A family occupied the facing seats across the aisle—a mother and three children. They were poor. Their clothing was cheap and threadbare, and the woman's face was worn. One of her children was sick and lay across her lap, sucking his thumb. He was two or three years old, but it was hard to guess his age, he was so pale and thin. There were sores on his forehead and sores on his thin legs. The lines around his mouth were as deep as those on the face of a man. He seemed sick and miserable, but stubborn and obdurate at the same time, as if he held in his fist a promise of something bewildering and festive that he would not relinquish in spite of his sickness and the strangeness of the train. He sucked his thumb noisily and would not move from his position in the midst of life. His mother bent over him as she must have done when she nursed him, and sang him a lullaby as they passed Parthenia, Gatesbridge, Tuxon Valley, and Tokinsville.

Gertrude said, "I don't understand people who lose their looks when they don't have to. I mean what's the point of going through life looking like an old laundry bag? Now, take Molly Singleton. She goes up to the Club on Saturday nights wearing those thick eyeglasses and an ugly dress and wonders why she doesn't have a good time. There's no point in going to parties if you're going to depress everyone. I'm no girl and I know it, but I still have all the partners I want and I like to give the boys a thrill. I like to see them perk up. It's amazing what you can do. Why, one of the grocery boys wrote me a love letter. I wouldn't tell Eddie— I wouldn't tell anyone—because the poor kid might lose his job, but what's the sense of living if you don't generate a little excitement once in a while?"

Jessica was jealous. That the rush of feeling she suffered was plainly ridiculous didn't diminish its power. She seemed, unknowingly, to have convinced herself of the fact that Emile worshipped her, and the possibility that he worshipped them all, that she might be at the bottom of his list of attractions, was a shock. It was all absurd, and it was all true. She seemed to have rearranged all of her values around his image, to have come unthinkingly to depend upon his admiration. The fact that she cared at all about his philandering was painfully humiliating.

She left New York in the middle of the afternoon and called Narobi's when she got back. She ordered a loaf of bread, garlic salt, endives—nothing she needed. He was there fifteen or twenty minutes later.

"Emile?" she asked.

"Yes."

"Did you ever write a letter to Mrs. Bender?"

"Mrs. who?"

"Mrs. Bender."

"I haven't written a letter since last Christmas. My uncle sent me ten dollars and I wrote a letter and thanked him."

"Emile, you must know who Mrs. Bender is."

"No, I don't. She probably buys her groceries somewhere else."

"Are you telling the truth, Emile?"

"Sure."

"Oh, I'm making such a damn fool of myself," she said, and began to cry.

"Don't be sad," he said. "Please don't! I like you very much, I think you're fascinating, but I wouldn't want to make you sad."

"Emile, I'm going to Nantucket on Saturday, to close up the house there. Would you like to come with me?"

"Sure, I'd love to."

He didn't, in the end, have to do anything.

When he had gone, she was alone in the dark house. She had done what she wanted; she had acted on her deepest instincts, and who would be harmed? . . . Who wouldn't? Her husband, her son, her friends, her neighbors, even her old Uncle Lawrence, dying in Palo Alto, would suffer, but the person who seemed most vulnerable to her then was Emile's mother. She had never seen Mrs. Cranmer. She could not imagine what the woman looked like. She got into the car and drove to the florist shop on Green Street. There was a bell attached to the door and, inside, the smell of flowers. Mrs. Cranmer came out of the back, taking a pencil from her bleached hair and smiling like a child.

Emile's mother was one of those widows who keep themselves in a constant state of readiness for some call, some invitation, some meeting that will never take place, because the lover is dead. You find them answering the telephone in the back-street cabstands of little towns, their hair freshly bleached, their nails painted, their high-arched shoes ready for dancing with someone who cannot come. They sell nightgowns, flowers, stationery, and candy, and the lowest in their ranks sell movie tickets. They are always in a state of readiness, they have all known the love of a good man, and it is in his memory that they struggle through the snow and mud in high heels. Mrs. Cranmer's face was painted brightly, her dress was silk, and there were bows on her high-heeled pumps. She was a small, plump woman, with her waist cinctured in sternly, like a cushion with a noose around it. She looked like a figure that had stepped from a comic book, although there was nothing comic about her.

Jessica ordered some roses, and Mrs. Cranmer passed the order on to someone in the back and said, "They'll be ready in a minute." The doorbell rang and another customer came in—a thick-featured man with a white plastic button in his right ear that was connected by an electrical cord to his vest. He spoke heavily. "I want something for a deceased," he said. Mrs. Cranmer was diplomatic, and through a series of delicate indirections tried to discover his relationship to the corpse. Would he like a blanket of flowers, at perhaps forty dollars, or something a little less expensive? He gave his information readily, but only in reply to direct questions. The corpse was his sister. Her children were scattered. "I guess I'm the closest she had left," he said confusedly, and Jessica, waiting for her roses, felt a premonition of death. She must die—she must be the subject of some such discussion in a flower shop, and close her eyes forever on a world that distracted her with its beauty. The image, hackneyed and poignant, that came to her was of life as a diversion, a festival from which she was summoned by the secret police of extinction, when the dancing and the music were at their best. I do not want to leave, she thought. I do not ever want to leave. Mrs. Cranmer gave her the roses, and she went home.

Emile went to the airport alone on Saturday morning. Jessica had bought the plane tickets and made all the arrangements, and she had asked him not to speak to her on the plane. He wore new shoes and a new pair of pants, and walked with a bounce in order to feel the thickness of the new soles and to feel the nice play of muscle as it worked up his legs and back into his shoulders. He had never been on a plane before, and he was disappointed to find that it was not as sleek as the planes in magazine advertisements, and that the fuselage was dented and stained with smoke. He got a window seat and watched the activity on the field, feeling that as soon as the plane was airborne he would begin a new life of motion, comfort, and freedom. Hadn't he always dreamed of going here and there and making friends in different places and being easily accepted as a man of strength and intelligence and not a grocery boy without a future or a destiny, and had he ever doubted that his dreams would come true? Jessica was the last but one to get on. She was wearing a fur coat, and the dark skins made her appear to him like a visitor from another continent, where everything was beautiful, orderly, and luxurious. She didn't look in his direction. A drunken sailor took the seat beside Emile and fell asleep. Emile was disappointed. Watching the planes that passed over Parthenia and Proxmire Manor, he had assumed that the people who travelled in them were of a high order. In a little while they were off the ground.

It was charming. At the distance of a few hundred feet, all the confused and mistaken works of man seemed orderly and charming, and the higher they got above the roofs of Long Island the more it seemed to him that the lives lived there must be full of love and happiness, and he smiled down broadly at the earth and its population. The sensation he had looked forward to, of being airborne, he did not have; flying was not what he had anticipated, and it seemed to him that the engines of the plane were struggling to resist gravity and hold them in their place among the thin clouds. The sea they were crossing was dark and colorless, and as they lost sight of land he felt in himself a corresponding sense of loss, as if at this point some sustaining bond with his green past had been cut. The island, when he saw it below them on the sea, with a cuff of foam on its northeast edge, looked so small and flat that he wondered why anyone should want to go there. When he left the plane, she was waiting for him by the steps, and they walked through the airport and got a cab. She told the driver, "First I want to go into the village and get some groceries, and then I want to go to Madamquid."

"What do you want to go to Madamquid for?" the driver asked. "There's nobody out there now."

"I have a cottage out there," she said.

They drove across a bleak landscape, but one so closely associated with her youth and her happiness that the bleakness escaped her. In the village, they stopped at the grocery store where she had always traded, and she asked Emile to wait outside.

When she had bought the groceries, a boy wearing the white
apron and bent in exactly the same attitude as Emile was when
she first saw him carried them out to the taxi. She gave him
a tip and looked up and down the street for Emile. He was
standing in front of the drugstore with some other young men
his age.

Her courage left her then. The society of the bored and the
disappointed, from which she had hoped to escape, seemed
battlemented, implacable, and splendid—a creation useful to con-
cert halls, hospitals, bridges, and courthouses, and one that she
was not fit to enter. She had wanted to bring into her life the
freshness of a journey and had achieved nothing but a galling
sense of moral shabbiness.

"You want me to get your boy friend?" the cabdriver asked.

"He's not my boy friend," Jessica said. "He's just come out to
help me move some things."

Emile saw her then, and crossed the street, and they started
for Madamquid. She felt so desperate that she took his hand,
not expecting him to support her, but he turned to her with
wonderful largess, a smile so strong and tender that she felt the
blood pour back into her heart. They were heading out to the
point, where there was nothing to see but the cream-colored dunes,
with their scalp locks of knife grass, and the dark autumn ocean.
He was perplexed by this. One of the several divisions in his
world was that group of people who went away for the summer—
who closed their houses in June and bought no more groceries
until September—and, never having enjoyed any such migratory
privileges himself, he had imagined the places where they went as
having golden sands and purple seas, the houses palatial and pink-
walled, with patios and swimming pools, like the houses he saw
in the movies. There was nothing like that here, and he couldn't
believe that even in the long, hot days of summer this place
would look less of a wilderness. Were there fleets of sailboats, deck
chairs, and beach umbrellas? There was no trace of summery furniture now. She pointed out the house to him and he saw a big,
shingled building on a bluff. He could see that it was big—it was
big, all right—but if you were going to build a summer house, why
not build something neat and compact, something that would
be nice to look at? But maybe he was wrong, maybe there was

something to be learned here; she seemed so pleased at the sight of the old place that he was willing to suspend judgment. She paid off the cabdriver and tried to open the front door, but the lock had rusted in the salt air and he had to help. He finally got the door open, and she went in and he carried in the bags and then, of course, the groceries.

She knew well enough that the place was homely—it was meant to be—but the lemony smell of the matchboard walls seemed to her like the fragrance of the lives that had been spent there in the sunny months. Her sister's old violin music, her brother's German textbooks, the water color of a thistle her aunt had painted seemed like the essence of their lives. And while she had quarrelled with her brother and her sister and they no longer communicated with each other, all her memories now were kind and gentle. "I've always been happy here," she said, "I've always been terribly happy here. That's why I wanted to come back. It's cold now, of course, but we can light some fires." She noticed then, on the wall at her left, the pencil markings where each Fourth of July her uncle had stood them up against the matchboard and recorded their growth. Afraid that Emile might see this incriminating evidence of her age, she said, "Let's put the groceries in the icebox."

"That's a funny word, icebox," he said. "I never heard it before. It's a funny thing to call a frigidaire. But you speak differently, you know—people like you. You say lots of different things. Now, you say 'divine'—you say lots of things are 'divine'—but, you know, my mother, she wouldn't ever use that word, excepting when she was speaking of God."

Frightened by the chart in the hallway, she wondered if there was anything else incriminating in the house, and remembered the gallery of family photographs in the upstairs hall. Here were pictures of her in school uniforms, in catboats, and many pictures of her playing on the beach with her son. While he put the groceries away, she went upstairs and hid the pictures in a closet. Then they walked down the bluff to the beach.

It was surprisingly warm for that time of year. The wind was southerly; in the night it would probably change around to the southwest, bringing rain. All along the beach, the waves from Portugal rolled in. There was the noise of a detonation, the roar

of furling water, and then the glistening discharge fanned out on
the sand, faded, and sank. Ahead of her, at the high-water mark,
she saw a sealed bottle with a note inside and ran to pick it up.
What did she expect? The secret of the Spada treasure, or a
proposal of marriage from a French sailor? She handed Emile the
bottle and he broke it open on a stone. The note was written
in pencil. "To whomever in the whole wide world may read this I
am a 18 yr old college boy, sitting on the beach at Madamquid on
Sept. 8. . . ." His sense of the act of setting his name and address
adrift on the tide was rhapsodic, but the bottle must have returned to where he stood a little while after he had walked away.
Emile asked if he could go swimming, and then bent down to
unlace his new shoes. One of the laces knotted and his face got
red. She dropped to her knees and undid it herself. He got out of
his clothes hurriedly in order to display his youth and his brawn,
but he asked her earnestly if she minded if he took off his under-
pants. He stood with his back to her while he did this, and then
walked off into the sea. It was colder than he had expected. His
shoulders and his buttocks tightened and his head shook. Naked
and shivering, he seemed pitiful, vain, and fair—a common young
man trying to find some pleasure and adventure in his life. He
dove into a wave and then came lunging back to where she stood.
His teeth were chattering. She threw her coat over him and they
went back to the house.

    She had been right about the wind. After midnight, or later,
it came out of the southwest, spouting rain, and as she had done
ever since she was a child, she got out of bed and crossed the room
to close the windows. He woke and heard the sound of her bare
feet on the wooden floor. He couldn't see her in the dark, but as
she came back toward the bed her step sounded heavy and old.

    It rained in the morning. They walked on the beach, and Jessica
cooked a chicken. Looking for a bottle of wine, she found a long-
necked green bottle of Moselle, like the bottle she had set out
in her dream of the picnic and the ruined castle. Emile ate most
of the chicken. At four they took a cab to the airport, and flew
back to New York. In the train out to Proxmire Manor he sat
several seats ahead of her, reading the paper. Tom met her at the
station and was pleased to have her back. The baby was awake,

and Jessica sat in a chair in their bedroom singing, "Sleep, my little one, sleep. Thy Father guards the sheep. . . ." She sang until both the baby and Tom were asleep.

Emile was at the house the next afternoon with a scheme. Some friends of his had a shack at the edge of town where they took girls, and Jessica and he could meet there. He admitted that it wasn't much of a place, but he could get a clean blanket and some curtains for the windows. He might even paint the inside. He was excited, and she saw that there wouldn't be any point in stating her objections, although the idea disgusted her. He told her the next afternoon that he was going ahead with his plans for improving the shack. He had bought some paint and a roller and was going to do the walls that night. It would be ready for the weekend. She put him off that weekend, but he was angry. The next Saturday, they met in Boston. She told Tom that she had to go north to see her aunt. Her aunt was not in Boston— she was in Florida—but Tom didn't question her explanation.

She and Emile flew in separate planes. He arrived an hour later than she, and went to her room, where they spent the afternoon. Later they went out for a walk. It was very cold, and, looking at the façades and campaniles of Copley Square, she was moved by the thought that Boston had once thought itself the sister city of Florence, that vale of flowers. The wind scored her face. He stopped to look at a ring in a jeweller's window. It was a man's ring, a star sapphire set in gold. The ring did not interest her, but it seemed to hold him. She shook with the cold while he admired the stone. "It's pretty, isn't it," he said. "I mean the star caught in the stone. I wonder how much it costs. I'm going in and ask."

"Don't, Emile," she said. "I'm frozen. And anyhow, those things are always terribly expensive."

"I'll just ask. It won't take a minute."

She waited for him in the shelter of the door. "Eight hundred dollars!" he exclaimed when he came out. "Think of that. Eight hundred dollars."

"I told you it would be expensive."

"Eight hundred dollars. But it was pretty, though, wasn't it? And I suppose if you needed money you could always sell it. I mean, they must fix the price on things like that, don't you think? It would be sort of like an investment. You know, if I had eight hundred dollars, I might buy a ring like that. I just might. People, when they saw the ring, they would always know that you were worth eight hundred dollars. Waiters. Like that. I mean they would respect you when you were wearing a ring like that."

It seemed to her that he was deliberately debasing their relationship and forcing her into the humiliating position of buying him the ring, but she was mistaken; the idea had never occurred to him.

"Do you want me to buy you the ring, Emile?"

"Oh, no, I wasn't thinking about that. It just caught my eye. You know how things catch your eye."

"I'll buy it for you."

"No, no, forget about it."

They had dinner in a restaurant and went to a movie. Walking back to the hotel, he bought a newspaper, and he sat reading it in her room while she undressed and brushed her hair. "I'm hungry," he said suddenly. His tone was petulant. "At home I get a bowl of cornflakes or a sandwich—something before I go to bed." He stood up, put his hands on his stomach, and shouted, "I'm hungry! I just don't get enough to eat in these restaurants. I'm still growing. I have to have three big meals a day and sometimes something in between!"

"Well, why don't you go down and get something to eat?"

"Well."

"Do you need money?"

"Sort of."

"Here," she said. "Here's some money. Go down and get some supper."

He went out, but he didn't return. At midnight she locked the door and went to sleep. In the morning she dressed, went to the jeweller's, and bought the ring. "Oh, I remember you," the clerk said. "I saw you last night. I saw you standing outside the door when your son came in to ask the price." It was a blow, and she supposed she could be seen to flinch. She thought that perhaps the winter dark and pale light in the street had made her seem old. "You're a very generous mother," the clerk said when he took her check and passed her the box. She called Emile's room and when he came down she gave him the ring. His pleasure and gratitude were not, she thought, mercenary and crass but only a natural response to the ancient tokens of love, the immemorial power of stones and fine gold. It was a foggy afternoon, all the planes were grounded, and they went back on the train, sitting in different cars.

He sat by the window, watching the landscape. Somewhere south of Boston, the train passed a suburban tract of houses. They were new, and although the architects and the gardeners had rung a few changes here and there, the effect was monotonous. What interested him was that rising in the center of the development was a large, ugly, loaf-shaped, and colorless escarpment of granite, too steep to hold the foundations of a house. It was the only form on the landscape that had not succumbed to change. It could not be dynamited. It could not be quarried and carried away piecemeal. It was useless, and it was invincible. Some boys his age were climbing the steep face, and he guessed this was their last refuge.

It was late and it was getting cold, and he could remember the sense of the season and the hour when it was time to leave off playing and go home to study. Near where he lived, there was a similar rock, and he had climbed it on winter afternoons, to smoke cigarettes and talk with his friends about the future. He could remember grasping for handholds on the steep face, and how the rough stone pulled at his best school clothes, but what he remembered most clearly was how once his feet were on the ground he had a sense of awakening to a whole new life, the arrival at a new state of consciousness, as clearly unlike his past as sleep is unlike waking. Standing at the foot of the cliff at that hour and season—about to go home and study but not yet on the path—he would stare at the yards and the trees and the lighted houses with a galvanic sense of discovery. How forceful and interesting the world had seemed in the early winter light! How new it all seemed. He must have been familiar with every window, roof, tree, and landmark in the place, but he felt as if he were seeing it all for the first time.

How old he had grown since then.

They met ten days or two weeks later, in a New York hotel.
She was there first and ordered some whiskey and roast-beef sandwiches. When he came in, she poured herself a drink and made
one for him, and he ate both the sandwiches she had ordered.
She was wearing a bracelet, made of silver bells, that she had
bought long ago in Casablanca. She had been given a Mediter-
ranean cruise as a Christmas present by a rich elderly cousin, and
in her travels she had never been able to escape a genuine and
oppressive sense of gratitude to the old lady. When she saw
Lisbon, she thought, Oh, Cousin Martha, I wish you could see
Lisbon! When she saw Rhodes, she thought, Oh, Cousin Martha,
I wish you could see Rhodes! Standing in the Casbah at dusk, she
thought, Oh, Cousin Martha, I wish you could see how purple
the skies are above Africa! Remembering this, she gave the silver
bells a shake.

"Do you have to wear that bracelet?" he asked.

"Of course not," she said.

"I hate that kind of junky stuff," he said. "You've got lots of
nice jewelry—those sapphires. I don't see why you want to wear
junk. Those bells are driving me crazy. Every time you move
they jingle. They get on my nerves."

"I'm sorry, darling," she said. She took off the bracelet. He
seemed ashamed or confused by his harshness; he had never before been harsh or callous with her.

"Sometimes I wonder why it happened to me like this," he
said. "I mean, I couldn't have had anything better, I know that.
You're beautiful and you're fascinating—your're the most fascinating woman I ever saw—but sometimes I wonder—wondered—
why it should happen to me this way. I mean, some fellows—right
away they get a pretty young girl, she lives next door, their folks
are friendly, they go to the same schools, the same dances, they
go dancing together, they fall in love and get married. But I
guess that's not for poor people. No pretty girls live next door to
me. There aren't any pretty girls on my street. Oh, I'm glad it
happened to me the way it did, but I can't stop wondering what
it would have been like some other way. I mean like in Nantucket
that weekend. That was the big football weekend, and I was thinking, there we were, all alone in that gloomy old house—that was

a real gloomy place, rainy and everything—while some fellows were driving in convertibles to the football game."

"I must seem terribly old."

"Oh, no. No, you don't. It isn't that. . . . Only once. That was in Nantucket, too. It was raining in the night. It began to rain and you got up to shut the window."

"And I seemed terribly old?"

"Just for a minute. . . . Not really. But you see, you're used to comfort, you're different. Two cars, plenty of clothes. I'm just a poor kid."

"Does it matter?"

"Oh, I know you think it doesn't, but it does. When you go into a restaurant, you never look at the prices. Now, your husband, he can buy you all these things. He can buy you anything you want, he's loaded, but I'm just a poor kid. I guess I'm sort of a lone wolf. I guess most poor people are. I'll never live in a house like yours. I'll never get to join a country club. I'll never have a place at the beach. And I'm still hungry," he said, looking at the empty sandwich plate. "I'm still growing, you know. I have to have lunch. I don't want to seem ungrateful or anything, but I'm hungry."

"You go down to the dining room, darling," she said, "and get some lunch. Here's five dollars." She kissed him, and then as soon as he was gone she left the hotel herself.

She wandered around the streets—she had no place to go—wondering what had been the first in the chain of events that had brought her to where she was. The barking of a dog, the dream of a castle, or her boredom at Mrs. Wishing's dance? She waited for the crushing pain of guilt and retribution, but the blow seemed suspended, and the thought of Emile eating his lunch put some blessed distance between her and him; they were individuals once more. She took a train home, her only anxiety then being that he would follow her and insist on some roaring confrontation—insist at least on a scene—although she should have known him better than this. The afternoon passed quietly, and they never met again except in passing. Driving down Green Street one evening, she saw him with a big blonde—a girl two or three inches taller than he. Tom never once suspected what had been going on, and she bought her groceries someplace else.

J. C. OATES is an instructor at the University of Detroit where she lives with her husband. Her fiction has appeared in several magazines and was included in the 1963 O. *Henry Awards* and the 1963 *Best American Short Stories*. Her first book of short stories was published by Vanguard and she is currently at work on a novel.

Stigmata

Though his father had been at St. Jerome's Home for the Aged for five or six years now, Walt Turner had never seen the home before—he had seen his father, of course, at various Christmases, at various houses of brothers and sisters, and the old man had journeyed down out of these saintly hills one fall to attend a Sunday High Mass sung by his second oldest son, newly ordained a priest—but Walt had never visited him at the home and had never imagined visiting him, since he did not like his father particularly. He had guessed that a visit to the home, with those faint mountains and hills peering in the old man's window, and that blue sky that was so fraudulently pure it offended one's credulity, would be, as his sister Clara had reported sadly, "A visit to him in Heaven—all he does is smile."

Walt had driven alone up to the home, in spite of his distrust of this second-hand car, refusing a ride with his brothers—who drove carefully and looked at the scenery and talked about their jobs and their children and their father—and as he approached the nursing home the impact of its high, rigid, ascetic opulence struck him so that he felt the car slowing, as if weakened by the vision. St. Jerome's, as its worthy brochure had shown, was built on a hill: a kind of drumlin, perhaps, at any rate a freakish hill which lifted high above the level of the immediate area. It was jarring: a photograph or a vision made real. Oh, there were frills of nature

attendant upon it, fir trees and slimly elegant shrubs; there were
foothills and real mountains behind it, suggesting its location in
nature; but the building itself, a heavy rectangular structure that
surrendered nothing to art, that, constructed of some deliberate
anonymous colorless rock, looked centuries old and simultaneously
unrelated to time, showed by the very bluntness of its reality
the illusion that nature conspired—there were meek dying trees
beneath that green, and hills fated to erode beneath those slivers
of left-over snow, and mountains so vague they might be erased
by hand. And had not nature's great contribution to history, the
wooden cross, become transformed into brilliant silver, gleaming
over there above the chapel? It was human creation that would
survive all worldly accidents.

Walt turned up the long gravel drive. The big building waited
coyly atop its hill: the drive leaned this way, now that way, as if
teasing. As it rose slowly Walt began to seek the parking lot
behind the home; there were a large number of cars parked there,
and he noticed in his rear view mirrow that a station wagon was
just turning in from the road. He drove faster. On the bumper of
the station wagon was a sticker with orange fluorescent letters
—a politician's name? But it was months too early for that. Walt
drove faster and heard with satisfaction gravel being picked up
and churned around his wheels. He supposed the driver behind
him had taken in, carefully, this car and was wondering about it
—St. Jerome's, though planned as near-charity, was aristocratic,
after all, and bluntly expensive. And who else would there be to
wonder at him? There would be reporters and doctors and one
or two psychiatrists and a university professor from downstate,
not to mention his two frail sweet sisters whose letters he did
not answer and his two successful brothers whose offers of money
he refused (the third brother was now in Rome, regretted violently
that he could not come). Walt parked along the edge of the
driveway; his heart was pounding. The station wagon passed him,
headed for the parking lot, and he found himself staring at the
orange sticker: OBSERVE EASTER.

Walt was met inside by a young nun in a brown outfit, who
smiled like his father smiled. He introduced himself with an absurd yet faintly proud sense of being important; he had noticed,
sitting about the foyer on cheap modern chairs, men who must

certainly be reporters. Other people drifted by, dumpy women in furs, young women holding back straining children, visitors to lesser patients, who looked about wonderingly. Was it possible a miracle might occur, and in this building? Walt's blood throbbed foolishly as he ascended the stairs.

But it was for nothing: his father was not in his room. A nurse explained politely, another young woman in a brown outfit, hardly more than a girl. No, not out in the sun porch either, this was his time of devotion; she spoke in short snatched enthusiastic phrases. "But your family is inside waiting. Won't you wait with them?" She was obviously shy and pleased and embarrassed.

As Walt knocked he heard his brother Art's voice, a solemn murmur that must be dragging down the corners of his mouth. The door opened—a dazzling flash of white like a glimpse of another world, beautifully white walls—his sister standing there chic in a dark tweed suit with black fur about its collar. "Walt, dear," she cried. She embraced him and he held his breath against the odor of cologne, though he liked Clara immensely: had she not always taken his side, the side of the youngest, the weakest, the nastiest? "It's so good to see you again," she said in her family-gathering voice. The others were on their feet and crowding in; welcomes were general. There was Carolyn and her husband, Carolyn now getting old—nearly forty—but smiling bravely, defying all wrinkles, trusting to a new complex sort of make-up: but Carolyn was a fine woman, a fine mother, wasn't that true? Walt accepted her embrace and saw over her shoulder the embarrassed expressions of his brothers. Then as he was released to them their expressions clicked into proper looks of solemn, cautious welcome, the professional greeting between older brothers. "Walt," Art said, shaking hands and cuffing his shoulder; Ronald did the same. "If only Tom had been able to come!" Clara said. In the awkward group they jostled about for a while, lighting cigarettes, helping Walt off with his coat; Carolyn and her husband exchanged domestic murmurs, nothing important, the sort of thing expected between husband and wife; Art—who was putting on weight, a round, well-fed, red-faced stranger—went back to his position by the window, where the fine glare burned around his head and blurred his features. "Here, sit down. I suppose you've driven all the way?" Clara said, leading him somewhere. "We're staying in

town, at the hotel. *The* hotel. There's only one but it's rather nice
—big and white with a veranda. It was built in 1850." Walt made
his way through the odor of cologne and cigar smoke and sat
down. "So where is he?" he said. "Holding a press conference or
something?"

He saw that look of pain shoot in several directions, ricochet
off one face and hit another, become absorbed finally in Clara's
shrill chatty voice. "He's at his devotions now," she said. "All
the old people spend quite a bit of time at their devotions, especially during Holy Week. But Father more than anyone—you
understand." Walt showed no understanding but lit a cigarette
and everyone watched him drop the match into a dirty ashtray.

The room was smaller than he had expected: the brochure had
hinted at larger rooms. This room, despite the esteem of its in-
mate, was hardly more than a cell—with a large window, it was
true, viewing the parking lot; its walls were starkly white, a white
so relentlessly clean and featureless that it turned Walt's eyes
continually away from it and to the security of flesh—the familiar
unfamiliar faces of his family. Their mother had died years ago
and so there was only a brother missing, Tom, who was tall,
angular, bony-faced, with a gift of venomous wit—Tom in Italy
now humbling himself in a study of marriage law, Tom who had
wanted to teach college: Walt missed him. How much easier these
people were without him lurking in the background to ridicule
and love them—how much straighter they stood! "If only Tom
had been able to get permission!" Clara said, looking at Walt.

"The discipline is too strong," Carolyn's husband suggested
without enthusiasm. Walt could not remember if he was Catholic
—maybe a convert. Didn't they have five children? Everyone murmured over this, perhaps agreeing, perhaps disagreeing. "A bul-
wark against anarchy," Ronald said. He wore a grey vest that
bulged gently about his abdomen. "But it is too strong!" Clara
said. "What are you talking about, anarchy? His own father is a
saint and the Church won't let him come! What are you talking
about?" Clara's nose seemed to grow sharper; a dull red flush
overtook her cheeks. "For God's sake don't start on that, that
saint business," Art said. He looked at Walt. "We've been instructed about that. They've made it clear. Nobody's a saint when

he's living, and there's no evidence—no final—" "But in your heart what do you feel?" Clara cried trimphantly.

An excited, embarrassed silence fell upon them. Walt's fingers were cold. "Oh, for Christ's sake," he said. "So you believe in this." They were too fond of him, or too dignified, to answer; Ronald, twelve years Walt's senior, blinked benignly at him as if at a child. It was odd that Walt's remark should hang in the air so clearly, as if it were cherished by them, examined by them, distinguishing him from them and their successful lives. . . . Walt, his face burning with anger and shame, felt catapulted back in time, sitting again at that big dinner table in the old parlor, with a napkin on his lap. Food being passed elegantly, in white dishes; his sisters' young faces, hair recently washed; his brothers in suits and ties; his mother with her heavy pearls; his father, there at the head of the table with his back reflected in the glass of the mahogany china cabinet: his father! While they murmured happily with the full fierce impersonal glare of their father's love falling upon them without distinction, like the sun's rays on the blind earth, Walt had grovelled backwards like a crab, staring down at his food and his dirt-edged fingernails, thinking that he was not related to them, could recognize nothing of himself in them, why did they pretend love for him? His mind shifted backward steadily, away from the candlelight, he retreated inside his bowed head from that half-smile on his father's lean attractive face. His father smiled that smile to all of them, Art who was so good in math, and Walt who had been caught stealing comic books in the drug store!

"It isn't the reporters I mind," Carolyn was saying. "I thought I would. It's the psychiatrist, the one from Chicago. Did you meet him? He's staying at the hotel." "He seemed cordial," Art said. "But they don't believe—any of them!" Carolyn said. "And," said Art carefully, "it's better that way—they'll be forced to believe. Why do you think they allow them here, to examine Father? They've been analyzing him for a week. —The bishop has finally come around, Walt, did you hear that?" Walt shrugged his shoulders. He had crossed his legs and noted now, with indifferent curiosity, that the cuffs of his trousers were dirty. "There's going to be a procession of the faithful on Friday, if everything is well," said Art. "If he starts to bleed on time," Walt said.

"Walt, how is Linda?" Carolyn said. She wore a hat with a seagreen feather twisting about it; it seemed to tense with the anticipation of putting Walt down.

"Fine, last time I saw her."

They looked at him sadly. "She was a sweet girl, but maybe a little too young. Immature," Clara offered.

"Not was but is. *Is* a sweet girl." Now that they watched him so closely he gloried, despite himself, in their attention. "And it hadn't anything much to do with her. Don't blame her."

"I wasn't blaming her," Clara said sharply.

"Well, don't. I know you all do." He leered at them, grinning. That would pierce their benevolent hearts. Or had they learned from their father that august generous indifference, that godly calm that stifles all anger, all love? He believed he could see something of their father in each of them, even in Clara, a girl forced into a woman, with bracelets and rings and clouds of perfume, to whose pretty smile so many young men had been drawn, eager at first, later perplexed, bored, retreating to firmer women. Especially in Art, the oldest, who leaned back against the window sill sucking at a cigar with the same look of tender concern their father had directed toward his own cigars, or his food, or Clara's recitations, at family reunions, of sprightly verse from *Alice in Wonderland*. "I used to think it would be strange to be a father," Walt said. "But it isn't anything, is it? That's the hell of it. It meant something to Linda, having the baby—but not to me. That's the way it is, isn't it?"

They looked at him blankly; this was too personal. With a frown Art stretched his arm so he could consult his watch: "Twenty past five. He stays in the chapel from one until five-thirty. On his knees, a man that age. Do you know he's been fasting all this year? Since last Easter, Walt." Walt shivered, not at this sinister information, but at his own name; what kin was he to such insanity? "He insisted that communion every morning would be enough for him to live on, but they wouldn't allow it—there was quite a controversy, all the way up to the chancery office. It was thought to be too extreme—I think I agree—"

"He's such an old man now, Walt, wait till you see him! He's lost so much weight," Clara said.

"But if *he* feels communion would be enough they should let

him fast," Carolyn pointed out. The sisters did not look at each
other but toward each other, obliquely; their glances crossed in
mid-air. "He knows more than they do. I *don't* care if they are the
church, this is something special, obviously. It's a direct revelation
from God."

"It isn't going through channels, that's sure," Ronald said.

"But if he were to die—!" Clara whispered.

"He's got to die," said Walt. "Then he's got to be resurrected,
Sunday morning. Isn't that how it goes, and isn't he under con-
tract to a television network for it?"

"Look, why the hell did you come?" Art said. Their father's
look slid off his face and he stared over at Walt. "Just what are you
doing here?"

Walt glanced away—at the unfinished bureau, the crucifix above
it. His hands became loose and self-conscious. "I don't know."

"I know you've been under a strain, Walt, with the divorce and
all," Art said slowly. "I don't want any quarrels. Not here.
There's too much at stake. It's just that you don't seem to realize
what this is—what's really happening and how important it is."

"Walt, the whole world is waiting," Clara said.

The horror of this remark calmed Walt. It was true that he believed in nothing, benevolence neither divine nor human; he expected nothing but age, perhaps cancer, perhaps a failing heart,
since nature runs only one way; he expected no more abortive
gestures of love; he was too ironical to care, really, about the
college degrees he had never been able to use. He had begun to
drink too much, as if fulfilling a role; it was true that his mind
had no refuge: thoughts before sleep could center on nothing,
neither the future nor the past nor the distant past, that sunless
perplexing area of his childhood. On his mother? But she was
dead too long, it was not a person he remembered but an image,
an American formula. And yet, he wanted to assure them, there
was something in him to which they could address themselves—if
they wanted— They could speak with him singly, honestly, they
could reveal the truth about their secret lives and he would listen
—greedily, gratefully— He was not hard, his heart was not dead,
he was waiting and vulnerable. He muttered, "Sorry."

Carolyn was speaking, slowly and elaborately, about the political machinations in the diocese, when the door was opened rather

roughly, given these still surroundings—and a heavy white-faced nun stared in at them. "Could you please wait downstairs? Could you— You must leave, something has happened to your father—" The women cried out; Walt got to his feet. Another nun appeared, an older woman. "Yes, your father has collapsed in the chapel but he is being attended. He is being attended. The doctors are going to bring him back up here and so we would like the room empty —you'll be able to visit him soon— No, it's nothing critical, he has regained consciousness. You understand he will have the best of medical care."

The women breathed audibly, trembling, the brothers moved tentatively toward the door: all stared at the nuns. "We weren't prepared for this," the older nun said suddenly, "since it—it began last year on Friday— And today is only Thursday— We weren't prepared—your father was not prepared, exactly, but he seems well —he is conscious, perfectly conscious— Pray for him. Pray for him," she said in excitement. "He is praying for us. God has visited this blessing upon him for us, for all of us, your father prays for all the world—"

Her fierce controlled hysteria followed Walt out into the hall. Ahead of him his sisters and brothers walked along in frightened obedience, like children; staring at their stiff backs, Walt was sickened with fear—was it possible that this miracle was going to happen? A miracle advertised in cheap Catholic pamphlets, a miracle insisted upon by factions within the Church—hinted at in his own newspaper, a sophisticated large-circulation daily? He saw the figures of old men in doorways, watching them as they passed, envious old men in bathrobes and slippers whose sunken mouths showed their despair over being no more than ordinary, dying old men.

They checked Walt into the hotel and had dinner there that evening with Father Mann—an old priest with a heavy, drooping head and an apologetic smile—and a writer introduced as a "special friend of the Church," a well-fed young man who did not take notes but listened to their conversation as if he were recording it. "Your father has concentrated his life upon Christ and the passion of Christ," the priest told them gently. They were at dinner, eating perfunctorily; an odor of baked fish rose about the table. "It was for this reason that he wanted to come to St.

Jerome's. We know the unhappiness this caused—you felt that
a man's children should take care of him in his old age. All this
is true, true," he said, nodding, as Walt remembered the shrill
quarrels that had shot back and forth from child to child, nervous
refutations of earlier remarks, or accusations, insistences upon love,
duty. No one had really wanted him since all were afraid of him,
and yet all—except Walt—had wanted him desperately and
viciously, afraid to surrender him to anyone else. "All this is
true ordinarily, but you have always known that your father is no
ordinary man. The miracle of his faith, the physical miracle, is
but a symptom—you understand. A sign, a manifestation of inner
faith. Here at St. Jerome's he was able to withdraw as far as
possible from the world; he could contemplate Christ and the
bitter crucifixion of Christ without having to return, except
incidentally, to the world. . . ."

"He never recognized the world," Walt said.

"Never recognized it?" The reporter leaned forward.

"Never recognized it, yes, a good expression," Father Mann
said. "Perhaps he spoke of his faith to you? Yes, he is a saintly
man, a holy man—by contrast with us who are secular," he added
carefully. "It's believed, you may have heard, that the manifestation of Our Savior's wounds came to him earlier than last year.
As long as three years ago. . . . One of the nurses has told us she
remembered your father falling sometime during Holy Week, and
suffering headaches, but of course nothing was suspected, nothing
supernatural. And last year the wounds appeared unmistakably,
on both hands, his feet, in his side. They bled slightly for about
three hours on Good Friday, but your father did not seem to
regain consciousness until Sunday morning. He came back to us
as if from a great distance, and the wounds faded. . . . A miracle."
The old man looked moved by his own words; his jaw had begun
to tremble finely. A small piece of fish, newly cut from the rest,
lay cooling on his plate. "Except for the miracle of the Mass
there's never been anything like it, in my life— Never so clear
a sign of God's love, so obvious a blessing. The sharing of Christ's
suffering by a human being, an ordinary man—this will be
acclaimed as a miracle, this will be a lever for conversion and
strengthening of faith all over the world."

"But why today? Why has it happened today?" Clara interrupted.

"God's time is not necessarily our time," the priest said coldly.

There was a long, intricate quarrel over the check, but Walt,
who excused himself to head for the bar, did not notice who won.
In the half-deserted lounge he sat at a small table in the rear, grateful for the dark. His eyes had begun to sting. He drank slowly,
while the yawning bartender read through a newspaper, turning
the pages noisily in the red glow from a neon sign. A little after
ten Clara joined him. She had changed from the suit to a dark
wool dress; gold jewelry tinkled about her wrist. "I'm going to
try to make it with them for six o'clock services," she said, "but I
couldn't sleep just now, I don't want to take more pills. . . ."
She chattered on with the nervous coquettish energy that Walt
had always pitied, knowing it must end slumped before a dressing
table mirror, nose a little shiny, powder smeared subtly by perspira-
tion, lips heavy. She skipped from topic to topic, person to person,
circling but steadily nearing the center of their worlds, the
accident that bound them there together, at a small cheap-surfaced
table in this dreary lounge— "I'm afraid that this will injure him,"
she said seriously. Her innocence alarmed Walt. "You mean you
don't think he's suffering?" Walt asked. "Suffering? Suffering?"
Clara murmured, looking in her purse for something. In the dull
red light she looked suddenly young; she allowed him the calculated impact of her simplicity. "Why, yes, he's suffering . . . some.
. . . That's part of it, I've done some reading and I was talking
to the Mother Superior, she. . . . But how does he suffer?"

Her fingers paused inside her purse. Walt could see a tangle of
objects, silver and gold, leather, the neat oval gleams of Clara's
enameled nails. "Like Christ," said Walt with a grin. But Clara
had begun to retreat. She took out a compact, opened it and
looked at herself, dutifully, licking her lips; then she snapped it
shut and replaced it. Her expression had the look of assurance that
comes from having just been checked in a mirror. "But I hope it
doesn't injure him so that he's different, so that he doesn't know
us anymore," she said. "I've been up to see him, Walt, more
than anyone, once a month, and he's so remote—always so remote
—I could hardly talk to him. Oh, he wasn't impolite; you know
Father, he's incapable of hurting anyone. . . . But he was so dis-

tracted that I felt later he wouldn't remember I had come. Or he wouldn't remember who had come." "Then why do you come to see him?" said Walt. "Because I love him," Clara said. "But why do you love him?" said Walt. "Because I love him," Clara said sharply. "He's our father."

They sat in silence for a while. Walt noticed a waitress with silver-blond hair uplifted and ballooning over the top of her head. She teetered skillfully on high heels. "I can't bear to think of anything happening to him," Clara went on, apologetically. "Anything to change him. What if he forgets? I can't sleep sometimes, or I wake up at night, thinking—what if he forgets me? Because I've always waited for him—I've always thought he might— Well, he might tell me something," she said, confused, "he might talk about home, when we were children, or he might ask me how I am, what my life is now— How could I have ever given everything over to some other man, some stranger, when— I thought he might tell me something, some secret about myself." They stared in embarrassment at each other. The kinship between them was so strong that Walt, to control his sudden nervousness, had to light a cigarette. "Do you understand?" Clara said. "Do you understand?"

Around three that morning, unable to sleep, Walt thought of calling his wife—his ex-wife—and had picked up the receiver, was dreamily awaiting the outside line, when he saw his reflection in the bureau mirror like a policeman popped up to accuse him: it was always a surprise to see that he was no longer really young, that last year between twenty-nine and thirty must have exhausted his youth. He had black hair, cut close against his head so that it looked like a cap, giving him an appearance of innocence— jocularity. His eyes, which were drooping like his brother Tom's, belied any innocence; they took in most things, including themselves, without enthusiasm. Yet he had a gift for irony, and if he prized it rather too much—if he sought in himself an academic salvation through it—it was because there was nothing else for him, really nothing. He had never believed in himself, any more than he had believed in the world: alien shapes, lines, colors, conversations, toothed smiles that convey whole dialogues, patterns of living, even passion—all had drifted by his sight with the watery instability of distractions in dreams, mere trifles to divert

STIGMATA 41

the mind from its true object. But what was this object? He had never been able to discover it, as his father so easily had; and perhaps it was only after struggle, relinquishing a part of their heritage, that his brothers had blinked away the glorious threat of this ideal and had surrendered to the complex material charms of the world. For these charms were complex and frightening; it was no coward who succumbed to them. Walt could appreciate the courage it took to sink oneself in the world, in its ponderous ways, yet he could not make the leap—any more than he could make the leap to the pleasant ghostly universe his father inhabited, gentlemanly man! He saw his fright in the mirror before he felt it: the telephone was speaking to him. "No, sorry, I've changed my mind." He put the receiver back. And he felt, then, half-smiling at the telephone, that he had, indeed, escaped—a clever escape—and that his father, if he had known, would have been pleased.

Walt woke after eight, feeling drugged, and drove alone up to St. Jerome's. The air was cold, there was no hint of spring; slivers of ice lay in the ditches. There were already cars in the parking lot, and about the damp front steps groups of people stood, families, breathing in the cold air. A young man with an acne-ravaged face and a maroon scarf approached Walt. "You are a member of the Turner family?" he said. "No," said Walt. Evidently they were waiting for the doors to be opened. He looked around at the mild faces, country people like domesticated animals, calmed by impending excitement. Some, older women, were saying rosaries to themselves. Walt heard the man with the scarf and another man, who wore a hat, talking behind him. "Supposed to be an inside story," one said. "Born without eyes, the skin just growing over. Radiation poisoning. It's going to break in a week." "Is this the same one, the one in California?" the other said.

The meek crowd moved along up the wide stone steps, watching their feet. Inside the building was gleaming with cleanliness: the floor shone, windows shone in the brittle light, the nuns' shoes, when they peeked out from beneath the heavy brown skirts, were polished a shiny black. Walt met his sister Carolyn upstairs. She took his arm. "They've put Father in another room, in the sun porch," she whispered. Her face was pale and not very pretty:

she had sacrificed lipstick for Good Friday. "He knows us, Walt.
He knows us." Her whisper became throaty with triumph; Walt
felt her shiver. "The tourists are here," Walt said brutally. "They're
downstairs." "The audience of the faithful," Carolyn said, as if
reading a sign on the wall. Walt looked up: there was a sign there,
but it said NO SMOKING.

When he entered the antiseptic-smelling room—which was
crowded quietly in the background—Walt understood that he had
been preparing for this meeting for months. Carolyn urged him on
as his heart thudded, and, yes, there was his father—no stranger
after all, but his father, their father, familiar man!—that face leapt
to Walt with the serenity of habit, the face of Walt's dreams, day-
dreams, and nothing in him protested as he approached the bed
and sank to his knees on the tiled floor. . . . Was he supposed to
pray? He supposed it was proper to pray a little, to mutter harm-
lessly, and to cross oneself; he crossed himself with care. He peered
up at his father, who did not seem to notice him. There the old
man lay, real as life! Weight gone out of his chest; his cheeks
sunken (as if the stubborn rotted old teeth had finally been
pulled); his face was pale, mottled slightly, mild, peaceful,
charmed with itself or with this blessing, his eyes fastened upon
something in the air, his throat quivering as if sustaining an
inaudible dialogue. White, frail hair, that of a professional old
man; and arms poking out of bony shoulders, narrow as rods,
hands turned upward to catch the precise gleam of bright spring
air from the great windows on the side wall—palms covered with
blood! Beneath them, on a paper-thin bluish plastic sheet that
protected the bedclothes, little beads of blood.

Walt felt a queer, half-pleasant paralysis. His legs were dead,
his eyes fastened themselves greedily upon that shining blood and
—to be recalled later with shame—he drew in a breath, slowly,
sniffing to catch the odor of blood, legitimate blood. He smelled
only antiseptic. "But the feet," he wanted to cry, "and the bleeding side—where are they? If I don't see them I won't believe!"
But he simply got to his feet, allowed Carolyn to lead him away.
He thought he was smiling, grinning, but the family—the nuns—
the strange men—looked at him tenderly, with understanding.

The phenomenon continued throughout the day, the old man
in a trance, and several hundred frightened visitors were allowed,

singly, in the room to drop to their knees, pray, stare, and leave; but the bleeding did not abate, neither that evening nor the next day, and the audience of the faithful continued. There was an alarming swell on Saturday afternoon. Walt waited out these hours at the hotel, in the lounge, reading newspapers about the miracle at St. Jerome's, which the Church, though refusing comment, was viewing "with benevolent interest." There were side articles about other miracles, most of them in Italy, one in southern France. Opinions of doctors, who were baffled, opinions of other author- ities, one of them—Walt read with anger—who attributed the bleeding to psychosomatic blisters! Walt did not see his brothers and sisters, they were at the home, near the old man, so he began to mutter to himself as he drank. Sometimes his mind, jolted naked by the insanity of this experience, called for flight, escape: if he did not escape soon he would be doomed. He forgot to eat and the inertia of half-pleasant nausea overtook him. On Saturday afternoon he was sick off and on for hours, waiting patiently on the edge of the bathtub, then he drank a little more until dinner. He came upon Ronald in the hotel lobby: Ronald looked aged, his hair had fallen loose about his forehead. But he smiled and grip- ped Walt's shoulders passionately. "He knows us!" he said. "The way he looks when we kneel by him—when you knelt too, did you see it? He recognizes us!"

Walt woke the next morning, oddly relaxed. Then he remem- bered that it was Sunday; all was over. Resurrection. He felt drained, pleased, his stomach ached with hunger. Perhaps his father would die before next Easter. Perhaps he would die. He ordered breakfast from room service, showered, shaved, hung out the door looking for someone familiar—saw no one—saw, out the window, people dressed for Easter Sunday, resplendent in the sun- shine. On an impulse he opened the window, grunting. There was a sound of remote bells.

He ate ravenously—eggs fried in butter, bacon, toast with jelly of two sorts, grape and apple. Cups of hot coffee, sweetened with cream. He watched the food lovingly as he ate, later he brushed his teeth and watched himself in the mirror with approval, then he dressed himself with a sense of pleasure and freedom: some catharsis had taken place after all, the miracle had touched him.

He sped out of town to St. Jerome's, which jutted out of the earth in a glory.

The foyer was radiant with lilies. Walt passed them, through the aisle which they bounded, frail white proud things that had blossomed out of the nursing home air itself. He exchanged greetings with young nuns, with strangers, men and women decked in fine warm clothes, little girls in patent leather shoes. It occurred to him, ascending the stairs for the last time, that he had not yet thought about his father—facing him now would be more difficult than facing him on Friday, when he was transfigured, another person. What did one say to such a being? But the Sunday air buoyed him, cheered him. Doors were opened upon domestic scenes—families sitting around beds, around old men in wheelchairs. Radios played, television sets were on. By one doorway a pile of breakfast dishes, plate smeared with hardened egg, were set carelessly on the floor—such was the vagabond holiday mood of Easter! But the door to his father's old room was closed, locked, and Walt wandered on, puzzled, down the corridor to the sun porch . . . which was blocked off by bureaus and bedframes dragged down from the attic, surely, and seeing this Walt's blood seemed to slow.

There were his brothers standing by a railing, looking down over a stairway, smoking. And Carolyn on a leather couch, legs crossed and stockings straining with muscle—legs nearly as girlish as ever. Ronald came up to Walt gravely. "Well, have you heard? It isn't over." "Isn't over?" Walt said. He saw immediately, in his mind's eye, a calendar; perhaps there was a confusion of dates. "The bleeding hasn't stopped," Ronald said, looking significantly at Walt. Walt wanted to say, "God's time is not necessarily man's time," but Ronald was so frightened—so *disappointed*—that Walt only stared abruptly down at his feet, as if something had dragged his gaze that way. "No one knows what's wrong," Ronald said. "Clara's in there with him, they can't get her to leave. It's been hell, Walt, you don't know—we think Clara might be—might need — You're so goddamed lucky, aren't you, off in your corner when things get tough!" Ronald's sickish face was puffy and distorted, like that of a bulldog. "Leave us to worry about it like you've always done!"

Walt pulled away and approached Ronald from another side,

as if executing a dance step; this seemed to work. "What have they done about it? Do the newsmen know?" he whispered. "It's been kept a secret," Ronald said. "They expect it to stop soon. Today. For God's sake why hasn't it stopped? It's only supposed to bleed a few hours on Friday." "Is he in pain?" said Walt. But Ronald shrugged his shoulders. "Money couldn't get him any better care. I've got to get started back, my wife called, she's worried as hell," he said, "and if Art wants a ride, and Carolyn and. . . . The responsibility of it. . . . Could you take Clara home? It's sure to stop today, it started earlier and maybe that's why it kept on longer." "How's Clara?" said Walt. "Oh, God, Clara. . . . You remember the time she ripped some evening dress with her heel, putting it on? The same thing. . . ." "Does he talk?" said Walt. "Yes, he talks," Ronald said abruptly. "Art," he said, holding out his arm, "what time do you have?"

Walt stared at the closed door. He felt dizzy, isolated. Everything spun away from him, even time: here he was back on Friday again, forced to enter that door, approach that bed, kneel, cross himself, sniff at the blood. . . . He argued gently with a nun who came at him out of nowhere, was admitted, saw with shock Clara's disorderly figure jerking to its feet as he entered the room. There was his father in bed, the same position! Nothing had changed except that the room was empty now of people, filled sweetly with lilies. Clara, on the other side of the bed, stared resentfully across at Walt. The old man was covered now with a brown blanket—lovingly darned at one corner, by a solitary, smiling old nun—his hands still out, though bandaged thickly, face propped up against the pillows. There was a small metal crucifix propped up against a fold in the blanket. The old man squinted at Walt as he approached. The room was silent, only from afar could they hear the pleasant muffled sounds of televisions, conversations, children's cries. At the bedside Walt saw the old man's lips move. Walt stared, transfixed, he awaited his name . . . the old man said something but Walt's ears were deafened by blood, he had to stoop like a little old man himself and say, "I didn't hear." The old man's throat quivered and the lips moved again. "I hurt," he said. Walt, still bent, stared at nothing—at the pillow. "I hurt," his father said again.

Walt stared. Again he felt the sensation of being alone, of being

lost, as if ordinary time and the ordinary people it involved had
been sucked violently away from him; even Clara, ravaged by
despair, looked on without involvement or comprehension. It was
at that moment, judging finally that old, handsome, dying face,
that Walt understood what had happened to his father. Safe in his
old age, before that safe in his tranquillity, he had refined himself
out of life—he had had, so easily, six children, he had given them
nothing, not his own identity, not identities of their own, he had
not distinguished one from the other, he had moved as a ghost
among the mild, ghostly illusions of this world, as a young man
and, now, an old man; he had never been a man; and he was
being educated now in the pain of being human. "Why, this is a
punishment," Walt said at once, almost laughing at the surprise of
his discovery. "This isn't a blessing, who told you that? This is a
punishment. A punishment." He looked up: Clara stared with
hatred at him. And his father, was that not a sly look, sly and
knowing behind the wincing pain? "You're being punished!"
Walt cried.

There were others around him, nurses, and a man he had not
seen before; they propelled him around. "A punishment! Or a
penance—your word for it!" he shouted into the face of one of the
nuns. "*He* knows! Ask *him!*" he said, jerking around to point
with his jaw back at the old man. At the opened door they
scuffled. Walt looked around again at the bed. Tears burned his
eyes. "Punishment that you deserve! Goddam selfish old bastard,
now you're getting it! God's on the right track! Got your number
—never loved us, did you? Took all our love from us and—" They
had pushed him out the door but he continued, laughing, seeing
the faces of his brothers rush toward him— "Took it and kept
taking it, a goddam sewer! a drain! down a toilet, anything we gave
you! Now you're getting it good! —He is, he's getting it good,"
Walt was crying at his brothers. "He's laying in there and told me
how he changed his mind and doesn't want the miracle any more,
he told me it with his eyes. He says he hates God, hates Christ,
says Christ had it easier than he does, if there ever was a real
Christ—which he doubts! Told me it with his eyes!" He felt a
sharp pain through his sleeve—a needle? He spun around and
grabbed something—the doctor's jacket—and with rage borne out
of revenge for his father, for the joke played upon him, began to

tear violently. Tears spilled out over his face, onto his own thresh-
ing hands.

Walt was not allowed in St. Jerome's again, so he waited down
at the hotel, in his room, lying on his rumpled bed. He found out
that Ronald and Art had gone—that was Monday afternoon. No
change in his father. He tried to get in touch with Carolyn but
there was never anyone in her room, his notes were never answered. . . . On Wednesday he paid part of his hotel bill, aware
that the management was suspicious of him; he paid with a check
which was worthless, but they would not know that immediately;
he was elated with his own cunning. But as if to give him away his
hands trembled as he made out the check. Upstairs he waited the
hours away, lying on his bed. He forgot to drink. His eyes grew
sore as if weakening from disuse. On Thursday he understood the
peculiar inertia, the heavy calm that had dulled his brain for so
long, when he was told of his father's death.

A professional-looking stranger who had knocked gently, whose
eyes, in spite of the message of gravity to be given, could not help
but wander about the smelling, cluttered room. If there were toast
crusts on the floor there, those eyes would seek them out! The
stranger spoke gently to Walt. "He managed to get out of the
room during the night and found his way down to the visitors'
restroom, the men's room, the room by the stairs— Strips of sheet
he tore from his bedclothes—did harm to himself— If you'd like to
get dressed and come with me— He was found in the morning—"
Walt lay on the bed, his legs outstretched. Though he had heard
only part of the man's speech he could see his father's skinny
body dangling in the air as clearly as if the old man had hanged
himself in the hotel closet, pushing the hangers to one side. Walt
felt neither surprise nor relief. "Did the bleeding stop, then?" he
said. "Your father was out of his mind with the pain, he wasn't
responsible for what he did," the man said. "My father was responsible for what he did," Walt said with dignity.

The man waited for him outside. Time went slowly, it took
time to dress. He ran his razor, dry, over his jaw, lost interest,
turned around in the white cramped bathroom as if looking for
something—forgot what it was— The white walls blurred and
dazzled his vision; a roaring began in his ears. What legacy had
his father left him? His father had recognized him! He had known

him, had talked to him—he had left him a legacy of death, spiteful death, but a work of art! Walt turned his palms up close to his face and stared at them. No blood. Nothing. No marks, no scars, no hints of anything, not even blisters. Clean as a life never quite lived. There were wrinkles there, and hints of soft, blue veins beneath, far beneath, pinkish-grey skin that looked, upon examination, more like wood than flesh—the same hands he remembered looking at, idly, one day, as a child, as if those innocent palms might tell him something about the life to come.

MARGARET SHEDD was born in Iran, of missionary parents. Known for her short stories appearing in *The New Yorker*, *Harper's* and many other magazines, she has written several novels as well: the first, *Hurricane Caye*, published in 1942 by Harper's, and more recently *Return to the Beach* and *Run*, both published by Doubleday. She spends much of her time in Mexico City, where she is Director of Centro Mexicano de Escritores, a binational organization for writers.

The Everlasting Witness

They three were eating breakfast on the terrace, a thousand and one felicitous birds in the garden trees. The coffee was exactly right, poured from its American electric percolator. In unsullied damp brown circles of soft earth the roses bloomed serenely against the pink Mexican wall. Marian's brother-in-law read the English page, as dedicated as a nice little boy reading the funnies, and Theresa, Marian's sister, chatted softly and merrily about their next Cuernevaca week-end. Theresa's bright smile had always been her mark and now, childless and with a husband beyond war age, and a life both ordered and gay, it looked as if that smile had justified itself.

Marian opened her mouth to tell them what she had done the night before and then she closed it on brioche, no words. What she had done was to try and find the film again, the war news-reel in which she had seen Jerry, her son. Or had she seen him? They ought to be told that the uncertainty had not been removed by this trip to Mexico. If she could explain the plain necessity to them maybe they would help her. But her next and clearer thought, untouched by terrace, food, and birds, was that this matter was all her own and had to be accomplished without help. Evidence of that was her husband's letting her come down

alone; the trip to Mexico was for her to find herself, get back on
her feet, return to him healed.

Well, she had not expected to look for the film, had not even
known she could look with only her smattering of Spanish. But
the night before—the first time her sister and brother-in-law had
left her alone—she had gone to the dictionary and got the two
words *cine* and *guerra*, and combining them with a question mark
had asked them over and over on the phone, going down the
movie houses in the yellow section of the book. At one of the
box offices a golden Mexican voice told her in perfect English
that the word she wanted was not *cine* but *noticias*, so she had
had to call the first part of the list over again. She now knew,
whether correctly or not, that three places had news-reels about
the war. Probably she had missed some but she was going to start
with these. She had not been able to understand the showing times
so she would have to go to the theatre and sit through whatever
came. Probably she could only manage one in a day because of
Theresa's persistence in helping her towards equanimity; it was
doubtful whether more than a few hours' absence would be
possible.

The Olimpia, the del Prado, and the Cine Mexico. She found
out exactly where each one was on the map in her red guide-
book. For that matter she could get into a taxi and say the
name of the theatre but she thought she would rather drive herself and keep the whole event within her control. Maybe this
was why she had brought her car to Mexico. Her husband had
wanted her to fly and she had said no, obstinately and without
being able to explain. And he (who was Jerry's stepfather and
therefore involved multifoldly in her suffering, not singly as a real
father would have been) gently accepted her decision and drove
her as far as Memphis. Although they didn't talk about it, she
knew he never would have let her go away from him except
that her sister was in Mexico, and also because he was pretty sure
she wouldn't be able to see the film there. But that part of it
had not worked because she hadn't been able to let it work.

Five months ago she had had the notice that Jerry was
missing in action. Twenty-and-a-half years old. His father had
died early in the other war. Jerry was seven then and she had had

to manage him alone, had sometimes failed him, had sometimes been burdened too greatly, but she had always loved him. Maybe that had not been enough. She had married again when he was seventeen but this had not given him a retroactive father for the twelve-thirteen-fourteen-year-old times of crisis. So he was not ready for the army when he had to go. He had been mixed up and scared. And in six months he was missing in action.

She could hardly remember now what happened to her right after the notification. Nightmare rides of balking misery which clattered over wide fields and hills of the rubbled dying. She was looking for him, finding his hand with his father's ring on the little finger, holding the hand to give it warmth, reaching to the wrist; and then the sweat of terror which brought her back to what she supposed must be reality. If this happened at night, her husband was there and his arms came around her, his hand on the side of her head, holding her to his shoulder. But that was also when she reached the ebb of pain because she had comfort and Jerry, wherever he was, had none.

It was like that until she saw the picture the first time. They went to the movies fairly often. Her husband always knew what they were going to see, asked the times carefully, got to the main picture and avoided news-reels. She had hardly noticed this and did not want to. Once two indolent people in the seats next to theirs delayed them, and the news-reel started. From the beginning it was about the war. She sat down again, her hands tight in her lap. Her husband was lost to her. She was alone. They were showing the finest new weapons, grand, shining, and built perfectly for death. Whoever summoned and made palpable all that force and skill knew death was best and would be earless to the little voice of mothers whose sons were their children before they got to be targets or heroes. Her hands and her neck began to sweat. But she knew that no emotion was pertinent.

And then some soldier boys came on the screen. They were prisoners of war. Someone had got a chance to take their pictures at a prison-compound gate. They were thin, young, sick American soldiers moving bemused. She said to herself they don't want to look right at the camera; they are angry or ashamed or both and their guards are saying to them, albeit in a different language, "Smile now so your mother can see you." So they will not smile. Why should they? Who took the picture, she was asking herself, was it an American who got permission or one of their own? Or maybe the boys didn't know the picture was being taken. They lolled against a gate frame and a plank wall. The narrator voice was full of professional pity but it gave no information.

She felt her blood pricking along her temples; now it was pounding, and there was pressure in her chest below the hollow. Jerry could be there. So strong a hope must play delaying games. He was not there.

He was there. One boy stood with his back to the camera, leaning stooped against a gate lintel, and on the finger of the hand that held the post there was a ring she recognised. There wouldn't be another like it. She had had it made for Jerry's father. The boy with his back to the camera began to straighten up; he was turning. But the picture was over.

The next was a roller-skating race. The tailored voice left behind it the sentiment siphoned in for the boys and went with gusto into a wild chant about sports. She got out of the seat still unconscious of her husband, excused herself politely to the people who had held them up, and went to the ladies' room where she vomited and then, immediately, in a renewal of energy, was full of plans.

Her husband went with her three times to see the film, and after that asked her to promise not to go any more. She made the promise but she could not keep it. The first time she saw the picture alone she was sure there was more action, only a flicking motion, but more. That was hope and she had to feed it.

Her husband made inquiries. The War Department answered they had no record of Jerry in a prison camp. Of course the enemy's reports on prisoners of war were not necessarily accurate. And they said they knew about the film. It was taken by American photographers who had been given permission because somehow the enemy thought it was good propaganda, but they had been forced to shoot from outside the gate only what they could catch that way and in a few minutes. The man who wrote said that as far as he had been able to find out nothing had been cut from the film.

But she was sure there was more. She followed the film to

every booking in town, second run, in the suburbs, in the drive-ins. Sometimes she stayed afterwards to see the roller-skating queens, Miss Hoboken and Miss Los Angeles. Sometimes she came out quickly, blinking in the light, leaving her boys behind her in the dark. It made her think they were safe there. That was not altogether the point but it was maybe three-quarters of it: that if she saw the picture it meant they were there (and Jerry) not dead on some chewed-up hill. She knew them all and they were Jerry's friends. She thought they were talking to him, "Why don't you turn around, kid? We ain't going to play up to this and grin from ear to ear to make out we're well off, but you better at least turn around. Your mother might be glad to see you." He was obstinate as he always had been, and a little slow, but he had been getting ready to turn. No, she was sure he had turned.

That was the way it was. It had got so that even if she knew the time was past to find it any more, she kept looking and looking as if she had transferred the nightmare battlefield search into this other kind and as if she might have to go back to the first if she stopped this.

And how could she have imagined that Mexico would be any different? The Olimpia, the del Prado, and the Cine Mexico. None of them first run so it was possible. She wanted to ask her brother-in-law behind his newspaper what they did to American news-reels here, cut them more? But the risk was too much. They might lie to her or in some other way keep her from going.

When she arrived a fortnight before she had asked her sister to give her a duty in the house. So Theresa gave her the flowers to arrange. The house was not far from the Dolores market, half a traffic circle of pure flowers. Marian had gone there every few days. Up to now Theresa went with her, or dropped her and picked her up. To-day she would go in her own car, she told them.

"Are you sure you know the way, Marian?"

"Of course, across the park and around that museum the opposite way from the one that looks right, and then the turn and out the gate. I know it perfectly." Her voice was sensible and secure.

But she had dallied, first on the terrace and then on the way across the park. This was the day. But what day?

When she had spent the eighty-four hours alone—from the morning she left her husband in Memphis to the evening she met Theresa, who flew to Monterrey to ride into Mexico with her —she had kept hoping that the long flat way would be a highway out of confusion, levelling it, thinning it down to understanding, as if the moving air would whip through the car and dissolve the granulated mass of unanswered worries. She wanted one firm answer: yes, they have a right to take him, no matter what; yes, the clatter and chatter of arms and the frail tremor of boys' fear, lost in a bunker or a new shrapnel-proof vest or wherever however, is a combination of sounds in some way acceptable to a mother. How? But the only thing she discovered on that ride was that there is no firm answer. Some place near Corpus Christi, Texas, she found out that the haze of grey questions was not going to lift.

When Jerry's father had died it was precise: a ring sent back to her; and event reported; sad notes on a gliding trumpet which said that pink gingham, rosebud, golden night love was gone. It broke her heart. After a while that mended in its own way. So if now she could only take her heart in her two hands to break it in a jagged line a little to one side of the middle . . . Was it different for mothers than for wives, this stream of grief muddied by the clay that children are made of? There was no answer for a mother; that was all she found out on the long ride.

She summed it up now on the short ride across the park to the flower market. She did this rather slowly, driving slowly too. And she pulled her car to a curb, because it came to her (like another trumpet call, like a call to duty?) that there was indeed an answer, and that this was why she had followed the movie treadmill around and around. The trouble was that she had never been willing to accept the clear issue of death or life.

Now, stopped by the road in the park, she decided categorically, hitting the back of one hand into the palm of the other over and over, that if she found him, found the picture here and now, maybe even that very day (unreasonably unquestioning that she would see it) then she would know he was alive and she would simply make waiting womanly and rational. And if she did not see it in the del Prado, Olimpia, or Cine Mexico then she would say he was dead. Because war is death or life. The line must be drawn, and if it was on death's side then her heart would have to break and she would have to go on, go back to life, get back to her husband who was waiting for her patiently and with love. It was a decision. The uncertainty was at last behind her.

At the flower market she walked up and down in front of the stalls, and saw more clearly because of her decision, so she thought. First she looked at the flowers: pansies, purple iris, marigolds, and sweet peas—amplitude—some that were like feathers, fluffy and silent, and some like banners, and all marshalled by skilful hands. Behind everything the backdrop of gladioli which because of their colours could be forgiven their pretensions.

She looked at the people. There was a family at the farthest stand. She had just found fresh violets there, and the gladioli were less blatant and unshriven probably because it was a poor stand and a poor family that could not afford the finest and tallest of anything. The woman's face was sad. She was sick. But her hands were beautiful. She was nursing a baby.

Marian wanted no grand flowers, only the soft and touchable. She browsed to other stands and pansies and peonies. She bought a big wheel of red carnations, and some little gentle-petalled primroses with shiny dark green leaves. She was loaded down beyond the vases or even the places for flowers in her sister's house. She turned away at last and ran head on into the man who opened car doors (but he had missed hers when she parked) and who was now tottering out to the curb for someone else.

He had a shaking sickness and his face looked old and bloated under the tremors and jerking muscles. Theresa never seemed to mind him and always gave him two pesos, for nothing, because he shook too much to carry flowers or really even to open car doors. But he was always there, and now Marian, on her own, sincerely hated him. The disgust and horror of him she had suppressed on others visits welled up unchecked.

He seemed to recognise her although he looked all of an idiot.
He came back from the curb to her and when she veered away
from him he puttered to her car which was parked in front
of the stand belonging to the family with the sick mother.
He fumbled for her car door.

"No," she said sharply, and shuddered because she could not
stand the touch of his hand on her door.

The nursing mother looked up. There was no disapproval in
her face but she called to the idiot, "Ven, ven, Pepito."

Marian felt ashamed, only because the other woman had seen
her disgust, but she could not have controlled that. Then
she turned back, not knowing exactly why—telling herself that it
was because to carry that load of flowers and leave them in a
parked car for possibly some hours, was absurd. Standing in
front of the flower-stand woman she knew she would not have to
explain that she wanted to leave them.

The other said, "Si, señora, si," and with lovely gestures asked
her husband to take the flowers and put them in the shade
behind the stand. The idiot meantime stood to one side awkwardly, and unpleasantly chewed a piece of cocoanut he had
picked up in the gutter.

So now she was going to the del Prado. Now she could go,
whatever was that need for buying flowers, taken care of. She
banged her car door and the idiot trembled but the nursing
woman looked up from the baby and smiled.

Down town, she had to park her car in a garage. She would
have liked not to go through the grind, clatter, jitter of the narrow
entryway. She needed quiet. Everything was getting ready for this
moment. She did not carry the flowers in her car but she carried
them in her heart. Now she was going to find out whether it
was death or life. Either she could tolerate. Again it did not
occur to her that the news-reel might not be there.

It was there.

She came in in the middle of a French costume picture about
love-making in a big bed with a mirror over it. She wondered
how they got the fabric sheen that always goes with movie
lasciviousness, whether the cloth was really stiff satin or if there

was some cheap material which photographed like that? The
actress' breasts looked as though they had been gilded to match
the gleam of the stuffs around her. The French words were finely
enunciated. The audience tittered in Spanish. A young man guffawed over and over on the same pitch. A French gentleman in
top hat and cane sang something which ended the picture and
tied it all together, judging from the louder laughing and audible
translation. Then the theatre was dark. There was the jerking
flicker of a reel starting and stopping, conglomerate unhuman
figures and motion, whistles from the audience. It started. She
saw the word *noticias* and this did not match the way the word
had looked in her mind's eye. She corrected the mental image.

She was burning hot from head to foot. The prisoner of war
scene opened the news-reel. Here they had omitted the cannons.
The boys were before her eyes. She had not doubted she was
going to see them but this did not keep her from being frightened.

She had long ago given the boys names. Chris was a slender
blond who was whittling away. He stood there all during the
picture, the one or two long dear moments. "I love him with all
my heart," she whispered to herself, forming the words to make
them solid. (She knew she loved Chris that much because of
her pent-up love and terror for Jerry.) She looked sideways to
the right but without shifting her head. Now it was Walter on the
screen, dear Walter with a deep stubble on his face and a scarf
wrapped around his neck. "He has a cold," she thought, this
time not saying it, and wondering why she had never thought it
before. She remembered faster than lightning many and many a
cold-remedy including steaming eucalyptus oil. Jerry had always
had colds when he was little, and that had worked the best. She
smelled eucalyptus. The smell was a barrier she was holding on to,
to keep the movie from going ahead. And she managed to keep
it back. But all the same it did come to the boy who might be
Jerry.

How many times had she thought about that ring: by the law
of averages could another wife have designed another exact ring
for her husband? Or could it maybe have been that she herself
did not design it, but that the drawing she took into the jeweller
was skilfully changed and incorporated by him into some ring he

had in stock and she had thought it was hers, and so some other person might have had one like it? There was the hand on the gate post, and the ring. The hand looked chapped and wizened, not a boy's.

The boy to whom it belonged began to turn. Her eyes blinked, waiting for the end, anxious now for the roller-skaters that came after and whom she knew almost as well as she knew the boys. He turned farther round. With her eyes riveted on him she could still see that Chris, in the back, looked up for the first time, and that he lifted his hand from whittling, abruptly, as if he were saying, don't do it, don't take the picture. The face of the boy who turned, now filling the camera, unmercifully filling the screen, was Jerry's face, but it was blank, as empty as an idiot's. He grimaced with his mouth and the hand with the ring was lifted to catch the twitching, trying to hold it. His eyes were focused straight out and his mother drowned in those vacant eyes.

There was an indrawn breath of horror from the audience and then the anxious and everlasting titter. And Marian heard everything. She saw everything.

Then a man was talking to her. "May I help you, madam? May I not help you?"

She heard her own breathing which was like someone gasping for the last of life. The man, and then a woman, took her gently arm-in-arm. She had been plucking at her mouth. The helping woman entwined her fingers with hers, and they brought her out into the light.

"Please madam, to where may we take you? Are you in this hotel?"

She shook her head, unable yet to speak.

"May I not call a doctor?"

"No, no." She knew now she would be able to take care of herself. She wanted to drive her car, in motion and tension to find rest. She gave them the parking tag. Once she looked at them while they were all waiting for the car and she saw she would always and forever know them and be known by them. Probably there would never be a chance for more than this four minutes in a garage waiting-room, but because of her pain and her trouble they did not try to conceal themselves. She did not have to describe them to herself. She knew them and and they her.

"Madam, is it for you to drive all right?" He said the double *l* against the *r* as if it were a caress that one known stranger was permitted to give another.

"Yes," she said, and "Goodbye and thanks." For the first time she felt like crying; it was because she had to say goodbye to them. The man said goodbye and the woman said nothing.

She drove out to the park and around for a while. And then she knew she must go to a place—the flight was ended. She had no place to go except the flower stands. She had marked that for return and she must return to it.

She went around the Dolores traffic circle once not finding any room to park. The second time there was a place; and right in front of it, the opener-and-closer of doors, the idiot, sat on the curb with his knees doubled over into the gutter. He was sleeping, his head thrown back against a telephone pole. His hands were thrown down on the cement of the sidewalk, no longer trembling, but abandoned. Nor was his head trembling and shaking. His face asleep was beautiful. He was not old, no, not old nor bloated as she had thought him, but thin and defenceless as the sleeping young are, beautiful, and an idiot.

BERNARD MALAMUD, now on the faculty of Bennington College, won the National Book Award in 1959 for his short stories, *The Magic Barrel*. His novels include *The Natural*, *The Assistant*, and *A New Life*. *Idiots First*, his second book of short stories was published in the fall of 1963. His short stories have appeared in several magazines both in the United States and in London.

The Jewbird

The window was open so the bird flew in. Flappity-flap with its frazzled black wings. That's how it goes. It's open, you're in. Closed, you're out and that's your fate. The bird wearily flapped through the open kitchen window of Harry Cohen's top-floor apartment on First Avenue near the lower East River. On a rod on the wall hung an escaped canary's cage, its door wide open, but this black-type long-beaked bird—its ruffled head and small dull eyes, crossed a little, making it look like a dissipated crow—landed, if not smack on Cohen's thick lamb chop, at least on the table close by. The frozen-foods salesman was sitting at supper with his wife and young son on a hot August evening last year. Cohen, a heavy man with hairy chest and beefy shorts; Edie, in skimpy yellow shorts and red halter; and their ten-year-old Morris (after her father)—Maurie, they called him, a nice kid though not overly bright—were all in the city after two weeks out, because Cohen's mother was dying. They had been enjoying Kingston, New York, but drove back when Mama got sick in her flat in the Bronx.

"Right on the table," said Cohen, putting down his beer glass and swatting at the bird. "Son of a bitch."

"Harry, take care with your language," Edie said, looking at Maurie, who watched every move.

The bird cawed hoarsely and with a flap of its bedraggled wings—feathers tufted this way and that—rose heavily to the top of the open kitchen door, where it perched staring down.

"Gevalt, a pogrom!"

"It's a talking bird," said Edie in astonishment.

"In Jewish," said Maurie.

"Wise guy," muttered Cohen. He gnawed on his chop, then put down the bone. "So if you can talk, state your business. What do you want?"

"If you can't spare a lamb chop," said the bird, "I'll settle for a piece of herring with a crust of bread. You can't live on nerve forever."

"This ain't a restaurant," Cohen replied. "All I'm asking is, What brings you to this address?"

"The window was open," the bird sighed, adding after a moment, "I'm running. I'm flying but I'm also running."

"From whom?" asked Edie with interest.

"Anti-Semeets."

"Anti-Semites?" they all said.

"That's from whom."

"What kind of anti-Semites bother a bird?" Edie asked.

"Any kind," said the bird. "Also including eagles, vultures, and hawks. And once in a while some crows will take your eyes out."

"But aren't you a crow?"

"Me? I'm a Jewbird."

Cohen laughed heartily. "What do you mean by that?"

The bird began dovening. He prayed without Book or tallith, but with great passion. Edie bowed her head though not Cohen. And Maurie rocked back and forth with the prayer, looking up with one wide-open eye.

When the prayer was done Cohen remarked, "No hat, no phylacteries?"

"I'm an old radical."

"You're sure you're not some kind of a ghost or dybbuk?"

"Not a dybbuk," answered the bird, "though one of my relatives had such an incident once. It's all over now, thanks God. They freed her from a former lover, a crazy jealous man. She's now the mother of two wonderful children."

"Birds?" Cohen asked slyly.

"Why not?"

"What kind of birds?"

"Like me. Jewbirds."

Cohen leaned back in his chair and guffawed. "That's a big laugh. I've heard of a Jewfish but not a Jewbird."

"We're once removed." The bird rested on one skinny leg, then on the other. "Please, could you spare maybe a piece of herring with a small crust of bread?"

Edie got up from the table.

"What are you doing?" Cohen asked her.

"I'll clear the dishes."

Cohen turned to the bird. "So what's your name, if you don't mind saying?"

"Call me Schwartz."

"He might be an old Jew changed into a bird by somebody," said Edie, removing a plate.

"Are you?" asked Harry, lighting a cigar.

"Who knows?" answered Schwartz. "Does God tell us everything?"

Maurie got up on his chair in his excitement. "What kind of herring?" he asked the bird.

"Get down, Maurie, or you'll fall," ordered Cohen.

"If you haven't got matjes, I'll take schmaltz," said Schwartz.

"All we have is marinated, with slices of onion—in a jar," said Edie.

"If you'll open for me the jar I'll eat marinated. Do you have also, if you don't mind, a piece of rye bread—the spitz?"

Edie thought she had.

"Feed him out on the balcony," Cohen said. He spoke to the bird. "After that, take off."

Schwartz closed both bird eyes. "I'm tired and it's a long way."

"Which direction are you headed, north or south?"

Schwartz, barely lifting his wings, shrugged.

"You don't know where you're going?"

"Where there's charity I'll go."

"Let him stay, Papa," said Maurie. "He's only a bird."

"So stay the night," Cohen said, "but not longer."

In the morning Cohen ordered the bird out of the house but

Maurie cried, so Schwartz stayed for a while. Maurie was still on vacation from school and his friends were away. He was lonely and Edie enjoyed the fun he had, playing with the bird.

"He's no trouble at all," she told Cohen, "and his appetite is very small."

"What'll you do when he makes dirty?"

"He flies across the street in a tree when he makes dirt and if nobody passes below, who notices?"

"So all right," said Cohen, "but I'm dead set against it. I warn you he ain't gonna stay here long."

"What have you got against the poor bird?"

"Poor bird, my ass. He's a foxy bastard. He thinks he's a Jew."

"What difference does it make what he thinks?"

"A Jewbird, what a chuzpah. One false move and he's out on his drumsticks."

At Cohen's insistence Schwartz lived out on the balcony in a new wooden birdhouse Edie had bought him.

"With many thanks," said Schwartz, "though I would rather have a human roof over my head. You know how it is at my age. I like the warm, the windows, the smell of cooking. I would also be glad to see once in a while the *Jewish Morning Journal* and have an occasional schnapps because it helps my breathing, thanks God. But whatever you give me, you'll hear no complaints."

However, when Cohen brought home a bird feeder full of dried corn, Schwartz said, "Impossible."

Cohen was annoyed. "What's the matter, Cross-eyes, is your life getting too good for you? Are you forgetting what it means to be migratory? I'll bet a helluva lot of crows you happen to be acquainted with, Jews or otherwise, would give their eyeteeth to eat this corn."

Schwartz did not answer. What can you say to a grubber yung?

"Not for my digestion," he later explained to Edie. "Cramps. Herring is better even if it makes you thirsty. At least rainwater is free." He laughed sadly in breathy caws.

And herring, thanks to Edie, who knew where to shop, was what Schwartz got, with an occasional piece of potato pancake, and even a bit of soup meat when Cohen wasn't looking.

When school began in September, before Cohen could once again suggest giving the bird the boot, Edie prevailed on him to wait a little while until Maurie adjusted.

"To deprive him right now might hurt his school work, and you know what trouble we had last year."

"So okay, but sooner or later the bird goes. That I promise you."

Schwartz, though nobody had asked him, took on full responsibility for Maurie's performance in school. In return for favors granted, when he was let in for an hour or two at night, he spent most of his time overseeing the boy's lessons. He sat on top of the dresser near Maurie's desk as the boy laboriously wrote out his homework. Maurie was a restless type and Schwartz softly kept him to his studies. He also listened to him practice his screechy violin, taking a few minutes off now and then to rest his ears in the bathroom. And they afterwards played dominoes. The boy was an indifferent checker player and it was impossible to teach him chess. When he was sick, Schwartz read him comic books though he personally disliked them. But Maurie's work improved in school and even his violin teacher admitted his playing was better. Edie gave Schwartz credit for these improvements though the bird pooh-poohed them.

Yet he was proud there was nothing lower than C minuses on Maurie's report card, and on Edie's insistence celebrated with a little schnapps.

"If he keeps up like this," Cohen said, "I'll get him in an Ivy League college for sure."

"Oh, I hope so," sighed Edie.

But Schwartz shook his head. "He's a good boy—you don't have to worry. He won't be a shicker or a wife beater, God forbid, but a scholar he'll never be, if you know what I mean, although maybe a good mechanic. It's no disgrace in these times."

"If I were you," Cohen said, angered, "I'd keep my big snoot out of other people's private business."

"Harry, please," said Edie.

"My goddamn patience is wearing out. That Cross-eyes butts into everything."

Though he wasn't exactly a welcome guest in the house, Schwartz gained a few ounces, although he did not improve in appearance. He looked bedraggled as ever, his feathers unkempt, as though he had just flown out of a snowstorm. He spent, he admitted, little time taking care of himself. Too much to think about. "Also outside plumbing," he told Edie. Still there was more glow to his eyes so that though Cohen still called him Cross-eyes he said it less emphatically.

Liking his situation, Schwartz tried tactfully to stay out of Cohen's way, but one night when Edie was at the movies and Maurie was taking a hot shower, the frozen-foods salesman began a quarrel with the bird.

"For Christ sake, why don't you wash yourself sometimes? Why must you always stink like a dead fish?"

"Mr. Cohen, if you'll pardon me, if somebody eats garlic he will smell from garlic. I eat herring three times a day. Feed me flowers and I will smell like flowers."

"Who's obligated to feed you anything at all? You're lucky you get herring."

"Excuse me, I'm not complaining," said the bird. "You're complaining."

"What's more," said Cohen, "even from out on the balcony I can hear you snoring away like a pig. It keeps me awake at night."

"Snoring," said Schwartz, "isn't a crime, thanks God."

"All in all you are a goddamn pest and free-loader. Next thing you'll want to sleep in bed next to my wife."

"Mr. Cohen," said Schwartz, "on this rest assured. A bird is a bird."

"So you say, but how do I know you're a bird and not some kind of a goddamn devil?"

"If I was a devil you would know already. And I don't mean because of your son's good marks."

"Shut up, you bastard bird!" shouted Cohen.

"Grubber yung!" cawed Schwartz, rising to the tips of his talons, his long wings outstretched.

Cohen was about to lunge for the bird's scrawny neck but Maurie came out of the bathroom, and for the rest of the evening, until Schwartz's bedtime on the balcony, there was pretended peace.

But the quarrel had deeply disturbed Schwartz and he slept badly. His snoring woke him, and awake, he was fearful of what would become of him. Wanting to stay out of Cohen's way, he kept to the birdhouse as much as possible. Cramped by it, he paced back and forth on the balcony ledge, or sat on it, staring into space. In the evenings, while overseeing Maurie's lessons, he often fell asleep. Awakening, he nervously hopped around exploring the four corners of the room. He spent much time in Maurie's closet, and carefully examined his bureau drawers when they were left open. And once when he found a large paper bag on the floor, Schwartz poked his way into it to investigate what the possibilities were. The boy was amused to see the bird in the paper bag.

"He wants to build a nest," he said to his mother.

Edie, sensing Schwartz's unhappiness, spoke to him quietly.

"Maybe if you did some of the things my husband wants you, you would get along better with him."

"Give me a for instance," Schwartz said.

"Like take a bath, for instance."

"I'm too old for baths," said the bird.

"He says you have a bad smell."

"Everybody smells. Some people smell because of their thoughts or because who they are. My bad smell comes from the food I eat. What does his come from?"

"I better not ask him or it will make him mad," said Edie.

In late November Schwartz froze on the balcony in the fog and cold, and especially on rainy days he woke with stiff joints and could barely move his wings. Already he felt twinges of rheumatism. He would have liked to spend more time in the warm house, particularly when Maurie was in school and Cohen at work. But though Edie was goodhearted and might have sneaked him in in the morning, just to thaw out, he was afraid to ask her. In the meantime Cohen, who had been reading articles about the migration of birds, came out on the balcony one night after work when Edie was in the kitchen preparing pot roast. Peeking into the birdhouse, he warned Schwartz to be on his way soon if he knew what was good for him. "Time to hit the flyways."

"Mr. Cohen, why do you hate me so much?" asked the bird. "What did I do to you?"

"Because you're an A number 1 troublemaker, that's why. Now scat or it's open war."

But Schwartz stubbornly refused to depart, so Cohen embarked on a campaign of harassing him, meanwhile hiding it from Edie and Maurie. Maurie hated violence and Cohen didn't want to leave a bad impression. He thought maybe if he played dirty tricks on the bird he would fly off without being physically kicked out. The vacation was over; let him make his easy living off the fat of somebody else's land. Cohen worried about the effect of the bird's departure on Maurie's schooling but decided to take the chance, first because the boy now seemed to have the knack of studying—give the black bird-bastard credit—and second because Schwartz was driving him bats by being there always, even in his dreams.

The frozen-foods salesman began his campaign against the bird by mixing watery cat food with the herring slices in Schwartz's dish. He also blew up and popped numerous paper bags outside the birdhouse as the bird slept, and when he had got Schwartz good and nervous, though not enough to leave, he brought a full-grown cat into the house, supposedly a gift for little Maurie, who had always wanted a pussy. The cat never stopped springing up at Schwartz whenever he saw him, one day managing to pull out several of his tailfeathers. And even at lesson time, when the cat was usually excluded from Maurie's room, though somehow or other he found his way in at the end of the lesson, Schwartz was desperately fearful of his life and flew from pinnacle to pinnacle—light fixture to clothestree to doortop—in order to elude the beast's wet jaws.

Once when the bird complained to Edie how hazardous his existence was, she said, "Be patient, Mr. Schwartz. When the cat gets to know you better he won't try to catch you any more."

"When he stops trying we will both be in Paradise," Schwartz answered. "Do me a favor and get rid of him. He makes my whole life worry. I'm losing feathers like a tree loses leaves."

"I'm awfully sorry but Maurie likes the pussy and sleeps with it."

What could Schwartz do? He worried but came to no decision, being afraid to leave. So he ate the herring garnished with cat food, tried hard not to hear the paper bags bursting like firecrackers outside the birdhouse at night, and lived terror-stricken closer to the ceiling than the floor, as the cat, his tail flicking, endlessly watched him.

Weeks went by. Then on the day after Cohen's mother had died in her flat in the Bronx and Maurie came home with a zero on an arithmetic test, Cohen, enraged, waited until Edie had taken the boy to his violin lesson, then openly attacked the bird. He chased him with a broom on the balcony and Schwartz frantically flew back and forth, finally escaping into his birdhouse. Cohen triumphantly reached in, and grabbing both skinny legs, dragged the bird out, cawing loudly, his wings wildly beating. He whirled the bird around and around his head. But Schwartz, as he moved in circles, managed to duck in and catch Cohen's nose in his beak, and hung on for dear life. Cohen cried out in great pain, punched the bird with his fist, and tugging at its legs with all his might, pulled his nose free. Again he swung the yawking Schwartz around until the bird grew dizzy, then with a furious heave flung him into the night. Schwartz sank like stone into the street. Cohen then tossed the birdhouse and feeder after him, listening until they crashed on the sidewalk. For a full hour, broom in hand, his heart palpitating and nose throbbing with pain, Cohen waited for Schwartz to return but the brokenhearted bird didn't.

That's the end of that dirty bastard, the salesman thought, and went in. Edie and Maurie had come home.

"Look," said Cohen, pointing to his bloody nose swollen three times its normal size, "what that sonofabitchy bird did. It's a permanent scar."

"Where is he now?" Edie asked, frightened.

"I threw him out and he flew away. Good riddance."

Nobody said no, though Edie touched a handkerchief to her eyes and Maurie rapidly tried the nine-times table and found he knew approximately half.

In the spring when the winter's snow had melted, the boy, moved by a memory, wandered in the neighborhood, looking for Schwartz. He found a dead black bird in a small lot near the river, his two wings broken, neck twisted, and both eyes plucked clean.

"Who did it to you, Mr. Schwartz?" Maurie wept.

"Anti-Semeets," Edie said later.

SALLIE BINGHAM is a graduate of Radcliffe, 1958. She began writing fiction while in college and won the Dana Reed Prize for 1957 for a story that was reprinted in *Best American Short Stories* in 1959. Several others have appeared in *Atlantic Monthly*. Her novel, *After Such Knowledge,* was published by Houghton Mifflin in 1960.

The Banks of the Ohio

Every afternoon that summer, rain or shine, the yellow taxi would turn into Pion Way at six minutes past six o'clock and stop in front of the house. Lutie's mother would spot it from the window seat where she had spent the day, licking envelopes for charity and watching the world go by, and she would call, "Lamb Tail, I believe I see him." Given a chance, she would add, "Lutie, I'm not at all sure he should park there. It's marked No Parking, and you know I try to be impartial." So Lutie was nearly always ready when Shriver came, and she would run downstairs and out the door with the long day coiled like a spring behind her.

Outside, she would calm down and walk slowly, under the weight of her mother's watching, across the strip of burned grass to the yellow taxi. Shriver had never been known to get out for her, but he would lean across the seat to open the door.

Several times a week, Lutie brought a picnic hamper packed with tuna fish sandwiches and hard-boiled eggs—the same meek food she and her mother took every April to Burning Bush State Park when they went to see the wild flowers. For Shriver's sake, she would add a pickle jar of gin and ginger ale; the picnic was to be eaten in his rowboat, the *Dolly*.

The *Dolly* was the only thing Shriver owned. The taxi, of course, was borrowed—he was a college graduate, the taxi job was only for the time being—and he lived in a boardinghouse on

Third Street. Even the town he worked in, the town where Lutie bought every stitch she wore and ate cottage cheese salads with girls she had known in school, had no claims on Shriver. He had hitch-hiked up from Florida, stopping in Louisville because the trucker he was riding with had a load to deliver at a cigarette factory. After two years, Shriver still did not know the names of the city streets, and he usually had to ask his passengers to direct him. When they did not know, he would telephone Lutie from a diner—"Ah, hello, did you ever hear of a place called Shawnee Parkway?"—cutting into her quiet morning with a question about a place she might have heard of, but would surely never want to be. For some reason, most of Shriver's customers wanted to go to the South End.

He would never have kept his job for so long if his boss, a man named Daddy Armstrong, had not had such respect for education. Daddy had never had a college graduate driving for him before, and he was so impressed that he let Shriver keep the taxi at night, after work. Lutie sometimes thought of telling Daddy, in a joking way, that she knew every crack and seam in that taxi's cocoa-colored plastic upholstery. But that was ancient history—before the first of July, when Shriver bought the rowboat for twenty-five dollars and christened it with a bottle of ginger ale.

One afternoon toward the end of August, when the heat was at its height, they parked the taxi on Henny's Public Pier and took out the picnic and carried it down to the *Dolly*. Lutie got in first and settled herself in the stern. She was chary of her white piqué dress; the *Dolly's* seats were still not really clean, although she had gone after them with a scrubbing brush. Shriver cast off from the iron ring and gave the shore a shove with his foot, and they drifted out into the oily river.

It was hot enough to raise the smell of the yellow mud which the spring flooding of the river had left caked on the low-hanging trees. Under the trees, the banks were beaten bare except for poison ivy, lovely in autumn; back farther, green corn nobody owned grew as high as forests. The bare roots which humped along the banks were used for moorings by the houseboats. Lutie and Shriver drifted past one, the *Sugar Belle*, snubbed up tightly against the bank; there were geraniums in her window boxes

under blue-striped awnings, and deep inside, a radio was playing
softly. Next they passed an inhabited barge, with laundry limp
on a line and a woman hunched over, stirring dinner in a tin
pot.

Shriver dropped the mooring rope in a wet tangle on the bottom of the boat, and Lutie said, "If this is my house, you should
make more effort," as she bent to pick it up. Shriver said, "Be
careful, now," and started for the rowing seat. He was a tall person,
not heavy but large, and each time he put his foot down the boat
dipped to that side. At last he sat down and fitted the oars,
which were not even a pair—one was blue, and a foot longer—into
the oarlocks. He pulled the boat around in a tight circle. "I never
thought to see the day when I'd put up with a person afraid to
dirty her skirt," he said, watching the way Lutie was handling the
wet rope.

"Every time I come home with a spot on my skirt, Mother thinks
she's lost me," Lutie said. "Look out for that boat." The river
was crowded in the late afternoon, and half the people on it didn't
know beans. The big motor cruisers were just excuses for mindless
lechery; they were always running aground on Hog Island with an
unmarried couple in every berth.

Shriver pulled the *Dolly* to the left just in time. He did not
lower himself to look over his shoulder at the houseboat they
had barely missed. "Did your mother give you a lot of jaw about
getting in late last night?" He sounded practically hopeful.

Lutie did not answer until she had taken a good look at the
houseboat they were passing, the *Doreen Ann*, and drawn her
own conclusions from the beer bottles and the fat women sitting
with their legs up. It was Shriver's river, not hers. The only river
she knew was the protected stretch below the yacht club, where
her father used to sail his Lightning every Sunday until he died.

"She didn't say anything, except she had gotten a little lonely,"
she answered Shriver finally, and when he huffed she decided
not to tell him that her mother had drawn her down onto her
bed: "Lambie, these nights go on and on." Her mother's sweet
wistfulness, as well as the pink crepe de Chine nightgown she
was wearing, had reminded Lutie of the nights just after her
father's death, when they had been close and sorrowful as two
birds in a nest. Shriver did not know anything about the sweet-

ness of that bedroom, where the shades were always down and the drawers were full of hand-embroidered underwear and lavender sachets, breathing. Shriver was always saying she could not eat her cake and have it, but her mother needed her, and for more reasons than one.

"It would be better if she did get angry with us," Shriver was droning on. "Then at least something could be discussed." He failed to understand that nothing could be discussed with her mother except clothes or the weather, which covered a good deal of ground. "Eighty-nine at six forty-five; I heard it on the radio," her mother would say, and if Lutie replied, "I didn't suffer," it meant her evening with Shriver had been nice and well behaved. Twice her mother had almost lost her, when the humidity had risen as high as the heat and the only thing Lutie could think of was to shed her clothes and her complications and lie back in cool passion, allowed if not admired.

"Duck," Shriver warned, and he leaned on the oars while they floated under a low limb. "The funny thing is, I sort of like her," he said, beginning to thrash the oars again, "and she sort of likes me. Remember that time I came to dinner? She kept saying, 'Thank you, Mr. Ellis, for giving my little girl some excitement.'"

Lutie laughed. "Excitement!"

He leaned on the oars. "That's all it's been, isn't it, Lutie?"

"Oh, Shriver, we've been over and over that ground."

"We're spared a lot," he said, going back to joking. He never would drive her to the wall. "Think if she actually liked me and we had to go there to dinner every other night. Over the peach-walnut soufflé she'd be asking me my intentions."

"It's not that I mind Shriver Ellis being poor and half educated and having no future," Lutie mimicked what he must think her mother would say. "It's just he's such a *plain* person."

"Does she mean my face or my soul?"

She looked at him. It hurt, to have to say. She knew his face so well she couldn't defend it, even from her own spite. He was yellow-brown from a summer on the river, and his eyelashes and eyebrows were bleached out white, so that he looked as though he were always startled and staring. Yet it was a plain face, one she wouldn't have had any trouble losing in a crowd. He had spotted brown eyes which still did not really interest her—his soul?

—and his cuticles rose halfway over his nails, and she never could think of his size with any comfort. Sometimes she thought it was his sheer bulk which prevented her from wanting to see him without clothes and not, as he was always hinting, the look she would find afterward in her mother's eyes. He would simply have too much flesh to bear, once he was naked. And such solemn flesh! She had known from the first time she rode out from town in his taxi that Shriver was different from the well-bred boys she knew, who would roll all over you on the country club golf course and then go back to college and send you a post-card: "How's tricks?"

"Your soul, I guess she means," she said, and then she hated herself for a minute, because after three months of necking and straining she was still holding him down to jokes. "Oh, Shrive," she said, "it looks like we never can be serious."

That was a mistake. He dropped the oars and came for her, getting over the seat on all fours like a bear getting over a log. The boat dipped to one side, and she held on with both hands. "Go back, Shriver. You'll sink us both." But he was already kissing her on the ear and leaning his full weight on her shoulders until she thought she would cave in. "How about some supper, it must be way past seven o'clock," she said, reaching under his arm for the picnic basket.

He sat back then. "All right, church social. How much am I bid for this box?"

Unwrapping the sandwiches, she pressed each piece of waxed paper out flat and laid it back in the hamper. "You should have married a poor man," Shriver said, "with your ways."

"Don't get ugly with me, Shriver. Shall we tie up to the shore?" For the last five minutes, they had been floating sideways across the river.

"If we tie up, I'll try to get you to go on the bank, and you'll fight me about it for an hour."

I am just a girl, she wanted to say. I am just frightened. I wear elastic garter belts with blue roses and white cotton petticoats with eyelet embroidery, and although I really like you, I do not know your ways. But he had shamed her out of using those excuses. "All right, then, we'll just float wild in the river," she said, handing him a tuna fish sandwich to plug his mouth.

Watching him eat, she knew that was what she really wanted: to feed him, with homemade lemon cupcakes and gummy cheese pies, with hot love and cool affection, beef stew and jellied broth, until he was finally filled up and could let her be. "I guess it doesn't mean anything," she said, to rile him, peeling an egg. "All the good meals we've eaten together, the picnics and the casseroles and the blue-plate steak dinners. I guess nothing means anything, to you, except *that*."

"It's pretty thin pickings."

"Not for me, it isn't."

"Well, maybe not, but you have your house and your mother, and pretty soon, that job practically running L. A. Leak Dry Goods. And all your other neat little things."

"I don't see why you have to be so pitiful. You have your job, your life—" She had to stop there. His life had no more to it than a gnat's. Hitch-hiking up from the South with his family dead or gone; he didn't even have a picture to show her of the place where he'd been born. Thin pickings, indeed!

"You're right," he said. "All my life, I've had my job and my life and the whole weight of myself on my hands. It's not a satisfaction."

"Have another tuna sandwich," she said. She refused, of all things, to pity him.

As she held out the sandwich, she heard the drumming of a big boat. "That reminds me, we haven't seen another boat for an hour," she said, and she shaded her eyes to admire the big blue motor cruiser coming toward them slowly and trailing a wide wake. "*L'Heure Bleu*, Port of Lou," the gold letters along the bow read. Lutie remembered the name; the boat docked at her father's club. Now she saw three people laid out in lounge chairs on the top deck. As the boat came closer, one of the people leaned down and said something to the man who was steering, and they all laughed. The big horn honked rudely, twice.

"*Blat, blat*," Shriver said, making a face over his shoulder. He turned back to Lutie. "You're bound to know I can't go on this way forever."

That made Lutie angry; she wouldn't stand for threats. "You know what I wish?" she said. "I wish for just one second I was laid out in a deck chair on that boat, with a Tom Collins in one hand and about six dozen peanuts in the other. Just for one minute, so I could enjoy myself."

"All right, Miss Priss," Shriver said. "I thought it was something else holding you back, but I guess it's nothing but goddamned prissiness."

"Don't you curse at me, boy," she said, flushing.

Blat, the horn said, over her head.

Shriver grabbed an oar and began to thrash the water. Lutie looked up and saw the big boat hanging over them.

She reached for the blue oar. Shriver was pulling them around in a circle. The motor cruiser hummed and thumped as the engines were reversed. She screamed at Shriver, but he gave a last desperate thrash and they turned in under the blue crusier's bow. Lutie reached to fend it off, and then she felt Shriver's hand in the small of her back and she fell, scraping her shin on the side of the rowboat.

Coming up with a gasp in the warm water, she thought, thank God, no more arguments.

Then a wave slapped her in the mouth and she drew in a long gasp of water. Choking, she spat out, and then remembered to breathe through her nose. It felt stripped. She had been in the water all summer, and now it felt more comfortable than the air. Treading water, she began to work off her shoes.

The stern of the big boat was already some distance away, but the loud thumping of the screws was still vibrating in the water around her. Hearing that, Lutie realized for the first time that she was in danger, and she heaved onto her back and began to kick for the shore.

After a few kicks, she thought of Shriver and came upright in the water, pushing her wet hair out of her eyes and looking.

He was floating about ten yards downstream, hanging onto the *Dolly*, which had capsized. The blistered brown hull rose and fell gently on the water. "Go for the shore," Shriver called in an ordinary voice. "I'll hang on to the boat." Then he turned his head away, as though he had seen her hesitating.

Lutie hung a minute, treading water. One day on the pier, Henny had asked Shriver, "Can you swim?", and he had answered, "Don't you know I was raised at a country club?"

Then she turned over on her back and began to kick toward him.

The river, so calm and oily on the surface, was fierce a few inches underneath with an offshore current. Each time Lutie kicked, the current caught her foot and dragged it sideways. Soon she turned over on her stomach to measure the distance.

Shriver and the boat had already floated farther away. This time Lutie did not hesitate; she turned over on her back and began to kick hard, dragging her arms up over her head and down through the water to make time against the current. Mrs. Leland, the lady swimming teacher, had given her a lesson every Monday in the shallow end of the country club pool; each time she had learned a stroke, Mrs. Leland had given her a lemon lollipop. The thought of the lemon lollipop made Lutie feel lost, and she tried to fix her attention on the small, the very small chop her feet were setting up in the water.

A long way upstream, the big blue motor cruiser was nosing along the bank, and for the first time she thought, the bastards! They never even bothered to stop.

A little later she began to notice the weight of her dress, and she let her feet drop and came upright in the water, to work on the side fastening. Clumsily, she wrenched at the tiny hooks and finally eased the dress off one shoulder and then off the other, sinking, as she did so, below the surface. The dress was hanging around her waist when it occurred to her that she was about to put her foot on the filthy muddy bottom. She pumped hard with her legs and came back up. She rested for a minute, then doubled over and worked the dress down over her knees. It fell away and hung in a white clot just below her feet. Free at last, she leaned back and swam on.

Soon she grew tired and turned over on her stomach to try the crawl. She had never really mastered the stroke, and her legs kept sinking below the surface of the water. Each time she turned her face to take a breath, she looked at the shore. After ten breaths, she had to admit that she was not getting anywhere; the big white sycamore which had been opposite her head when she started was now just off her knee. So she lay and floated, giving herself up to the tug of the current, until the thought of Shriver drifting farther and farther away started her up again, hammering through the water. This time she had to stop almost immediately. Her legs had become limp and soft, and the current was pulling her out to the middle of the river. Dry panic clung to the roof of her mouth. Raising her arms once more, she thought, here I am in the middle of the Ohio River, drowning, and nothing has ever happened to me. That seemed more important than anything else. A feeling of great luxury was sweeping over her, and she raised her arms languidly over her head, knowing it was for the last time.

Shriver caught her by the wrist and pulled her to the side of the rowboat. "Hang on," he gasped, "I can't hold you." He folded her fingers over the narrow ridge of the keel, and then he let go of her and hung from both his hands for a moment, and then he put his left hand back over hers. She shook her head, to tell him that she could hang on by herself—she knew, from his face, how long he had been waiting—but he kept his hand clamped over hers. So for a while she lay with her legs streaming out behind her and her cheek resting on the scaly hull of the *Dolly*.

Then she raised her head and said, "We better get started." She looked around the end of the boat to gauge the distance to the shore. It did not look too far. She took a new grip on the keel and began to kick, and after a moment, Shriver started too, and the *Dolly* lumbered forward.

Their combined kicking seemed very strong, and she turned her head to smile at Shriver. "It's you should have gotten the lemon lollipop." He did not smile, and she wondered why he had to look so white and stricken when the shore was practically within reach. Then he turned his head toward her and laid his cheek on the side of the boat, and she heard his kicking falter and stop. "Too heavy," he gasped. "You swim. I'll wait."

Lutie looked around the end of the boat and saw that they still had some way to go. "I don't know about you, but I'm not leaving the *Dolly*," she said.

"She's served," he whispered, and she saw that his eyes were closing.

"Not yet, she hasn't." She was frightened; his voice sounded so peaceful and dull. "I take back what I said about the lollipop," she told him, trying to sound angry, and then at some expense she made a loud thrashing in the water with her feet. Without Shriver kicking, the boat hardly moved at all, but she went on working, out of pride, not daring to look at him. After a long time, she heard him begin to kick. But with only one foot. At least, that was the way it sounded. After her own pair of kicks, she listened for his, and the little soft splash he made, like a twig falling into the water, almost drove her mad. "Kick with both feet, you nuthead," she gasped. "You're supposed to be the strong one." But he did not even lift his head off the boat.

Then the other side of the *Dolly* butted into something solid, jarred, hung still, and began to rock in place as peacefully as a porch swing.

Very slowly, with heavy paddling motions which had no connection with any stroke she had ever learned, Lutie eased around the end of the boat, holding on with one hand. She saw the branch they had hit, jutting like a horn out of the brown water. But when she tried to stand, the sweet soft mud sank away beneath her, and so she had to leave the boat nodding against the branch and paddle farther in. When she had found a place where she could stand, chin-deep in still water, she marked it in her mind and swam slowly back to the boat, where Shriver was hanging.

"Come on. We're there." She had to unbend each of his big fingers to get him off the keel. "Swim." But he hung, a dead weight, off her hands until at last she grew angry and said, "At least make some effort." It was quite a way to the shore, and she had to drag him the whole distance, hitched in the crook of her elbow. Even then, he kept slipping away from her, stiff and unmanageable as a waterlogged piece of tree. At last she was standing and he was sitting or crouching beside her in the shallow water.

She stood beside him, mechanically wringing out her hair.

Presently he looked up, and she saw that his eyes were bloodshot from the water. "Can you make it from here?" she asked formally.

He nodded, and when she leaned down and hooked her hands under his arms, he struggled to his knees and finally to his feet. Standing, he leaned his whole weight on her, and she felt, with strange wonder, his weight, and his weakness. Then he leaned away from her and walked carefully to dry ground and sat down. She followed and sat down near him.

After a while, she asked, "Why didn't you look at me all that time I was trying to get to you?" She made it sound as though he had been rude.

He shook his head, knocking water out of his ears. "I guess pride cometh," he said in a husky voice.

"I thought you could swim. I thought that day on the pier you told Henny you could swim."

"I thought you weren't going to make it, and all I could do was hold onto that boat and try to push it toward you."

Then she began to shiver. Her fingernails were purple, and her teeth clacked loudly in her head. "I'm too cold," she complained, and she kneeled and pulled off her wet white slip.

"Here," he said, and he took the slip from her and wrung it out. She looked at him. His white shorts were pasted to him with water, and water was running down his thighs, combing the dark hair straight. She watched him wringing out the slip, and then she looked down and saw the tops of her stockings and the metal hook of her garter. She sat down and tried to cover herself.

"Oh, Lutie, you're freezing," Shriver said, and he took off his shirt, which was soaking wet, and wrung it out and laid it across her shoulders.

She thought of saying, It's late in the day for that, but instead she thought of his great weight when he had leaned on her, and his weakness. It seemed a wonderful mixture, wonderful and terrifying.

Then he got up and went to spread her slip out to dry. Lutie watched him and pulled the sleeves of his shirt down to cover herself. He slapped the wet rag against his knee and spread it carefully on a rock, where the last sunlight lay in a little pool. He untangled the slip straps and draped them over the edge of the stone as though he had been doing this kind of thing for her for many years. Finally he turned around and came toward her, shaking river water out of his hair.

LILLIAN ROSS, born in Syracuse, New York, is on *The New Yorker* magazine for which she has written numerous articles and short stories. She is the author of four books: *Picture* (a factual account of Hollywood film-making that takes the form of a novel), *Portrait of Hemingway*, *The Player*, and *Vertical and Horizontal*.

Night and Day, Day and Night

A few weeks after Phyllis and Larry Elmendorf had Dr. Spencer Fifield over to meet Barbara Kirsch, Phyllis telephoned Spencer at his office to say she wanted to come in about her ulcer, and at the same time she invited him out to their place in Connecticut for the weekend. Phyllis suggested that Spencer pick up Barbara Kirsch and her three-year-old daughter, Bunny, and drive them out for the weekend, too. Barbara's husband had been killed in an automobile accident the previous winter, leaving her with Bunny and a six-year-old boy. Barbara's mother was taking the boy for the weekend, Phyllis said; Barbara's mother was a doll. "You two kids need a weekend with us," Phyllis said over the telephone.

She sounded so friendly, her intonation joining him so warmly to Barbara, that Spencer's heart flipped. He didn't have to stop and think about it at all, he realized; he knew immediately that he really *wanted* to do it. He made a quick note to himself that he was sensing real development, real progress, in himself; this was one decision he did not need to work out first with Dr. Blauberman, his psychoanalyst.

"Bobbie tells me that you two kids have been dat-ing," Phyllis went on, in a singsong.

It was true; they had been dating. Everything was going so easily and so quickly. Soon after he had met Barbara at the Elmendorfs', she called him up and invited him to go to the opening of a Broadway play that Larry Elmendorf had invested in.

Spencer just couldn't believe that it was happening to *him*. Ever since then, his mind seemed to be floating several feet above his body, and he kept trying to get back into himself so that he could really take part in what was going on. Spencer was facing his fortieth birthday, and Barbara was a good ten years younger, but Phyllis was putting him back in time, where he felt he belonged, where he had missed his life. He was full of wonder and gratitude, but he was too excited to talk. He felt so many strange, untried sensations that he was unable to utter more than a choked cough.

"I hear you and Bobbie have discovered that you're both rabid liberals—left of the New Frontier," Phyllis said. She had a hoarse voice, which she used loudly, in the manner Spencer had learned belonged to the confident rich. The voice knocked against his eardrum, but Spencer liked it.

"She's a lovely individual," he said.

"So get with it, boy, get with it," Phyllis said, with a rasping laugh. "If you don't mind a little *in loco parentis*ing push."

"Bobbie has very real values, frankly," Spencer said, and gave another nervous cough.

"Wait till you meet Benny, her father," Phyllis said. "Benny's on the right-wing side, part lower-echelon John Loeb, part Uris Brothers, and with a dash of Barry Goldwater. But a real sweet guy. Bobbie got a twenty-five-dollar contribution out of him for Sailboat Seltzer's special study project on 'Psychoanalysis and Negro Integration.'"

"Frankly, she got ten out of me," Spencer said.

Dr. Seltzer had analyzed Phyllis and had been very helpful to Larry, too, Phyllis had told Spencer, and now the Elmendorfs and Dr. Seltzer and his wife, Effie, spent a lot of time together. Dr. Seltzer was very influential in psychoanalytic circles, Spencer knew from Dr. Blauberman, who often referred to Sailboat, in a rather hostile way, Spencer thought, but with admiration, as "a key figure in modern analysis." He was called "Sailboat" because of his enthusiasm for sailing. For one reason or another, Dr. Seltzer had not been able to obtain more than three thousand dollars from a private foundation—only enough to cover a secretary—for his project, so he had gone ahead on his own, with a full-time researcher on salary, as well as nine volunteers, including

Phyllis and Bobbie. Phyllis wanted to help Sailboat lead what he described as "the movement to bring Psychic Apparatus closer to everyday American life." To date, Sailboat's project consisted of four separate studies, called "Overdevelopment of Ego Cathexis in Mississippi"; "Racism, Problems of Acting Out in the Pentagon and the White House, and the Superego"; "Color, Job Discrimination, and Pregenitality"; and "Phylogenetic Thrust, Dr. Martin Luther King, Jr., and the Democratic Party."

"Benny thinks that Ego Cathexis is a new listing on the market," Phyllis was saying on the phone. "You'll be mad for Benny."

Spencer smiled at the mouthpiece of the telephone and rubbed his eye with his knuckle. This gesture was habitual, and he had discovered, with Dr. Blauberman's help, that it dated back to when he was three years old and that it was connected with his mother's insistence that he keep his knees clean.

"We're going to start the weekend off with a cocktail party—the informal bit," Phyllis was saying. "With only people we like."

"No drinking for *you*, dear," Spencer said, amazed at his own manner with Phyllis, who was not only older than he but much, much richer and more sophisticated. He swallowed the fright he felt at his own authority with her. Though he had not yet told her, he planned to have her operated on for her ulcer very soon. He was sure about the chronic, penetrating ulcer and the damage, but her intractable pain and other symptoms just might indicate several interesting possibilities. He would make tests for all of them, once he had her in the hospital. As long as fifteen years ago, in the days of his interneship, Spencer had discovered that doing a lot of tests made a good impression on patients. After all, if the tests turned out to be negative, Phyllis and Larry wouldn't complain. Like most patients, they would be too busy feeling relief and thankfulness, especially if they had thought there might be something worse than an ulcer.

"I promise to be good," Phyllis said.

Her eagerness to accept his authority added to his sense of fright. He felt scared, actually, every time he called her by her first name. The Elmendorfs were still "new" patients to him. Their former internist had given up his practice after suffering Coronary No. 2, and had, for a compensation, turned over his practice to several younger men. Dick Freisleben, Phyllis's der-

matologist, had alerted Spencer, who had taken about three dozen
of the patients, all of them well heeled. Larry and Phyllis
Elmendorf had hit it off with Spencer from the start, and Spencer
had become very fond of them. Both had talked to him about a
sexual problem that Spencer just happened to have some inside
dope on, thanks to Dr. Blauberman, and Spencer was able to be
very helpful to the Elmendorfs. Consequently, they had opened
their Park Avenue apartment and their place in Connecticut to
him. They gave a lot of dinner parties, many of them having to
do with the good liberal causes, and they invited Spencer to all
of them. Spencer couldn't get over the fact that both Elmendorfs
were deep-seated liberals, even though Larry was in Wall Street.
Yet there wasn't anything seedy or unpleasant about their
progressiveness, and everybody they knew seemed to be liberal
or rich or attractive or interesting, and sometimes all four at once.
It was hard for Spencer to believe, in the light of all this, that the
Elmendorfs would be so interested in *him*. But nevertheless Phyllis
and Larry both were always asking him to be with them. Slowly,
and pushing down the fear that what was happening might at
any moment be taken away from him, he began to feel he belonged
with them. It made him feel proud.

"They really *need* me," he reported to Dr. Blauberman. "They
want me around socially. It reassures them."

"Give and take," Dr. Blauberman replied. "Take and give.
Mmmm?"

"I *like* Phyllis," Spencer said. "You'd never guess she had all
that money."

"The pool you say they are building in Connecticut," Dr.
Blauberman said. "It is a *heated* pool?"

"Heated and constantly changing water," Spencer said. "It cost
so much dough, it isn't even funny."

"So. Probably they got a special price," Dr. Blauberman said.
"He is in chemicals in Wall Street? Chlorine, maybe?"

"You want me to talk about chlorine?" Spencer said, resentfully.
At the end of the previous hour, they were trying to get at the
meaning of another aspect of his childhood relationship to his
mother—the battles-before-the-kisses—and he wanted Dr. Blauberman to remember that they had been talking about this and ask
him to get going again.

To his amazement, instead of remarking upon his hostility, Dr. Blauberman laughed and said, "Everybody likes to have a pool, a heated pool—even a psychoanalyst. Psychoanalysts are human, too. Yes?"

"The other night . . ." Spencer began. The other night, he had been looking at photographs of himself at the wistful, unsmiling, thin-faced age of three, during one of his infrequent visits to his parents. The albums had been dragged out to impress their dinner guests, the Hiram Stones. Mr. Stone, the electronics king, had once bought a policy from Spencer's father, who sold life insurance. Spencer had discovered on his arrival—ahead of the Stones, fortunately—that his father planned to urge Mr. Stone to increase the size of his policy. "What makes you think you can get Mr. Stone to add to his coverage?" Spencer told his father. "I notice you've been selling less lately, not more. Don't overdo it. Don't push your luck."

It was a lousy evening. There was forced interest and enthusiasm over the photographs in the albums. Mr. Stone, who had some rather special condition that required a weekly treatment, which Spencer attended to, on a retainer, repeatedly exclaimed that he never would have recognized Spencer from the albums. "You look anemic," he said, "even in your hair." As a child, Spencer had been blond.

"Spencer had such tiny, gorgeous ears," Spencer's mother said. "He still has them. Very tiny ears for a man."

"That's why he can't hear my troubles," Spencer's father said. Then Mr. Fifield, who had a great repertoire of Borscht Circuit jokes, decided to tell a joke. "Two Jews are going to be shot," he said to Mr. Stone. "So one of the Jews asks for a blindfold. The other Jew turns to him and says, 'Sh-h-h! Don't make trouble!'"

Mr. Stone was not amused. "Being Jewish myself," he said, "I'm entitled to say the Jews never know when they're well off."

Soon after that, Spencer made some excuse about having to go to the hospital and left his parents to entertain the Stones.

Toward the end of the hour, Dr. Blauberman got the discussion back to Larry and Phyllis, and Spencer found himself telling Dr. Blauberman that the Elmendorfs had "a very sound relationship." It was a second marriage for Phyllis; she had a married daughter by her first marriage and no children with Larry.

"The Elmendorfs are good together, even though Phyllis is the one with the original dough," Spencer explained. "Larry used to be her caddie at the country club, but she really fell in love with him anyway."

"But you say that Larry makes money now on the market?" Dr. Blauberman said. "He did not use her money for that?"

"Originally," Spencer said. "He's younger than she is, but they're very close. They have everything in common. All the forward-looking interests."

"To them everybody is human?" Dr. Blauberman said. "Mmmm? They are ideal patients. And maybe you are gaining new insight into your patients. Yes?"

"Yes," Spencer said.

After fifteen years with Dr. Blauberman, Spencer should not have questioned even for a minute that the Doctor had his interests at heart when he asked about the Elmendorfs, and really was concerned about Spencer's medical practice. With the Elmendorfs, at last, his life was on the right track. Now he didn't have to bother—as he had for years and years—with trying to reach out to patients who offered him nothing but their own neurotic fears and dependencies, and never paid their bills on time, and always seemed to wind up throwing a barrage of confusing feelings at him, feelings he could never comprehend. He had always been so baffled by patients who seemed to be pulling at him, trying to get something out of him that he couldn't give, and so making him feel that he had failed them. With patients like the Elmendorfs, every thing was clear, simple, and, as Dr. Blauberman said, rewarding.

Now the Elmendorfs were rewarding him with Barbara Kirsch and her children. A few days after bringing Barbara and him together, the Elmendorfs had given another of their inimitable dinner parties, and Barbara was seated next to Spencer. On his other side Phyllis had placed Mrs. Bertha Cornwall Durlingham-Smith, the famous Negro psychiatric social worker.

"The Elmendorfs are up on the latest," Spencer had reported to Dr. Blauberman. "They're deeply involved in the Negro question, and they really *work* at it."

Across the table at the dinner party were Sailboat Seltzer and Effie. And Barbara was perfect. For one thing, she knew the Seltzers very well and was very casual with them, taking over for Spencer, who felt so shaky in the analyst's presence that he couldn't look him in the eye. In his nervousness, Spencer started talking about his own analysis, and Barbara smoothly switched the conversation to some minor point in *her* own analysis, and got Spencer off the hook. Barbara was so damn poised. Over the Baked Alaska, Spencer got into a terrific discussion with Mrs. Durlingham-Smith about the recent increase of V.D. cases, mostly Negroes, being treated in the hospital clinic, and Barbara contributed a lot to the discussion. Afterward, over brandy, Phyllis took Spencer and Barbara aside and asked, "How did you two kids get on with Bertie Smith?"

"Frankly, she's a very real person," Spencer said. "I've got to hand it to you."

"We just like each other," Phyllis said. "Larry and I only invite people we like."

"Bertie knew more about syphilis than I do, frankly," Spencer said. "And this young lady"—he grabbed Barbara by the back of the neck—"knows a lot about it, too."

"I did a paper about it at Barnard," Barbara said. "And I've got the kind of mind, facts always stick."

"I'm that way, too, actually," Spencer said.

"Bertie is a gem," Phyllis said. "We'll all do it again soon."

That night, when Spencer took Barbara home, he told her all about his Cousin Bonnie in Bridgeport, who won a beauty contest a couple of years before as Miss Brass Hardware of that city, and how Cousin Bonnie had known a wonderful Negro boy in high school, very handsome, an honor student and captain of the football team, who was "very clean-cut." The boy had asked Bonnie to go to a school dance with him, precipitating a family crisis. Bonnie's mother had put the kibosh on the date. So Bonnie had gone to the dance with another boy, but she had *danced* with the Negro boy twice. "It took a lot of guts," Spencer said to Barbara.

"Phyllis has guts," Barbara said. "It took guts to marry Larry. He was just this poor, ordinary Jewish boy."

In a vague way, Spencer felt he was being complimented. "One

thing I don't completely understand—maybe you can help me,"
he said. "Is Dr. Seltzer supposed to socialize with Phyllis? As her
analyst, I mean?"

"She's finished," Barbara said. "It's all right to socialize now."

Spencer had found, more and more, that he could really depend
on Barbara for guidance and help. She knew as many answers
as Dr. Blauberman. Every morning, when he arrived for his analytic hour, Dr. Blauberman greeted him with a smile and made no
secret of the fact that he was pleased with the changes in
Spencer's life. Dr. Blauberman entirely dropped his program of
spurring Spencer on to make love objects of various other young
women. It had got so that Dr. Blauberman started every session off with inquires about the Elmendorfs and Bobbie Kirsch.
"It's all opening up now, Dr. Blauberman," Spencer would say.
"Basically," Dr. Blauberman said, cheering him on, "you have
all the makings of an ordinary, conventional, normal person."
Most wonderful of all, Spencer actually began to *feel* different.
All his senses were heightened. He thought he could see so much
more. He thought he could hear more. He even thought he could
feel.

"So," Phyllis said, by way of concluding the telephone conversation, "you drive Bobbie out in time for the party?"

"Will do," Spencer said. "Will do."

Looking forward to Friday afternoon, Spencer felt a special
kind of exhilaration, and it didn't turn out to be momentary.
It stayed with him. The next morning, at the start of his analytic
hour, when he told Dr. Blauberman about the coming weekend,
the analyst was all approval.

"Phyllis says that Larry is bringing an investment specialist up
for the weekend who will give me some advice on buying stocks,"
Spencer said.

Dr. Blauberman said, in a kidding tone, that he wished he could
go along.

"You know, Bobbie is getting very interested in *you*," Spencer
said. "She keeps asking me. She wants to know everything. I think
I feel a little jealous."

"So," Dr. Blauberman said. "Bobbie transfers to *me* now.
Mmmm?"

"I think I'm *jealous*," Spencer said.

"The Elmendorfs—they ask about me, too?" Dr. Blauberman inquired, and Spencer said of course, the Elmendorfs always asked about him, too.

"They must have a big place, the Elmendorfs, to hold so many guests," Dr. Blauberman said. "No?"

"Fourteen rooms and a guesthouse sleeping six," Spencer said. "The guesthouse has these double-decker beds. The whole motif is nautical. Reminds me of my days in the Navy."

"Forget associating!" Dr. Blauberman said sternly. "You go for a fun weekend. Forget the analysis, mmmm?"

"Funny about 'Bobbie' and 'Bunny' and 'Benny'—they sound so much like my Cousin Bonnie," Spencer said. "And my mother is Beattie."

"Forget associating, I said! We do not bring up any of that material today."

"Phyllis is crazy about Bobbie," Spencer said. "Phyllis says that Bobbie won't take any foolishness—that Bobbie knows how to lay down the law, you know? Phyllis says I need that."

Dr. Blauberman said nothing.

"She gives me a feeling of security, something to hold on to," Spencer said.

"Phyllis?"

"Bobbie," Spencer said.

"The investment man Larry is bringing," Dr. Blauberman said. "He will give you market tips?"

"Frankly, I really *feel* like making a lot of money now," Spencer said. "After all, Phyllis and Larry do good things with their money. I mean, they give to all the good causes. All the latest movements that are important. They're not defensive about their money, like some rich people, who act as though you're always trying to get some of it. I want to make money for Bobbie. I really do. It's a healthy sign, isn't it?"

"Forget about healthy. What is healthy?" Dr. Blauberman said. "Take the market tips. And forget about healthy. Forget about the analysis. Until after the weekend."

Spencer left the couch in a state of bliss.

Phyllis had arranged her visit to Spencer's office for just before lunch, and, after he had examined her, Spencer took her to the

Kwik Kitchen around the corner from his office for a bite. He wanted to avoid telling her about going into the hospital for tests until after the weekend, and this wasn't difficult. They both, it turned out, wanted to talk about Bobbie. Phyllis had almost finished a pastrami sandwich before Spencer noticed what she was eating. She was talking about a beautiful little piece of property that Bobbie liked that was next to the Elmendorfs' place in Connecticut. Larry could get the property for Spencer for hardly anything.

"It has a nice little house," Phyllis was saying. "Nothing special, but functional. And you'll be spending most of your time at our place anyway—Dammit, Spencer, I've got this rotten, gnawing pain!" She clutched at her midriff with her left hand, and the pastrami sandwich, in her other hand, was right in front of Spencer's face, and that's how he happened to notice it.

"Naughty," Spencer said decisively, and took the sandwich out of her hand and set it on the plate.

He saw for the first time, after all the months he had been looking at her, that Phyllis had a mole over her left eyebrow. She wore a large diamond-and-emerald turtle pin on the lapel of her lavender wool suit; the turtle's head emerged from the diamond-studded shell with two rubies for eyes.

"It can't be from the pastrami," Phyllis said. "That takes an hour before you feel it."

And suddenly he realized that she was looking at him like any other patient in trouble. He felt wonderful.

"Let's find out what in Christ's name is going on with my whatsis and get it over with," Phyllis said.

Spencer lit a cigarette. "We'll get the picture on your whatsis soon," he said.

"What do I have to do first?" Phyllis said.

"Leave everything to me," Spencer said.

"I want you to get rid of this damn pain for me," Phyllis said. "I want to stick around. Promise me?"

"I promise you," Spencer said. "You'll dance at my wedding."

Friday started with a hilarious hour and a half in the operating room. As an attending physician on the staff of the hospital, Spencer was in charge of a medical ward, and one of the ward patients was being operated on for gallstones. Spencer stood by with Max Pooley, who was operating. The patient was a husky young man who had a tattoo in four colors across his stomach. The tattoo showed a large heart enclosing the words "True Love. Mom. Dad. Flo." Pooley was about to start cutting on "Mom," but Spencer stopped him. Spencer was feeling more at ease with Pooley than he could ever remember. It just wasn't right, he told Pooley, to start by cutting "Mom." One of the young surgical residents giggled so violently that a nurse had to help him change his mask. "Why not start with 'Flo'?" Spencer said.

"All right, why not?" Pooley said. "I can afford to be charitable. I just won the Metrecal Award. The No-Belly Prize."

Everybody was laughing so hard it was a wonder that Pooley could hold the knife steady, Spencer thought. But, of course, he did. He was a marvel, that Pooley. A genius. He really knew how to cut. Afterward, while they were washing up, Pooley told Spencer that he had promised to take a couple of his grandchildren to California, to visit Disneyland, during Christmas week. Now it seemed to Spencer that he was seeing Pooley for the first time, too. Pooley's pince-nez and bushy white hair gave him such an elegant, elder-statesman appearance.

"I'm playing Papa this weekend," Spencer said. "Taking a friend and her three-year-old out to the country." He helped himself to a few of the paper containers from the O.R. "Insurance," he said, winking at Pooley. "You know the way kids get. In a car."

From the O.R., Spencer made it downstairs to Private a few minutes too late to see the Davidson boy out of this world.

"We tried to page you, but he went out too fast," the resident told Spencer.

The parents of the boy stared at Spencer, stunned. Spencer had spent a lot of time with them, preparing them for the fact that their son would never leave the hospital alive. He had had dinner with them twice a week for the past ten weeks. It was amazing, Spencer had told Dr. Blauberman, how the parents plied him with questions about their son's illness. "They're overcompensating because of guilt feelings," Spencer said, and was congratulated on his insight into the situation.

Mrs. Davidson held a gift—a white handkerchief box tied with a blue silk ribbon. "We got it for you last night, to give to your girl friend maybe," she said. "Because we took you away from her so much."

Spencer got loose from the Davidsons as fast as possible. He decided not to look in on Rod Miller. Rod had a persistent infection in a broken leg. As a boy, Spencer had gone to camp with Rod, who was an English teacher. Until a month or so ago, Spencer had given a lot of time to Rod and his wife, but now he found Rod just too burdensome.

"Poor Rod," Spencer said to Barbara once, when they were discussing the patients he had in the hospital. "He just resumed psychoanalysis, and he's scared stiff people at his school will find out. He made me promise to keep it confidential."

"You can tell *me*," Barbara said.

"He's such a downbeat character," Spencer said. "He just found out his wife can't have any children."

"Poor Rod," Barbara said.

Luckily, the door to Rod's room was closed, so he wouldn't know Spencer had been in that day without stopping to see him.

In his office, Spencer saw about ten patients. He brushed them off crisply when they started talking about matters not directly related to the business at hand. He was especially abrupt with Mrs. Stone, who started her usual routine with him of asking whether he knew this doctor or that. She always had two or three new names to ask about. Although Spencer ordinarily liked to gossip with Mrs. Stone, today he said coldly, "I haven't heard of them, frankly. I have to go now," he added, ushering her out. Mrs. Stone would just have to adjust. Her husband ran the show, and Spencer was not afraid of anything that Mrs. Stone might do.

The only patient Spencer gave a little extra time to was Pete Himmel, who was on a weekend in town from college. He was in his first year. He had a number of questions he wanted to ask about sex. Spencer was touched by Pete's innocence, his complete faith in Spencer, and his automatic assumption that Spencer knew all the answers. In particular, Pete wanted to know whether it was all right to go up to a certain establishment with a reputation for kindness to college boys.

"Go ahead, don't worry about it," Spencer said, feeling very paternal and protective. "Someday you'll have a real relationship with a woman, but in the meantime, frankly, we all have our physical needs."

"I can really *talk* to you," Pete said. "You really understand."

"The thing to remember," Spencer said, speaking the words that Dr. Blauberman had taught him, "is don't feel guilty about anything that happens."

Spencer was still exhilarated on the drive up to Connecticut, with Bobbie alongside him and Bunny stretched out on the shelf above the back seat, under the rear window, asleep. After reaching the Merritt Parkway, Spencer stopped to get some gas. The attendant cleaned the front window and then told Spencer that he would skip the rear one. "I might wake up your little girl," he said. Spencer was delirious, and gave the man a fifty-cent tip. Driving in the heavy traffic, he absent-mindedly turned out of his lane without looking behind him. Another driver had to swerve away from Spencer to avoid hitting him, and shouted an insult. Spencer laughed. He felt like laughing at everything. Bobbie said she had brought along a new pair of slacks, and he laughed at *that*. With this strong, confident, good-looking, dependable girl next to him, his head pounded as he drove. If he ever wanted anything at all in his whole life, he wanted Bobbie and everything she had to offer. She was perfect wife material. And patients would be crazy about her, too. That is, his new type of patient—not those screwballs of both sexes who had given him so much trouble in the past. If somebody very sick called up and got Bobbie, he knew she wouldn't be thrown by it; she wasn't the type to get upset. She never tired of hearing the medical details of his day. She wanted to know everything about how the Davidson boy went out, and Spencer told her.

"Frankly, it was rough," he said. "I spent a lot of time with his parents that I might have spent with you."

"I had a feeling it would happen today," Bobbie said.

"Patient Griselda," Spencer said to her, and with one hand he took the handkerchief box from the rear of the car and handed it to her. "Open it, Patient Griselda," he said. "Mrs. Davidson said it's for you."

Bobbie untied the blue silk ribbon and opened the box. Inside was a white lace handkerchief with a blue lace border. "It's beautiful," she said, and put the handkerchief in her purse.

"The Davidsons have good taste," Spencer said.

They talked about other patients as they drove, and Spencer told her of the particular service he performed for Mr. Stone each week. "But I think I'm growing away from that," Spencer said. "After all, he doesn't really need a doctor to do that. Anybody can do that for him. It's just that he feels confidence in me." Spencer rubbed his eye. "I worry about taking all that money from him for it."

"You need it more than he does," Bobbie said. He smiled at her. She lit a cigarette. "You think too much," she said, and exhaled a stream of smoke at him. "Every time you start to intellectualize, stop. Don't think. *Feel.*"

It was amazing the way she put her finger on things. He confided to her how he had skipped looking in on Rod Miller that morning. "I feel so sorry for guys like Rod whose desire for normalcy is constantly being frustrated," he said.

"Remind me to show the handkerchief to Phyllis," Bobbie said.

They then discussed Phyllis's ulcer, and he said he wanted to lure her into the hospital for tests.

"Tell her what you want to do and why," Bobbie said. "Phyllis can take it. She has guts."

"I really *care* what happens to Phyllis," Spencer said.

"Identifying with her husband, hmmm?" Bobbie said.

"I've gained a lot of insight into love relationships," Spencer said.

Under the rear window, Bunny mumbled something in her sleep. Spencer glanced back at the child and told Bobbie he thought Bunny looked like little Caroline Kennedy. And Bobbie, he suddenly realized, had her hair combed just like Jackie's. My God, he thought, here I am, identifying with the President of the United States. For the first time in his life, he was sure he was happy.

Phyllis Elmendorf came up to them as soon as they arrived. The cocktail party was going strong on the patio, with most of the people dressed casually; the men, as well as the women, were in Bermuda shorts.

"Don't take the time to change now, Spencer," Phyllis said, putting her arm through his. "Bobbie will put Bunny to bed upstairs. I want you down here."

"Pucci?" Spencer said, looking at Phyllis's gold gauzy-silk slacks and matching jacket, both stamped with large butterflies and grasshoppers in green and purple. The ruby-eyed diamond-studded turtle now squatted on her collar.

"Pucci," Phyllis said, looking pleased. "Had this set made in Hong Kong, actually. The two days we spent there on our world tour. They copied my aquamarine Puccis overnight. For about two dollars and fifty cents." She introduced him to a number of people. He wished that Bobbie had stayed with him for support. He felt lost. As Phyllis led him quickly from one young-middleaged couple to another, he catalogued the impressive jewels—impressive but in good taste—pinned, like Phyllis's turtle, on Pucci shirts and cashmere sweaters with white mink collars. Everybody smiled friendship at Spencer. Then Phyllis left him in order to greet someone else.

An upright piano, painted in red enamel, had been moved out to a corner of the patio, but no one was playing. A young Negro butler held a tray of Martinis-with-lemon-peel out to Spencer. He took one. A Negro maid, with a stiff little white cap on her head and a tiny white apron over a black uniform, stood holding a bowl of shrimp dip in one hand and in the other a bowl of giant potato chips. Spencer took a potato chip and scooped up some of the shrimp paste.

"Spence! Long time no see!" It was Dick Freisleben. He was in training on the side to become a full-time psychoanalyst, but Spencer thought he ought to stick to dermatology. Freisleben went around these days acting as though he was in on special secrets, and had some official right to be euphoric. He was also in the process of divorcing his wife. "Isn't this great?" Freisleben said, looking around with Martini-inspired enthusiasm. "What a joint! Some layout, no, Spence? Here, meet Sophie. Soph is a candidate in training with me." Sophie, a small, stocky woman wearing floral-print shorts, disengaged herself from the shrimp dip and nodded

at Spencer. "Soph is working with Sailboat on the big project!"
Freisleben went on. "You seen Sailboat yet, Spence?"

There was something irritating about the way Freisleben was
so relaxed, so at home with everybody. Spencer doubted if
Freisleben *really* addressed Dr. Seltzer by the nickname. He looked
around for Barbara.

"Sailboat!" Freisleben called out. "Stranger! Long time no see!"

"Dick!" Sailboat said. "Sophie!" Then he noticed Spencer and
said, "Hi there."

"Spencer Fifield," Spencer said, feeling very uncomfortable. "I
was just going to look for Bobbie."

Effie came along and said that they were getting up a sailing
party to leave at eight in the morning. "Bobbie wants to go,"
she said to Spencer.

"In that case—" Spencer said. For the first time, he was able
to look straight into Sailboat's eyes, and now Sailboat also smiled
on Spencer.

"It's a deal," Effie said.

"Not us!" Freisleben shouted, patting Sophie on the floral-
print shorts. "We got various things to do to report back on to
our analysts Monday morning." He and Sophie both went for
more shrimp dip.

"Isn't Phyllis some*thing?" Effie said to Spencer. "Who else in
Fairfield County would have the nerve to invite a Negro up for
the weekend?"

"Where?" Spencer said.

Sailboat tilted his Martini in the direction of a very handsome
young man with light-brown skin. He was wearing tartan-plaid
wool Bermuda shorts and a camel's-hair jacket with gold buttons,
and he had just sat down at the upright piano. Several of the
guests began edging over toward him. Just then, Larry Elmendorf
joined Spencer and the Seltzers. In one hand Larry was carrying
an ashtray, and in the other a highball. A lady's coat was slung
over one shoulder. There was still a touch of the caddie about
Larry Elmendorf. Although he had a rather obtrusive potbelly
and was almost completely bald except for a few wisps of hair
at the base of his skull, he had the freckled face of a barefoot
boy on a calendar going fishing down a sunlit country road. Bow-
ing pleasantly at everybody, he managed to crook the arm holding

the ashtray around Spencer's shoulders in greeting. Not since the days when his maternal grandfather was alive had Spencer felt so favored. His grandparents had lived with his father and mother—or, rather, the Fifields and Spencer, who was an only child, had lived with the grandparents, in the latter's town house—for the first seventeen years of Spencer's life. Only last spring, Spencer had devoted half a dozen sessions with Dr. Blauberman to his grandfather. "Grandpa *liked* me," was the way Spencer summed up what he had learned at the end of the sessions. Larry Elmendorf liked him, too. He kept his arm around Spencer, hanging on while swaying back and forth gently in conversation with the Seltzers.

"Shet mah mouth, Larry, you trying to get the K.K.K. to crash this wingding?" Sailboat said. "I've got to hand it to you."

"You're wonderful," Effie said. "Larry, you and Phyllis are wonderful."

"You mean Johnny?" Larry said, indicating the young man at the piano. "We only invite people we like. I know Johnny's big brother, Tom. Tom is the most influential broker in Harlem. You'd be surprised what the weekly figure is of what they buy up there in Harlem."

"Wouldn't surprise *me*," Sailboat said. "Not after our study on the Phylogenetic Thrust."

"The middle-class Negro has drive," Spencer said. "I have a Negro patient, a lawyer, and the suppressed hostility—"

But Larry, his arm still crooked around Spencer, wasn't paying attention. Neither was anybody else, and Spencer dropped what he was trying to say and looked around for Bobbie.

"Tom sent Johnny over to me to see if there's anything I can do for the kid," Larry was saying to Sailboat Seltzer. "Seems the kid gets into trouble. Overshadowed by successful powerhouse older brother—that sort of thing, you know?"

"I try not to work on weekends," Sailboat said.

Larry laughed. "The kid got thrown out of Harvard," he said. "Drank, and flunked out, you know?"

"He probably needs help," Spencer said.

"I need a refill," Sailboat said, turning the stem of his empty Martini glass. "Where's that butler of yours?"

There was a rumor around that Sailboat had gone sailing during

the summer with the Kennedys at Hyannis Port. Sailboat hadn't
exactly quashed the rumor. Dr. Blauberman had found out, however, with considerable satisfaction, that Sailboat had indeed
visited Hyannis Port in August, but only to see an actress patient
of his who was playing in the Cape Cod Melody Tent. "Dr.
Seltzer is a brilliant doctor, but he gets ahead of himself," Dr.
Blauberman had told Spencer.

"This patio reminds me of my grandfather's house," Spencer
now said. "My grandfather had a town house in the city, with
a patio just like this one in the back. A town house is the only
way to live in the city." Sailboat owned a town house where
he both lived and kept his office. The house was also the head-
quarters of the study project on "Psychoanalysis and Negro Integration." He ought to have been interested in the subject of town
houses, but apparently he didn't feel like discussing it with
Spencer. Larry, however, said, "Nice," and gave Spencer a friendly
hug. "Our investment buddy with the hot tips we want will be
along later," he said. "I'll get you a drink, Sailboat."

Dick Freisleben came back with Sophie. "Sailboat!" he shouted.
"You'll love this! Tell him, Soph!"

"The latest on why people in Great Neck aren't building any
fallout shelters," Sophie said.

"This'll kill you!" Freisleben shouted.

"Because they figure they won't *need* them," Sophie said. "They
figure if war comes the men will all be at their offices in New
York, the women will all be out shopping, the kids will be in
school. So why build? For the *help?*"

Everybody laughed the same kind of laugh, united and exact,
a laugh that was divided clearly into two parts, two syllables—
an "ah" that went uphill quickly into a knowing "hah."

"Isn't that wild?" Freisleben shouted joyously. He used to live,
with his about-to-be-divorced wife, in Great Neck.

"I hear Kim Novak is building a fallout shelter," Sailboat
said. "They're big in California."

"Frankly, don't you find Kim Novak a very superficial individual?" Spencer said, but again his remark got lost. He began to
droop. He noticed it immediately. It was frightening. If only
Bobbie would come.

"Where's that drink?" Sailboat said, turning away, and found himself face to face with a Japanese floor lamp. "Don't scare me like that," Sailboat said to the lamp.

Spencer heard exuberant laughter coming from some people standing at the piano. He glanced around. The Negro maid was between the piano and him. There was a particularly blank expression on her face as she stood looking toward the young man at the piano and extending the bowls of shrimp dip and potato chips to Spencer. He took a potato chip, and scooped it into the mixture. Then he nodded in the direction of the piano and said, "Johnny going to start playing now?"

"I don't know, sir," the maid said.

"I mean, did Johnny play before?" Spencer said. "Frankly, I just got here."

"I don't know, sir," the maid repeated.

Spencer put down the potato chip on a table and looked desperately toward the stairway, which he could see through the French doors that opened onto the patio. Possibly he should run upstairs and *find* Bobbie—give her a hand, maybe, with Bunny. He tried to focus on the faces of people he had been introduced to a few minutes before. He tried to remember their names, but he couldn't. As he was pushing his way through the crush toward the stairway, he suddenly encountered Phyllis.

"Kitty Lenz, Dr. Spencer Fifield," Phyllis was saying, and he realized that she was introducing him to a young woman who was wearing tight, fuchsia-colored toreador pants.

Kitty Lenz gave Spencer her hand to shake. It was cold. She looked ill at ease and alone. She kept wetting her lips. Her white lace overblouse fell a couple of inches short of the top of the toreador pants, exposing a smooth, tanned strip of skin. She wore high-heeled gold sandals, her face was heavily made up, and she had long fingernails painted to match the color of her pants. She presented Spencer with an expression of gaiety—an expression that she had probably taken to many other cocktail parties where she had wandered ill at ease and alone. Spencer recognized the expression. In the past, at other parties, he had often found himself drawn to women like her.

"Did you see Bobbie?" Spencer said to Phyllis. "Will Bobbie be down soon?"

"Soon as she gets Bunny to bed," Phyllis said.

"What a trip!" Spencer said expansively. "I expected Bunny to oops in the car, but she slept practically all the way."

"Keep the windows of the car open," Kitty Lenz said. "Don't let them know you're worrying about it, and just don't make a big production out of it. Cute kid at the piano there. I like his gold buttons. Who brought the cute kid at the piano, Phyl?"

"She's three," Spencer said. "And she looks exactly like little Caroline Kennedy." Turning to Phyllis, he said, "I'd better run upstairs and see if I can help Bobbie."

"You stay right here with us, darling," Phyllis said, leaning against him. And then, answering Kitty Lenz, she said, "Johnny's brother is one of our favorite people. Larry does a lot of business with him."

"Such cute buttons," Kitty Lenz said, and gave Spencer a smile.

"Johnny's brother that investment man?" Spencer said.

Phyllis let out a shriek of laughter. "No, darling," she said. "Johnny's brother is relatively small potatoes. We've got something special lined up for you."

"What's up, Doc?" Kitty Lenz said, trying to make herself sound comical. "You need a new stethoscope?"

Phyllis gave another shriek, which was echoed by a burst of laughter from the vicinity of the piano. Spencer saw Sailboat Seltzer pumping Johnny's hand. "My tan is better than your tan!" he said jovially to the young Negro.

Johnny took a newly lighted cigarette out of his mouth and threw back his head and laughed. He laughed for an unusually long time. Everybody around the piano tried to laugh along with him. Then Larry held out his ashtray to Johnny, who snapped the whole cigarette into the tray, scattering sparks on the front of Larry's shirt. Larry picked up the cigarette and put it out, and Johnny threw back his head again and laughed some more.

"Play something, Johnny," Phyllis called out. Larry saw her and came over, and she gave him a wifely peck on the cheek.

"Johnny sure is adorable," Kitty Lenz said, as though speaking to herself, but looking wistfully at Spencer. "That lad has got beautiful choppers."

Spencer looked away from her without answering.

"Pul-lay som-a-thing!" Phyllis called out to Johnny.

"Does he play?" Larry asked. "I didn't know he played."

"He *must* play," Phyllis said.

"Why?" Kitty Lenz said.

Spencer edged away from her. She was making him feel nervous. He wanted to stand with Phyllis and Larry without being disturbed by this oddball-screwball.

"How about some Cole Porter, man?" Sailboat said. " 'Night and Day.' How about 'Night and Day'?" Sailboat motioned with his drink to the Elmendorfs to come over to the piano. Spencer started to go with them, but Kitty Lenz held him back by saying quickly, "Dr. Fifield—or am I expected to call you by your first name?"

"Spencer," he said stiffly.

"Relax, Spencer, I'm harmless. Do you mind if I ask what kind of doctor are you?"

"An internist," Spencer said.

"My ex-husband was an internist. My ex-husband moved out to the Coast. He had this theory that all his patients needed him to mother them—that he was their mother figure. That was his theory. So we got divorced. Maybe you knew him—Dr. Donald Lenz. *Summa cum laude*, Harvard, 1940. Harvard Med School, 1944. His office was on Seventy-third and Park."

"I'd better go up and get Bobbie," Spencer said, but he couldn't move.

On the other side of the piano, Phyllis was asking Johnny to play some Twist music. "Play Chubby Checker," she said.

"How about Joey Dee?" Johnny said softly, and he put his head back and laughed.

"Twist, Johnny!" Phyllis yelled.

"Ray Charles' 'Do the Twist' is better than any of Chubby Checker, frankly," Spencer said.

"What do you know, a Ray Charles man!" Kitty Lenz said.

There was something in her tone that Spencer heard as mockery. He lit a cigarette, and he saw that his hands were trembling. He felt an old panic. Then, inhaling deeply, he forced himself to concentrate on what he had to remember: He was over the hump now. Dr. Blauberman had led him to his graduation from the lame-duck school of the Kitty Lenzes. He had graduated from the Rod Millers. He had now reached what Dr. Blauberman had assured him was the adult level of the Elmendorfs, of Bobbie Kirsch.

He was one of them now. He had finally joined what Dr.
Blauberman liked to call the human race. And Dr. Blauberman
had shown him how to fight for his position.

"You wear too much makeup," he heard himself say to Kitty
Lenz. She gave him a look of astonishment. He left her and went
over to Larry and Phyllis.

"Cole Porter," Sailboat was saying to Johnny. "'Night and
Day.'"

Johnny started banging meaninglessly on the piano keys. Then
he lifted his hands high above the keyboard and held them poised
there, and burst into a laugh. The audience began laughing, too.

"Yeah, man!" Sailboat said, and, reaching across a couple of
guests, he took a fresh drink from the Negro butler.

"'Night and day . . .'" Johnny began, in a high, strained voice,
and he brought both hands, fingers spread out, down at random,
without playing real chords, "'Night and day . . . day and night
. . . night and day . . .'" He seemed to sing in bits and pieces of
the accepted styles of several popular singers. Then he lifted his
head way up high, closed his eyes, and brought his head way down
low, until his chin practically rested on the keyboard.

Kitty Lenz joined the group at the piano. "He doesn't know
the song, Phyl," she said to Phyllis, but Phyllis had her eyes closed,
and was busy nodding and tapping her foot.

"He's not playing the piano," Kitty Lenz said, touching Phyllis
on the arm. "He's just hitting the keys."

Phyllis opened her eyes, but looked at Sailboat, who was slapping
the side of the piano drunkenly. "Cool, man, cool!" Sailboat
said, to the piano.

"'You are the one . . .'" Effie Seltzer put in, lifting her head as
Johnny was doing and closing *her* eyes, too.

"'You are the one . . . you are the one . . . you are the
one . . .'" Johnny repeated, and struck a few more would-be
chords, at opposite ends of the keyboard.

"Why don't you all leave him alone?" Kitty Lenz said, to no
one in particular. "He's not playing the piano. There's nothing
there. Stop pushing him."

Phyllis gave her a look of annoyance and joined Sailboat in a
slapping duet on the wood of the piano. Kitty Lenz was right,
Spencer realized. Johnny wasn't really singing, and he wasn't really

playing the piano. Spencer looked at Phyllis and Larry and the Seltzers. All four of them now were nodding and foot-tapping a would-be beat to the nonexistent rhythm, the nonexistent melody, the abortive lyrics. Spencer looked back at Kitty Lenz blankly. She could *afford* to stand around telling the truth. She was on the outside of everything anyway.

Just then, Bobbie came into the room. Spencer signalled to her to work her way in alongside him. "How's Bunny?" he said to her, in a loud voice. He took hold of the back of Bobbie's neck and looked over at Kitty Lenz.

"She's fast asleep," Bobbie said.

"Martini, dear?" Spencer said.

"With lemon peel," Bobbie said.

As Spencer headed for the butler and the drinks, he passed Phyllis, who was still tapping her foot enthusiastically, going through all the motions of keeping time, or what she thought was time, to the nonexistent music. For a moment, Spencer felt his panic returning, but then he saw clearly that it didn't matter whether Johnny was playing music or not; the important thing was that everybody *acted* as if he was. Who needed Kitty Lenz?

"Cool?" Phyllis said, smiling at Spencer, smiling at Bobbie, smiling at Johnny at the piano.

"Real cool," Spencer said.

DAVID STACTON is the author of verse, a biography, a history of the collapse of Byzantium and nine novels, of which the latest to appear in America are *Sir William* in the fall of 1963 and *Old Acquaintance,* scheduled for the spring of 1964. "The Metamorphosis of Kenko" is from a series of studies of religious experience which he has been working on for the past few years.

The Metamorphosis of Kenko

It is about Kenko. Kenko is known for, in fact he is famous because of, a collection of random thoughts called the *Tsure-Zure Gusa,* which he did not write. The book was compiled from scraps of paper found pinned up with old maple leaves on the walls of his house which, through sparse, was nothing but the hermitage of a well-to-do Buddhist recluse. To judge by the *Tsure-Zure Gusa,* the life Kenko lived there was a serene and contented one, and he a serene and contented man.

Actually, he hated his life there so much that he feared to go mad. It was how he had been put there that demented him most.

At forty-two Kenko was the most distinguished—though not the most important—member of his family, the Urabe, whose pomp and power came from the fact that, almost alone of the nobles at Kyoto, they had their ancestral estates (which also meant their armed retainers), only a short distance from the capital. Nonetheless they were losing their preëminence. Kenko, though that was the cause of his discomfiture, could not see that that loss of position affected him. He was, to tell the truth, a little selfish. And besides, he was an official at court, and at court nothing affects them.

Unmarried and reasonably rich, he liked the prettiness of women as he liked plum blossom and his tea whisk or a single crocus in the snow. His interest in the world stopped there. At court they were not interested in the world. They were interested in the arts. At court, far from maintaining the nation, the Emperor was maintained by it. They were so idle there that they had no time to think for themselves. To think for them was Kenko's function. The Empress, when she took a walk to admire the gardens (which were in disrepair), always sent ahead of her a lady in waiting, who, in her turn, asked Kenko to choose the particular spot from which some particular spruce or bed of iris was to be viewed that day, rather than be put to the fatigue of choosing the spot for herself.

Of course Kenko saw through all that. He was not a fool. But he had been arbiter elegantiarum and nursemaid to these people for twelve years. He was accustomed to the life. It suited him.

Then came the family crisis. His brothers wanted him to marry. To his brothers, that was only sensible. They knew there was a revolution to come soon, and, to ride through it, they would have to make an alliance with the winning side. The Yoshida had the power to win, and a marriageable daughter besides. It was, his brothers said, only his duty.

His duty did not interest him. He had seen the daughter. She had moth eyebrows and a certain fragile manner. He did not object to her, but he was set in his ways. He loved solitude. With women in the house, you never knew what would happen, but at least you knew that things would never be as they had been. A conservative, he liked things the way they were. He said no.

That monosyllable wrecked his life. Or so he thought at the time. The Yoshida were furious, they felt themselves snubbed, and the Urabe were afraid of having their estates confiscated in retaliation, once the revolution came. There was only one way out. Kenko, in his refusal to the marriage intermediary, had provided it for them. He was, he had said, a recluse. He was already beginning to leave the affairs of his world. His feet were on another path. It was merely a polite formula. It was also a solution. His brothers proposed to clap him into a monastery. The best compromise he could manage was that he should be allowed to retire to a solitary hermitage instead. Monks did not wash often enough, at least not their robes, and he loathed to recite sutras. He owned a small property in the hills above Kyoto. Might he not go there?

Of course he might, said his brothers, if he went at once; and when he dawdled, they took him there themselves with all the pomp they could manage, further to convince the Yoshida of his probity and of no snub to themselves. In this they succeeded, but Kenko would never forget that moment when the jangle of the escort died away, the trees suddenly seemed closer and blacker, and he was alone.

He found it altogether horrible.

The silence of a great house, which he loved, tucked away in his own wing of it, was not the same as being tucked away in some corner of a silent world. Always, after he had seen too many people, he was grateful for solitude. He liked to be alone at night.

But this was different. He had no objection to a sameness of days, but these days were empty. He tried to keep himself busy with small tasks: the grinding of ink, the writing of letters. But no matter how busy he kept, he could not help but hear the silence. It kept welling up around the edges of consciousness, with the inexorability of a backed-up drain. There was also an awareness in his head of some gadfly question as visible as words: "When you have finished your letters," it said, "what do you do next?"

"There will be visitors," he said. "It won't be so bad."

So there were, at first. But it was a long climb up to that hill, and court ladies and gentlemen do not like to climb hills.

Kenko threw down his writing brush, saw it was almost evening, left the house, and went over to admire the view. It was a fine view. The sea was visible over folds of wooded hills. But look as he might, there was no glimpse of Kyoto. Kyoto, he realized, he would never see again.

Sunset was almost over. Because of the cloud formation, the sky resembled a horizontally barred window high up in a wall. Someone must be burning wood somewhere, for the bars of light were purple and pale green. They faded, the window was shuttered, and the night became a solid wall.

He did not want to go back to his hermitage. From the screen of maples, he looked at that barren, flickering, inhuman room, and did not like the look of it. But neither could he stay outdoors all night.

The next two years were not agreeable.

He could appreciate the comedy of it, if he kept his nerves steady, but sometimes his nerves snapped. He had to fill the time up somehow. Unfortunately, religious texts bored him. "How trivial," he had written once, "is a life full of nothing but immensities." We are always told the life of a retired sage is serene and untroubled. He sits upon his hill; he meditates upon the glories of the Tao or the nature of the Buddha; he writes a little; he drinks a little more; sometimes he sees old friends; he becomes a wise man; he is venerated. His life is not empty, for he is absorbed, even delighted, by the Great Void of Being. But what on earth does he do?

What on earth *does* he do?

Kenko could not spend the rest of his life rearranging the same four tea cups, one pot, and two scrolls. He had devoted most of his life to the intricacies of gossip. Now nobody answered his letters. And though one may, in the very best prose, compare a woman's beauty to a young pine tree, what do you say about the pine tree when there is no woman to compare it to?

He decided to write a book—small, full of style and insight and wistful wisdom. If this life is unendurable, he would do what he suspected all others who had taken up this existence did: pretend to the world as one pretends about everything that what was vile was in actuality calm and beautiful. True, he had nothing to write about, but by describing a few things well one hints at those one cannot describe at all; and for a limited talent, this artifice makes it possible to accomplish more than one can do. Anyone can be abstract, but it takes skill to define the particular— those discontinuous moments of awareness which, in the discomforts of life's journey, show us what is around us in the fog. It is the essential secret of Japanese literature, that approach. It has excused many and augmented the rest.

Unfortunately he did not have such moments. He was reduced, on many an endless afternoon, to scribbling meaningless marks on pieces of paper and then trying to figure out what characters they resembled, in the hope that those, strung together, might say something. It was a method peculiar to one Taoist monastery in China, a source of Zen painting, a form of trance writing, but for him it did not work. He derived only a senseless squiggle.

He found himself glowering at the maple trees. His poems had been about the subtleties of make-up, the ripple of a woman's skirt, the transience of life, in the contented knowledge that there was nothing transient about his own. What could one say about a maple tree? It was meaningless. As he watched, the bronze leaves dropped from its branches, and it became even more boring than it had been before.

He became slovenly. Sometimes he forgot to pluck the slight hairs of his chin. From irony he passed to the sardonic. To infrequent visitors, he explained that he was growing the beard of a sage. Very well then. That is what he would become, a sage. He would study and meditate. It would help fill up the time.

It filled up two more years, but nothing happened. He was incurably secular. When he tried to achieve *samadhi*, all he got was a cramp in his left shin. When he contemplated The Void, all he could see was that it was empty.

And then there came a change.

One day he decided to wander in the woods, up a little draw. It had not, up till now, occurred to him to explore his surroundings, for nature had never appealed to him. He preferred gardens.

His hermitage was on the edge of wild country so he had to pick his way over fallen trees and push through prickly shrubbery. The draw was the course of a stream, dried up now because it was autumn. He followed the stream bed through the late, dust-filled afternoon light until he reached a place where the going was rough. To go on it would be necessary to climb a steep bank treacherous with an ancient pile of dead leaves. He hesitated, but he had nothing else to do and was so bored that there was nothing to do but go on. He began to climb and came out, after a good deal of puffing, at a place almost level, where, being out of breath, he sat down to look around him.

The sunlight hit a wall of exposed rock which a smooth trickle of water had turned a glistening black. On either side stood slim trees. At the bottom of the trickle there was a tiny pool perhaps two feet wide and no more than six inches deep. Rocks were piled at random in the empty stream bed. While he watched, a leaf detached itself from somewhere high above his head and seesawed down, waywardly, showing first its bright yellow side and then its brown. He followed its course until it settled beside a stone.

He jumped. It seemed to him the stone was staring back at him and was ready to hop towards him.

Then he bent closer.

The stone was conglomerate. It had a certain accidental resemblance, and on two of its nodules the water from the trickle had left it wet, so that, those two places glistening, it looked exactly like a large frog. Perhaps it was a frog. Why should it not be? He knew the world to be full of dropped objects, for, whereas other Gods may cast down manna, the Japanese *kami* are always dropping *things*, and who knows what they really are or what they really contain in Heaven? If a frog can be a rock, a rock a frog, then a frog may be a person, and a person, in turn, a rock; for we all want some kind of immortality, we want to survive, and of all things in this world, a rock survives the longest.

So why should it not be a frog? Smiling, he got up and cast it into the pool at the bottom of the exhausted waterfall. A frog likes to be wet. He went over to the pool and saw (for once it was wet the frog had disappeared back into ordinary rock) a single minnow in the pool and the one or two weeds on which it fed.

That minnow was very like himself. It was trapped in a world that had shrunk around it, and it had too little to do, too little to feed on. Besides, he had an eye for proportion and the pool was too small in relation to the wall of rock behind it. He saw what could be done. Hoisting up his skirts, he worked until twilight, moving stones and filling the chinks with leaves and pebbly soil. The task fascinated him so that he was sorry when it grew dark and he had to leave.

On his way down, he kept glancing back, for through the trees he could still catch a glint of that wet wall. Why had he not noticed it on the way up?

Next morning he went back again to finish the pool.

Day after day, he rearranged the stones to change the shape of the banks. Snow began to fall. Winter had taken him by surprise. But those rocks which looked to be in the right place in autumn did not look so in the snow. He spent days studying the problem. And then months. How could they be arranged to look right at all seasons and achieve by artifice that natural look which is what the Japanese esteem in nature and which they achieve by altering ever so subtly the natural relationships between stones, water, moss, trees, and shrubs, so that, though the mind is not disturbed by incongruity, still the minute incongruity between where a thing naturally is and where it has been put makes them the more aware of the natural order of the world for having reshaped it into what they think it should be?

He would have to see the pool at all four seasons, first of all. He could hardly wait for spring, when, instead of a mere trickle, the waterfall would be in spate.

When it was in spate, he spent every day there, studying the thrust and spray of the water, moving a boulder, a rock or two, to keep the right trickle from a subsidiary pool. The trees came into leaf. The flowers began. And then, in summer, the current slackened. It went down and down, and once more he went to work. Once more he watched the last autumn leaf float down before him as he sat there.

The stream bed was done, but now he saw, looking around him, that the trees would have to be thinned. He was grateful for winter. Winter is nature skeletalized and abstract. That made it easier to grasp the relationships among the trees.

He hired a woodsman. He had less and less time for those terrific letters of admonishment to his family which, until now, had taken up so much of his existence.

He thought he had found a tree which contained a *kami*. And though he had sometimes tried to find that stone that looked like a frog, he never could. It did not greatly matter. Now the pool had widened, real frogs had taken to appearing, and he found it fascinating to watch them. The way they moved meant something. He set himself to try to define it.

Their imperturbable longevity, perhaps. Finding a scrap of paper, he wrote that down and pinned the paper to the wall of the hermitage. The words were not quite correct. Perhaps if he thought about them during the winter, he could find the exact phrase.

Spring was late that year, but he did not find the phrase. He would have to study the frogs again, next summer, to find it out.

The snow became mushy at the crust, plopped from branches to make moon craters on the dirty ground drifts, and the spring break-up came a week and a half after the deciduous trees had put out their first trial buds.

As he worked his way up to the waterfall, for the first time this season the water roared around him in the heaviest flood for fifteen years. A little worried, he hurried on and saw it was as he feared: all his work had been swept askew.

At first he was filled with dismay, then he remembered those passages in the *Tao te Ching* which compare the process of life and the nature of wisdom to the passage of water, which, unchanged itself, changes all things in its path simply by its own nature, and yet it has no nature.

He had always thought that philosophic nonsense, and, besides, the *Tao te Ching* was obviously a political tract, but now he saw that there was a great deal of sense in it. It might not be true, but it was the way life was.

He had adjusted this place for the ebb and flow of the seasons. Now he saw that he had overlooked the larger cycle of the ebb and flow of life itself, and there could be no order in the world unless one took into account not only the usual tenor, but also the sudden verve, of being.

Meanwhile, until the water had gone down enough so that he could get to work again, there was still much to be done with the wood and with the landscape around his hermitage.

That year his brothers wrote to say that now the Ashikaga were in power and the Hojo out, they had had to sell off some of his land. His income would be diminished. No doubt they had sold his before parting with their own which would once have made him furious. Now he merely shrugged his shoulders. He needed little. Even his reduced income was more than adequate, and, besides, he had other things to do. More important things.

He had begun to notice so much. The tree slugs, for instance, though no doubt they had always been there. Why had he not seen them before? That summer the dragonflies skimming over the pool as he worked seemed more numerous and more iridescent than usual. What impressed him most was the resemblance of their bodies to a whittled wooden peg with a broad end, or to fishbones of a certain sort.

But fishbones of what sort? That night at supper he found out. To the backbone of an eel.

He wrote it down.

The walls of the hut were littered with such small scraps of paper now, but somehow he never got around to putting them in order. He had not the time.

He had eaten it so often that he had forgotten how delicious was the taste of eel. Like carp, it had the muddy taste of wisdom. He must install carp in the pool. But also eel tasted lithe. Was it possible (perhaps it had something to do with their musculature) that game and fish had the taste of their function, plants of those things which they took from and then restored to the soil?

Life had taken him unawares. He had been so busy that he had not perceived the change. But sometimes now, sitting at dusk, on the veranda, waiting for the rising of the moon which was sometimes yellow and sometimes not (one could never be sure which it would be); he realized that he was not only content, but often happy. He was certainly never bored. There was the whole world to watch, and he felt so at ease with it that he often woke in the morning with the snug, warm feeling of someone who knows where he belongs.

In 1349, when he was fifty-seven, he heard that the Lady Aoi had died. That was the girl he had been supposed to marry, the girl who had gotten him here. So he supposed he had much to thank her for.

But no. What had gotten him here was a total ignorance of love. He could see that now. To make amends, he began, when he had the time, to set down little sketches of people he had once known, equipping them with principles and a morality which perhaps they had, perhaps they had not, but which he had discovered at the waterfall.

Why not? People, animals, the elements, a waterfall, a tree— they all live in the world, they all follow the same process of birth and decay, so that, willy-nilly (and even if discordant) they have no choice in the matter: they are all part of the harmony of the world. As for transience, that does not matter either. When the wind blew, one went with it as one said "leaf" out of politeness and the wonder of a recognized affinity, to the last autumn leaf as it dwindled down, yellow on one side, brown on the other, to settle by a stone.

The death of the Lady Aoi reminded him, for some reason,

that the time had come to take the training wires off the maple trees, for they were now confirmed in their new shape and would grow that way without any interference from him.

And so he went to do it. It is what nature has to teach.

IRWIN SHAW is famous for his short stories, plays, and novels, *The Young Lions, The Troubled Air, Lucy Crown,* and *Two Weeks in Another Town.* He received the O. Henry Memorial Award in 1944 and took second place in 1945. He now lives in Klosters, Switzerland.

The Inhabitants of Venus

He had been skiing since early morning, and he was ready to stop and have lunch in the village, but Mac said, "Let's do one more before eating," and, since it was Mac's last day, Robert agreed to go up again. The weather was spotty, but there were a few clear patches of sky, and the visibility had been good enough for decent skiing most of the morning. The *téléférique* was crowded, and they had to push their way in among the bright sweaters and anoraks and the bulky packs of the people carrying picnic lunches and extra clothing and skins for climbing. The doors closed and the cabin swung out of the station, over the belt of pine trees at the base of the mountain.

The passengers were packed in so tightly that it was hard to reach for a handkerchief or light a cigarette. Robert was pressed, not unpleasurably, against a handsome young Italian woman with a dissatisfied face, who was explaining to someone over Robert's shoulder why Milan was such a miserable city in the wintertime. "*Milano si trova in un bacino deprimente,*" the woman said, "*bagnato dalla pioggia durante tre mesi all'anno. E, nonostante il loro gusto per l'opera, i Milanesi non sono altro che volgari materialisti che solo il denaro interessa.*" Robert knew enough Italian to understand that she was saying that Milan was in a dismal basin which was swamped by rain for three months a year and that the Milanese, despite their taste for opera, were crass and materialistic and interested only in money.

Robert smiled. Although he had not been born in the United
States, he had been a citizen since 1944, and it was pleasant, in
the heart of Europe, to hear somebody else besides Americans
being accused of materialism and a singular interest in money.

"What's the Contessa saying?" Mac whispered above the curly
red hair of a small woman who was standing between him and
Robert. Mac was a lieutenant on leave from his outfit in Germany. He had been in Europe nearly three years and, to show
that he was not just an ordinary tourist, he called all pretty Italian girls Contessa. Robert had met him a week before in the
bar of the hotel where they were both staying. They were the
same kind of skiers, adventurous and looking for difficulties; they
had skied together every day, and they were already planning to
come back at the same time for the next winter's holiday, if
Robert could get over again from America.

"The Contessa is saying that in Milan all they're interested in
is money," Robert said, keeping his voice low, although in the
babble of conversation in the cabin there was little chance of
being overheard.

"If I was in Milan," Mac said, "and she was in Milan, I'd
be interested in something besides money." He looked with open
admiration at the Italian girl. "Can you find out what run she's
going to do?"

"What for?" Robert asked.

"Because that's the run I'm going to do," Mac said, grinning.
"I plan to follow her like her shadow."

"Mac," Robert said, "don't waste your time. It's your last day."

"That's when the best things always happen," Mac said. "The
last day." He beamed—huge, overt, uncomplicated—at the Italian
girl, who took no notice of him. She was busy now complaining
to her friend about the natives of Sicily.

The sun came out for a few minutes, and the cabin grew hot,
with 40 people jammed into such a small space, and Robert half-
dozed, not bothering to listen to the voices speaking French,
Italian, English, *Schweizerdeutsch* and German, on all sides of
him. Robert liked being in the middle of this informal congress
of tongues. It was one of the reasons he came to Switzerland to
ski whenever he could take time off from his job. In the angry days
through which the world was passing, there was a ray of hope in

this good-natured, polyglot chorus of people who smiled at strangers, who had collected in these shining white hills merely to
enjoy the innocent pleasures of sun and snow.

The feeling of generalized cordiality that Robert experienced
on these trips was intensified by the fact that most of the people
on the lifts and runs seemed more or less familiar to him. Skiers
formed a kind of loose international club, and the same faces
kept turning up year after year in Mégève, Dovas, St. Anton,
Val d'Isére, so that after a while you had the impression you knew
almost everybody. There were four or five Americans in the
cabin whom Robert was sure he had seen at Stowe at Christmas.
The Americans had come over in one of the chartered ski-club
planes that Swissair ran every winter on a cut-rate basis. They
were young and enthusiastic, and none of them had ever been to
Europe before, and they were noisily appreciative of everything—
the Alps, the food, the snow, the weather, the peasants in their
blue smocks, the chic of the lady skiers and the skill and good
looks of the instructors. They were popular with the villagers because they were so obviously enjoying themselves. Besides, they
tipped generously, in the American style with what was, to Swiss
eyes, an endearing disregard of the fact that a service charge of
15 per cent had been added automatically to every bill before it
was presented to them. Two of the girls were very attractive, in a
youthful prettiest-girl-at-the-prom way, and one of the young men,
a lanky boy from Philadelphia, the informal leader of the group,
was a beautiful skier who guided the others down the runs and
helped the dubs.

The Philadelphian, who was standing near Robert, spoke to him
as the cabin swung high over a steep, snowy face of the mountain.
"You've skied here before, haven't you?" he said.

"Yes," Robert said, "a few times."

"What's the best run down this time of day?" the Philadelphian
asked. He had the drawling, flat tone of the good New England
schools that Europeans use in their imitations when they wish to
make fun of upper-class Americans.

"They're all OK today," Robert said.

"What's this run everybody says is so good?" the boy asked.
"The—the Kaiser something-or-other?"

"The Kaisergarten," Robert said. "It's the first gully to the right after you get out of the station on top."

"Is it tough?" the boy asked.

"It's not for beginners," Robert said.

"You've seen this bunch ski, haven't you?" The boy waved vaguely to indicate his friends. "Do you think they can make it?"

"Well," Robert said doubtfully, "there's a narrow, steep ravine full of bumps halfway down, and there are one or two places where it's advisable not to fall, because you're liable to keep on sliding all the way if you do."

"We'll take a chance," the Philadelphian said. "It'll be good for their characters. Boys and girls," he said, raising his voice, "the cowards will stay on top and have lunch. The heroes will come with me. We're going to do the Kaisergarten."

"Francis," one of the pretty girls said, "I do believe it is your sworn intention to kill me on this trip."

"It's not as bad as all that," Robert said, smiling at the girl.

"Say," the girl said, looking with interest at Robert, "haven't I seen you someplace before?"

"On this lift, yesterday," Robert said.

"No." The girl shook her head. She had on a black, fuzzy, lambskin hat, and she looked like a high-school drum majorette pretending to be Anna Karenina. "Before yesterday. Someplace."

"I saw you at Stowe," Robert confessed. "At Christmas."

"Oh, that's where," she said. "I saw you ski. Oh, my, you're *silky*."

Mac broke into a loud laugh at this description of Robert's skiing style.

"Don't mind my friend," Robert said, enjoying the girl's admiration. "He's a coarse soldier who is trying to beat the mountain to its knees by brute strength."

"Say," the girl said, looking puzzled, "you have a funny little way of talking. Are you American?"

"Well, yes," Robert said. "I am now. I was born in France."

"Oh, that explains it," the girl said. "You were born among the crags."

"I was born in Paris," Robert said.

"Do you live there now?"

"I live in New York," Robert said.

"Are you married?" the girl asked anxiously.

"Barbara," the Philadelphian said, "behave yourself."

"I just asked the man a simple, friendly question," the girl protested. "Do you mind, *Monsieur?*"

"Not at all."

"*Are* you married?"

"Yes," Robert said.

"He has three children," Mac added helpfully. "The oldest one is going to run for President in the next election."

"Oh, isn't that too bad?" the girl said. "I set myself a goal on this trip. I was going to meet one unmarried Frenchman."

"I'm sure you'll manage it," Robert said.

"Three children," the girl said. "My! How old are you, anyway?"

"Thirty-nine," Robert said.

"Where is your wife now?" the girl said.

"In New York."

"Pregnant," Mac said, more helpful than ever.

"And she lets you run off and ski all alone like this?" the girl asked incredulously.

"Yes," Robert said. "Actually I'm in Europe on business, and I'm sneaking off for ten days."

"What business?" the girl asked.

"I'm a diamond merchant," Robert said. "I buy and sell diamonds."

"That's the sort of man I'd like to meet," the girl said. "Somebody awash with diamonds. But unmarried."

"Barbara!" the Philadelphian said.

"I deal mostly in industrial diamonds," Robert said. "It's not exactly the same thing."

"Even so," the girl said.

"Barbara," the Philadelphian said, "pretend you're a lady."

"If you can't speak candidly to a fellow American," the girl said, "who can you speak candidly to?" She looked out the plexiglass window of the cabin. "Oh, dear," she said, "it's a perfect monster of a mountain, isn't it? I'm in a fever of terror." She turned and regarded Robert again. "You do look like a Frenchman," she said. "Terribly polished. You're definitely sure you're married?"

"Barbara," the Philadelphian said forlornly.

Robert laughed, and Mac and the other Americans laughed, and the girl smiled under her fuzzy hat, amused by her own clowning and pleased at the reaction she was getting. The other people in the car, who could not understand English, smiled good-naturedly, happy, even though they were not in on the joke, to be the witnesses of this youthful gaiety.

Then through the laughter Robert heard a man's voice say, in tones of quiet, cold distaste, "*Schaut euch diese dummen amerikanischen Gesichter an! Und diese Leute bilden sich ein, sie waren berufen, die Welt zu regieren.*"

Robert had learned German as a child from his Alsatian grandparents, and he understood what he had just heard, but he forced himself not to turn to see who had spoken. His years of temper, he liked to believe, were behind him, and, if nobody else in the cabin had overheard or understood the words, he was not going to be the one to force the issue. He was here to enjoy himself, and he didn't feel like getting into a fight or dragging Mac and the other kids into one. Long ago he had learned the wisdom of playing deaf when he heard things like that, and worse. If some bastard of a German wanted to say, "Look at those stupid American faces. And these are the people who think they have been chosen to rule the world," it made very little real difference to anybody, and a grown man ignored it if he could. So he didn't look to see who had said it, because he knew that if he picked out the man he wouldn't be able to let it go. This way—as long as the hateful voice was anonymous—he could let it slide, along with many other things that Germans had said during his lifetime.

The effort of not looking was difficult, though, and he closed his eyes, angry with himself for being so disturbed by a scrap of overheard malice. It had been a perfect holiday up to now, and it would be foolish to let it be shadowed, even briefly, by a random voice in a crowd. If you came to Switzerland to ski, Robert told himself, you had to expect to find some Germans. But each year now there were more and more of them, massive, prosperous-looking men and sulky-looking women with the suspicious eyes of people who believe they are in danger of being cheated. Men and women both pushed more than was necessary in the lift lines, with a kind of impersonal egotism, an unquestioning assumption of precedence. When they skied they did it grimly, in large groups as if under military orders. At night, when they relaxed in the bars and *Stüblis*, their merriment was more difficult to tolerate than their dedicated daytime gloom and *Junker* arrogance. They sat in red-faced platoons, drinking gallons of beer, volleying great bursts of heavy laughter and roaring glee-club arrangements of student drinking songs. Robert had never heard them sing the Horst Wessel song, but he had noticed that long ago they had stopped pretending they were Swiss or Austrian, or that they had been born in Alsace. Somehow to the sport of skiing, which is, above all, individual and light and an exercise in grace, the Germans seemed to bring the image of the herd. Once or twice when he had been trampled in the *téléférique* station he had let some of his distaste show to Mac, but Mac, who was far from being a fool under his puppy-fullback exterior, had said, "The trick is to isolate them, lad. It's only when they're in groups that they get on your nerves. I've been in Germany for three years, and I've met a lot of good fellows and some smashing girls."

Robert had agreed that Mac was probably right. Deep in his heart he wanted to believe that Mac was right. Before and during the war the problem of the Germans had occupied so much of his waking life that V-E Day had seemed a personal liberation from them, a kind of graduation ceremony from a school in which he had been forced to spend long years trying to solve a single boring, painful problem. He had reasoned himself into believing that defeat had returned the Germans to rationality. So, along with the relief he felt because he no longer ran the risk of being killed by them, there was an almost-as-intense relief that he no longer had to think about them.

After the war he had believed in establishing normal relations with the Germans as quickly as possible, both as good politics and as simple humanity. He drank German beer and even bought a Volkswagen, although he would not have favored equipping the German army with the hydrogen bomb. In the course of his business he had few dealings with Germans, and it was only here, in this village in the Graubünden where their presence was becoming so much more apparent each year, that the idea of Germans disturbed him anymore. But he loved the village, and the thought of abandoning his yearly vacation because of the prevalence of license plates from Munich and Düsseldorf was repugnant to him. Maybe, he thought, from now on he would come at a different time, in January instead of late February. Late February through early March, when the sun was warmer and shone until six o'clock in the evening, was the German season. The Germans were sun gluttons, and they could be seen all over the hills, stripped to the waist, sitting on rocks, eating their picnic lunches, greedily absorbing each precious ray of sunlight. It was as though they came from a country perpetually covered by mist, like the planet Venus, and had to soak up as much brightness and life as possible during their short holidays in order to endure the harsh gloom of their homeland and the conduct of the other inhabitants of Venus for the rest of the year.

Robert smiled to himself at this tolerant concept and felt better disposed toward everyone around him. *Maybe*, he thought, *if I were a single man I'd find a Bavarian girl and fall in love with her and finish the whole thing off.*

"I warn you, Francis," the girl in the lambskin hat was saying, "if you do me to death on this mountain there are three juniors at Yale who will track you down to the ends of the earth."

Then he heard the German voice again. "*Warum haben die Amerikaner nicht genügend Verstand*," the voice said, low but distinctly, near him, the accent clearly *Hochdeutsch*, not *Zurichois* or any of the other variations of *Schweizerdeutsch*, "*ihre dummen kleinen Nutten zu Hause zu lassen, wo sie hingehören?*"

Now he knew there was no avoiding looking and there was no avoiding doing something about it. He glanced at Mac first, to see if Mac, who understood a little German, had heard. Mac was huge and could be dangerous; and, for all his easy good nature, if he had heard the man say, "Why don't the Americans have the sense to leave their silly little tramps at home where they belong?" the man would have been in for a beating. But Mac was still beaming placidly at the Contessa. *That was all to the good*, Robert thought. The Swiss police took a dim view of fighting, no matter what the provocation, and Mac, enraged, would wreak terrible damage in a fight and would more than likely wind up in jail. For an American career soldier stationed in Frankfurt a brawl like that could have serious consequences. *The worst that can happen to me*, Robert thought as he turned to find the man who had spoken, *is a few hours in the pokey and a lecture from the magistrate about abusing Swiss hospitality.*

Almost automatically Robert decided that when they got to the top he would follow the man out of the car, tell him quietly that he, Robert, had understood what had been said about Americans, and swing immediately. *I just hope,* Robert thought, *that whoever it is isn't too damned big.*

For a moment Robert couldn't pick out his opponent-to-be. There was a tall man with his back to Robert, on the other side of the Italian woman, and the voice had come from that direction. Because of the crowd Robert could see only his head and shoulders, which looked bulky and powerful under a black parka. The man had on the kind of black cap that had been worn by the Afrika Korps during the war. Beneath the cap the blond hair, which was thick and very low on the back of his neck, was plentifully streaked with gray. The man was with a plump, hard-faced woman who was whispering earnestly to him but not loudly enough for Robert to hear what she was saying. Then the man said crisply in German, replying to her, "I don't care how many of them understand the language. Let them understand," and Robert knew that he had found his man.

A tingle of anticipation ran through him, making his hands and arms feel tense and jumpy. He regretted that the cabin wouldn't arrive at the top for another five minutes. Now that he had decided the fight was inevitable he could hardly bear waiting. He stared fixedly at the man's broad, black-nylon back, wishing the fellow would turn and show his face. Judging by the man's height and the width of his shoulders he was at least 20 pounds heavier than Robert, but Robert was wiry and in good condition, and in the days when he still got into fights he had been a stubborn performer with a punch surprisingly damaging for someone his size. He wondered if the man would go down with the first blow, if he would apologize, if he would try to use his ski poles. Robert decided to keep his own poles handy, just in case, although Mac could be depended upon to police matters thoroughly if he saw weapons being used. Deliberately Robert took off his heavy leather mittens and stuck them in his belt. Bare knuckles would be more effective. He wondered fleetingly if the man was wearing a ring. He kept his eyes fixed on the back of the man's neck, willing him to turn. Then the plump woman noticed his stare. She dropped her eyes and whispered something to the man in the black parka, and after several seconds he turned, pretending that it was a casual, unmotivated movement. The man looked squarely at Robert, and Robert thought, *If you ski long enough you meet every other skier you've ever known.* At the same moment he knew that it wasn't going to be a nice, simple little fistfight on top of the mountain. For the first time in his life he wanted to kill a man, and the man he wanted to kill was the one whose icy blue eyes, fringed with pale, blond lashes, were staring challengingly at him from under the black peak of the Afrika Korps cap.

It was a long time ago, the winter of 1938, in the French part of Switzerland, and he was 14 years old. The sun was setting behind another mountain, and it was 10 below zero, and he was lying in the snow with his foot turned in that funny, unnatural way, although the pain hadn't really begun yet, and the eyes were looking down at him.

He had done something foolish, and at the moment he was more worried about what his parents would say when they found out than about the broken leg. He had gone up alone, late in the afternoon when almost everybody else was off the mountain. And even so he hadn't stayed on the packed snow of the regular runs, but had started bushwhacking through the forest, searching for powder snow that hadn't been tracked by other skiers. One ski had caught on a hidden root, and he had fallen, hearing the sickening, dry cracking sound from his right leg even as he pitched forward.

Trying not to panic, he had sat up, facing in the direction of the normal track, seeing the markers 100 meters away through the pine forest. If any skiers happened to come by they might just, with luck, be able to hear him if he shouted. He did not try to crawl toward the line of poles, because when he moved a queer feeling flickered from his ankle up his leg into his stomach, making him want to throw up.

The shadows were very long in the forest, and only the highest peaks were rose-colored now against a frozen green sky. He was beginning to feel the cold, and from time to time he was shaken by spasms of shivering.

I'm going to die here, he thought. *I'm going to die here tonight.*
He thought of his parents and his sister comfortably seated this
moment, probably having tea, in the warm dining room of the
chalet two miles down the mountain, and he bit his lips to keep
back the tears. They wouldn't start to worry about him for another
hour or two yet, and then when they did, and started to do something about finding him, they wouldn't know where to begin. He
had known none of the seven or eight people on the lift with
him on his last ride up, and he hadn't told anyone what run he
was going to take. There were three different mountains, with
separate lifts and numberless variations of runs that he might have
taken, and finding him in the dark would be an almost hopeless
task. He looked up at the sky. There were clouds moving in from
the east, a high black wall covering the already darkened sky. If it
snowed that night there was a good chance they wouldn't even
find his body before spring. He had promised his mother that no
matter what happened, he would never ski alone, and now he had
broken the promise, and this was his punishment.

Then he heard the sound of skis coming fast, a harsh, metallic
sound on the iced snow of the run. Before he could see the skier
he began to shout with all the strength of his lungs, frantically, "*Au
secours! Au secours!*"

A dark shape appeared high above him for a second, disappeared
behind a clump of trees, then shot into view much lower down,
almost on a level with the place where he was sitting. Robert
shouted wildly, not uttering words anymore, just a senseless,
passionate, throat-bursting claim on the attention of the human
race, represented, for this one instant at sunset on this cold mountain, by the dark, expert figure plunging, with a scraping of steel
edges and a *whoosh* of wind, toward the village below.

Then, miraculously, in a swirl of snow, the figure stopped.
Robert shouted. The sound of his voice echoed hysterically in the
forest. For a moment the skier didn't move, and Robert shook
with the fear that it was all a hallucination, a mirage of sight and
sound, that there was no one there on the beaten snow at the
edge of the forest, that he was only imagining his own shouts,
that despite all the fierce efiort of his throat and lungs he was
mute, unheard.

Suddenly he couldn't see anything. He had the sensation of

something sinking somewhere within him, of a rush of warm liquid inundating all the ducts and canals of his body. He waved his hands weakly and sank slowly over in a faint.

When he came to, a man was kneeling over him, rubbing his cheeks with snow. "You heard me," Robert said in French. "I was afraid you wouldn't hear me."

"*Ich verstehe nicht*," the man said. "*Nicht parler Französisch.*"

"I was afraid you wouldn't hear me," Robert repeated, in German.

"You are a stupid little boy," the man said severely, in clipped, educated German. "And very lucky. I am the last man on the mountain." He felt Robert's ankle, his hands hard but deft. "Nice," he said ironically, "very nice. You're going to be in plaster for at least three months. Here—lie still. I am going to take your skis off. You will be more comfortable." Working swiftly, he undid the long leather thongs and stood the skis up in the snow. Then he swept the snow off a stump a few yards away, got behind Robert and put his hands under Robert's armpits. "Relax," he said. "Do not try to help me." He picked Robert up. "Luckily, you weigh nothing. How old are you—eleven?"

"Fourteen," Robert said.

"What's the matter?" the man said, laughing. "Don't they feed you in Switzerland?"

"I'm French," Robert said.

"Oh." The man's voice went flat. "French." He half-carried, half-dragged Robert over to the stump and sat him down gently on it. "There," he said, "at least you're out of the snow. You won't freeze—for the time being. Now, listen carefully. I will take your skis down with me to the ski school, and I will tell them where you are and tell them to send a sled for you. They should get to you in less than an hour. Now whom are you staying with in town?"

"My mother and father. At the Chalet Montana."

"Good." The man nodded. "The Chalet Montana. Do they speak German too?"

"Yes."

"Excellent," the man said. "I will telephone them and tell them that their foolish son has broken his leg and that the patrol is taking him to the hospital. What is your name?"

"Robert."

"Robert what?"

"Robert Rosenthal," Robert said.

"Please don't say I'm hurt too badly. They'll be worried enough as it is."

The man didn't answer immediately. He busied himself tying Robert's skis together and slung them over his shoulder. "Do not worry, Robert Rosenthal," he said. "I will not worry them more than is necessary." Abruptly he started off, sweeping easily through the trees, his poles held in one hand, balancing Robert's skis across his shoulders with the other hand.

His sudden departure took Robert by surprise, and it was only when the man was a considerable distance away, almost lost among the trees, that he realized he hadn't thanked the man for saving his life. "Thank you," he shouted into the growing darkness. "Thank you very much."

The man didn't stop, and Robert never knew whether his cry had been heard or not. Because after an hour, when it was completely dark, with the stars covered by the clouds that had been moving in from the east, the patrol had not yet appeared. Robert had a watch with a radium dial. Timing himself, he waited exactly one hour and a half, until 10 minutes past seven, and then decided that nobody was coming for him and that if he hoped to live through the night he would have to crawl out of the forest somehow and make his way down to the town by himself.

He was rigid with cold by now, and suffering from shock. His teeth chattered in a frightening way, as though his jaws were part of an insane machine over which he had no control. There was no feeling in his fingers anymore, and the pain in his leg came in ever-enlarging waves. He had put up the hood of his parka and let his head sink as low on his chest as he could, and the cloth of the parka was stiff with his frosted breath. He heard a whimpering sound somewhere around him, and it was only after what seemed like several minutes that he realized the whimpering sound was coming from him, and that there was nothing he could do to stop it.

Stiffly, with exaggerated care, he tried to lift himself off the tree stump without putting any weight on his injured leg, but at the last moment he slipped and twisted the leg as he went down into the snow. He screamed twice and lay with his face in the snow and thought of just staying that way and forgetting the whole thing, the whole intolerable effort of remaining alive. Later on, when he was much older, he came to the conclusion that the one thing that had kept him moving was the thought of his mother and father waiting for him, with an anxiety that would soon become terror, in the town below.

He pulled himself along on his belly, digging at the snow with his hands, using rocks, low-hanging branches and snow-covered roots to help him, meter by meter, out of the forest. His watch was torn off somewhere along the way, and when he finally reached the line of poles that marked the packed snow and ice of the run he had no notion of whether it had taken him five minutes or five hours to cover the 100 meters from the place where he had fallen. He lay panting, sobbing, staring at the lights of the town far below, knowing that he could never reach them, knowing that he had to reach them. The effort of crawling through the deep snow had warmed him, though, and his face was streaming with sweat, and the blood coming back into his numbed hands and feet jabbed him with a thousand needles of pain.

The lights of the town guided him now, and here and there he could see the marker poles outlined against the small, cozy, Christmasy glow of the lights. It was easier going, too, on the packed snow of the run. From time to time he managed to slide 10 or 15 meters without stopping, tobogganing on his stomach, screaming occasionally when his broken leg banged loosely against an icy bump, or twisted as he went over a steep embankment to crash down on a level place below. Once he couldn't stop himself and fell into a swiftly rushing small stream and pulled himself out of it five minutes later with his gloves and mid-section and knees soaked with icy water. And still the lights of the town seemed as far away as ever.

Finally, after he had stopped twice to vomit, he felt he couldn't move anymore. He tried to sit up, so that if the snow came that night there would be a chance somebody might see the top of his head sticking out of the new cover in the morning. He was struggling to push himself erect when a shadow passed between him and the lights of the town. The shadow was very close and with his last breath he called out. Later on, the peasant who had rescued him said that what he had called out was "Excuse me."

The peasant had been moving hay on a big sled from one of the hill barns down to the valley, and he rolled the hay off the sled and put Robert on instead. Then, braking carefully and taking the sled on a path that cut back and forth across the run, he brought Robert down to the valley and the hospital.

By the time his mother and father had been notified and reached the hospital, the doctor had given him a shot of morphine and was already setting the leg. So it wasn't until the next morning, as he lay in the gray hospital room, sweating with pain, his leg in traction, that he could get out any kind of coherent story for his parents about what had happened.

"Then I saw this man skiing very fast, all alone," Robert said, trying to speak without showing how much the effort was costing him, trying to take the look of shock and agony from his parents' set faces by pretending that his leg hardly hurt at all, and that the whole incident was of small importance. "He heard me and came over and took off my skis and made me comfortable on a tree stump, and he asked me what my name was and where my parents were staying, and he said he'd go to the ski school and tell them where I was and to send a sled for me, and that he'd call you at the chalet and tell you they were bringing me down to the hospital. Then after more than an hour—it was pitch dark already —nobody came, and I decided I'd better not wait anymore and I started down and I was lucky and I saw this farmer with a sled and——"

"You were very lucky," Robert's mother said flatly. She was a small, neat, plump woman with bad nerves, who was at home only in cities. She detested the cold, detested the mountains, detested the idea of her loved ones running what seemed to her the senseless risk of injury that skiing involved, and she came on these holidays only because Robert and his father and sister were so passionate about the sport. Now she was white with fatigue and worry, and if Robert had not been immobilized in traction she would have had him out of the accursed mountains that morning on the train to Paris.

"Now, Robert," his father said, "is it possible that when you hurt yourself the pain did things to you and that you just imagined you saw a man and just imagined he told you he was going to call us and get you a sled from the ski school?"

"I didn't imagine it, Papa," Robert said. The morphine had made him feel hazy and heavy-brained, and he was puzzled that his father was talking to him that way. "Why do you think I might have imagined it?"

"Because," his father said, "nobody called us last night until ten o'clock, when the doctor telephoned from the hospital. And nobody called the ski school either."

"I didn't imagine him," Robert repeated. He was hurt that his father seemed to think he was lying. "If he came into this room I'd know him right off. He was wearing a white cap, he was a big man with a black anorak, and he had blue eyes. They looked a little funny because his eyelashes were almost white, and from a little way off it looked as though he didn't have any eyelashes at all."

"How old was he, do you think?" Robert's father asked. "As old as I am?" Robert's father was nearly 50.

"No," Robert said. "I don't think so."

"Was he as old as your Uncle Jules?" Robert's father asked.

"Yes," Robert said. "Just about." He wished his parents would leave him alone. He was all right now. His leg was in plaster, and he wasn't dead, and in three months, the doctor said, he'd be walking again, and he wanted to forget everything that had happened last night in the forest.

"So," Robert's mother said, "he was a man of about twenty-five, with a white cap and blue eyes." She picked up the phone and asked for the ski school.

Robert's father lit a cigarette and went over to the window and looked out. It was snowing. It had been snowing since midnight, heavily, and the lifts weren't running today because a driving wind had sprung up with the snow and up on top there was danger of avalanches.

"Did you talk to the farmer who picked me up?" Robert asked.

"Yes," said his father. "He said you were a very brave little boy. He also said that if he hadn't found you you couldn't have gone on more than another fifty meters."

"Sssh." Robert's mother had the connection with the ski school now. "This is Mrs. Rosenthal again. Yes, thank you, he's doing as well as can be expected," she said, in her precise, melodious French. "We've been talking to him, and there's one aspect of his story that's a little strange. He says a man stopped and helped him take off his skis last night after he'd broken his leg, and promised to go to the ski school and leave the skis there and ask for a sled to be sent to bring him down. We'd like to know if, in fact, the man did report the accident. It would have been some-where around six o'clock."

She listened for a moment, her face tense. "I see," she said, and listened again.

"No," she said, "we don't know his name. My son says he was about twenty-five years old, with blue eyes and a white cap. Wait a minute. I'll ask." She turned to Robert. "Robert, what kind of skis did you have? They're going to look and see if they're out in the rack."

"Attenhofer's," Robert said. "One meter seventy. And they have my initials in red up on the tips."

"Attenhofer's," his mother repeated over the phone. "And they have his initials on them. 'R. R.' In red. Thank you. I'll wait."

Robert's father came back from the window and doused his cigarette in an ashtray. Beneath the holiday tan his face looked weary and sick. "Robert," he said with a rueful smile, "you must learn to be more careful. You are my only male heir, and there is very little chance that I shall produce another."

"Yes, Papa," Robert said. "I'll be careful."

His mother waved impatiently at them to be quiet and listened again at the telephone. "Thank you," she said. "Please call me if you hear anything." She hung up. "No," she said to Robert's father, "the skis aren't there."

"It can't be possible," Robert's father said, "that a man would leave a little boy to freeze to death just to steal a pair of skis."

"I'd like to get my hands on him," Robert's mother said, "just for ten minutes. Robert, darling, think hard. Did he seem—well —did he seem normal?"

"He seemed all right," Robert said, "I suppose."

"Was there any other thing about him that you noticed? Think hard. Anything that would help us find him. It's not only for us, Robert. If there's a man in this town who would do something

like that to you, it's important that people know about him before
he does something even worse to other boys."

"Mama," Robert said, feeling close to tears under the insistence
of her questioning, "I told you just the way it was. Everything.
I'm not lying, Mama."

"What did he sound like, Robert?" his mother said. "Did he
have a low voice, a high voice, did he sound like us, as though he
lived in Paris, did he sound like any of your teachers, did he sound
like the other people from around here, did he——"

"Oh," Robert said, remembering.

"What is it? What do you want to say?" his mother said sharply.

"I had to speak German to him," Robert said. Until now, what
with the pain and the morphine, it hadn't occurred to him to
mention that.

"What do you mean, you had to speak German to him?"

"I started to speak to him in French, and he didn't understand.
We spoke in German."

His parents exchanged glances. Then his mother said gently,
"Was it real German? Or was it Swiss German? You know the
difference, don't you?"

"Of course," Robert said. One of his father's parlor tricks was
giving imitations of Swiss friends in Paris speaking first French
and then Swiss German. Robert had a good ear for languages,
and, aside from having heard his Alsatian grandparents speak German since he was an infant, he was studying German literature in
school and knew long passages of Goethe and Schiller and Heine
by heart. "It was German, all right," he said.

There was silence in the room. His father went over to the
window again and looked out at the snow falling like a soft,
blurred curtain outside. "I knew," his father said quietly, "that it
couldn't just have been for the skis."

In the end, his father won out. His mother wanted the police to
try to find the man, even though his father pointed out that there
were perhaps 5000 skiers in the town for the holidays, a good
percentage of them German-speaking and blue-eyed, and that
trains arrived and departed with them five times a day. Robert's
father was sure that the man had left the very night Robert broke
his leg, but during the remainder of his stay in the town Mr.

Rosenthal prowled the snowy streets and went in and out of bars searching for the face that would answer Robert's description of the man on the mountain. He said it would do no good to go to the police and might do harm, because once the story got out there would be plenty of people to complain that this was just another hysterical Jewish fantasy. "There are plenty of Nazis in Switzerland, of all nationalities," Robert's father told his mother in the course of an argument that lasted for weeks, "and this will just give them more ammunition—they'll be able to say, 'See, wherever the Jews go they start trouble.'"

Robert's mother, who was made of sterner stuff and who had relatives in Germany who smuggled out disturbing letters, wanted justice at any cost, but after a while even she saw the hopelessness of pushing the matter further. Four weeks after the accident, when Robert finally could be moved, as she sat beside her son, holding his hand, in the ambulance that would take them to Geneva and then on to Paris, she said in a dead voice, "Soon we must leave Europe. I cannot stand to live anymore on a continent where things like this are permitted to happen."

Much later, during the war, after Mr. Rosenthal had died in occupied France and Robert and his mother and sister were in America, a friend of Robert's, who had also done a lot of skiing in Europe, heard the story of the man in the white cap and told Robert he was almost sure he recognized the man from the description Robert gave. It was a ski instructor from Garmisch, or maybe from Oberndorf or Freudenstadt, who had a couple of rich Austrian clients with whom he toured each winter from one ski resort to another. Robert's friend didn't know the man's name, and the one time Robert got to Garmisch it was with French troops in the closing days of the war, and of course nobody was skiing then.

Now the man was standing just three feet from him, on the other side of the pretty Italian woman, his face framed by the straight black rows of skis, looking coolly, with insolent amusement, but without recognition, at Robert from under his almost-albino eyelashes. He was approaching 50 now, and his face was fleshy but hard and healthy, with a thin, set mouth that indicated control and self-discipline.

Robert hated him. He hated him for the attempted murder of a 14-year-old boy in 1938; he hated him for the acts he must have condoned or collaborated in during the war; he hated him for his father's death and his mother's exile; he hated him for what he had said about the pretty little American girl in the lambskin hat; he hated him for the impudence of his glance and the healthy, untouched robustness of his face and neck; he hated him because the man could look directly into the eyes of someone he had tried to kill and not recognize him; he hated him because he was here, bringing the idea of death and vengeance into this silvery bubble climbing through the placid holiday air of a kindly, welcoming country.

And most of all he hated the man whose cap was black now because the man betrayed and made a sour joke of the precariously achieved peace that Robert had built with his wife, his children, his job, his comfortable, easygoing, generously forgetful Americanism since the war.

The German deprived him of his sense of normality. Living with a wife and three children in a clean, cheerful house was not normal; having your name in the telephone directory was not normal; lifting your hat to your neighbor and paying your bills was not normal; obeying the law and depending upon the protection of the police was not normal. The German sent him back through the years to an older and truer normality—murder, blood, flight, conspiracy, pillage and ruin. For a while Robert had deceived himself into believing that the nature of everyday things could change. The German in the crowded cabin had now put him to rights. Meeting the German had been an accident, but the accident had revealed what was permanent and nonaccidental in his life and in the life of the people around him.

Mac was saying something to him, and the girl in the lambskin hat was singing an American song in a soft, small voice, but he didn't hear what Mac was saying, and the words of the song made no sense. He had turned away from the German and was looking at the steep stone escarpment of the mountain, now almost obscured by a swirling cloud. He felt confused and battered, and the images that raced through his mind were shadowy, veiled, like his glimpses of the mountain through the cloud—the man in the black cap lying in the snow, in a spreading red stain, himself standing over the man with a pistol in his hand (where could he find a weapon on this peaceful mountain?), the man struggling beneath him, the feel of the crushed, gasping throat between his strangling hands, the last terrified look of recognition and understanding, the man in the black cap sliding, skis flailing, hands clutching at the icy surface, going toward the brink, screaming as he went over and whirled down toward the rocks below.

And he himself? What? The plotter of a perfect crime? The joyous murderer? The just executor? The prisoner in the dock, explaining his justifiable crime? Condemned and waking, morning after morning for the rest of his life, in a prison cell? Or exonerated and going back, as though nothing had happened, to his neat white house and ordering his wife and children to believe that nothing had changed, that although there was blood on his hands he was still the same husband, the same thoughtful father he had always been?

Murder. Murder. Men killed every hour for much less reason. They killed in the course of burglaries in which the loot was no more than 10 or 15 dollars. They killed in bars for differences of opinion. They killed in support of abstract political ideas; they killed for love, for religion, jealousy, out of exasperation.

In other times men had killed for a slight, for a glass of wine thrown in the face. Was he civilized beyond the point of avenging slights? What had to be thrown in his face before he acted, what sneers was he prepared to endure?

Was it cowardice that made him hesitate? Was he like his father, holding back because he was worried about the opinion of neighbors who said Jews made trouble wherever they went?

Other Jews had killed without compunction, careless of all opinion. The Stern gang terrorists in Palestine, Jewish gangsters in the United States. Not all Jews were like his father.

And in Europe and Africa and Asia there was constant slaughter —Algerian revolutionaries shooting policemen on the bustling streets of Paris, a student in Japan running a sword through a political leader, Congolese sergeants bayoneting tribal opponents. After all, murder was a commonplace event. Even in the United States, every hour of every day in the year, a murder was reported to the police.

During the war he had been ready enough to kill—for an ideal, for a country, for the safety of men who wore the same uniform he did. But it was harder to think of killing for himself, to avenge a wound out of his own past. Was it modesty on his part? Did he feel that he was not important enough for so grave and irrevocable an act? Was he finally the victim of his mother's fussing and tender love, of nannies saying "Naughty boy," of polite schools, of rabbis dreaming about Jerusalem, of children's books, of coaches on long-forgotten athletic fields talking about fair play, of that vague, comfort-shaped, false, all-pervading doctrine by which Americans lived, whose key word was "arbitrate"?

What was there subject to arbitration between him and the man in the black cap who had left him on the mountainside to die?

It was not even a terribly special case. In the world of hatred and agony that the Germans had created, meetings between persecutors and victims were unavoidable. There had been so many persecutors, and for all their zeal they had left so many victims alive. There were the stories, so frequent in Europe, of men who had been in concentration camps who had confronted their torturers after the war and turned them in to the authorities, and had the satisfaction of witnessing their execution. But to whom could he turn this German over—the Swiss police? For what crime, under what criminal code?

He could do what an ex-prisoner had done in Budapest three or four years after the war when he had met one of his former jailers on a bridge over the Danube and had simply picked the man up and thrown him into the water and watched him drown. The ex-prisoner had explained who he was and who the drowned man was and had been let off and treated as a hero. But Switzerland was not Hungary, the Danube was far away, the war had been finished a long time ago.

Robert moved tensely in the crowded cabin. He could feel the sweat running unpleasantly down his ribs under his heavy sweater. The presence of so many people, chattering away with nothing on their minds but lunch or how to perfect the new Austrian ski technique, disturbed him and made it difficult for him to think. And he had to think. In a few minutes they would be on top of the mountain and a decision would have to be made, a decision which would change the course of his life.

No matter what he did, he had to get rid of Mac. This was something he could only solve alone. With Mac out of the way he could follow the man and wait for events to push him to one action or another. He might even surprise the man alone somewhere on the slopes and contrive a murder that would look like an accident. Maybe the man would insult him, enrage him to a point where instinct would take over, swamping all hesitation.

Whatever he did that day, Robert knew that he was not going to make it any kind of a duel. It was punishment he was after, not a symbol of honor. He closed his eyes and envisaged himself finishing the man off in some isolated place, hidden from all eyes by the enveloping cloud—how the finish would come he didn't know. Somehow. Then he would pull the body off into the forest, leave it there for the snow to cover, for weeks, months

(VICTIM OF SKIING ACCIDENT DISCOVERED BY FARMER
TWO MONTHS AFTER DISAPPEARANCE),

then get out of the country fast, divulging nothing to anyone.

Robert had never killed a man. During the war he had been assigned by the American Army as part of a liaison team, to a French division, and, though he had been shot at often enough, he had never fired a gun in Europe. When the war was over he had been secretly thankful that he had been spared the question of whether or not he was capable of killing. Now he understood—he had not been spared. The question was still open. His war was not over.

And if he didn't kill—then what? Get the man alone, beat him to the ground, kick in his head with the big, heavy ski boots, leave him disfigured, marked for life with a broken face to bear witness to the vengeance he had so thoroughly deserved?

Maybe that, Robert thought; *maybe that. Let him go to the police and complain. I would like that*. He had a feeling that no matter what happened, the man would keep the police out of it if he could.

So, Robert decided, *follow him. See what develops. Don't let him out of your sight. Let what happens happen.*

And swiftly—it had to happen swiftly, before the man realized that he was the object of any special attention, before he began to wonder about the American on his tracks, before the face of the skinny 14-year-old boy on the dark mountain in 1938 emerged in his memory from the avenging face of the grown man before him now.

"Say, Robert." It was Mac's voice finally breaking into his consciousness. "What's the matter? I've been talking to you for thirty seconds and you haven't heard a word I said. Are you sick? You look awfully queer, lad."

"I'm all right," Robert said. He made a great effort to make his face look like the face of the man Mac had skied with every day for a week. "I have a headache. That's all. Maybe I'd better eat something, get something warm to drink. You go ahead down by yourself."

"Of course not," Mac said. "I'll wait for you."

"Don't be silly," Robert said, trying to keep his tone natural and friendly. "You'll lose the Contessa. Actually I don't feel much like skiing any more today. The weather's turned lousy." He gestured at the cloud that was blanketing the mountain. "You can't see a thing. I'll probably take the lift back down."

"Hey, you're beginning to worry me," Mac said anxiously. "I'll stick with you. You want me to take you to a doctor?"

"Leave me alone, please, Mac," Robert said. He had to get rid of Mac. If it meant hurting his feelings he'd make it up to him someway later. "When I get one of these headaches I prefer being alone."

"You're sure now?" Mac asked.

"I'm sure."

"OK. See you at the hotel for tea?"

"Yes, Robert said. *After murder*, he thought, *I always have a good tea. After murder—or whatever.* He prayed that the Italian girl would put her skis on and move off quickly once they got to the top so that Mac would be gone before he started off after the man in the black cap.

The cabin was swinging over the last pylon now and slowing down to come into the station. The passengers were stirring, arranging clothes, testing bindings in preparation for their descent. Robert stole a quick glance at the German. The woman with him was knotting a silk scarf around his throat with little wifely gestures. She had the face of a cook, splotchy, with a red nose. Neither she nor the man looked in Robert's direction. *I will han-*

dle the problem of the woman when I come to it, Robert thought.

The cabin stopped, and the skiers began to disembark. Robert was close to the door and was one of the first out. Without looking back he walked swiftly away from the station and into the shifting grayness of the mountaintop. The mountain dropped off in a sheer, rocky face on one side of the station, and Robert went over and stood at the edge, looking out. If the German for any reason happened to come near him, to see how thick the cloud was on that side or to judge the condition of the snow on the Kaisergarten, which had to be entered farther on, but which cut back under the cliff lower down where the slope became more gradual, there was a possibility that a quick move on Robert's part would send the man crashing down to the rocks 100 meters below, and then the whole thing would be over. Robert turned and faced the station exit, searching the crowd of brightly dressed skiers for the Afrika Korps cap.

He saw Mac come out with the Italian girl. He was talking to her and carrying her skis, and the girl was smiling warmly. Mac waved at Robert and then knelt to help the girl put on her skis. Robert took a deep breath. Mac, at least, was out of the way. And the American group had decided to have lunch on top and had gone into the restaurant near the station.

The Afrika Korps cap was not to be seen. The German and the woman had not yet come out. There was nothing unusual about that. People often waxed their skis in the station where it was warm or went to the toilets downstairs before starting down the mountain. It was all to the good. The longer the German took, the fewer people there would be hanging around to notice Robert when he set out after the man.

Robert waited at the cliff's edge. In the swirling, cold cloud, he felt capable, powerful, curiously light-headed. For the first time in his life he understood the profound, sensual pleasure of destruction. *I think I can do it,* he thought; *I really think I can do it.* He waved gaily at Mac and the Italian girl as they moved off together on the traverse to one of the easier runs on the other side of the mountain.

Then the door to the station opened again, and the woman who had been with the German came out. She had her skis on, and Robert realized that they had been so long inside because they were putting their skis on in the waiting room. In bad weather people often did that so they wouldn't freeze their hands outdoors on the icy metal of the bindings. The woman held the door open, and Robert saw the man in the Afrika Korps cap coming through the opening. But he wasn't coming out like everybody else. He was hopping, with great ability, on one leg. The other leg had been cut off at mid-thigh. To keep his balance the German had miniature skis fixed on the ends of his poles, instead of the usual thonged baskets.

Through the years Robert had seen other one-legged skiers, veterans of Hitler's armies who had refused to let their mutilation keep them off the mountains they loved, and he had admired their fortitude and skill. But he felt no admiration for the man in the Afrika Korps cap. All he felt was a bitter sense of loss, of having been deprived at the last moment of something that had been promised him and that he had wanted and desperately needed, because he knew he was not strong enough to murder or maim a man already maimed, to punish the already punished, and he despised himself for his own weakness. Now he understood why the German had been so carelessly loud in expressing his contempt for the Americans in the cabin. His severed leg conferred on him a cripple's immunity, and, cynically, he had enjoyed it to the full.

Robert watched as the man made his way across the snow with crablike cunning, hunched over the poles with the infants' skis on their ends. Two or three times, when the man and the woman came to a rise, the woman got behind the man silently, and pushed him up the slope until he could move under his own power again.

The cloud had been swept away, and there was a momentary burst of sunlight. In it Robert saw the man and the woman traverse to the entrance of the steepest run on the mountain. Without hesitating, the man plunged into it, skiing skillfully overtaking the more timid or weaker skiers who were picking their way cautiously down the slope.

Dully Robert watched the two of them descend the mountain, the man hideously graceful, wounded and invulnerable, and soon the couple became tiny figures on the white expanse below. Now

Robert knew there was nothing to be done, nothing more to wait for except a cold, hopeless, everlasting forgiveness.

The two figures disappeared out of the sunlight into the solid bank of cloud that cut across the lower part of the mountain.

Then Robert went back to where he had left his skis and put them on. He did it clumsily. His hands were cold because he had taken off his mittens in the *téléférique* cabin in that hopeful and innocent past 10 minutes ago when he had thought the German insult could be paid back with a few blows of a bare fist.

He went off fast on the run that Mac had taken with the Italian girl, and he caught up with them before they were halfway down. It began to snow when they reached the village, and they went into the hotel and had a hilarious lunch with a lot of wine, and the girl gave Mac her address and said he should be sure to look her up the next time he came to Milan.

HORTENSE CALISHER has an established reputation as a fiction writer with two volumes of short stories, *In the Absence of Angels* and *Tale for the Mirror*, and two novels, *False Entry* and *Textures of Life*. She has written reviews and articles, lectures occasionally, has won two Guggenheim Fellowships and in 1958 toured Southeast Asia under a State Department American Specialist Grant. She and her husband are residents of New York.

The Scream on 57th Street

When the scream came, from downstairs in the street five flights below her bedroom window, Mrs. Hazlitt, who in her month's tenancy of the flat had become the lightest of sleepers, stumbled up, groped her way past the empty second twin bed that stood nearer the window, and looked out. There was nothing to be seen of course—the apartment house she was in, though smartly kept up to the standards of the neighborhood, dated from the era of front fire escapes, and the sound, if it had come at all, had come from directly beneath them. From other half-insomniac nights she knew that the hours must be somewhere between three and four in the morning. The 'all night' doorman who guarded the huge façade of the apartment house opposite had retired, per custom, to some region behind its canopy; the one down the block at the corner of First, who blew his taxi whistle so incessantly that she had for some nights mistaken it for a traffic policeman's, had been quiet for a long time. Even the white-shaded lamp that burned all day and most of the night on the top floor of the little gray town house sandwiched between the tall buildings across the way—an invalid's light perhaps—had been quenched. At this hour the wide expanse of the avenue, Fifty-seventh Street at its easternmost end, looked calm, reassuring and amazingly silent for one of the main arteries of the city. The crosstown bus

From *Tale for the Mirror* © 1962 by Hortense Calisher. Reprinted by permission of Little, Brown and Company and Brandt and Brandt. Originally published in *Harper's Bazaar*.

service had long since ceased; the truck traffic over on First made
only an occasional dim rumble. If she went into the next room,
where there was a French window opening like a double door,
and leaned out, absurd idea, in her nightgown, she would see,
far down to the right, the lamps of a portion of the Queensboro
Bridge, quietly necklaced on the night. In the blur beneath them,
out of range but comfortable to imagine, the beautiful cul-de-sac
of Sutton Square must be musing, Edwardian in the starlight, its
one antique bow-front jutting over the river shimmering below.
And in the façades opposite her, lights were still spotted here
and there, as was always the case, even in the small hours, in
New York. Other consciousnesses were awake, a vigil of anonymous neighbors whom she would never know, that still gave one
the hive-sense of never being utterly alone.

All was silent. No, she must have dreamed it, reinterpreted in
her doze some routine sound, perhaps the siren of the police car
that often keened through this street but never stopped, no doubt
on it way to the more tumultuous West Side.

Until the death eight months ago of her husband, companion
of twenty years, her ability to sleep had always been healthy and
immediate; since then it had gradually, not unnaturally deterio-
rated, but this was the worst; she had never done this before.
For she could still hear very clearly the character of the sound,
or rather its lack of one—a long, oddly sustained note, then a
shorter one, both perfectly even, not discernible as a man's or
woman's, and without—yes, without the color of any emotion—
surely the sound that one heard in dreams. Never a woman of
small midnight fears in either city or country, as a girl she had
done settlement work on some of this city's blackest streets, as a
mining engineer's wife had nestled peacefully within the shriek-
ing velvet of an Andes night. Not to give herself special marks
for this, it was still all the more reason why what she had heard,
or thought she had heard, must have been hallucinatory. A harsh
word, but she must be stern with herself at the very beginnings
of any such, of what could presage the sort of disintegrating
widowhood, full of the mouse-fears and softening self-indulgences
of the manless, that she could not, would not abide. Scarcely a
second or two could have elapsed between that long—yes, that
was it, soulless—cry, and her arrival at the window. And look,

down there on the street and upward, everything remained motionless. Not a soul, in answer, had erupted from a doorway. All
the fanlights of the lobbies shone serenely. Up above, no one
leaned, not a window had flapped wide. After twenty years of
living outside of the city, she could still flatter herself that she
knew New York down to the ground—she had been born here,
and raised. Secretly mourning it, missing it through all the hap-
piest suburban years, she had kept up with it like a scholar, building a red-book of it for herself even through all its savage, in-
continent rebuilding. She still knew all its neighborhoods. She
knew. And this was one in which such a sound would be policed
at once, such a cry serviced at once, if only by doormen running.
No, the fault, the disturbance, must be hers.

Reaching into the pretty, built-in wardrobe on her right—the
flat, with so many features that made it more like a house (fire-
place, high ceilings), had attracted her from the first for this
reason—she took out a warm dressing gown and sat down on
the bed to put on her slippers. The window was wide open and
she meant to leave it that way; country living had made unbearable the steam heat of her youth. There was no point to winter
otherwise, and she—she and Sam—had always been ones to enjoy
the weather as it came. Perhaps she had been unwise to give
up the dog, excuse for walks early and late, outlet for talking aloud
—the city was full of them. Unwise too, in the self-denuding impulse of loss, to have made herself that solitary in readiness for a
city where she would have to remake friends and no longer had
kin. And charming as this flat was, wooed as she increasingly was
by the delicately winning personality of its unknown, absent
owner, Mrs. Berry, by her bric-a-brac, her cookbooks, even by her
widowhood, almost as recent as Mrs. Hazlitt's own—perhaps it
would be best to do something about getting the empty second
twin bed removed from this room. No doubt Mrs. Berry, fled to
London, possibly even residing in the rooms of yet a third woman
in search of recommended change, would understand.

Mrs. Hazlitt stretched her arms, able to smile at this imagined
procession of women inhabiting each other's rooms, fallen one
against the other like a pack of playing cards. How could she
have forgotten what anyone who had reached middle age through
the normal amount of trouble should know: that the very

horizontal position itself of sleep, when one could not, laid one open to every attack from within, on a couch with no psychiatrist to listen but oneself. The best way to meet the horrors was on two feet, vertical. What she meant to do now was to fix herself a sensible hot drink, not coffee, reminiscent of shared midnight snacks, not even tea, but a nursery drink, cocoa. In a lifetime, she thought, there are probably two eras of the sleep that is utterly sound: the nursery sleep (if one had the lucky kind of childhood I did), and the sleep next or near the heart and body of the one permanently loved and loving (if one has been lucky enough for that too). I must learn from within, as well as without, that both are over. She stood up, tying her sash more firmly. And at that moment the scream came again.

She listened, rigid. It came exactly as remembered, one shrilled long note, then the shorter second, like a cut-off Amen to the first and of the same timbre, dreadful in its cool, a madness expended almost with calm, near the edge of joy. No wonder she had thought of the siren; this had the same note of terror controlled. One could not tell whether it sped toward a victim or from one. As before, it seemed to come from directly below.

Shaking, she leaned out, could see nothing because of the high sill, ran into the next room, opened the French window and all but stood on the fire escape. As she did so, the sound, certainly human, had just ceased; at the same moment a cab, going slowly down the middle of the avenue, its light up, veered directly toward her, as if the driver too had heard, poised there beneath her with its nose pointed toward the curb, then veered sharply back to the center of the street, gathered speed, and drove on. Immediately behind it another cab, top light off, slowed up, performed exactly the same orbit, then it too, with a hasty squeal of brakes, made for the center street and sped away. In the confusion of noises she thought she heard the grind of a window sash coming down, then a slam—perhaps the downstairs door of the adjoining set of flats, or of this one. Dropping to her knees, she leaned both palms on the floor-level lintel of the window and peered down through the iron slats of her fire escape and the successive ones below. Crouched that way, she could see straight back to the building line. To the left, a streetlamp cast a pale, even glow on empty sidewalk and the free space of curb either side of a hydrant; to the right, the shadows were obscure, but motionless. She saw nothing to conjure into a half-expected human bundle lying still, heard no footfall staggering or slipping away. Not more than a minute or two could have elapsed since she had heard the cry. Tilting her head up at the façades opposite, she saw that their simple pattern of lit windows seemed the same. While she stared, one of the squares blotted out, then another, both on floors not too high to have heard. Would no one, having heard, attend? Would she?

Standing up, her hand on the hasp of the French window, she felt herself still shaking, not with fear, but with the effort to keep herself from in some way heeding that cry. Again she told herself that she had been born here, knew the city's ways, had not the *auslander's* incredulity about some of them. These ways had hardened since her day, people had warned her, to an indifference beyond that of any civilized city; there were no 'good' neighborhoods now, none of any kind really, except the half-hostile enclosure that each family must build for itself. She had discounted this, knowing unsentimentally what city life was; even in the tender version of it that was her childhood there had been noises, human ones, that the most responsible people, the kindest, had shrugged away, saying, 'Nothing, dear. Something outside.' What she had not taken into account was her own twenty years of living elsewhere, where such a cry in the night would be succored at once if only for gossip's sake, if only because one gave up privacy—anonymity—forever, when one went to live in a house on a road. If only, she thought, holding herself rigid to stop her trembling, because it would be the cry of someone one knew. Nevertheless, it took all her strength not to rush downstairs, to hang on to the handle, while in her mind's eye she ran out of her apartment door, remembering to take the key, pressed the elevator button and waited, went down at the car's deliberate pace. After that there would be the inner, buzzer door to open, then at last the door to the outside.

No, it would take too long, and it was already too late for the phone, by the time police could come or she could find the number of the superintendent in his back basement—and when either answered, what would she say? She looked at the fire escape. Not counting hers, there must be three others between herself and the street. Whether there was a ladder extending from the lowest one, she could not remember; possibly one hung by one's hands and dropped to the ground. Years ago there had been more of them, even the better houses had had them in their rear areaways, but she had never in her life seen one used. And this one fronted directly on the avenue. It was this that brought her to her senses—the vision of herself in her blue robe creeping down the front of a building on Fifty-seventh Street, hanging by her hands until she dropped to the ground. She shut the long window quickly, leaning her weight against it to help the slightly swollen frame into place, and turned the handle counterclockwise, shooting the long vertical bolt. The bolt fell into place with a thump she had never noticed before but already seemed familiar. Probably, she thought, sighing, it was the kind of sound—old hardware on old wood—that more often went with a house.

In the kitchen, over her cocoa, she shook herself with a reminiscent tremble, in the way one did after a narrow escape. It was a gesture made more often to a companion, an auditor. Easy enough to make the larger gestures involved in cutting down one's life to the pattern of the single—the selling of a house, the arranging of income or new occupation. Even the abnegation of sex had a drama that lent one strength, made one hold up one's head as one saw oneself traveling a clear, melancholy line. It was the small gestures for which there was no possible sublimation; the sudden phrase, posture—to no auditor; the constant clueing of identity in another's—its cessation. 'Dear me,' she would have said—they would have come to town for the winter months as they had often planned, and he would have just returned from an overnight business trip—'what do you suppose I'd have done, Sam, if I'd gone all the way, in my housecoat, really found myself outside? Funny how the distinction between outdoors and in breaks down in the country. I'd forgotten how absolute it is here—with so many barriers between.' Of course, she thought, that's the simple reason why here, in the city, the sense of responsibility has to weaken. Who could maintain it, through a door, an elevator, a door and a door, toward everyone, anyone, who screamed? Perhaps that was the real reason she had come here, she thought, washing the cup under the faucet. Where the walls are soundproofed there are no more 'people next door'

with their ready 'casserole' pity; at worst, with the harbored glow
of their own family life peering from their averted eyelids like the
lamplight from under their eaves. Perhaps she had known all
along that the best way to learn how to live alone was to come
to the place where people really were.

She set the cup out for the morning and added a plate and
a spoon. It was wiser not to let herself deteriorate to the utterly
casual; besides, the sight of them always gave her a certain pleasure, like a greeting, if only from herself of the night before. Tomorrow she had a meeting, of one of the two hospital boards on
which, luckily for now, she had served for years. There was plenty
more of that kind of useful occupation available and no one would
care a hoot whether what once she had done for conscience' sake
she now did for her own. The meeting was not scheduled
until two. Before that she would manage to inquire very
discreetly—careful not to appear either eccentric or too friendly,
both of which made city people uneasy—as to whether anyone
else in the building had heard what she had. This too she would
do for discipline's sake. There was no longer any doubt that the
sound had been real.

The next morning at eight-thirty, dressed to go out except
for her coat, she waited just inside her door for one or the other
of the tenants on her floor to emerge. Her heart pounded at the
very queerness of what she was doing, but she overruled it; if
she did feel somewhat too interested, too much as if she were
embarking on a chase, then let her get it out of her system at
once, and have done. How to do so was precisely what she had
considered while dressing. The problem was not to make too
many inquiries, too earnest ones, and not to seem to be making
any personal overture, from which people would naturally withdraw. One did not make inconvenient, hothouse friendships in
the place one lived in, here. Therefore she had decided to limit
her approaches to three: the first to the girl who lived in the
adjacent apartment, who could usually be encountered at this
hour and was the only tenant she knew for sure lived in the
front of the building—back tenants were less likely to have heard.
For the rest, she must trust to luck. And whatever the outcome,
she would not let herself pursue the matter beyond today.

She opened the door a crack and listened. Still too early. Actually the place, being small—six floors of four or five flats each—had a more intimate feeling than most. According to the super's wife, Mrs. Stump, with whom she had had a chat or two in the hall, many of the tenants, clinging to ceiling rents in what had become a fancier district, had been here for years, some for the thirty since the place had been built. This would account for the many middle-aged and elderly, seemingly either single or the remnants of families; besides various quiet, well-mannered women who, like herself, did not work, she had noticed at times two men who were obviously father and son, two others who from their ages and nameplate, noticed at mailtime, might be brothers, and a mother with the only child in the place—a subdued little girl of about eight. As soon as a tenant of long standing vacated or died, Mrs. Stump had added, the larger units were converted to smaller, and this would account for the substratum of slightly showier or younger occupants: two modish blondes, a couple of homburged 'decorator' types—all more in keeping with the newly sub-theatrical, antique-shop character of the neighborhood—as well as for the 'career girl' on her floor. Mrs. Berry, who from evidences in the flat should be something past forty like herself, belonged to the first group, having been here, with her husband of course until recently, since just after the war. A pity that she, Mrs. Berry, who from her books, her one charming letter, her own situation, might have been just the person to understand, even share Mrs. Hazlitt's reaction to the event of last night, was not here. But this was nonsense; if she were, then she, Mrs. Hazlitt, would not be. She thought again of the chain of women, sighed, and immediately chid herself for this new habit of sighing, as well as for this alarming mound of gratuitous information she seemed to have acquired, in less than a month, about people with whom she was in no way concerned. At that moment she heard the door next to hers creak open. Quickly she put on her coat, opened her door and bent to pick up the morning paper. The girl coming out stepped back, dropping one of a pile of boxes she was carrying. Mrs. Hazlitt returned it to her, pressed the button for the elevator, and when it came, held the door. It was the girl she had seen twice before; for the first time they had a nice exchange of smiles.

"Whoops, I'm late," said the girl, craning to look at her watch.
"Me too," said Mrs. Hazlitt, as the cage slid slowly down. She
drew breath. "Overslept, once I did get to sleep. Rather a noisy
night outside—did you hear all that fuss, must have been around
three or four?" She waited hopefully for the answer: 'Why yes
indeed, what on earth was it, did you?'

"Uh-uh," said the girl, shaking her head serenely. "'Fraid the
three of us sleep like a log, that's the trouble. My roommates
are still at it, lucky stiffs." She checked her watch again, was
first out of the elevator, nodded her thanks when Mrs. Hazlitt
hurried to hold the buzzer door for her because of the boxes,
managed the outer door herself, and departed.

Mrs. Hazlitt walked briskly around the corner to the bakery,
came back with her bag of two brioches, and reentered. Imagine,
there are three of them, she thought, and I never knew. Well,
I envy them their log. The inner door, usually locked, was propped
open. Mrs. Stump was on her knees just behind it, washing the
marble floor, as she did every day. It was certainly a tidy house,
not luxurious but up to a firmly well-bred standard, just the sort
a woman like Mrs. Berry would have, that she herself, when the
sublease was over, would like to find. Nodding to Mrs. Stump,
she went past her to the row of brass mail slots, pretending to
search her own although she knew it was too early, weighing
whether she ought to risk wasting one of her three chances on
her.

"Mail don't come 'til ten," said Mrs. Stump from behind her.

"Yes, I know," said Mrs. Hazlitt, recalling suddenly that they
had had this exchange before. "But I forgot to check yesterday."

"Yesterday vass holiday."

"Oh, so it was." Guiltily Mrs. Hazlitt entered the elevator and
faced the door, relieved when it closed. The truth was that she
had known yesterday was a holiday and had checked the mail
anyway. The truth was that she often did this even on Sundays
here, often even more than once. It made an errand in the long
expanse of a day when she either flinched from the daily walk
that was too dreary to do alone on Sunday, or had not provided
herself with a ticket to something. One had to tidy one's hair,
spruce a bit for the possible regard of someone in the hall, and

when she did see someone, although of course they never spoke, she always returned feeling refreshed, reaffirmed.

Upstairs again, she felt that way now; her day had begun in the eyes of others, as a day should. She made a few phone calls to laundry and bank, and felt even better. Curious how, when one lived alone, one began to feel that only one's own consciousness held up the world, and at the very same time that only an incursion into the world, or a recognition from it, made one continue to exist at all. There was another phone call she might make, to a friend up in the country, who had broken an ankle, but she would save that for a time when she needed it more. This was yet another discipline—not to become a phone bore. The era when she herself had been a victim of such, had often thought of the phone as a nuisance, now seemed as distant as China. She looked at the clock—time enough to make another pot of coffee. With it she ate a brioche slowly, then with the pleasant sense of hurry she now had so seldom, another.

At ten sharp she went downstairs again, resolving to take her chance with whoever might be there. As she emerged from the elevator she saw that she was in luck: the owner of a big brown poodle—a tall, well set-up man of sixty or so—was bent over his mail slot while the dog stood by. It was the simplest of matters to make an overture to the poodle, who was already politely nosing the palm she offered him, to expose her own love of the breed, remarking on this one's exceptional manners, to skip lightly on from the question of barking to noise in general, to a particular noise.

"Ah, well, Coco's had stage training," said his owner, in answer to her compliments. She guessed that his owner might have had the same; he had that fine, bravura face which aging actors of another generation often had, a trifle shallow for its years perhaps but very fine, and he inclined toward her with the same majestic politeness as his dog, looking into her face very intently as she spoke, answering her in the slender, semi-British accent she recalled from matinee idols of her youth. She had to repeat her question on the noise. This time she firmly gave the sound its name—a scream, really rather an unusual scream.

"A scream?" The man straightened. She thought that for a moment he looked dismayed. Then he pursed his lips very judiciously, in almost an acting-out of that kind of response. "Come to think of it, ye-es. I may have heard something." He squared his shoulders. "But no doubt I just turned over. And Coco's a city dog, very blasé fellow. Rather imagine he did too." He tipped his excellent homburg. "Good morning," he added, with sudden reserve, and turned away, giving a flick to the dog's leash that started the animal off with his master behind him.

"Good morning," she called after them, "and thanks for the tip on where to get one like Coco." Coco looked back at her, but his master, back turned, disentangling the leash from the doorknob, did not, and went out without answering.

So I've done it after all, she thought. Too friendly. Especially too friendly since I'm a woman. Her face grew hot at his probable estimate of her—gushy woman chattering over-brightly, lingering in the hall. Bore of a woman who heard things at night, no doubt looked under the bed before she got into it. No, she thought, there was something—when I mentioned the scream. At the aural memory of that latter, still clear, she felt her resolve stiffen. Also—what a dunce she was being—there were the taxis. Taxis, one of them occupied, did not veer, one after the other, on an empty street, without reason. Emboldened, she bent to look at the man's mailbox. The name, Reginald Warwick, certainly fitted her imaginary dossier, but that was not what gave her pause. Apartment 3A. Hers was 5A. He lived in the front, two floors beneath her, where he must have heard.

As she inserted the key in her apartment door, she heard the telephone ringing, fumbled the key and dropped it, then had to open the double lock up above. All part of the city picture, she thought resentfully, remembering their four doors, never locked, in the country—utterly foolhardy, never to be dreamed of here. Even if she had, there were Mrs. Berry's possessions to be considered, nothing extraordinary, but rather like the modest, crotchety bits of treasure she had inherited or acquired herself— in the matter of bric-a-brac alone there was really quite a kinship between them. The phone was still ringing as she entered. She raced toward it eagerly. It was the secretary of the hospital board, telling her that this afternoon's meeting was put off.

"Oh . . . oh dear," said Mrs. Hazlitt. "I mean—I'm so sorry to hear about Mrs. Levin. Hope it's nothing serious."

"I really couldn't say," said the secretary. "But we've enough for a quorum the week after." She rang off.

Mrs. Hazlitt put down the phone, alarmed at the sudden sinking of her heart over such a minor reversal. She had looked forward to seeing people of course, but particularly to spending an afternoon in the brightly capable impersonality of the boardroom, among men and women who brought with them a sense of indefinable swathes of well-being extending behind them, of such a superfluity of it, from lives as full as their checkbooks, that they were met in that efficient room to dispense what overflowed. The meeting would have been an antidote to that dark, anarchic version of the city which had been obsessing her; it would have been a reminder that everywhere, on flight after flight of the city's high, brilliant floors, similar groups of the responsible were convening, could always be applied to, were in command. The phone gave a reminiscent tinkle as she pushed it aside, and she waited, but there was no further ring. She looked at her calendar, scribbled with domestic markings—the hairdresser on Tuesday, a fitting for her spring suit, the date when she must appear at the lawyer's for the closing on the sale of the house. Beyond that she had a dinner party with old acquaintances on the following Thursday, tickets with a woman friend for the Philharmonic on Saturday week. Certainly she was not destitute of either company or activity. But the facts were that within the next two weeks, she could look forward to only two occasions when she would be communicating on any terms of intimacy with people who, within limits, knew 'who' she was. A default on either would be felt keenly, much more than the collapse of this afternoon's little—prop. Absently she twiddled the dial back and forth. Proportion was what went first 'in solitary'; circling one's own small platform in space, the need for speech mute in one's own throat, one developed an abnormal concern over the night cries of others. No, she thought, remembering the board meeting, those high convocations of the responsible, I've promised—Lord knows who, myself, somebody. She stood up and gave herself a smart slap on the buttock. "Come on, Millie," she said, using the nickname her husband always had. "Get on with it." She started to leave the room, then remained in its center, hand at her mouth, wondering. Talking aloud to oneself was more common than admitted; almost everyone did. It was merely that she could not decide whether or not she had.

Around eleven o'clock, making up a bundle of lingerie, she went down to the basement where there was a community washing machine, set the machine's cycle, and went back upstairs. Forty minutes later she went through the same routine, shifting the wet clothes to the dryer. At one o'clock she returned for the finished clothes and carried them up. This made six trips in all, but at no time had she met anyone en route; it was Saturday afternoon, perhaps a bad time. At two she went out to do her weekend shopping. The streets were buzzing, the women in the supermarket evidently laying in enough stores for a visitation of giants. Outside the market, a few kids from Third Avenue always waited in the hope of tips for carrying, and on impulse, although her load was small, she engaged a boy of about ten. On the way home, promising him extra for waiting, she stopped at the patisserie where she always lingered for the sheer gilt- and-chocolate gaiety of the place, bought her brioches for the morning, and, again on impulse, an eclair for the boy. Going up in the elevator they encountered the mother and small girl, but she had never found any pretext for addressing that glum pair, the mother engaged as usual in a low, toneless tongue lashing of the child. Divorcée, Mrs. Hazlitt fancied, and no man in the offing, an inconvenient child. In the kitchen, she tipped the boy and offered him the pastry. After an astonished glance, he wolfed it with a practical air, peering at her furtively between bites, and darted off at once, looking askance over his shoulder at her "See you next Saturday, maybe." Obviously he had been brought up to believe that only witches dispensed free gingerbread. In front of the bathroom mirror, Mrs. Hazlitt, tidying up before her walk, almost ritual now, to Sutton Square, regarded her image, not yet a witch's but certainly a fool's, a country-cookie-jar fool's. "Oh well, you're company," she said, quite consciously aloud this time, and for some reason this cheered her. Before leaving, she went over face and costume with the laborious attention she always gave them nowadays before going anywhere outside.

Again, when she rode down, she met no one, but she walked with a bracing step, making herself take a circuitous route for health's sake, all the way to Bloomingdale's, then back along the

Fifty-eighth Street bridge pass, and the dejectedly frivolous shops that lurked near it, before she let herself approach the house with the niche with the little statue of Dante in it, then the Square. Sitting in the Square, the air rapidly blueing now, lapping her like reverie, she wondered whether any of the residents of the windows surrounding her had noticed her almost daily presence, half-hoped they had. Before it became too much of a habit, of course, she would stop coming. Meanwhile, if she took off her distance glasses, the scene before her, seen through the tender, Whistlerian blur of myopia—misted gray bridge, blue and green lights of a barge going at its tranced pace downriver—was the very likeness of a corner of the Chelsea embankment, glimpsed throughout a winter of happy teatime windows seven years ago, from a certain angle below Battersea Bridge. Surely it was blameless to remember past happiness if one did so without self-pity; better still, of course, to be able to speak of it to someone in an even, healing voice. Idly she wondered where Mrs. Berry was living in London. The flat in Cheyne Walk would have just suited her. 'Just the thing for you,' she would have said to her had she known her. 'The Sebrings still let it every season. We always meant to go back.' Her watch said five and the air was chilling. She walked rapidly home through the evening scurry, the hour of appointments, catching its excitement as she too hurried, half-persuaded of her own appointment, mythical but still possible, with someone as yet unknown.

Outside her own building she paused. All day long she had been entering it from the westerly side. Now, approaching from the east, she saw that the fire escape on this side of the entrance did end in a ladder, about four feet above her. Anyone moderately tall, like herself, would have had an easy drop of it, as she would have done last night. Shaking her head at that crazy image, she looked up at the brilliant hives all around her. Lights were cramming in, crowding on, but she knew too much now about their nighttime progression, their gradual decline to a single indifferent string on that rising, insomniac silence in which she might lie until morning, dreading to hear again what no one else would appear to have heard. Scaring myself to death, she thought (or muttered?), and in the same instant resolved to drop all limits, go down to the basement and interrogate the Stumps, sit on the

bench in the lobby and accost anyone who came in, ring door-
bells if necessary, until she had confirmation—and not go upstairs
until she had.

"Excuse me," said someone. She turned. A small, frail, elderly
woman, smiling timidly, waited to get past her through the outer
door.

"Oh—sorry," said Mrs. Hazlitt. "Why—good evening!" she
added with a rush, an enormous rush of relief. "Here—let me,"
she said more quietly, opening the door with a numb sense of
gratitude for having been tugged back from the brink of what
she saw now, at the touch of a voice, had been panic. For here
was a tenant, unaccountably forgotten, with whom she was almost
on speaking terms—a gentle old sort, badly crippled with arthritis,
for whom Mrs. Hazlitt had once or twice unlocked the inner
door. She did so now.

"Thank you, my dear—my hands are that knobbly." There was
the trace of brogue that Mrs. Hazlitt had noticed before. The old
woman, her gray hair sparse from the disease but freshly done in
the artfully messy arrangements used to conceal the skulls of old
ladies, her broadtail coat not new but of an excellence properly
maintained, gave off the comfortable essence, pleasing as rose-
water, of one who had been serenely protected all her life. Unmarried—for she had that strangely deducible aura about her even
before one noted the lack of ring—she had also a certain
simpleness, now almost bygone, of those household women who
had never gone to business: Mrs. Hazlitt had put her down as
perhaps the relict sister of a contractor, or of a school superintendent of the days when the system had been Irish from top to
bottom—at the top, Irish of just this class. The old lady fumbled
now with the minute key to her mailbox.

"May I?"

"Ah, if you would now. Couldn't manage it when I came down.
The fingers don't seem to warm up until evening. It's 2B."

Mrs. Hazlitt, inserting the key, barely noticed the name—Finan.
2B would be a front apartment also, in the line adjacent to the
A's.

"And you would be the lady in Mrs. Berry's. Such a nicely
spoken woman, she was."

"Oh yes, isn't she," said Mrs. Hazlitt. "I mean . . . I just

came through the agent. But when you live in a person's house—
do you know her?"

"Just to speak. Half as long as me, they'd lived here. Fifteen
years." The old lady took the one letter Mrs. Hazlitt passed her,
the yellow-fronted rent bill whose duplicate she herself had
received this morning. "Ah well, we're always sure of this one,
aren't we?" Nodding her thanks, she shuffled toward the elevator
on built-up shoes shaped like hods. "Still, it's a nice, quiet building, and lucky we are to be in it these days."

There was such a rickety bravery about her, of neat habit long
overborne by the imprecisions of age, of dowager hat set slightly
askew by fingers unable to deal with a key, yet living alone, that
Mrs. Hazlitt, reluctant to shake the poor, tottery dear further, had
to remind herself of the moment before their encounter.

"Last night?" The old blue eyes looked blank, then brightened.
"Ah no, I must have taken one of my Seconals. Otherwise I'd
have heard it surely. 'Auntie, my niece always says—what if there
should be a fire, and you were sleeping away?' Do what she says,
I do sometimes, only to hear every pin drop 'til morning." She
shook her head, entering the elevator. "Going up?"

"N-no," said Mrs. Hazlitt, "I—have to wait here for a minute."
She sat down on the bench, the token bench that she had never
seen anybody sitting on, and watched the car door close on the
little figure still shaking its head, borne upward like a fairy god-
mother, willing but unable to oblige. The car's hum stopped, then
its light glowed on again. Someone else was coming down. No,
this is the nadir, Mrs. Hazlitt thought. Whether I heard it or
not, I'm obviously no longer myself. Sleeping pills for me too,
though I've never—and no more nonsense. And no more
questioning, no matter who.

The car door opened. "Wssht!" said Miss Finan, scuttling out
again. "I've just remembered. Not last night, but two weeks ago.
And once before that. A scream, you said?"

Mrs. Hazlitt stood up. Almost unable to speak, for the tears
that suddenly wrenched her throat, she described it.

"That's it, just what I told my niece on the phone next morning.
Like nothing human, and yet it was. I'd taken my Seconal too
early, so there I was wide awake again, lying there just thinking,
when it came. 'Auntie,' she tried to tell me, 'it was just one of

the sireens. Or hoodlums maybe.'" Miss Finan reached up very
slowly and settled her hat. "The city's gone down, you know.
Not what it was," she said in a reduced voice, casting a glance
over her shoulder, as if whatever the city now was loomed behind
her. "But I've laid awake on this street too many years, I said,
not to know what I hear." She leaned forward. "But—she . . .
they think I'm getting old, you know," she said, in the whisper
used to confide the unimaginable. "So . . . well . . . when I
heard it again I just didn't tell her."

Mrs. Hazlitt grubbed for her handkerchief, found it and blew
her nose. Breaking down, she thought—I never knew what
a literal phrase it is. For she felt as if all the muscles that usually
held her up, knee to ankle, had slipped their knots and were
melting her, unless she could stop them, to the floor. "I'm not
normally such a nervous woman," she managed to say. "But it
was just that no one else seemed to—why, there were people with
lights on, but they just seemed to ignore it."

The old lady nodded absently. "Well, thank God my hearing's
as good as ever. Hmm. Wait till I tell Jennie that!" She began
making her painful way back to the car.

Mrs. Hazlitt put out a hand to delay her. "In case it—I mean,
in case somebody ought to be notified—do you have any idea
what it was?"

"Oh, I don't know. And what could we—?" Miss Finan
shrugged, eager to get along. Still, gossip was tempting. "I did
think—" She paused, lowering her voice uneasily. "Like somebody
in a fit, it was. We'd a sexton at church taken that way with
epilepsy once. And it stopped short like that, just as if somebody's clapped a hand over its mouth, poor devil. Then the next
time I thought—no, more like a signal, like somebody calling.
You know the things you'll think at night." She turned, clearly
eager to get away.

"But, oughtn't we to inquire?" Mrs. Hazlitt thought of the
taxis. "In case it came from this building?"

"This build—" For a moment Miss Finan looked scared, her
chin trembling, eyes rounded in the misty, affronted stare that the
old gave, not to physical danger, but to a new idea swum too
late into their ken. Then she drew herself up, all five feet of
her bowed backbone. "Not from here it wouldn't. Across from that

big place, maybe. Lots of riffraff there, not used to their money.
Or from Third Avenue, maybe. There's always been tenements
there." She looked at Mrs. Hazlitt with an obtuse patronage that
reminded her of an old nurse who had first instructed her on the
social order, blandly mixing up all first causes—disease, money,
poverty, snobbery—with a firm illogic that had still seemed somehow in possession—far more firmly so than her own good-hearted
parents—of the crude facts. "New to the city, are you," Miss
Finan said, more kindly. "It takes a while."

This time they rode up together. "Now you remember," Miss
Finan said on leaving, "You've two locks on your door, one downstairs. Get a telephone put in by your bed. Snug as a bug in
a rug you are then. Nothing to get at you but what's there already. That's what I always tell myself when I'm wakeful.
Nothing to get at you then but the Old Nick."

The door closed on her. Watching her go, Mrs. Hazlitt envied
her the simplicity, even the spinsterhood that had barred her from
imagination as it had from experience. Even the narrowing-in of
age would have its compensations, tenderly constricting the
horizon as it cramped the fingers, adding the best of locks to
Miss Finan's snugness—by now on her way to the triumphant
phone call to Jennie.

But that was sinful, to wish for that too soon; what's more it
was sentimental, in just the way she had vowed to avoid. Mrs.
Hazlitt pushed the button for Down. Emerging from the building, she looked back at it from the corner, back at her day of
contrived exits and entrances, abortive conversations. People were
hurrying in and out now at a great rate. An invisible glass
separated her from them; she was no longer in the fold.

Later that night, Mrs. Hazlitt, once more preparing for bed,
peered down at the streets through the slats of the Ventian blind.
Catching herself in the attitude of peering made her uneasy.
Darkening the room behind her, she raised the blind. After dinner
in one of the good French restaurants on Third Avenue and a
Tati movie afterward—the French were such competent dis-
pensers of gaiety—she could review her day more as a convalescent does his delirium: 'Did I really say—do—that?' And even
here she was addressing a vis-à-vis, so deeply was the habit in-
grained. But she could see her self-imposed project now for what

it was—only a hysterical seeking after conversation, the final breaking point, like the old-fashioned 'crisis' in pneumonia, of the
long, low fever of loneliness unexpressed. Even the city, gazed
at squarely, was really no anarchy, only a huge diffuseness that
returned to the eye of the beholder, to the walker in its streets,
even to the closed dream of its sleeper, his own mood, dark or
light. Dozens of the solitary must be looking down at it with her,
most of them with some *modus vivendi*, many of them booking
themselves into life with the same painful intentness, the way
the middle-aged sometimes set themselves to learning the tango.
And a queer booking you gave yourself today, she told herself,
the words lilting with Miss Finan's Irish, this being the last
exchange of speech she had had. Testing the words aloud, she
found her way with accents, always such a delight to Sam, as good
as ever. Well, she had heard a scream, had discovered someone
else who had heard it. And now to forget it as promised; the
day was done. Prowling the room a bit, she took up her robe,
draped it over her shoulders, still more providently put it on.
"Oh Millie," she said, tossing the dark mirror a look of scorn as
she passed it, "you're such a *sensible* woman."

Wear out Mrs. Berry's carpet you will, Millie, she thought,
twenty minutes later by the bedroom clock, but the accent,
adulterated now by Sam's, had escaped her. Had the scream had
an accent? The trouble was that the mind had its own discipline;
one could remember, even with a smile, the story of the man
promised all the gold in the world if he could but go for two
minutes not thinking of the word 'hippopotamus.' She stopped
in front of the mirror, seeking her smile, but it too had escaped.
"Hippopotamus," she said, to her dark image. The knuckles of
one hand rose, somnambulist, as she watched, and pressed against
her teeth. She forced the hand, hers, down again. I will say it
again, aloud, she thought, and while I am saying it I will be
sure to say to myself that I am saying it aloud. She did so.
"Hippopotamus." For a long moment she remained there, staring
into the mirror. Then she turned and snapped on every light in
the room.

Across from her, in another mirror, the full-length one, herself
regarded her. She went forward to it, to that image so irritatingly
familiar, so constant as life changed it, so necessarily dear. Fair

hair, if maintained too late in life, too brightly, always made the most sensible of women look foolish. There was hers, allowed to gray gently, disordered no more than was natural in the boudoir, framing a face still rational, if strained. "Dear me," she said to it. "All you need is somebody to talk to, get it out of your system. Somebody like yourself." As if prodded, she turned and surveyed the room.

Even in the glare of the lights, the naked black projected from the window, the room sent out to her, in half a dozen pleasant little touches, the same sense of its compatible owner that she had had from the beginning. There, flung down, was Mrs. Berry's copy of *The Eustace Diamonds*, a book that she had always meant to read and had been delighted to find here, along with many others of its ilk and still others she herself owned. How many people knew good bisque and how cheaply it might still be collected, or could let it hobnob so amiably with grandmotherly bits of Tiffanyware, even with the chipped Quimper ashtrays that Mrs. Berry, like Mrs. Hazlitt at the time of her own marriage, must once have thought the cutest in the world. There were the white walls, with the silly, strawberry-mouthed Marie Laurencin just above the Beerbohm, the presence of good faded colors, the absence of the new or fauve. On the night table were the scissors, placed, like everything in the house, where Mrs. Hazlitt would have had them, near them a relic that winked of her own child-hood—and kept on, she would wager, for the same reason—a magnifying glass exactly like her father's. Above them the only floor lamp in the house, least offensive of its kind, towered above all the table ones, sign of a struggle between practicality and grace that she knew well, whose end she could applaud. Every-where indeed there were the same signs of the struggles toward taste, the decline of taste into the prejudices of comfort, that went with a whole milieu and a generation—both hers. And over there was, even more personally, the second bed.

Mrs. Hazlitt sat down on it. If it were moved, into the study say, a few things out of storage with it, how sympathetically this flat might be shared. Nonsense, sheer fantasy to go on like this, to fancy herself embarking on the pitiable twin-life of leftover women, much less with a stranger. But was a woman a stranger if you happened to know that on her twelfth birthday she had received a copy of Dr. *Doolittle*, inscribed to Helena Nelson from her loving father, if you knew the secret, packrat place in the linen closet where she stuffed the neglected mending, of another, in a kitchen drawer, full of broken Mexican terrines and clipped recipes as shamefully grimy as your own cherished ones; if you knew that on 2/11/58 and on 7/25/57 a Dr. Burke had prescribed what looked to be sulfa pills, never used, that must have cured her at the point of purchase, as had embarrassingly happened time and again to yourself? If, in short, you knew almost every endearing thing about her, except her face?

Mrs. Hazlitt, blinking in the excessive light, looked sideways. She knew where there was a photograph album, tumbled once by accident from its shunted place in the bookshelf, and at once honorably replaced. She had seen enough to know that the snapshots, not pasted in separately, would have to be exhumed, one by one, from their packets. No, she told herself, she already knew more than enough of Mrs. Berry from all that had been so trustfully exposed here—enough to know that this was the sort of prying to which Mrs. Berry, like herself, would never stoop. Somehow this clinched it—their understanding. She could see them exchanging notes at some future meeting, Mrs. Berry saying, 'Why, do you know—one night, when I was in London—' —herself, the vis-à-vis, nodding their perfect rapprochement. Then what would be wrong in using, when so handily provided, so graciously awaiting her, such a comforting vis-à-vis, now?

Mrs. Hazlitt found herself standing, the room's glare pressing on her as if she were arraigned in a police lineup, as if, she reminded herself irritably, it were not self-imposed. She forced herself to make a circuit of the room, turning out each lamp with the crisp, no-nonsense flick of the wrist that nurses employ. At the one lamp still burning she hesitated, reluctant to cross over that last shadow-line. Then, with a shrug, she turned it out and sat down in the darkness, in one of the two opposing boudoir chairs. For long minutes she sat there. Once or twice she trembled on the verge of speech, covered it with a swallow. The conventions that guarded the mind in its strict relationship with the tongue were the hardest to flaunt. But this was the century of talk, of the long talk, in which all were healthily urged to confide. Even the children were encouraged toward, praised for, the imaginary companion. Why should the grown person, who for circumstance beyond his control had no other, be denied? As she watched the window, the light in the small gray house was extinguished. Some minutes later the doorman across the way disappeared. Without looking at the luminous dial of the clock, she could feel the silence aging, ripening. At last she bent forward to the opposite chair.

"Helena?" she said.

Her voice, clear-cut, surprised her. There was nothing so strange about it. The walls remained walls. No one could hear her, or cared to, and now, tucking her feet up, she could remember how cozy this could be, with someone opposite. "Helena," she said. "Wait till I tell you what happened while you were away."

She told her everything. At first she stumbled, went back, as if she were rehearsing in front of a mirror. Several times she froze, unsure whether a sentence had been spoken aloud entirely, or had begun, or terminated, unspoken, in the mind. But as she went on, this wavering borderline seemed only to resemble the clued conversation, meshed with silences, between two people who knew each other well. By the time she had finished her account she was almost at ease, settling back into the comfortably shared midnight post-mortem that always restored balance to the world— so nearly could she imagine the face, not unlike her own, in the chair opposite, smiling ruefully at her over the boy and his ginger-bread fears, wondering mischievously with her as to in which of the shapes of temptation the Old Nick visited Miss Finan.

"That girl and her *log!*" said Mrs. Hazlitt. "You know how, when they're that young, you want to smash in the smugness. And yet, when you think of all they've got to go through, you feel so maternal. Even if—" Even if, came the nod, imperceptibly—you've never had children, like us.

For a while they were silent. "Warwick!" said Mrs. Hazlitt then. "Years ago there was an actor—Robert Warwick. I was in love with him—at about the age of eight." Then she smiled, bridling slightly, at the dark chair opposite, whose occupant would know her age. "Oh, all right then—twelve. But what is it, do you suppose, always makes old actors look seedy, even when they're not? Daylight maybe. Or all the pretenses." She ruminated. "Why . . . do you know," she said slowly, "I think I've got it.

The way he looked in my face when I was speaking, and the way the dog turned back and he didn't. He was lip-reading. Why, the poor old boy is deaf!" She settled back, dropping her slippers one by one to the floor. "Of course, that's it. And he wouldn't want to admit that he couldn't have heard it. Probably doesn't dare wear an aid. Poor old boy, pretty dreary for him if he is an actor, and I'll bet he is." She sighed, a luxury permitted now. "Ah, well. Frail reed—Miss Finan. Lucky for me, though, that I stumbled on her." And on you.

A police siren sounded, muffled less and less by distance, approaching. She was at the window in time to see the car's red dome light streak by as it always did, its alarum dying behind it. Nothing else was on the road. "And there were the taxis," she said, looking down. "I don't know why I keep forgetting them. Veering to the side like that, one right after the other, and one had his light out, so it wasn't for a fare. Nothing on the curb either. Then they both shot away, almost as if they'd caught sight of something up here. And wanted no part of it—the way people do in this town. Wish you could've seen them—it was eerie." There was no response from behind her.

She sat down again. Yes, there was a response, for the first time faintly contrary.

"No," she said. "It certainly was *not* the siren. I was up in a flash. I'd have seen it." She found herself clenching the arms of the chair. "Besides" she said, in a quieter voice, "don't you remember? I heard it twice."

There was no answer. Glancing sideways, she saw the string of lights opposite, not quite of last night's pattern. But the silence was the same, opened to its perfect hour like a century plant, multiple-rooted, that came of age every night. The silence was in full bloom, and it had its own sound. Hark hark, no dogs do bark. And there is nobody in the chair.

Never was, never had been. It was sad to be up at this hour and sane. For now is the hour, now is the hour when all good men are asleep. Her hand smoothed the rim of the wastebasket, about the height from the floor of a dog's collar. Get one tomorrow. But how to manage until then, with all this silence speaking?

She made herself stretch out on the bed, close her eyes. "Sam," she said at last, as she had sworn never to do in thought or word, "I'm lonely." Listening vainly, she thought how wise her resolve had been. Too late, now she had tested his loss to the full, knew him for the void he was—far more of a one than Mrs. Berry, who, though unknown, was still somewhere. By using the name of love, when she had been ready to settle for anybody, she had sent him into the void forever. Opening her eyes, adjusted now to the sourceless city light that never ceased trickling on ceilings, lancing from mirrors, she turned her head right to left, left to right on the pillow, in a gesture to the one auditor who remained.

"No," she said, in the dry voice of correction. "I'm not lonely. I'm alone."

Almost at once she raised herself on her elbow, her head cocked. No, she had heard nothing from outside. But in her mind's ear she could hear the sound of the word she had just spoken, its final syllable twanging like a tuning fork, infinitely receding to octaves above itself, infinitely returning. In what seemed scarcely a stride, she was in the next room, at the French window, brought there by that thin, directional vibration which not necessarily even the blind would hear. For she had recognized it. She had identified the accent of the scream.

The long window frame, its swollen wood shoved tight by her the night before, at first would not budge; then, as she put both hands on the hasp and braced her knees, it gave slowly, grinding inward, the heavy man-high bolt thumping down. Both sounds, too, fell into their proper places. That's what I heard before, she thought, the noise of a window opening or closing, exactly like mine. Two lines of them, down the six floors of the building, made twelve possibles. But that was of no importance now. Stepping up on the lintel, she spread the casements wide.

Yes, there was the bridge, one small arc of it, sheering off into the mist, beautiful against the night, as all bridges were. Now that she was outside, past all barriers, she could hear, with her ordinary ear, faint nickings that marred the silence, but these were only the surface scratches on a record that still revolved one low, continuous tone. No dogs do bark. That was the key to it, which her own hand, smoothing a remembered dog collar, had been trying to give her. There were certain dog whistles, to be bought anywhere—one had hung, with the unused leash, on a hook near a door in the country—which blew a summons so high above the human range that only a dog could hear it. What had summoned her last night would have been that much higher, audible only to those tuned in by necessity—the thin, soaring decibel of those who were no longer in the fold. *Alone-oh. Alone-oh.* That would have been the shape of it, of silence expelled from the mouth in one long relieving note, cool, irrepressible, the second one clapped short by the hand. No dog would have heard it. No animal but one was ever that alone.

She stepped out onto the fire escape. There must be legions of them, of us, she thought, in the dim alleyways, the high, flashing terraces—each one of them come to the end of his bookings, circling his small platform in space. And who would hear such a person? Not the log-girls, not for years and years. None of any age who, body to body, bed to bed, either in love or in the mutual pluck-pluck of hate—like the little girl and her mother— were still nested down. Reginald Warwick, stoppled in his special quiet, might hear it, turn to his Coco for confirmation which did not come, and persuade himself once again that it was only his affliction. Others lying awake snug as a bug, listening for that Old Nick, death, would hear the thin, sororal signal and not know what they had heard. But an endless assemblage of others all over the city would be waiting for it—all those sitting in the dark void of the one lamp quenched, the one syllable spoken— who would start up, some from sleep, to their windows. Or were already there.

A car passed below. Instinctively, she flattened against the casement, but the car traveled on. Last night someone, man or woman, would have been standing in one of the line of niches above and beneath hers—perhaps even a woman in a blue robe like her own. But literal distance or person would not matter; in that audience all would be the same. Looking up, she could see the tired, heated lavender of the midtown sky, behind which lay that real empyrean into which some men were already hurling their exquisitely signaling spheres. But this sound would come from breast to breast, at an altitude higher than any of those. She brought her fist to her mouth, in savage pride at having heard it, at belonging to a race some of whom could never adapt to any range less than that. *Some of us,* she thought, *are still responsible.*

Stepping forward, she leaned on the iron railing. At that moment, another car, traveling slowly by, hesitated opposite, its red dome light blinking. Mrs. Hazlitt stood very still. She watched until the police car went on again, inching ahead slowly, as if somebody inside were looking back. The two men inside there would never understand what she was waiting for. Hand clapped to her mouth, she herself had just understood. She was waiting for it—for its company. She was waiting for a second chance—to answer it. She was waiting for the scream to come again.

GEORGE LANNING, assistant editor of *The Kenyon Review*, is author of a novel, *This Happy Rural Seat*, and co-author with Robie Macauley of *Technique in Fiction*, scheduled for publication by Harper and Row in early 1964. His stories have appeared in several magazines.

Something Just for Me

Jack met Mrs. Michigan one summer in Connecticut—at a writers' conference, as it happens, though given Jack's kind of luck the same misfortune could have hit anywhere. He was an instructor and Mrs. Michigan, arriving straight from the breakup of her marriage, was a student. That put them at once, in her view, on a suitable footing for whatever arrangement they might come to. If she was older, he was *better*.

Knowing no one when he arrived on campus, Jack smiled anxiously, placatingly in every direction—placatingly because he was a flop as a writer and was sure the whole conference would be on to him in a matter of days: a fraud passing himself off as a success in front of trusting people who'd paid a lot of money to get the straight word. Mrs. Michigan was not alone in smiling back, but she was alone in also smiling first. Jack was trapped instantly between those two smiles, and from that moment on their intimacy increased at a fast clip.

"Call me Mildred," she said. "I'm going back to my maiden name right after the divorce, and already I don't feel like a Michigan. Just think of me as that friendly Mildred, hardly able to wait for your classes to start."

Except for registration, she scarcely left his side during the rest of the opening day. That evening, at the reception which officially launched the conference, she managed briefly to insert herself into the faculty receiving line, between Jack and "noted juvenile writer" Lily Potter Plummer. Only Lily's experienced and ample hip, smoothly closing the gap between her brown lace gown and Jack's dinner jacket, prevented Mrs. Michigan from doing her share to make the new students welcome. Even so, as she yielded to social pressure, she managed to whisper, "You look gorgeous. I bleed to see you tethered to such a cow."

Mrs. Michigan was, as she herself said, in the full flower of maturity at the time they came together. "Would you guess I'm 59?" she asked. "Take a look at my chest."

They were alone when Mrs. Michigan—Mildred—got on this subject of her age and chest, and Jack was pretty sure he was expected to pooh-pooh the former and run his hands over the latter. Honesty forbade astonishment, and despite all the continental novels he'd read, in which youth (comparative) and age share a moment of exquisite fulfillment, he couldn't bring himself to gratify Mrs. Michigan's only slightly veiled invitation. (She had, soon after their first meeting—while lying on his bed, in fact—quoted Benjamin Franklin to him. Or had it been Lord Chesterfield? The advice to younger men, anyway, about seeking out older women, who are not only better but more grateful. Jack remained vague about the source of the quotation because, at the time, he was preoccupied with trying to remember how she'd managed to get into his room and onto his bed, and worrying about getting her off and out again.)

The trouble was, or so Jack told himself, that she was exactly his own mother's age. Mrs. Michigan did not seem at all motherly —although she had a son, she said, "years younger" than Jack was—but still her importunity struck him as not quite respectable.

He wondered, as he often had in the past under similar circumstances, what gave mature ladies so much strength of persistence? But he knew, tiredly, that the speculation was futile. Where he was concerned, at least, they all exhibited a wonderful energy and single-mindedness, and a tendency toward the horizontal. It had begun, at 18, with the pleasant elderly lady of 43 whom he'd visited for the purpose of reading aloud his stories for criticism. She had almost instantly got flat on his arrival, and she'd never risen again except to open a fresh bottle of wine when the first one on the floor at her side went dry. As the evening progressed and her clothing, inexplicably, achieved a state of sad disorder, he'd been much disheartened by the acidity of her criticism.

Later, when others began to come along, he got to know their
bag of tricks: first they asked about his "work," next they clutched
his hands, then they stroked his nearest available knee and murmured of how "we understand each other," and finally they
scolded.

If the tack that Mrs. Michigan took was far from new to him,
her aggression was, for she observed none of the rules which her
predecessors had kept to. ("I walked by your window last night,
and you looked adorable, sitting at your desk with nothing but
your shorts on and that beautiful tan." Jack, occupying a ground
floor room, kept his shades pulled all the way down, and to get
such a comprehensive view Mrs. Michigan must have pasted herself against his screen and peered through the slit between the
edge of the shade and the casing of the window.)

She was, Jack admitted conscientiously, a handsome woman.
It wasn't just the chest that had held its own. The jawline had
too. Her hair was a bold, metallic orange which, certainly, Jack's
mother couldn't have carried off with Mrs.—Mildred's—aplomb.
As the relationship became increasingly a matter of public interest, some of Jack's students urged him to do the decent thing by
the old girl. There were times (when she appeared at the pool in
a white bathing suit, for instance) when he wavered. But later
on, spread once more across his bed and fully clothed, she didn't
look the same. And he couldn't love her for her mind, that was
for sure. The last books she'd read were a couple by Floyd Dell
and something pretty strong, though she didn't recall the title,
by Grace Lumpkin.

To be sure, she meant to catch up, and even had a list based
on recommendations by various literary friends: Rupert Hughes,
Viña Delmar, Ben Ames Williams, Adela Rogers St. John, and
Vincent Rose Benét. Since coming to the conference, she'd naturally added Jack's name, and meant to get to him first—in
fact, was on him right now. How on earth had she missed his
marvelous things all this time? How could she have settled for
Floyd Dell and Grace Lumpkin?

Jack had published a novel some years earlier, and, before that,
a scattering of dull but respectable stories—stories that even he,
in his sizable vanity, couldn't bear to look at. (Mildred could,
though; from the college stacks she hauled out dusty issues of

forgotten magazines, read his contributions devoutly, and pronounced them "tiny classics.") She meant to have a go at his
novel any minute now.

For some time Jack had been trying to finish a second novel—
for such a time, in fact, that most people had forgot about the
first one. He was, as a result, discouraged, defensive, belligerent
toward other and better writers, and conscious of his age and
failure. Willy-nilly, his new fan chinked up his morale. In future
he'd be linked, wherever she went, to Floyd Dell and Grace
Lumpkin: a kind of fame, for whenever people talked of Faulkner,
Proust, Dostoevsky, she'd haul out Floyd and Grace and Jack
and feel that she was more than holding her own. Word of
mouth publicity, Jack reminded himself. The trinity was so con-
founding that out of morbid curiosity a few people might look
them up.

Mrs. Michigan, having been such a great reader all her life,
had decided to join the ranks of those whose work had given her
so much pleasure. Besides, now that she'd cut off her husband
"like a cancer," as she put it—and didn't this bold use of figurative
language indicate a real talent?—she wanted to make a lot of
money. Someone had told her the heartwarming story of a
lady named Emilie Loring, who at 87 or thereabouts had taken
up the writing of fiction and had earned twenty-nine million
dollars before she died some thirty-six years and seventy-four novels
later. The story might be exaggerated, but nobody could say
you didn't run into Emilie Loring everywhere you went. Why
shouldn't she eventually move over and make room for some
spicier pieces by Mildred P. Michigan?

"Not Michigan, of course," she said. "My maiden name that
I'm going back to. Putzig. Mildred Putzig."

"Stick to Michigan," counseled Jack.

Mrs. Michigan said that that was just the kind of thing she'd
come to the conference to find out. She liked the quick way he
tackled a problem. It was what was so good about his lectures,
and made him show up that poor little hack he shared the period
with for the mess she was.

In the peculiar parlance of that particular summer school,
Jack was junior lecturer in "long fiction." The senior lecturer
was a middle-aged woman named Caroline Coulter who brought

out a romantic novel every year and was well thought of both
by the dollar book clubs and the bigger rental libraries. Before Mrs. Michigan's scorn Jack remained silent, but felt a twinge
of disloyalty. The poor little hack was a fixture at the school and,
despite the administration's preference for minor writers who came
cheap, was used to a partner of rather greater renown than she'd
been landed with this time. Yet she'd shown him every possible
kindness and gone out of her way to let him make an impression
on their joint class. In addition, she was plump, tiny, and pretty.
Although there was no attachment between them, he liked working with the kind of rosy little woman he could imagine growing old and fat with, and snuggling up against in bed: a delicious
goosedown pillow of a woman. More to the point, she had a
way of handling captious editors which commanded all his admiration— "I said I'd go to Doubleday if they took that scene out."
Also, he was dazzled by her ability to bone up on a subject and
get a book out of it within a twelve-month period. "I didn't know
if the Reformation would be too much or not; luckily, it wasn't."
    Still, he felt grateful to Mildred—why not call her Mildred?
—for understanding that this was not quite the method by which
one produced a *Bovary* or an *Ántonia*. Not that he was producing
a *Bovary* or *Ántonia* either, just at present, but Mildred obviously
meant to suggest that her money was riding on him, of the two,
and that *he* was the one whose advice would make her famous.
    It was moments like this which produced in Jack the softening
which led him to agree to little jaunts in the country in Mildred's
car, or to the shore, which was only thirty miles distant, or to a
funny bar she'd found. Little jaunts led to long drinks— "Let me
pay," said Mildred; "I haven't started writing yet, so I'm not
as poor as you are"—and further confidences: "My husband and
I didn't . . . *You* know. Not after the first week. Later, he got
a job traveling, and he used to come home and tell me about
the things he did. Then he'd cry and beg me to forgive him.
All the women were flat-chested. My analyst says that Victor is
really attracted to men, but flat-chested girls are as near as his
middle-class morality lets him get. This woman he's gone off
with is like the rest. And I stood it for twenty years."
    "Still," Jack countered the first time, "you have a son—"
    "That was by my *first* husband," said Mildred, and she smiled

in a way she had, as if they were (in this case) sharing a common recollection of how efficiently husband number one had been disposed of (some broken glass in the frozen Daiquiri?). Her eyes—hard, prominent, pale blue like winter sky reflected in ice—opened wide, wider. Jack drew as far backward as the rigid upright wall of the booth would permit. Those eyes might at any moment detach themselves from their sockets and dart at him and stare and stare until he gave in to their demands.

After this exchange, he went back, for a day or two, to addressing his disciple as Mrs. Michigan.

Husband number one had indeed gone beyond the veil, but to hear Mrs. Michigan he'd departed peacefully. Not really peacefully, of course, because he'd been shot down in a revolution; but *legitimately*, so to speak. He'd been, said his pious relict, a crack correspondent for the AP. A stray bullet had got him. Jack wanted to ask whether Mrs. Michigan—Mrs. Tischman, as she then was—had been accustomed to accompany her spouse on his reportorial jaunts, and from which camp the bullet had seemed to come: the government's or the rebels'? But as well as Mrs. Michigan assured him that they knew one another, he lacked the courage.

The subject of Mr. Tischman led, of course, to that of his sole surviving exploit: his and the present Mrs. Michigan's son. "Peter and I are very close," said Mrs. Michigan. "He tells me everything. Are you and your mother that close?"

"No," said Jack. "Yes, but no. She wouldn't be interested. Or I mean she wouldn't want to know that there was anything like that that she *might* be interested in."

"We're like brother and sister," Mrs. Michigan went on. She finished her old fashioned and he watched her chew a piece of glass. Ice, he meant. "Once he brought a little gal he'd been shacked up with home for the weekend. He'd written me about her and I was glad to have a look. He was glad, too. He wasn't sure, he said, until Mom said nix. Do you show your mother your girls, Jack?"

Not conscientiously, said Jack; and then (for he was under the impression that Peter was in his late 'teens) he asked her: "What does your son do?"

"He teaches at M.I.T. He's been there six years—ever since he finished his doctor's."

Mrs. Michigan was not officially enrolled in "long fiction." She was doing "short fiction" and "articles." But she appeared faithfully at Jack's classes, and she addressed all her questions pointedly to him, even when it was Caroline who was carrying the particular session. "I have this thing I've got to work out of me," she explained. "This hideous barren marriage. That's why I've sold my house and bought a trailer."

"You think that travel will? . . ."

"No. But I'm going to Arizona for the winter and live in my trailer and write the whole thing out. As a novel, of course. I'll change the names. Therapy for my trauma, the analyst says."

"You ought to talk to Caroline. She can give you some really practical advice about how to do it."

"I don't want to make this a hack job. It's my life. She'd give me a list of reference books to read. Pretty soon I'd find I was writing about passion in the Punic Wars, not about *me*. I want to get the thing over with so I can go on to more commercial stuff. That's why I hang on your every word."

Jack was surprised to learn that he struck his auditors as so conversant with the market. He even had a moment in which he determined to take his own advice, before it struck him that there was none to take. Whatever Mrs. Michigan's motive for attending a course she wasn't enrolled in, it wasn't the literary horse sense she claimed to find there.

There were only two periods in the day when Jack could be sure of being free of Mrs. Michigan's presence on his bed, at his side at the pool, before him in class, or approaching him at a rapid pace down corridor or across lawn. One period was lunch and the other was dinner, both of which he ate in the faculty dining room. At these meals his colleagues scolded him unmercifully for his tolerance of "that really appalling woman," as Mrs. Michigan had come to be known.

"People like that should be drowned in bags, like cats," said an elderly Jew, one of the lecturers in "articles" and therefore necessarily another of Mrs. Michigan's victims. "You think you're

the only one she's stalking? You're just the patsy when the rest
of us give her the freeze."

"But I *can't* . . ." Jack would protest miserably. And what was
it he couldn't?—cut her off? put her in her place? let her know,
through some unmistakable rudeness, that she was a spectacular
nuisance? He wished he could at least reply that he felt sorry
for her, but the fact was that he didn't. Maybe the relationship
was the more difficult to break off because he felt that he *should*
pity her early widowhood, her humiliating second marriage, her
present loneliness and resolve to get some mileage out of the
therapy recommended for her "trauma." Wasn't this sad? And
quoting Thomas Jefferson—or whoever the hell it was—and peeking in at windows, and prowling around waiting to grab somebody, anybody: weren't these just brave little things she did, a
way she had of flinging out a lifeline between herself and the
world?

As the conference moved into its closing week, Jack's life was
complicated by a second and equally unrewarding relationship.
He became the confidant of a lady poet and fellow lecturer named
Eunice. Ten years earlier, Eunice had won a major literary prize
for a long verse narrative on an Early American theme. It had
been published in two parts in either *Look* or *Life*, with Thomas
Hart Benton-like "paintings," and later had been the dual selection of a book club. "In all, I made $40,000 out of it," Eunice
told him, and her voice—normally that of an aging tenor reaching
for a series of high notes—grew plump, sleek, silken. Since
publication of A *Benevolence in Sudbury*, which was the unlikely
title of her book, Eunice hadn't been able to whip out even one
perfect iambic pentameter. ("I was distracted by dactyls," she
liked to explain—and invariably Jack saw prehistoric monsters
waving their flippers at her, hypnotizing her, drawing her from
her desk into a hideous metric wilderness. "*Dump* dump dump!"
Eunice would add. "The rhythm got into my blood; but I couldn't
write anything in it. *Dump* dump dump!")

Her long literary silence—longer than Jack's by four years—
may have been what first drew him to her. He thought that they
shared a common agony and humiliation, and it was good to find
a fellow sufferer. Also, it was bracing for him to remember that
Eunice was further along the road to failure than he was. Some-

thing would certainly happen for him in another four years, but
even if it didn't he'd be no worse off than Eunice was now—
whereas *she'd* be in the very devil of a fix (his sympathy was not
so great that he allowed Eunice, in his imagination, any second
triumph in the years ahead—not until he'd got in first with one,
anyway). The clincher was that even if time went by and nothing came right for Jack, either, there was Eunice always before
him, a figure ever-receding at a steady, dactylic *dump* dump dump!
In short, she gave him fresh courage.

Eunice, less affected by her failure than Jack might have wished,
was part of the regular faculty at the conference: another lecturer
on "articles," as it happened. (Her only experience in this field,
she told Jack, had been a brief piece called "Let's Explore Monument Avenue" which had appeared in one of those fancy magazines distributed by automobile manufacturers— "They paid me
$450," she said, once again sounding rich and plump.) She was
a woman of about 29, if you calculated on the basis of the chro-
nology she threw out with careful casualness, with a bony white
intense face, a lot of straight black hair which smelled strongly
of tobacco and always got loose from the single comb she held it
back with, and a body as trim as a fountain pen.

("You should see her in the shower," said Mrs. Michigan.
"Remember Slim Summerville? In fact, I wish you could get a
look at the whole bunch of them in there. I hold up good.")

Nevertheless, Eunice had such a deep faith in her own de-
sirability that she actually exuded a kind of hilarious allure. Jack
began by having lunch with her a couple of times; then dinner;
and finally both, with cosy walks and talks in between. Eunice
gave him useful advice about dealing with magazine editors and
book publishers, and Jack was flattered to be treated as someone
who actually had things to deal with them *about*. Sometimes,
though, he had the feeling that Eunice was really Clara Kimball
Young and he was really Wallace Reid, and they'd met at Hollywood and Vine to discuss all the television shows on which neither
of them would ever appear.

After three or four days of what Jack considered a prolonged
courtship, he invited Eunice to his room for a drink (Mildred, as
she'd once again turned into, was mercifully out; no doubt scout-
ing around for more funny bars). In public, Eunice had the

endearing habit of emphasizing her remarks by swatting whatever part of whatever male anatomy was adjacent to her, and
now, in private, Jack thought that she might enjoy being swatted
back. But Eunice, settling down with warm bourbon and water
in a paper cup, made plain at once that she had other matters on
her mind.

She had a problem, she said, and it did her good to talk it out.
She was in love with a worker in a nearby woollen mill whose
name was Ernest. They'd met during the first summer when
she'd lectured at the conference (Ernest, enrolled in "poetry,"
had sung some of his own work one evening to the accompaniment
of a guitar, and Eunice, metaphorically, had been ravished). "He's
a natural," she explained; and then, more thoughtfully, "A kind
of American primitive." That first summer, Ernest had still been
living with the frightful woman who was his wife. This unwhole-
some relationship had since been severed, but Ernest seemed no
closer to a divorce than ever. He was a stubborn, dyed-in-the-wool
Yankee—no pun intended—and he couldn't agree to a settlement
which gave his wife most of their property and the better part
of his subsequent income. Unfortunately, the youngest child
(there were five) was still a minor.

"My family, as you might guess, oppose the whole thing," said
Eunice.

"They don't like divorce?" asked Jack, pouring more bourbon
into her extended cup.

"Not just that. Ernest is twenty years my senior." Twenty?
Ernest, then, was . . . "He's 63," said Eunice. "I suppose they're
right. I ought to find a younger man." She looked coyly at Jack,
round the edge of her paper cup, and curled herself up on his
bed. "Like you."

Jack's intentions wavered. Twenty from 63 . . . Was he to
push out one Mrs. Michigan only to make room for the next?

"Have another drink," said Jack gloomily.

Eunice smiled at him. "Just like you," she giggled. "Like you,
like you, like you. . . . I've got a drink."

If arithmetic only made Eunice something besides 43, Jack
thought. The age revived so vividly the image of the lady who
had drunk wine and commenced to snap. And now here was

Eunice, too, uncurling with what might be purpose, settling her
flat little bones along the mattress.

"Then you only see Ernest when you're up here—in the
summer, I mean?" he asked hurriedly. (During the school year,
Eunice taught at a woman's college in Virginia.)

"Not quite." She closed her eyes and burrowed her head
luxuriously into Jack's pillow. The paper cup, balanced on her
chest, slopped its contents onto the peculiar blouse she was wearing. Really, a very peculiar blouse, now he took a good look at it:
the effect was of fishnet, through which large misshapen tropical
creatures—distant kin of the dactyl, possibly—peered glumly forth
from their green and orange depths. They wobbled and dipped
with Eunice's breathing. Her bony—fine-boned, he meant—
shoulder blades stuck out of the blouse like reefs. "He comes
down for a reading once every winter," she explained. "The girls
love him."

Jack, afflicted by the heat of the day or simply by too much
liquor, saw Ernest slowly swimming south along the green and
orange Atlantic shore, his guitar clutched under a fin; saw Eunice
cast out her net and haul him in as he got opposite Virginia.

"He usually stays a week," Eunice added, opening her eyes
and fixing him with one of those intense stares that Mildred was
so fond of. Jack didn't doubt the implication, but he found it
implausible. To begin with, Ernest would be so exhausted after
that long swim . . .

Eunice suddenly sat up and mopped at her shoulders with the
side of her cup. "You and I could have fun together," she went
on, once again immobilizing him with her direct gaze. "But what
would it lead to?"

A few speaking engagements, Jack thought. Except I can't play
a guitar.

"I need a father figure," she explained with manly frankness.
"You've guessed that from *Benevolence in Sudbury*, of course."
Jack hadn't, since Wallace Stevens was as far as he went with
popular poets, but he nodded sympathetically. Eunice required
a father figure and Mildred wanted a husband figure. As for
him, he needed a girl figure—and an enthusiastic editor. Look
what life had dished up. They were all the clowns of fate.

The next day Mildred proposed an expedition to one of the

more distant beaches. The conference would soon be over and
they might not have another chance to see something of the
countryside. En route, they could look for a literary shrine to
visit, thus justifying the fact that they'd be playing hookey from
an afternoon lecture by a New York publisher. Except for Wallace Stevens, Jack couldn't think of a single respectable author
who came—or ever had come—from Connecticut, unless you
counted Mark Twain. And they'd be going nowhere near Hart-
ford. Besides, he'd hoped to meet the publisher and make an
impression on him which later might be useful. He gave in, of
course—not with the best grace, but with the knowledge that Mildred was so used to refinements of attitude that she took no
notice of them.

"Wear that tiny *teeny* bathing suit of yours," she said joyously.
"I love your legs, and I want to get some pictures."

The trouble was, she probably *did* love his legs, and the more
he thought about them being all alone in a car with her, or
stretched naked and defenseless on a deserted beach, the more
apprehensive he got. Also, she belonged to the generation when
cars ran "out of gas" or "broke down" in convenient isolation, and
with the conference ending so soon there was no telling what old-
fashioned ingenuities she might dream up.

At noon that day, meeting Eunice as usual at the faculty dining
room, he said, "Would you like to go to the beach today?
Mildred wants to make up a party. I know what you think of
her, but we haven't much longer, and it won't be bad with the
two of us there. A little human kindness, you know . . ."

An hour later he said to Mildred: "Would you mind awfully
if Eunice came? Like a fool I mentioned it to her and she went
wild. It shouldn't be too painful since we'll have each other."

Mildred had worked out a picturesque route which led along
a series of teeth-jarring gravel roads. Since she'd brought her
camera, they paused regularly before abandoned farmhouses and
alongside stony out-croppings, and at each of these places Jack and
Eunice were photographed by Mildred; then Jack and Mildred
were photographed by Eunice. At the first stop, Jack offered to
take a picture of the girls, but the deafness which simultaneously
afflicted both of them was too striking to be risked a second time.

Jack was also photographed alone: leaning against a peeling gate
(his face carefully lifted to the sun, to erase the incipient double
chin), standing with one foot on a broken step, and looking
myopically toward the horizon from atop a spur of rock. It was
at this last place that Mildred suggested he get into his bathing
suit. They would just pretend that they were somewhere along
the shore. It would make a marvelous picture. But Jack, looking
below into two sets of voracious, glittering eyes, two mouths
thinned out by hunger and bafflement, managed again the laugh
by which he usually turned Mildred's proposals into jokes, and
shinnied down the rock and rejoined them.

The beach which Mildred achieved by her system of unmarked
roads was so crowded that they all turned in horror from the prospect of swimming there. It was perhaps the day's single moment
of rapport, if you didn't count Mildred and Eunice's common
glee as they pointed out to each other the pretty young mothers
chasing fat babies across the sand, the healthy young men tossing
beach balls back and forth or lying beside sunflushed and diapered
girls in an intimacy which perhaps was never realized in private.

Appalling, of course: that is, it was the sort of beach one never
went to. And yet, before the spectacle of so much health and
energy, before the imagined spectacle of happy, uncomplicated
people, people free of problems, people making promises of love
under a glittering August sky, Jack felt shabby; he felt old, and
disappointed in other than literary matters; he felt like a fool,
trailing these two cackling, malicious, scruffy hens in his wake. In
a moment the whole beach would rise and turn and point a collec-
tive finger at them, and laugh. Before such scorn the three of
them would dry up and blow away in the wind off the water.
How was it that these women found him better than what they
saw before them, along this sweep of coast? But of course they
didn't; they only thought that he, unlike the beauty they laughed
at, might be attainable. For he was of their kind—not as the
member of a common profession but as an outcast, an incompetent, a plain damned fool who was getting old.

They had a couple of beers in a roadhouse and then started back.
Somehow—maybe because of all the picture-taking—the afternoon was gone. To the west, thunderheads mounted. They stuck
to the highway this time, and Eunice pointed out the drive which

led to the house of one of the judges for the club which had taken *Sudbury*. She'd been to dinner there, soon after her book was published.

So after all, thought Jack, we've found our literary shrine, or one sufficient to the day. He wondered what the New York publisher had had to say—a good novel is hard to find?—and whether he might still be around tonight. He wondered how much further they had to go, and whether Mildred would insist on stopping for dinner somewhere. He thought of happy people on a beach. He decided that he never wanted to visit Connecticut again.

The last days of the conference passed swiftly. The director gave his annual party, at which the guests were served a warm wine punch with so much citric acid in it that whole groups succumbed to heartburn on the spot. Then there was a rather peculiar evening seminar featuring a man and woman who edited a writers' magazine. They were like a competent vaudeville turn, one speaker leading into the other's jokes, and each working hard to build the act. They had many valuable things to say about "the right market" and "current editorial needs." They brought along with them a woman with extraordinarily long legs who wrote plays for children. Her relevance to the general topic was never clear, but she held her own anyway: the successful author of 169 one-act plays, most of them in book form, who'd started out as nothing more than a Poughkeepsie housewife. With those legs, she should have gone farther, or at least in a different direction.

Also, there was the final dinner—lobster Newburg—in the women's gymnasium. This was enlivened by the hunt for a washroom for the men and a reading by the year's winner of the annual conference poetry-writing award. For Jack, it was also livened up by his hunt for a seat somewhere distant from both Eunice and Mildred. But Mildred was ever brisker and more alert than he, and when the assembly sat down he found that they were directly across the table from one another. The dinner was formal, and Mildred wore a taffeta dress in electric blue. It was off the shoulder, off the arm, and almost off the chest.

"I want to see you later," she said, leaning toward him. This was near the end of the meal, and the director of the conference was already on his feet, introducing the poetry winner. As a result, Jack was able to nod noncommittally.

The poetry winner began to read—from his prize poem, presumably.

"Oh, fecund earth, mother strong and fierce—"

". . . been good friends, haven't we?" whispered Mildred.

"The very best," said Jack warmly, thinking of how they'd all be dispersed come morning.

"And so revere your binding sheets of sperm!" cried the poet.

". . . last favor," said Mildred.

A favor in the sheets? No, no, that couldn't be what she meant. Still, she was giving him that hard look again. But surely not. The last night. They were all so *fed up!* And there was a room party in the students' dorm that he wanted to go to.

"Now toss your belly seaward to the wind!" the poet suggested.

You do that, thought Jack. You go back to the beach and just *do* that.

". . . time finding it, but I finally managed to get a copy," Mildred added.

"Fine," said Jack. Copy? Of his book, did she mean? "Swell," he said. She might mean anybody's book, of course: she was perfectly capable of handing him something by Grace Lumpkin— or even by Emilie Loring.

"And then with *ong dee plooey* do I rest," the poet declared in conclusion.

Ong dee plooey?

There was a quite unnecessary amount of applause.

". . . going on, is there?"

He'd lost the whole of that speech. "What?" he said.

"We could have a last chat, couldn't we? There's nothing going on tonight, is there?" Mildred had raised her voice just as the applause was dying away, and her words carried clearly to everyone in their vicinity.

"I know what's going on," said the elderly Jew, Jack's neighbor at the right, speaking from behind his napkin. With his elbow he struck Jack a sharp, brotherly blow in the ribs and then subsided into the napkin, coughing with laughter.

The poet, by God, was on his feet again, flushed with the pleasure of his success and ready to read something else, from the look of him. "*Ong dee plooey*," muttered Jack, and pushing his chair back softly he stood up. He waggled his head at Mildred, smiled sheepishly, and thought that he'd probably managed to get across the idea that he was off to the men's room. But what a bore, having to make a fool of himself in order to give her the slip. And she'd be along as soon as the dinner was over; straight for his bed she'd make, and a last "chat," book in hand—somebody's book. His strategy gained him nothing but a respite, a chance to think up a way of shaking her before the party really got going. "Come up early," one of his students had said (a young twig of 50 or so). "It'll be a ball—we'll maybe go on all night, the liquor holds out. But give the old girl the brush, will you? We've had it—and she's had it. Take her for a walk and drown her in the pool."

It wasn't as simple as that. For one thing, the gate to the pool was locked. And she'd never take a hint and exit gracefully; she didn't know a hint from a handrail, if that was the expression. He sighed in exasperation. Life was full of *ongst*. No wonder the poet shouted *plooey!* He understood exactly why the late Mr. Tischman had arranged to intercept a bullet. He congratulated Mr. Michigan on his taste for flat-chested girls. Go bind your belly deep within the sea, he thought. Oh, please, just for tonight, drop dead.

But Mildred had no consideration. She turned up in his room twenty minutes after he made it there himself. "I looked all *over* for you!" she cried happily.

"I couldn't very well go back in," he answered. "And I got tired of hanging around outside. . . ."

"No," she agreed. "You didn't miss a thing—except three more songs to mother and the sea. Thank heavens it's over." She tossed a large black plastic briefcase on his bed—containing, he decided gloomily, her nightgown and slippers, and possibly a few sandwiches. Freed of her encumbrance, she leaned against his door, her hands behind her, and crossed one foot over the other. The attitude, rather that of a voluptuous inclined plane, reminded him of the way some actress used to look—Carole Lombard, was it? or Constance Bennett?—in overwrought movies about women who'd got abandoned in the tropics. *Were* abandoned, so to speak. He regarded Mildred apprehensively. She was breathing heavily, but mercifully her eyes were closed. For the moment her attention was withdrawn from him. Then he realized that she was out of breath. Perhaps she'd run all the way from the women's gymnasium to her room, where presumably she'd acquired the briefcase, and then across the quadrangle to his building. In fact, she must have run—and at top speed—for not a sound came from the hallway beyond his partly-open door. No one else had returned yet.

Just then Mildred leaned farther backward and the door closed. She opened her eyes and smiled at him and he felt a spasm of unwelcome pity; no, not pity; kindred feeling, as if they'd come to share something that now they must talk about. She moved over to the bed and from the briefcase withdrew his book, neat and bright in its jacket, the orange and yellow ink only slightly faded from its years of storage in the publisher's warehouse or on the shelf in an out-of-the-way bookstore.

"I want you to write something specially for me," she said. "Nothing you've put in anybody else's."

There hadn't been anybody else, not lately, certainly not on this go-round. It struck Jack suddenly, as he took the book from her, that there hadn't been anybody else for anything at all for quite a while. What was there to choose between their situations, his and Mildred's? Nothing—except that she, like Eunice, was farther along the route, had less time to make it in—make whatever it was each of them wanted. This was the thing they shared; but it was unbearable and couldn't, after all, be acknowledged, let alone talked about.

"I'll have to find my pen," he said, going over to a suitcase which stood, partly packed, beneath a window. He groped in the pockets along each side and finally came upon the pen clipped to the rolled-up manuscript of his lecture notes. Then at last he felt the evening's finality; the end of summer. For those closely-written sheets represented not only the days of the conference but the weeks he had given to preparation. He *had* to make that party tonight, round off his summer with some kind of bang, however slight.

As he got up from his knees, he saw Mildred's face and body reflected in the windowpane. She was seated on the extreme edge of the bed, and, in the light of the unshaded overhead bulb, she looked like a skull in an orange wig propped on an electric-blue bolster. Her gaze was directed away from him, straight across the narrow room; her naked shoulders drooped and, as nearly as he could tell, her mouth had gone slack. He cleared his throat sharply, said "Found it!" in a voice too loud and hearty, and turned around.

He'd given her what time she needed—or it might be that he'd seen wrong, in the dark glass. She dazzled for him, light running like water off the folds of blue taffeta. Her bold eyes sought his boldly, without pretense; but without calculation, too. Her skin, sun-brown fading to yellowish-white, was a little moist. One long wild hair, which she couldn't see, curled outward from a mole on her back.

"A really special inscription," he said; making noise. Abruptly he was overcome by a lassitude more painful than irritation or even disappointment and loneliness. He looked at the book which had cost him so much effort but had brought him none of the praise and respect he'd longed for, none of the kindred spirits he'd hoped would find him through its pages.

"Something just for me to look at," she said. When he made no response, she leaned forward slightly, and one hand rose in wavering supplication. "We've had a lot of fun together, haven't we? I don't know that I've got much out of the conference—I suppose I'm too advanced for this kind of thing—but I've certainly learned from you, Jack."

Have you? he thought grimly.

"Jack," she said a moment later, into his continuing silence, "I could— Do you want me to give you a lift down to New York? With all the stuff you've got to carry . . . I'm going up to Peter's, but he doesn't know when I'm finished here. I mean—"

He had put the book on top of the chest of drawers and opened it to its endpaper. "You're distracting genius from its work," he told her, and hoped that he'd struck a tone of jocular ferocity. "If you want something just for you . . ."

Rather curiously, she seemed to find his words reassuring. She contrived a little girl's laugh and wriggled backward onto the mattress. She leaned sideways on one elbow, with a provocation which might not have been intended, and got a cigarette from the briefcase and lighted it.

What could he say in her damned book—*his* damned book. It was a desecration, to take this thing he'd loved so much and concoct a few lines to bloat her swollen vanity with. "For Mildred, who's getting out of my life and better stay there. In memory of all our lousy trips and talks." Will that do, Mildred? Milly, dearest Milly? "For Milly, whose scholarship has brought Benjamin Franklin to the awareness of a whole new generation." "For Mildred P. Michigan, the biggest case of summer complaint I've ever had."

"I always have trouble writing these things," he said.

"Let's have a little drinkie first, and maybe that'll warm you up." She opened the briefcase again and brought out a fifth of bourbon. "I got this in town today."

True, a fresh bottle. Did she picture them sitting here together, slugging it down? Warmed up for what?

Mildred knew exactly where he kept everything, and from the bottom drawer in his desk she extracted the venerable paper cups.

"That looks like Caroline's lipstick," she said, examining a fresh smear on one of them.

"Eunice's," said Jack while his mind sought frantically for an excuse to skip the drink, cut the session short. Look, there's a party I'm going to—a sort of private party. . . . No good. Mildred would just say she loved private parties.

"Did you notice," asked Mildred gleefully, "what Eunice had on tonight?"

"I didn't see her all evening."

"I think—I'm not *sure*—it was a pair of exercise bloomers. And I'll swear that the top was a black lace bra. She looked like the cleaning woman in a harem." With a whoop of laughter, Mildred opened the door and carried the cups out to the water fountain in the hall. Glumly, Jack tore the sealer off the bourbon. Mildred returned, her face flushed pink with laughter and the good feeling that the fun had started. "And her *shoes!* . . ." she exclaimed, but could say no more. Still whooping and hiccoughing, she took the drink he made for her and went back to the bed. She dabbed at her eyes and then, peeping at him over the rim of the cup much as Eunice had done earlier, she solicited his response.

He made a few perfunctory noises which, with Mildred, were

as good as the real thing—*were* the real thing for her, probably, since an authentic response was something she mustn't have encountered in years.

As silence closed in on them once more, and the animation and hope died from her face, he was seized with compassion. He said, "That's a beautiful dress"—and knew, before the words were out, that he'd said too much.

"I wore it for you," she replied. "I even bought it for you."

"For me?" he echoed in genuine astonishment.

"For the you I knew I was going to meet some day, I mean. I bought it right after Victor left me, but this is the first time I've had it on."

In a moment, he feared, she'd have it off. "My mother has—" he began, hoping the presence of his mother might regularize the situation. But what did she possess which could be brought out to meet Mildred's gown? His mother's clothes, made for her, would only be puzzled by this poor little machine-cut-and-stitched imitation of the high fashion of a season which had already gone into history.

It didn't matter, for Mildred had no intention of letting another woman get into the room. "I could see you looking at me in the mirror," she said lyrically. "Right there in the shop. And yes," —she examined him critically—"fantastic as it may seem, it really was *your* face. You nodded your head—this was the perfect one for my coloring."

Orange and blue, thought Jack dazedly. Wasn't there a college? . . . "Well, I should say so!" he declared, nodding his head— no, no, better not nod. That got them back to the mirror again. The power of suggestion: was this what she put her faith in? He bolted his drink and stood up. "I'd better see what I can write in this book of yours. I know you're tired, and you've got a long drive in front . . . Certainly enjoyed the drink. Better than a sleeping pill, any day."

He hastened across the room to the chest of drawers and once again took up his pen. Mildred, with the monolithic calm, the careful languor, of women who do not choose to be hustled off, only smiled and, bending over for the bottle which he'd placed beside her feet, filled her cup again. Straight.

He wrenched his mind away from the awful, portentous sight,

and stared at the endpaper. "From the me you was sure you'd meet some day, to the you I wish I hadn't." No, no, no. "For a darned good pal and a really snappy dresser. . . ."

"Look, Mildred," he said at last, desperately, "I draw a blank when I have to perform with somebody looking at me. And I want . . . I want to write a nice one."

"You'd better," she said. "One I can look at when I'm in my trailer this winter and remember the fun we had. When I'm trying to get that dirty dog out of my system. Twenty years, Jack! Jacky, twenty long miserable years! There are plenty of things I haven't told you yet. Things I didn't have the courage to tell my analyst, even."

"Well, that's just fine . . ." he said. "Or—"

"What's *really* fine," she declared, "is that it's just the two of us here. I'm so bored with those stupid room parties, and in the daytime Eunice follows you around like a hamster on the edge of menopause, and in class you're so polite to that fat sack with wind on her brain that she does all the talking. . . . Jack, aren't you glad we're alone, to have a real talk together? We're like two crazy kids, aren't we, Jack? We get so excited about ideas, I mean. Don't you think so? And, you know, things. I guess we understand each other—you do *me*, I know! And this is our last night!"

"When do you go to Arizona?" he asked.

"When do I? . . ." She appeared, briefly, bewildered. "Oh. I don't know. I'll probably spend the fall with Peter. We're going to take an apartment. Maybe you could come up for a weekend. Could you?"

"Wait a minute," he said. "Wait a minute now. I think I've got it."

"No, you wait," she said, with such urgency that he couldn't pretend to ignore her. "There's one thing I want to tell you. What you've done for me. I was in pretty low spirits when I started out for here. Victor and everything. Selling the house and all our furniture. Deciding about Arizona. I've never been to Arizona. Besides, the people here aren't very chummy, are they? It would have been horrible except for you. We could . . . That is, we're really friends, aren't we? We're among the lucky few who find something precious and have the good sense to recognize it. If you want . . . If there's anything you want, you know I'm right here, Jack."

Jack didn't reply. Throughout her speech he'd kept his eyes down, his face half-turned away from hers. Now, in rage and humiliation, he gripped the pen and bent above the book and began to write. "For our wonderful 'Mom,'" he put down, "the life of the Connecticut writers' conference and the wickedest old gal who ever set the whole East Coast on its ear. Long may she reign! From one sinner to another, with kindest personal regards." Then he signed his name and the date. He blew on the ink and handed the book to her, still open. He could feel sweat running down his arms, feel his hands turning cold, feel his stomach beginning already to revolt at the cruelty he'd done to her with this inscription, and to himself as well.

"Maybe you'd rather read it later," he told her, as a poisoner might urge his victim to finish the nice hot drink in bed.

She glanced at the words he had written and he thought he saw her stiffen. She, too, blew on the ink, and then she waved the book back and forth in the air.

"You're wonderful!" she said. "I love it! I just love it!" She laughed loudly and, laying the book on the coverlet, got up and brushed cigarette ashes off her lap. "You're the only person who ever seems to know when I'm kidding. It's what I like about you. 'Mom'!" she repeated. "Wait till Peter sees this. And it's just what I feel about all you kids. Old, wicked Mom! You've got my number, all right."

"Well, it's been grand," said Jack, feeling his sickness rising up behind his teeth. "Every minute of it. I wish I could have said it better."

"No, I wanted it like this, off the cuff. It's wonderful. It shows your wonderful humor." She looked down at the liquor which remained in her cup, started to drink it, and then changed her mind and set the cup on Jack's desk. "I guess old Mom's had enough." She took a deep breath and swung round to face him squarely. "Bad for the complexion. I want to look good so I can catch me a millionaire dude out West." She smiled. "I guess I'll see you in the morning to say goodbye."

"Oh, sure. Sure. We'll all see each other. Here." He stopped and picked up the bottle and the briefcase and put them in her hands.

She took them blindly, and blindly, it seemed, she started for the door. "Beauty sleep!" she cried. "Beauty sleep!"

"Wait a minute. Don't forget your book." He swept it off the bed and crossed the room to her.

"My? . . . Oh, yes. And after I came all the way over here just to get you to write in it." She went out into the hall.

"Goodnight, Mildred," he said, following her as far as the doorway.

She didn't answer. She had begun already to move away from him, down the empty, silent corridor. Her dress and her hair flamed up as she passed beneath a ceiling light. Then the vitality died away as she went beyond into a stretch of darkness. He was too exhausted, too near being sick, to cheer her out of sight, to call reassuring phrases which might ease both their savaged dignities. He did manage to say "See you at breakfast for sure!"—but she was at the stairs now; perhaps she didn't hear him. He saw her put one foot on a riser, teeter slightly as if she were dizzy, and then begin slowly to ascend.

He closed his door and leaned against it in a posture which, by accident, was a travesty of Mildred's own earlier travesty. And he thought: it's over, over! He moved across to the window and flung it up, although the night was cold for August, and leaned his forehead against the screen. He breathed deeply, damp earth and grass, clean impersonal air, and closed his eyes. Then he had an uneasy moment in which he imagined that another forehead was pressing against his—that of Mildred leaning in to tell him how adorable he looked leaning *out*. He closed the window and turned back into the room. There on the desk stood the drink she'd left. He lifted the cup in a toast. *Salud!* Mildred P. Michigan, he said silently. And goodbye forever. He drank off the bourbon in a gulp. It was time to get a move on. Time—oh, God! and more!—to go and have a ball.

GEORGE A. ZORN was born in Brooklyn, attended Hofstra College, Columbia University, and Indiana University. For the past several years he has been teaching, and at present is an assistant professor of English at Central Michigan University. He is married and has three sons. Three previous stories have been published in small magazines.

Thompson

> John is thy christen name, John,
> And thre bytter bytter hathe the bytten,
> Thre bytter bytter hathe the nyppen,
> And thre bytter bytter hathe the stryken

Besechying almyghty god, whedder itt were eye or tong or hert, the better shall be your heale and boote, the father the son and the holy gooste.

—An Old Witch Charm

When he drew up the car, a dog shot from around the shrubbery into the driveway, set its feet, and stood there, head up and jerked forward, barking viciously. Even from the distance, down at the curb, Thompson could distinguish the pink-purple mouth, the tongue, the two mean front teeth arcing down from the upper jaw. Not very big—mutt—with glossy black fur that curled over his back, waved down his chest: a little, he thought, like a dog he'd had as a kid—only (What was his name?) was as tame as a rabbit, wouldn't hurt a fly.

Though he didn't hear anything, he figured the woman must have shouted something, because after a few more yaps the dog spun about as if he'd been struck or caught with a stone and high-tailed it around to the back again.

He called out, stooping his head under the car window, but the woman apparently couldn't hear him because she just moved to the screen door of the porch, a blurred shadow, and stood looking down. He tried again, with no better success, and was annoyed to think he'd have to get out of the car when he heard the screen door slam and saw her coming toward him along the rutted concrete path that led from the house.

She seemed to be drying her hands, though when he first saw her he'd thought she was standing there, doing nothing, simply looking out at the road. She kept her head down, cocked, as if trying to hear.

Halfway along the path she stopped short, her hands jerking up irritably. "April!" she shouted back at the house. "Did you hear me, April!"

Then she was coming forward again, head still tilted that way, smiling the perplexed smile of a country woman addressed suddenly by a stranger parking his car, calling up to her.

Thompson slid over now to be nearer the open window. He'd grown heavy, almost fat in the past few years and as he shifted from behind the wheel he made what had become a habitual gesture: pulling his coat together before him and cupping his abdomen with his palm. At the window a sudden raw edge of pain cut across his temple from his bandaged left ear. He cursed quietly, filthily, and held his hand against it for a second.

She was careful on the short flight of steps leading down from the slope of the lawn—narrow steps, cracked, with weeds and moss eating through, still damp despite the bright sun that had, a little while back, broken through the gray November morning. At the last step the sweater she'd thrown about her slipped from her shoulders and she adjusted it, holding it in place with her arms crossed upon her breast until she reached the car.

She was about forty or so—thin, with one of those plump, pretty-little-girl faces which, as in her case, the wear and tear of life can sometimes give a sort of freakish look to.

"I'm sorry, I couldn't hear you," she said, brushing hair from her forehead. "My daughter had the radio on."

"I was just asking if this was the right way to East Bolin." He turned his head up, aslant, framed in the window opening. "I'm trying to get to East Bolin."

"East Bolin?" she said, leaning forward, placing her fingers on the sill. "Why look, you're way out of you way, Mister. That's Remus back there. You should have turned off at Parker—on the main street in Parker there—onto 41."

He *had* turned off on the main street in Parker, following Gillespie's directions to a T, and the sign had said 41.

"But then you must have kept right on going, past the Ratchokan school—that's the old building, all the windows broken, on your left—you must have gone past it and swung right around."

He had no idea what she was talking about. After the doctor had left last night, he'd asked Gillespie, the hotel manager, for directions, and the little geezer had pulled up a chair to the bed, crossed his legs in that sissy way of his, and given them to him. Explicitly. Describing each turn—left past the railroad, left again just before he got to the mill—slowly, sympathizing with his discomfort, trying to make it all clear. And despite the way he'd felt—he was still woozy from the drink and the whole left side of his head was numb from whatever the doctor had shot into him —he'd thought he'd got it straight. He'd even repeated everything two or three times before he'd fallen asleep, to be sure. And now she comes up with this Ratchokan school business.

"Then this isn't 41," he said.

"This?" She forgot her initial shyness and laughed.

His ear throbbed again, the pain shooting down this time, into his cheek, hooking its way across his chin.

Past her shoulder, up the slope of patchy lawn, stood the house, a narrow two-story stucco affair, in need of plastering around the corners, with a glassed-in porch, the flowers in the plot before it dead now, revealing, between the shrubs, the gray cement foundation. Behind the driveway stood a weathered farm shed. In the driveway itself a 1954 Chevy, rain-splotched, a dent in the rear fender, the trunk handle missing. In the strip between the driveway and the kitchen garden a kids' gym set, raw metal now, the paint roughnecked away, the ground beneath the swings scooped bare like that under his own kids' swing at home.

He was nuts, he told himself, to be fidgety about anything here.

"I guess I'm lost," he said.

"It looks like you are."

"You say I'm supposed to go back to Parker?"

"Well, there's an easier way from here—since you've come this far—and that's through Fullerton. All you have to do. . . . You know these parts at all?"

"No, I'm from up north, Wassau City. This place—at least this section (I know the Bolin area all right; my sister's got a cabin over there) but this section's new territory for me. I'm a salesman—been down to Carr and Franklin. Just come from Heltvei—been over there a couple of days. Just come from there this morning and now I'm trying to get back to East Bolin to head home."

It was a peculiar moment—but one of a kind, he realized afterwards, he'd experienced before. It was common enough. It was the sort of thing you feel on a dim stairway when you're certain another step is there and you bring down your foot only to discover—that moment of confusion when everything seems to drop away and you wonder where you are—that it isn't.

The point is that he thought, as he spoke, that she'd flicked up her eyes in some meaningful way at the road ahead. His sense of the movement was so vivid that he automatically glanced through the windshield expecting to see something—someone walking, a car coming toward them, anything. His surprise came when he could discover nothing that might have attracted her attention. The road was as empty as it had been since he'd parked there.

He turned an inquiring glance at her, but she not only ignored his question but seemed not even to notice it. "Well," she was going on, almost to herself, pensive, finger to her mouth. She tugged the sweater closer about her, as if she were chilly. "Well, I'd say the best way, all in all, is to just go back to Parker. That way's a little longer, but you know it, so maybe you won't get lost again. Just stay on Langdon road here—like you came—all the way back to Parker; then when you get to the town, when you come to the school—you'll recognize the school easily enough —go past it, and a little ways further you'll find the cutoff that you missed. It's called Ouida Road there."

As she spoke Thompson yanked his topcoat straight beneath

him and adjusted his bulk more comfortably in the seat. He wasn't, he told himself, at his age, going to start acting like a god-damned fool. Like a kid. The woman was perfectly all right. All he had to do was listen, get the directions straight this time, and he could still maybe make it home before night.

Still he couldn't prevent his eyes, as he sat there, attentive, listening to her, from wandering across to the windshield, away from her, out to the road . . .

It was like hundreds of roads he'd driven over—no different— a stretch of tar, lusterless, scaley, humping toward the center. On both sides were telephone poles, tilted this way and that, up a little, down. . . . Billboards—down farther an increasing clutter of them. Some road signs. A tottering barn in a waste field, the *Mail Pouch* ad half weathered away. Other fields. A large wood—almost leafless now—the bare branches netting darkly against the sky. Then down, where the road curved away, a big white farmhouse, trees on the lawn, neat fences—and above it all, way up, a television aerial, struck by the sun, shooting out bars of glare like neon.

He'd allowed his eyes to rove back over the billboards and signs —was trying to make out a sign—when the woman called out in that distraught tone she'd used up on the porch: "April! April. Do you hear me? You go in and put something on!"

The girl had come out and was standing on the stoop, her foot propping the screen door, peering down at them. She was eight or nine, skinny, in a faded cotton dress too large for her, her frizzled brown hair needing combing. In her right hand she held a violin tightly by the neck, like a bat or a breadboard, as if she were going to knock someone over the head with it.

"Who is it?" she yelled down.

"Go inside."

"Who is it?"

Her mother took a warning step and the girl screwed up her mouth, flung around, and slammed the door behind her.

"Kids," the woman said, shaking her head. "They can be the devil."

"I know what you mean," he told her. "I've got three myself."

Since she'd finished with the directions there was little more to say. She stepped back from the car but continued to lean forward from the waist, hugging herself. "Just be sure you stay on Langdon here . . . then past the school. You can't miss it."

Thompson thanked her and shifted over behind the wheel. "Well . . . ," she said.

In his hurry he fumbled with the handbrake. Then he was pushed back in the seat, settled, ready. At the realization that he wouldn't be going down the road, that he'd be pulling into the driveway, swinging around, he brightened and leaned across to the open window. "Well, thanks again. Thanks again for everything." But when he turned on the ignition and pressed the starter the engine ground hollowly for a moment, stuttered, and died.

She waited until he'd tried it again. "Something the matter?"

"No," he said. "It'll be all right." He'd had the same trouble that morning in the hotel parking lot. He tried it again—several more times. Once it almost caught. "It's nothing," he repeated. The woman moved forward, rested her fingers on the sill again. He was jabbing his foot down so hard now that he hardly gave the engine a chance to catch. "Damn!" he finally exploded.

"Maybe you've flooded it."

He sat back, distracted, uncertain what to do. "Same thing happened this morning," he said, as if that, in some way, would be of assistance to him now. He looked in the glove compartment, along the seat, in his topcoat—finally found his cigarettes where he should have expected them to be, in his jacket pocket. Only as he was lighting one did he realize that his hands were trembling and that there were beads of sweat on his chin. "I'll just wait a couple of minutes," he said.

He hadn't seen the girl come out, but she was up on the slope now, across the driveway, on one of the swings. It was too small for her and she twisted her feet out, letting them drag back and forth on the ground. She hadn't combed her hair, but she'd put on a green wool coat, heavy, like the dress before too large for her. Now and again she'd glance down indifferently at the car, then go back to watching the scrape of her feet on the ground.

The sun continued to glare down, but it couldn't, he thought, last; the horizon had already turned the leaden gray he'd driven against all morning. His ear was paining so much that he was

certain again—as he'd been that morning when he woke up—
that the doctor—arrogant and superior as he had acted—hadn't
known his business, that he was some kind of quack. The cut and
the stitches would account for some of the swelling, but not
this much—the pressure on the bandages like this, as if the ear
were trying to bloat its way right through. He made a tentative
gesture to touch it, trace his fingers over it, but remembering
the woman decided not to. He couldn't do anything about it
now, here—what the hell could he do? It would be better, for
the time, to forget it. It wasn't his ear he should be worrying about,
but the car—getting the car started so he could get the hell on
his way.

He had no better luck this time, but he'd already decided to
ask her to give him a push.

"A push might do it," he said.

"Yes. That's an idea. Maybe that's all you need."

At the same moment an old pick-up sped by on the road. It
passed behind him, but so quickly that although he turned his
head at the sound of the motor, he caught only the back of the
driver through the rear window: overalls, wrinkled brown neck,
limp engineer's cap, the peak turned up. But the woman, facing
the road, smiled and waved her handkerchief. And down farther,
where the girl was kicking around among the dead stalks in the
vegetable garden, the driver extended his hand through the window and pinched his fingers familiarly at her.

"Oh!" the woman suddenly exclaimed, staring at Thompson.
In her distress she struck her cheek lightly with her palm. "Oh,
what a fool—I should have stopped him!" She turned her head
and seemed, even now, to consider yelling down the road. But
the truck was already at the bend, curving out of sight. "That
was Mr. Flaxheim—a neighbor of mine—I should have stopped
him—to give you a push."

"That's okay," Thompson said, smiling. "No, that's all right.
Your car here will do all right."

It took her a moment. "Oh," she said. "Oh, no, you don't
understand. That's Will's. My husband's. He don't take it today,
Thursdays. He takes the company truck. I don't drive. I can't drive
a car."

He sat up at that and for the first time looked at her closely, searched her face—the pale brown eyes, the pale cheeks with their little-girl puff, the apologetic mouth. Because he didn't believe her, some instinct told him not to—she was lying. She drove. Of course she did. A country woman like her, away from town, away from everything. With kids. And a jalopy sitting parked right up there in the driveway. Of course she drove. . . . Then what did she think she was doing? What the hell did she think she was trying to pull?

"But there'll be another one along," she assured him. "You don't have to worry. It's lunch time—not so many now. But another will be along in a minute."

He sat there, his head aching, his ear paining, trying to think. He took the key from the ignition, held it idly in his hand staring down at it. Then he closed his eyes. And as he did—as if the vision had been waiting just behind his lids—he was back in his hotel room of the night before, shortly after he'd hurried up from that bitch's room below. The manager was there, Gillespie, tsk-tsking, pussyfooting about, telling him everything would be all right. Then a few minutes later the doctor had come—the one Gillespie had phoned. Lambert. Young, thin, drawn face, everything about him looking exhausted, in need of sleep, except the pale bright eyes. "He's been drinking," he'd said to Gillespie as soon as he came in, seeming not to care whether Thompson heard or not, flinging out of his raincoat, a big one, belted, flaps across the chest. German. Pronounced German accent. Then the two of them had whispered together, Lambert with his back to him, hand hooked, knuckle tight against his hip. Hairy wrist; watch band on thick. And later, when he had opened his bag and was preparing things and Thompson in his confusion had sat up straighter on the edge of the bed and tilted his head, Lambert saying to him curtly: "No, you'll have to lie down, Mr. Thompson. Push up, stick your head on the pillow." He'd stood by the desk preparing the hypodermic, the lamp shooting up at the bright eyes, at the row of small yellowed teeth. He took the bloody towel away. "This won't hurt much." It had hurt like hell—the pain clouding everything, making him even dizzier. "Turn your head down more, more down. You can't watch." He hadn't, of course, been able to watch, he hadn't wanted to, he'd closed his eyes. But he'd been aware, by the quick breathing, of the serious, mocking gray face descending above him, hovering over him—and he'd felt the first painless prick of the stitching needle. The next thing he knew it was over—the doctor stood there (he didn't see him, he was still turned away, only his shadow on the wall) wiping his hands on his handkerchief, touching his lips.

When Thompson was jolted awake—the dog was up on the lawn again, barking, and the girl was screaming at him, waving her arms—it was with the intuitive sense that no car was going to come. He recognized the insanity of the idea as soon as it came to him (he was parked here, talking to a woman, on a public road and sooner or later, on all public roads, a car passed). He knew that. Yet with the thought itself had come the impression that in some manner of which he was totally ignorant, in a way he couldn't even imagine, *that* made no difference. He'd been here a half hour—parked a half hour—and only one car had passed. One. That pick-up. And though she went on talking away, telling him— as if everything were all right, nothing out of the way—that another car would be along, he felt she knew it wasn't so, that she was deliberately lying. And he sensed too that they would go on like this, her lying and him sitting here, his panic mounting, until . . . When? . . . until what happened?

"Ho! Wo-ho! Hey!" She was up on her toes, flailing her arms. Thompson sat up. The girl, up on the lawn, jerked around too to see what was the matter. And in the next minute an old black Ford, gleaming like new, swung abruptly off the road and screeched to a stop about twenty yards in front of him.

"I told you," the woman said, bursting, happy for him, happy to have proved herself right. "I told you you wouldn't have to wait long."

For a moment Thompson had difficulty believing what he saw. Then: "I knew it!" he coughed, laughing out loud. "I knew it!" And in that explosion of reason and joy, all the suspicions, the wild thoughts of a minute before were blown away. He hopped out of the car and holding his topcoat closed against his paunch trotted quickly over to the other car. The woman followed slowly along up on the curb. Even the girl had become interested enough to stop what she was doing and come down and join them.

The driver was a little pug of a woman, so short she needed a cushion to get her up to the windshield. Middle-aged. In a brown tweed suit, silk blouse with a floppy polka dot bow at the collar, black felt hat pulled down to her ears. Eyes big as saucers, dark, alert, behind the steel-rimmed glasses.

"My car's stuck. I wonder if you could help me?" Thompson asked through the window.

"I can try," briskly, no monkey business about her.

"I don't know what's wrong with it. Maybe the battery. I think a push might do it."

She had already raised her backside from the cushion, was twisted around, getting ready to back up.

"I'll get her started," Thompson said.

"Stick out your hand, just wave it, when you're ready," she ordered.

She barely waited for him to get clear before she swung the car, in a swift, precise arc, behind his own.

"This ought to do it," he called to the woman at the curb.

But when he got behind the wheel, arranged himself in the seat, he couldn't find the key. He looked first in the ignition, then, not finding it, remembered he'd had it in his hand. But he didn't have it now. What the hell had he done with it! He stepped out of the car and felt in his pockets—his trouser pockets, jacket, topcoat. When he failed to find it, he began searching the pavement.

"What's wrong?" the woman called from the curb.

"I must have dropped the key."

Her eyebrows went up but she didn't comment; she merely stepped down from the curb and began looking about the road. "It can't be very far. You just walked this little way." The girl decided to help too—but she remained apart from them, aloof, searching on her own. Finally the pudgy woman got out of her car to see what was the matter.

"Now you had it in your hand," she said, feet set squarely, bull jaw set, staring up at him. She reminded him of a teacher he'd had in grammar school.

"I had it in my hand in the car," he told her again. "I took it out of the ignition— I remember that. And I was holding it."

"And you've looked in all your pants pockets?"

He looked again.

"I suppose there's no holes."

The suit was almost new.

"How about the floor of the car?"

He'd searched it thoroughly.

"Back of the seat?"

He nodded.

"Then you dropped it." There was no question. "Where else could it be?"

So they fanned out at her direction and went over the ground again. But they had no better luck this time.

"All right," she said when they'd got back to the car. "Any other ideas?"

"Maybe he lost it in your car," the girl suggested. "When he was over talking to you."

And with that they all became confident again. The four of them trotted back together and searched the seat. The woman even helped him lift it clear out. But they didn't find the key.

And it was the plump little woman who in the end was least willing to give up the search. While he stood with the other talking about using the phone to call a garage, he watched her, scowling, pacing the road, darting her eyes about, kicking over scraps with the side of her shoe. Finally she strode back to where they stood, fixed herself on the road below them—they were on a rise now above the curb—and tipped back the front of her hat like a man.

"You've looked in all your pockets."

He told her again that he had.

"Well then where in the hell do you think it is?"

"I wish I knew."

"Well, you had it," she told him disgustedly.

Finally, though, she left, zoomed the car away—the squat figure jerking back in the seat—smiling, waving good-bye to them. The sun continued to stream down, but it gave little heat and he realized now why the woman had seemed cold all this time in just the sweater. The girl had left them; he noticed her in the back by the garage, bouncing on an old bedspring over which she'd placed some boards.

"Come inside," the woman said.

His choice, he felt, lay between believing that in some inexplicable way he'd lost the key, or that it had been spirited away. It couldn't have been taken by either the woman or the girl, because neither of them, after he'd left the car, had been close enough to it to pick it up secretly and hide it. Why they should want to, he didn't know, but even granting them some crazy motive, they couldn't have. So there could be no doubt about it: he'd lost it somehow. Still he would rather not have gone into the house.

The porch had potted plants all over it, not very thriving, it seemed in his brief glance—dry yellowed leaves about the lips of the pots—but carefully attended. A group was in the deep tin tray of a wicker stand, an old-fashioned contraption like one his mother had. The hallway was dim, and when he stepped from it into the living room he struck his head sharply against some projecting object.

He must have let out a cry because the woman turned, eyes wide, hand to her face, as if in fear for her life. "What . . . !"

He couldn't answer. He'd almost toppled, his hat had dropped, and he had both hands pressed tightly against his bandaged ear. Head lowered, he kept screwing up his eyes, trying to see straight.

"Oh . . . !" the woman exclaimed.

He saw what it was then—a bird cage projecting into the doorway on a limb of metal. It still swung, in jerking arcs, the bird on the far perch, crouched against the side, its feathers ruffled, snapping out its bill at him.

"I didn't push it back," the woman said, aghast at the accident. "I mustn't have pushed it back. And it's the bad ear. I'm awfully sorry. I'm. . . ." She took a step forward, as if to assist him, then seeming to recognize the futility of the gesture just stood there, anxious, her face mirroring his agony.

His ear continued to throb, a pulsing, flaming swell and ebb, but the dart-tongued lights had begun to waver, flick out. He stopped and picked up his hat, shook himself, and told her he was all right.

The room, he saw, was little lighter than the hall. Single tall window, cream-colored enamel frame, the Venetian blind drawn. Heavy green rug with black scroll design, badly worn in spots. Lumpy furniture—probably her mother's stuff—but prettied up with doilies on the couch, on the armchair. Big Emerson radio on spindle legs, pull-open cabinet. Opposite that a small television set. Magazine rack—newspapers, comics, battered catalogues. On the cabinet of the radio a statue of Saint Theresa on an oval plaster base stuck all over with tinted seashells.

The phone book was on a wobbly end-table next to the couch. When she'd found the number she folded back the yellow page for him and excused herself.

"What number are you calling?" the operator asked. She sounded irritated, as if he'd interrupted something.

He told her.

"I'm sorry," she complained, "that number's been changed." She gave him the new one.

He was about to dial it when he noticed the girl standing in the doorway—not the one he'd come in by but one leading, it seemed, to a bedroom: there was a narrow bed or cot behind her, against the wall—dark covering over it, linoleum on the floor, toys scattered about. He imagined, seeing her, that she'd been standing just as she was for some time—not looking directly at him—he couldn't quite make out where she was looking—eyes wide and softly glazed, the small lips parted.

"What's the matter?" he said, cupping the phone to his chest.

His tone was harsher, more abrupt than he had intended and she immediately reacted, glanced away, across to the window, the radio, down at her feet. Finally she shot her eyes up at him again, as if she wanted to tell him something, then changed her mind and hurried, tripping over some toys, away to the back of the house.

He got the garage. The voice at the other end was chewing gum, big young man, buoyant, sympathetic. He wasn't sure what he could do—he might have to tow him in. But he'd be able to do something. But he was in the middle of a job at the minute. Give him, say, a half hour. How about that?

Thompson intended to say "Fine" and thank him, but found himself instead whispering, "Could you hurry!"

There was a pause. "Sure. I'm almost through. Twenty minutes. A half hour."

"I'll make it worth your while."

Silence again. "No need. I'll be out as soon as I'm done here."

Thompson came to himself.

"Fine," he said. "Thanks. Thanks. A half hour."

He hung up and walked quickly to get his hat from the couch where he'd laid it. The house oppressed him; he wanted to get outside. Still, once he'd caught up his hat, he hesitated. She was talking to her daughter—he could hear her; he couldn't just run out of the house without waiting for her. She'd want to know. How would it seem? So he stood there, ill at ease, exhausted, staring down at his feet (the broken shoelace; he'd broken it when he was hurrying into his clothes in the woman's room the night before—then this morning he'd had such a hell of a time tying it, making a knot)—glancing around at the pictures, the shabby furniture, the bird still hunched in its corner, its eyes on him, beak raised.

Finally she came in, smiling nervously, her brow creased. "Did you get him?"

"Yes. Fine. He's coming over."

And now, looking at her, he realized that the girl had been staring at his ear.

"Something the matter?"

"It's your ear. April said it was bleeding. I don't know what to say. I. . . . It was my fault. I should have pushed the cage back. I *always* do. Maybe you'd like to use the bathroom."

He reached up and touched the bandage delicately, allowed his fingers to creep over it until he found a soft warm spot. He traced the edge. It didn't seem much, not big; one of the stitches must have broken. He began to lower his hand, then brought it up, found the spot again. He couldn't think what was wrong.

"Thanks," he said.

He allowed her to show him where the bathroom was—down the dim hallway, past a door leading to a closet under the stairway. The bathroom was narrow, hardly wider than the hallway itself, with a tub stuck in a cut-out of the walls. Pipes running across the ceiling. The whole place green. Decals—ducks after dragonflies. Hamper. Small window with pebbled glass.

He switched on the light over the medicine chest, but it cast only a weak yellow glow. He had to twist his head up, around, to see decently. The bandage was no longer in place, a strand had slipped loose (Had it been like that all the while in the car, he wondered, hanging down the back of his neck?) and the gauze patch over the ear had become frayed and soiled from his touching it.

Luckily it wasn't, as he'd guessed, bleeding badly. There was a spot about the size of a nickel, and a thin streamer of flow, almost dried now, beneath it. But he saw what had disturbed him. The spot, as he made it out, seemed too high. Only the lobe, he'd imagined, had been severed and this was halfway up the shell. He craned about, jerking his neck, his face up. What the hell, he asked himself, was wrong now! And he experienced, in his sudden distress and anger, the same impulse he'd known that morning—when he'd wakened with its aching so, feeling so hot and bloated—to tear the dressing away to see what it looked like.

He restrained himself partially out of a simple recognition of his situation (Once he got it off, how could he get it on again? He couldn't ask *her* to help him.), and partially out of sense of fear. If something was wrong, he told himself, what could he do—here, so far from home, among people he didn't know? What could he do about it? In the morning his fear had focused itself more sharply: hand lifted to the bandage, he'd had a sudden vivid impression of Gillespie nodding his head understandingly and phoning Lambert. At the idea he'd swung abruptly from the mirror—so abruptly that he'd bruised his side on the edge of the dresser—and hurried to get into his clothes.

He pushed the loose bandage up under one of the tighter strands, then took his comb from his breast pocket and combed his hair as well as he could. He pulled his tie straight—tried to pinch a dimple into the knot. He'd been surprised, seeing himself in the mirror, at how shabby he looked. He was usually fussy about his clothes: too fussy, his wife liked to complain ("Who do you think you are, Frank, Romeo? Only in the opera these days, honey, where they like the big ones"—and she'd knocked the back of her hand against his stomach). But in his haste to leave the hotel in the morning he'd shaved hurriedly, knicking himself in a couple of places, and instead of bothering about a fresh shirt, he'd grabbed up the one on the back of the chair. His suit, too, looked rumpled—he tried to iron down one of the lapels that must have got folded over under his coat and jutted up now.

The hallway seemed darker after straining his eyes, staring up to the light in the bathroom: he had to feel his way along it. He moved through it cautiously, careful not to make a sound that might draw the woman's attention. There was no one in the parlor. He finished the rest of the length quickly, crossed the porch, and stepped out onto the front stoop.

The sun bathed everything more brightly than ever—the car parked below, the road, the field beyond. The sudden brightness surprised him: in the house he'd had the impression that the sky had grayed over, that it had perhaps begun to rain.

He couldn't think why, at the moment, it seemed important to act warily. Still he did. He remained at the top of the stoop, pulled his topcoat closed as if in preparation for something—checked the driveway, the lawn. A car zoomed past on the road, the sun flicking from the glazed top. Two well-dressed ladies—one with hair pulled back tight, earrings, a fur piece—talking away like sixty. Then, right on top of that, another car—swishing past the first one from the opposite direction—this time a kid driving. The woman or the girl must have turned on the radio, because he heard cracking music behind him, first very loud, then quickly muted. And down the road, out of the dilapidated barn, a farmer backed a tractor—high up in the seat, in overalls and a brown shirt, kicking his foot at the dog that chased back and forth about the heavy wheels.

Thompson told himself he was walking but he was actually trotting—huffing as he went—down the path. The key, he was certain now, was on the road or in the car: Where else could it be? And this time without any interference, any butting in from anyone, he'd find it. He'd just look and there it would be, right in front of his nose. And the damned car would start and he'd be on his way. Away from this place. Away from here. Headed home.

He saw the stone steps leading down from the lawn but he'd forgotten how narrow they were and tumbled down three of them. His one knee caught the gravel with his whole weight, and he scraped his hand badly, but he wasn't seriously hurt. Still the fall dazed him, and as he remained on all fours, panting, trying to catch his breath, he saw the girl's head pop up from the other side of the car. They were staring at one another through the car windows and the first thing they did—he did it too; he almost laughed out loud—was to grin at one another. Then the girl's expression quickly became solemn and she hurried around the rear of the car.

"Did you hurt yourself?" she asked anxiously.

"I don't think so. Not much."

He pulled himself stumblingly to his feet and dusted his clothes. He'd torn his trouser knee slightly; the stones had splayed the cloth. He tried to brush the spot, but the ground was still damp and there remained a thin caking of mud around it.

"My brother knocked a tooth out on those steps," the girl said. "He was coming down on his trike and he couldn't stop. This one." She opened her mouth, revealing a row of peculiarly small, even teeth, to show him.

But he was more interested in his palm.

"You hurt that too?"

She couldn't see, so he flapped down his hand to show her. It was his right palm. He'd scraped the heel when he'd shot the hand out to protect himself. There was a white patch, as if sandpaper had been rubbed over it, and three deeper cuts that were beading now with blood.

She pressed his hand down even farther to see better. Then, before he was aware of what she was doing, she'd dug a crumpled handkerchief from her pocket and dabbed the blood away.

He jerked his hand back. "No, that's all right. That's all right. I'll take care of it."

She examined the cloth in her hand, the lines of irregular red spots on it, then stuffed it back in her coat pocket.

They walked to the car together. He stood for a moment at the curb, thinking of the key, of looking for it, but decided he was too shaken: he needed to sit down, to recuperate a minute. He ducked into the seat, leaving the door open in case she wanted to keep him company. She slipped in right behind him, without hesitation, at ease in the car immediately, pushing back in the seat, testing it, leaning forward, fiddling with the lighter, the radio dials, finally settling upon the windshield, drawing on the dusty surface with her finger.

"How come you're not in school?" he asked, for something to say.

"Cold," she pouted.

"You have a cold?"

"I *had* a cold." She sat up at that. "I don't have one anymore, but Mamma says you have to be careful."

"I have to be careful?" he joked.

She found that so funny her shoulders hunched under the bulky coat. "Of course not. *Me!*" she exclaimed.

He hadn't, when he was in the house, seen any sign of the violin she'd had in her hand when he first noticed her, but he remembered it now.

"That isn't mine. It's my brother's."

"I played the violin—took lessons—when I was a kid."

It made no impression.

He could think of nothing else after that and the conversation dwindled. He looked at his watch: the man from the garage should be along soon. The girl had gone back to drawing on the windshield. Simple figures. A house. A flower. A bird. She'd printed some words. GIRL, BOY, DRAGON, SCHOOL, PIG. He said "Boy" to himself and looked out the window to where he'd seen the farmer with the tractor. He and the dog were gone now and the barn looked more deserted than ever. The word "Boy" sounded again in his thoughts and without actually hearing it he attempted to brush it aside. But it sounded again and pausing, hearing it now, he wondered why. Then, without any effort, indifferently— because the incident had aroused only the slightest curiosity in him—he recalled something that had happened on the night he arrived at the hotel in Heltvei.

It had been after seven when he got into the strange town and he was tired and hungry. He found the hotel easily and took the cheapest room as usual (it gave him a little leeway, a couple of extra bucks to play around with). Only this one was particularly dreary: one of the lights was blown, the shade was chewed raw along one side, the dresser top badly marred. He washed quickly and changed his shirt; then he lit a cigarette and yanked up the shade. And it was at that moment that he noticed the boy. The room was on the second floor and as he looked down he could see the corner opposite the hotel and part of the main street. The street itself was almost empty now, most of the store windows dark, big Penney's sign on a water tower standing out chalk white against the night, faint crescent of glow above a movie marquee. The few people who passed pulled their coats about them, kept their heads down against the raw wind.

The boy appeared suddenly from the hotel side, hopping across the street, his pale hands flapping behind him, seeming to be hurrying along with the rest. It was only because, once on the opposite curb, he stopped and appeared to change his mind that Thompson noticed him at all.

And in the end—though he had remained a long time at the window watching him—he never found out what he was about. He just stood along the curb, glancing across at the hotel windows now and again; then he'd saunter down to the tree in front of the gas station—stand there, motionless, poking his feet in the dead leaves; then move back the sixty or seventy feet to the corner.

The tree was almost opposite Thompson's window, and it was at this point that he saw him most clearly. But there appeared nothing unusual about him. Eight or nine, with a gangling thinness. Pale face with dark eyes. He smiled once when he got in the way of a car coming out of the station—a pinched, shy smile. He picked up a leaf and twirled it by the stem, once placed it to his mouth and blew it like a pinwheel. The mackinaw he was wearing seemed too small: he kept hunching his shoulders under it, pulling back his hands. He tilted up the peak of his cap now and then, a habitual gesture, with the back of his fingers.

After a time, when one of the station attendants came out, he asked him something and Thompson saw the man shake his head "no." The boy seemed disappointed, but he continued to pace along the curb. Once, as he had his head up again surveying the windows, Thompson caught the full face and was touched by the beauty of it. He thought, at that moment, their eyes met, but if they did, the boy gave no sign of recognition; his own simply passed on. Finally he walked slowly to the corner, remained there for a while longer, then, as if deciding that, despite some hope, he was wasting his time, he spun around and began chasing in the direction he'd been going when Thompson first saw him.

"But he asked me, Mamma," the girl was whining.

"Still, April. . . ."

"But he. . . ."

"Still. . . . I hope she hasn't been bothering you too much."

And by then he was back, turned away from the barn, staring over the frizzled head of the girl at the woman bending toward him in the car doorway.

"You must have called the Mobile station instead of Andy's," she went on without waiting for him to answer. "That's all the way down Langdon, almost to Remus. Andy's is just over on Fletcher, about two miles." He thought he'd called the number she'd shown him; apparently he hadn't and she was slightly put out. "It'll take almost fifteen-twenty minutes for the fellow from the Mobile station to get here." Then she came to the point. "But he called—he seems a nice fellow, considerate—to say something's come up. He said he didn't want you to think he'd forgotten you—that it would be about another half hour. You can come inside if you want—wait for him in there—it would maybe be more comfortable."

And suddenly Thompson felt—looking at her—at her tentative stand there in front of the door (seeming chilly again), at the eyes offering their friendly, weak invitation—more frightened than he had at any moment since last night in the other woman's room when, back to the door where she'd left him, he'd felt the first warm drip of the blood on his shoulder. She'd pinched a hair from his nipple and kissed him, and, in just the kimono she'd put on, had slipped out of the door. And a moment later, standing there, panting, reaching for her, hardly knowing she was gone, he'd felt the first drop, the trickle down his chest.

"Would you like to come inside?" The woman seemed disturbed by his expression. "Into the house?"

"No," he said.

"Well, that's all right," she said. "I just thought. . . ."

He knew that he'd been tricked—no repairman was coming—the whole thing, however it had been managed, was a hoax. And she drove the car. Oh, of course she drove the car—that was part of it so they could tease him along with the little fatso, the telephone business, the repairman coming. Part of whatever lousy game they were all playing. And he hadn't got lost—why should he, just this one time, get lost? No, that was Gillespie. Gillespie had purposely *led* him here—and *she* knew all about it, had known it all along, because that's what she was doing right from the first, when he first saw her: standing by the porch window *waiting* for him. And finally, with a convulsion of terror, he understood now why, when Lambert had straightened from beside the bed, he'd taken out his handkerchief and wiped his lips.

"What have I done?" he shouted angrily at the woman.

She stared at him, amazed.

"No. Now no, you listen . . . ," he demanded, beside himself, shifting quickly in the seat, closer to where she stood. "There's no use pretending. . . ."

"Here! Here!" the girl ducked under her mother's arm, holding up the car key. She stood directly in front of him, bright-eyed, glowing with her discovery. "It was where you fell."

"What, April?" her mother asked.

"I found it where he fell, right over there."

"Did he fall?" she asked.

"When you fell it came out," the girl went on to tell him, ignoring her mother. "Don't you see yet? Where it was?"

"In my cuff!" he exploded. He saw it, it was as clear as day. He was laughing and crying "It was in my cuff!"

He grabbed the key, impetuously reached out and hugged her, tousled her hair. "Thanks, kid. Oh, thank you, kiddoe!" He reached into his pocket and took out a handful of coins. "That's for you. All for yourself. Hear!"

"Thank *you!*"

He scooted over and thinking about nothing but having the key again placed it in the ignition and tried the car.

"Why, it's started!" the woman shouted. And it had, on the first try. There was a small explosion, as if something had been released, and a moment later it was humming away beautifully. "Keep it going. Keep it going," the woman warned excitedly. "If you let it stop you might have trouble again."

He pressed down on the gas, evened it off, pressed down again. He had never heard any sound sweeter.

"And imagine," the woman said. She seemed to relax—happy for him, happy to be on the verge of getting rid of him, to be allowed to get back to her own work. "And imagine—all this time and nothing was wrong with it."

"Oh, there's something wrong with it," he said, puffing himself out, sitting up importantly. "I'll have to take to the garage when I get home—have them look at it." He hardly knew what he said. He was just talking, boasting; he didn't care what came out now. It was all over, the car was running, he'd be turned round, headed home in a minute.

"You're sure you're all right?" the woman asked. "Your ear? I could go in and get you some aspirin if you don't have any."

"No, I'm fine," he said. "No. . . . Now, I just turn around and go the way I came. Right?"

"That's right. Stay on Langdon here to Parker. Then when you get. . . ."

He'd had his left hand hanging out the window. It felt as if a mosquito had bitten him.

"Oh, April!" the mother said, annoyed, thoroughly irritated by the child.

When he brought his hand in, to look at it, he saw that half the thumb had been severed.

At the sound of her mother's scolding, the girl had run away, up to the driveway, and there turned about, her eyes angry, wiping her mouth on her sleeve.

"You just wait," the woman went on, shaking her hand at her. "Just you wait."

The blood was flowing all over him—his topcoat, his trousers, the seat of the car. He didn't know what to do.

He began crying.

"Why?" he yelled at the woman.

She seemed hardly to hear. She was more interested in the girl.

"What?" she asked.

"Why!" He was holding up the bloody stump of the finger at her.

"Oh," she said, "you people. People like you." She seemed offended and, at the same time, to find him a little ridiculous. "Put something on it. Haven't you a handkerchief?"

"But why!"

"Why?" She could hardly be bothered. "April!" she shrilled. The girl was running across the garden patch, toward the wood. "April, you come back here. . . . Why?" She had to find something quickly before the girl got away. "Oh," she shook her head. "Just think of the boy and look at you. Look!" And with that she was through with him. "April . . . !"

He didn't wait to turn the car but pressed the gas and sped directly ahead. Still he wasn't going so fast that he didn't notice the sign, the one he'd remained vaguely aware of since he'd first searched down the road. It was a simple township marker telling him he was entering Heltvei. And with that, after a moment, he became all fear—and so, for Thompson, who had been for such a brief time aware that he'd known any fear at all, there was never to be fear again.

SARA is the pseudonym of a California writer. Her first published story, "Silence is Golden," appeared in *New Campus Writing.*

So I'm Not Lady Chatterley
So Better I Should Know It Now

That was the summer her mother kept badgering, "Be a little modern. Smoke a little." Which really meant, in her mother's back-hand fashion, it was high time she got married and got out of there. Or, more precisely, that it was high time she got out, moved around the corner into, maybe, one of the flats over the butcher shop, and started producing . . . babies. They should have a little pleasure in their old age.

It was also the summer the family took a flat on the Avenue and her room, even four flights up, joggled with the streetcars and flashed with sharp pin-points of light, was an agony of sound and movement, and it was no use pretending like Virginia Woolf. It was the summer of her last year in college, the summer when, all men gone—or at least those without ulcers and families—she'd been awarded the "lobster trick" at the United Press and was, finally, from midnight to eight, anyhow, a newspaperwoman. It was the summer when she'd first discovered that, in Boston, there were plenty of mothers who violently forbade smoking and the daughters did whether or no, that her Irish friend from Salem (lace curtain) had been happily knocked up by a V-12 student from Harvard, happily because he was rich, too, and they would get married, leave Boston forever. That her tight-bound New England friend, frail and fragile, stood pining for her professor—at a decent puritan distance—whilst swooning through D. H. Lawrence, and insisting that she swoon, too. That the only fellows available for dating, in any regular fashion, were guys on the order of Leslie and Maynard who liked their own company better. It was the summer when she'd changed her name from Dobkie to Dora to Dolly, and still felt there was something not quite right about the "Dolly," she wasn't the type. When she'd finished her first weeping opus titled "Mid Alien Corn" which was somehow related to herself and the Biblical story of Ruth in an obscure, symbolic, and highly rhetorical way. When, among newspaper people, she was gently learning to swear again, having—if not fully forgiven, perhaps reasonably forgotten—the days when the boys under the street lamp called her "queen of the shithouse." It was, in short, a summer of war, and of girls approaching womanhood in a time without men and a place fast loosening an outworn restraint.

She was nineteen, and the family was worried. Not since adolescence when her father had cracked a boy over the head for keeping her out after midnight, and her mother had spent all the following week talking marriage to the boy's grandmother, had she brought anything eligible around for inspection. She was too much with books, she worked too hard, it wasn't natural, she would die an old maid. And there were times, that summer, when she was afraid maybe they were right.

The battle of Moe Schlepp began in early June. Like he was the last man.

"Faege had a letter today," her mother timidly opened the door to her room as she sat studying for finals. "Her youngest is coming home in August. For furlough."

Dobkie-Dora-Dolly stayed with her books. She knew what her mother was pushing.

"He's a Private . . . First Class."

Her kid brother, who'd had to fake his age to get in at all, was a Seaman, Ordinary, and her big brother, who had a nagging wife and four snotty brats, was a taxi driver, plain. At that rate, Faege's youngest was pretty good pickings.

In July, when she was working midnight to eight, taking classes in summer session from eight-thirty to noon, sleeping from one to five and studying in whatever hours were left, her father, sneaking in from a pinochle game, stopped her on the stairs as she was leaving for the office. "You remember Schlepp?" he said.

She remembered all right. Schlepp was one of his pinochle partners from the Workmen's Circle. Also Faege's husband.

"His boy, Moe, is coming home next month."

"I know already."

"How come you know?"

"Ma."

"Oh. . . ." He shook his head, his mouth puckering and a frown furrowing. "He's not like the others," her father offered.

The others were the rest of the Schlepp boys, five of them, all built like icemen, big, fleshy, with huge red hands.

"He don't talk politics," her father said.

Old man Schlepp was a soapbox orator and the boys generally tailed along. At least before the war. She had a fleeting vision of the whole red-faced Schlepp clan, in the middle of Franklin Field, with handkerchiefs, sweating and exhorting.

She raced for her streetcar. "I'll be late." Then turning to her father, who still pondered on the stairs, "Stop worrying. I'm not a freak."

The summer was unendurably muggy and hot. She liked working nights, because it was cooler then. She was losing weight fast, which was all to the good; she had a tendency to heft which the family found "rosily blooming" but which left her aching for a little consumption, her ideal was Margaret Sullavan with a desperate, throaty, come-and-protect me voice. Sad, sagging circles were beginning to loop beneath her eyes and her face was turning the color of a stale, hard-boiled egg from the lack of sunlight and fresh air. On her, however, she felt it looked interesting. With the amount of reading she'd done, she figured there must be somebody, somewhere who would at least find her interesting. The trouble was, even traipsing around on streetcars and subways half the night and wandering through the sailors on Scollay Square, nothing ever happened. She was ripe for something to happen.

Looking back in later years, it seemed as if it had all been telescoped into that single, short, poignant summer. In truth, of course, it hadn't. There were the years before, years when, fleeing from the youth under the tree, the shock of physical fact, she

had burrowed in, walking the city sidewalks with steel arch sup-
ports and lisle stockings, trembling. With time, as she reached out,
the years when, clutching a box seat ticket, she sat in the dark
of the Colonial Theater and began to believe. And still later,
as she rode the subways from Newspaper Row, the wobbly movement into high heels and the tottering at the top of the stairs.

That summer, in late July, her brother, the taxi-cab driver, met
her one morning as she left the office, bound for school. They
drove down Commonwealth Avenue, broad and Bostonian, a clean
coolness at 8 A.M.

"Chaike sent me," he said. Chaike was his wife. "She's arranged
a little tête-à-tête. Something special."

"Moe Schlepp," said Dolly.

"But he's just your type, a bookworm," said her brother.

"I'll find my own worms," snapped Dolly. And inside she was
thinking, an accountant, or worse, an engineer. In her family,
books meant, not education, but vocation. It was all well enough
intentioned; they were seriously searching—really combing the
territory—for a high-type, clean-cut Jewish boy with white collar
prospects and limited expectations as to dowry and female glamor.
"Tell Chaike," she said, "that I'm planning to elope with a
Connecticut Yankee."

Which wasn't so funny, since her Irish friend, Meg, actually was
planning to elope and within two weeks, did, in the dark of a
summer's night, riding a motorcycle across the state line and into
the wilds of rural Connecticut.

The night that Meg eloped with Buff, she and Lydia, her Puritan friend, met in the bar and grill they called "Ptomaine Tavern."
It was a newspaper hangout, cobwebbed on the narrow block
between the press associations, the Boston Globe, and the Boston
Post. Lydia worked the 3:30 to midnight, on much the same basis
as Dolly got the midnight to eight. No men. At midnight, Lydia
generally stopped off for a few rounds of beer. It wasn't a matter
of gay abandon; she was hoping it would fatten her up. Whatever Dolly's notions of romance were, Lydia, bone thin, wanted a
bit of plumpness for her professor, however remote the possibilities
might be.

Dolly had a night off, and she felt edgy. She didn't need the beer, she wanted very much to get drunk. "You can't get drunk on beer," she kept repeating, it being the third round, and she already quite giddy.

"Have you read *Lady Chatterley's Lover* yet?" said Lydia, six books on the bench beside her.

"It's banned in Boston," said Dolly righteously. "Along with *The Decameron* and Elizabeth Barrett Browning."

"Oh, Dolly, you must, you simply must. . . ."

"I'm tired of reading," said Dolly, a drunken candor suddenly overflowing. "I think I would prefer a little something in the flesh."

And gray eyes searching brown, together, they wept.

The family took a room at the beach for the month of August— in one of those porch-fronted sagging seaside hotels where all the city neighbors, suddenly denuded and with knobby knees, bulging breasts, in dripping bathing suits, absurdly played the same pinochle and poker games and argued with the same butcher as if the entire neighborhood had, at one shot, been thrown, sweat, torment, turbulence and all, into the same hotel. She refused to go. Her work, she said. Work, she knew, was sacred. Not so sacred for a woman, but sacred enough. Her mother hedged, perplexed. Finally, said her mother, "I'll leave the sheets off the parlor, maybe you can entertain, private, on Sundays, when there's no school and you're not working." Her mother was a huge battleship of a woman, but Dolly confused her, and she always appeared querulous, uncertain, eyes dodging, when confronted by her daughter. "Faege's youngest. . . ." her mother began again. But Dolly cut her short. "I haven't the time."

So she stayed in the city, alone. The house was a little frightening, but she was hardly in it, except for Sundays, and she treasured the quiet, not that she was antisocial, just that the years of elbow rubbing, of loud and vocal humanity each pinching the next to make certain they were still alive, had left her with a desperate, inarticulate longing for separateness. And at the same time, as her body stirred with a new awakening, for a shared separateness, for one other.

Even Lydia, stiff, purple-veined Lydia, wrote passioned letters to the boy-from-next-door, who was, at the moment, in France. Dolly was sure it would all come to nothing, but at least Lydia was getting it off her chest.

Which was the reason, she supposed, she ever got hooked into that lousy USO picnic sponsored by the ladies of Junior Hadassah. She could beat Lydia at the passioned letter game any day of the week. Only, she needed a serial number.

She should have expected what happened; normally, she would have. But these weren't normal times. She knew the Junior Hadassah type—nine to five secretaries with a lunch hour spent at the cosmetic counter of Filene's Bargain Basement, *True Confessions* hidden under movie magazines, slacks on Sunday over gilt high heels. And long engagements, very long, very respectable engagements, with bewildered young men wearing the family's seal of approval. She bore them no ill will, but she had, unfortunately, outgrown them. From the vantage point of her midnight maturity, they seemed, servicemen escorts as well, incredibly young. It being Sunday, and she being tired, she found herself a rock, and went to sleep.

She woke to the ping of an acorn on her head. Then another, matched by a singsong refrain, "Giant oaks from acorns grow, yo-ho." Ping, went the acorn again.

Bending stealthily round the rock, she caught a glimpse of a slumped khaki shoulder flipping a handful of the seeds, desultory and desolate.

"Not on my head, they don't," she stood up, shaking her hair.

He was leaning against the rock, a crummy, paperbound book propped against his knees. His gray face was lost behind a pair of horn-rimmed glasses and his fresh, whiffle haircut stood screaming on edge. The uniform was a mistake, she decided, and went back to her berth.

She sensed him standing over her, though her eyes were closed. Opening them, she took a quick inventory, a Halloween skeleton rattling around in his big brother's soldier suit, and she closed them again. But he stood fixed. "So say something," she said, finally.

He extended a limp hand. "Moe Schlepp, Private, First Class."

As she said before, she should have expected it. Anyway, they hid there behind the rock, tossing acorns around, and moping. The paperbound book was *Lady Chatterley's Lover*.

"Any good?" she asked, feigning innocence.

"So-so," he mumbled.

"How come you're reading it then?"

He took his glasses off to look at her better. His eyes, she noted, were a nearsighted green. "Lady," he said, "you ain't in the army at-all without you've read *Lady Chatterley's Lover*."

On the beach below, arms and legs shining copper in the sun flashed tense and solid through the shifting sand. A multicolored ball hung in the air, suspended in aching brilliance against the more muted tones of lake and sky. And the sound of laughter, bouncing toward them, the fresh, clean smell of openness.

"Who's the black-haired beauty in the lemon bathing suit?" he asked, his eyes on the girl who at that moment had leaped to catch the ball.

"Engaged," said Dolly, "to my kid brother."

She herself was vaguely considering a tall, sensitive-looking blond in white.

"Engaged," said Moe, "to my niece."

They smiled, tentatively, at one another, a quick understanding established. Then the usual conversation as to what each did in real life, the pathetic parrying into hidden corners. He wasn't an accountant, or an engineer. He wasn't anything. "Ping-pong champion of Tallahassee, Florida," he said, when she asked him, with her candid bluntness. And she answered, in the same spirit, "I keep house with a teletype machine, nights."

He was chewing on a dried-up blade of grass, sort of musing and gazing, at nothing in particular, altogether too dreamy for a guy with five older placard-marching brothers. Plus the father.

"Looking for a bluebird?" she said.

"No," he said, and he was serious. "Just looking for myself."

"He went that-a-way," she gestured, flippantly, toward the docks. It was a silly thing to say, but after all, he'd left her hanging there, hadn't he, way out on a limb, looking, maybe, for *herself*?

There was a long pause while he looked, she supposed, some more. Finally he pointed, at a tangible speck on the lake. "We've

missed the boat," he said. The afternoon excursion. She was quite
happy to do without. "Maybe we can be athletic and rent one
of those little items." He didn't sound particularly eager.

"Ever been in one before?"

"Nothing like the present," he said. "Like we should wet our
feet at least now we're here."

It was an old rowboat fitted out with a second-hand outboard
motor. He had the right idea okay, shoved off neatly, but the
motor wouldn't start. "Here," he said, "you work the lever," and
he showed her how, "while I get us moving with the oars." She
was never sure later exactly why it happened, or what she'd done
wrong. But somehow her finger got wedged into the jamb, crack
went the lever, and the mashed finger-tip hung torn and bloody
in mid-air, the nail split wide open.

They got her patched up at the first-aid station, and he bought
her an ice-cream cone, worried and apologetic. She laughed it off.
"Anyway," she said, "It's my left hand. I can still peck at the
typewriter with my right." At her home, they parted, if anything
even more hopelessly gay than before, beneath the bantering,
an innocent despair. "So we're not meant for each other," they
grinned, "so you go your way, I'll go mine." But she didn't want
to see him again, and that was for real. She didn't even want his
serial number, for letters. He was being shipped overseas in two
weeks, and she had the feeling he didn't know any more about
guns and fighting than he did about rowboats. She had the really
awful feeling, like in a Greek play, that it was absolutely hopeless
from the start.

To avoid him, not that he was particularly persistent, he seemed
as willing as she to forget the whole business, but to avoid even
thinking of him, of the war and of all their lost youth, she went
further out of her way than usual, to keep herself busier—Shut-
it-out, shut-it-out, shut-it-out—busier, if that was possible, than
ever. At school, she added more hours to her already heavily
accelerated program; at the office, she took on features in addition
to the overnight desk. With all the strength of a wounded animal,
she was running away. No one in pursuit, particularly, except her
own pain.

Only he kept popping up, fated, Moe Schlepp, Private, First

Class, the ghost of her conscience, the other side of the coin.

She was interviewing Sally Keith, the strip-tease dancer who did it with tassels. She had talked to her momentarily in a mirror-covered, powder-littered cubbyhole of a room backstage, shocked to find her so young, she couldn't be much older than herself, yet already and for many years, she knew, a headliner and a sailor's byword. It was show time. "Stay, and catch the act," said Sally, "we can chew the fat again later." So she caught the act.

She stood timidly in a doorway, at the very edge of the man-crowded room, hugging her pencils and paper tightly in her hands and in full view of anyone who cared to see, they shouldn't mistake her for one of the girls in the line. The lights were on Sally. Otherwise, there was darkness all around, the feeling of too many people pushed together into too small a space, a heavy, labored breathing, and the smell of urine absolutely choking her, reminding her of tenement halls and her father's broken-down shop with the broken-down toilet in the back. It seemed like hundreds of heads in front of her, most of them in various states of balding, but plenty of healthy, young ones, too, belonging to the vast unknown and unnamed in battle dress who aimlessly walked that neon-lighted square on the long, lonely nights when she, with typewriter, sat.

Sally peeled slowly, the music thumping behind her. It took forever, Dolly thought, about ready to run again, for her to get down to flesh and gauze. Then the music stopped. And Sally stood there, stark, raving, naked. The tassels were a violent purplish-blue, embroidered in the center, with long silken threads, dangling from her white breasts. She twirled them, grinding, faster and faster, till all that was left was a circle of color, like one of those kid's toys that sends out sparks. A round of whistling, stamping applause, here and there men jumping and shouting, then the house lights went up, and Sally was gone.

She elbowed her way through the excitement, wishing her boss all kinds of damnation, wishing herself anywhere but where she was. Somebody grabbed her round the waist and started dragging her toward a table. And who should intervene? Moe Schlepp.

He had an empty beer bottle in his hand, and probably would have tried to use it.

"My Galahad," she said, bitterly.

"Well," he flung the bottle idiotically in erratic little circles, "what in hell are you doing in a dive like this?"

"I might ask the same," she blurted, close to tears.

They crawled out into the night. She forgot about "chewing the fat" with Sally again. She'd caught the act, which seemed, to her, quite sufficient.

He walked her back to the office, past the all-night penny arcades, the narrow, gaping movie houses with their continuous shows and their painted posters, the hamburger stands and the fish carts, and the shuffling of drunken feet. On Newspaper Row, it was, as always at this hour, deadly quiet. In the daytime there would be large crowds gathered before the chalk boards, lined faces and folded arms, waiting for the news. Was that the summer Rome was taken? But now there were only dim lights in empty city rooms, a lone green eye-shade with rolled sleeve occasionally bent over a single, littered desk. On the street, only the one-legged newsboy called "Niggy" hawking the latest editions to the black and silent night.

"Seems to me you can do better than sitting around ogling cheap floozies like Sally Keith," she said, hitting below the belt.

"Got any telephone numbers?" his eyes pierced hers.

She rang for the night janitor. "Listen," she said, "take care of yourself. I mean it." And she shook his hand. "I got work to do."

A few nights later, she ran into him again on the streetcar, shortly before midnight, on her way to the office. At that hour, in her neighborhood at any rate, the cars rattled their empty way to the city, driven by unseen motormen behind curtained shrouds, and nobody, but nobody, was ever in them.

He lay stretched out on one of the double benches at the back, hiccuping, and reading.

She sat down opposite, and he tipped his hat. "Welcome," he said. "Will you join me on my wagon ride to hell?" Hic.

Then he tottered over, cross the wooden slates, and handed her the book. "For you," he said. "Enjoy it."

It was a brand new, Modern Library edition of *The Sex Problem in Modern Society*.

"Moreover," he said, and he had to hang onto the straps above to keep from falling completely, "I bought it in Boston. Not banned."

She hated him at that moment, as much as she hated the city that had bred her, and all the stinking flesh that had warmed her, for never having allowed her either childhood or girlhood, or the comfort of not-knowing. She wanted to walk out and meet life pure in heart, with illusion and belief, and a reverence for the mystery that was her birthright. But it wasn't given so; perhaps it wasn't given to any in that time and place. There was no innocence, and there were no young.

The whole city lay clouded in humidity that summer, like one great big Turkish bath. And she, too, denuded, vulnerable, unable to see beyond the perspiring mist.

When she stopped off for a beer with Lydia before going up to the office later in the week, Moe sat there, ensconced, in a corner of the booth.

Like a bad and broken record, Lydia began the introductions again.

Dolly waved her off. "Enough," she said. "We've met."

"Let's drink to him in that case," said Lydia, "for he's off to the wars tomorrow."

Dolly stiffened. Had she then so successfully drowned the passing days?

His hand brushed hers.

There are those for whom conversation is just so much cheap lace. Moe and Dolly, in the pathetic inadequacy of their human frames, in the void they both recognized between the felt and the expressed, were of those.

Knowledgeable, with a candor shorn of any ornament, their hands clasped and held.

He stayed with her, in the office, through the night. Such a long night. While she took the fight results and clipped the morning editions and the desks stood empty all around. "This is being a newspaperwoman?" his eyes mocked her. "What did you expect . . . Broadway . . . ?"

In the morning, they went home to her room over the streetcars, as the sun rose and the day opened slowly to the heat. On the stairs, faces flushed, they awkwardly edged past Mr.

Teitelbaum, the second-floor tenant, heavy and lumbering and still dazed with sleep, as he stumbled on his way to the factory where he would stand, choked, and even more dazed, in the steam of the afternoon, pressing pants. "Tell me," says Mr. Teitelbaum, "how's the family?" Grimacing, "Fine, everybody's fine, thank you for asking," they climbed upward, to that room with its fading flowered wallpaper and its view looking out on steel tracks and concrete walks and murky shops and peeling billboards and the drugstore cowboys on the corner, what was left of them.

They stood in the doorway, uneasy. "You want something to eat?" she said.

The kitchen stared white and barren.

"Got anything to drink?" he said, turning away from her. "Tea."

"Nothing stronger?"

She was burrowing in the pantry. Sometimes her mother kept a crock of cherries fermenting beneath the cupboards, for the holidays. She dragged it out.

He laughed. "It takes two Jews to salute their virginity in Passover Wine."

The crock was too heavy to move. So they sat there, in the moldy pantry, Indian fashion, with legs crossed, gulping.

"God, it's sweet." His mouth was a wry, downward turned purple.

"I don't feel so good," she said.

"To tell you the truth, neither do I."

He held her as they unbent. She was wearing a thin cotton, sleeveless dress, and her arms burned. His uniform felt coarse and heavy against her skin.

"I'm going to take a bath," she said, wildly.

"Ashamed?" His eyes caressed her gently and softly.

"Yes," she said. "I don't think I like my body very well."

In her room, the sun beat through mercilessly. They pulled the torn yellow shades, but it only seemed to heighten the light, turned persimmon now and coursing through every corner. In the center, the bed spotlighted, waiting, like the stage before Sally Keith walked on.

Moe found some blankets in the closet and draped them over the windows.

"Thanks," she said, understanding that he understood.

"It's okay," he fumbled with the buttons on his jacket. "I got feelings too, you know," and he grinned. "Like maybe Moe Schlepp, Private, First Class, ain't exactly Mellors." His chest stood bared, a sickly blue, hairless and in-caved.

Beneath the covers, they hid, wet and sweaty, eyes closed and blood pounding. With all their bleak honesty, for all their tutored courage, who had told them and how were they to know that blunder, and ineptitude, and this moist despairing willed effort were also part of youth, and that their nakedness notwithstanding, they, too, stood innocent before the joining.

For her, there was pain, and nothing much else. Blood on the sheets, and they would have to be washed. Her family.

For him? "I'm sorry," he said.

"Don't be sorry," she said. "So I'm not Lady Chatterley. So better I should know it now, than later."

In the fall, she left Boston and went to New York City, armed with college degree, newspaper guild card, and a little experience. She still didn't know any better, if she wasn't queen of the shit-house, or Lady Chatterley, who she was, nor did she ever find out for sure. And since Moe died in the war, she supposed he never found out either. But she hoped that somewhere, before he died, if only on a German field with a German fraulein, bestial and uncaring, he'd had it where he wasn't sorry.

SHIRLEY W. SCHOONOVER'S stories have appeared in *New Campus Writing, Transatlantic Review,* and in the 1952 O. *Henry Prize Story Awards* with "The Star Blanket." Her novel, *Mountain of Winter,* is scheduled for publication by Coward-McCann in 1963.

Old and Country Tale

He had run away. Not so much run as walked, he thought, but it came to the same thing. However you did it, you went away from a place. He had taken the team to the north forty to finish the plowing, and all at once it had come to him that this was as good a time as any to go. Close after sunup it was, and she wouldn't be coming to check on him until noon. He had looked over his shoulder just in case, but the hill was empty of her; so he removed the bridles and hung them on the hames of the harness. "Let you have all you want without the bit in your way," he said to the horses. "She'll be coming soon enough to bring you back." The horses had begun to graze placidly, undisturbed by this change. He touched them once on their necks and then walked away.

He crossed the barbed-wire fence and left the Davidson property, always keeping to where the sun had burned off the morning mist in case she came early and looked to track him. He kept his eyes down to watch the grass spring up undamaged behind him. A lark flew up against the sky and, seeing no harm in him, returned to her nest. He went on until he reached the highway, where he stopped to look both ways—no cars in sight. He stepped across the pavement and walked along the bottom of the man-deep ditch. He'd hear cars this way and be out of sight. Five hours until noon, five hours of fast walking; then he'd have to find a place to rest until night. She'd have found the horses and, along

with her parents and brothers, would be looking for him. He held
no bitterness about that; only he wouldn't be brought back.

He was sweating from his pace and looked to where the sun
stood now. Nearly noon, and figure four miles an hour, he had
come something like twenty miles since morning. Time to find
a roost till night comes, he thought; and after a scrutiny of the
highway he left the protection of the ditch to duck under another
fence. Cornfield's good cover, least till somebody comes to start
the harvest. Stepping carefully between the rows of corn, he put
several yards between himself and the highway. He picked three
ears of corn and sat down to munch them raw. Sweet and milky,
they satisfied the hunger and thirst that had grown inside him.
Now that the belly mumbling had hushed he lay full length on the
ground. He could hear the passing cars; and if anyone wanted
to start taking this corn, well, he'd hear that too, and be gone
before they noticed him. He lay his forehead on an arm and let
the afternoon grow hot and moist.

A beetle worked its way out of the tumulus. He watched it as it
climbed down the bottom of the runnel between the rows of corn.
He blew at it to see if it would notice him. The beetle squared
around and stood motionless. "Aren't you going to clack your
mandibles at me?" he asked the beetle, and then remembered
where he was. Like a kid you are, he told himself sternly. Can't
keep a thing in your head any longer than a kid would. You,
hiding in a cornfield so she can't find you, and then you go talking
to beetles. All she'd have to do is walk quiet down the road,
and she'd hear you. Aggravated, he put his head down again.
After a moment he looked up. But the beetle was gone.

Late in the afternoon the tree frogs began calling for rain,
and he knew it had gone past five o'clock. *Whee-whee-ee*, the
tree frogs cried; and the sky hung heavy on the tops of the
hills. Higher up the scale came the wheedling of the locusts, de-
claring frost within six weeks and their own end. He sat up,
listening to the frogs and the locusts, and believed them, because
once in a while they were right and they believed so hard themselves.

When the sun had gone down he got up and ate some more
corn. Then he slipped from the cornfield down into the ditch
to walk all night. He stopped twice for a cigarette and to relieve

himself, but these stops were timed so that he could tell the hour by the stars. Orion had swung around to point northeast when he heard a car coming slowly along the highway. He pinched the cigarette out and lay down in the damp grass.

A band of light cleared the top of the ditch and illuminated the prickle-edged fence and the first rows of corn. He closed his eyes and ducked his face between his arms. The car went down the road without pausing. Spotlight on now, he thought, I'd forgotten that. He stood up carefully, watching the spotlight poke gently at the roadside. Well, he predicted, they'll come back the other side and look that over too. And tomorrow, early, they'll be like ants. I'd better make it over the Platte tonight, and then it's just one more night and I'm in Colorado. He walked quickly, watching the highway ahead and the ground beneath to keep from stumbling.

First it was just a fence to be crossed and a property line. Then a highway and now a river. Tomorrow a state line. How many lines will I have to cross before I've gone far enough? You'll not look long nor far, will you, Siiri? You'll give up soon and let me be wherever I land.

He saw the car coming back, beam touching the other side of the highway. He watched his wife driving past. Her father was with her. He could hear them talking above the car's monotone. Then they were gone.

North Platte. He skirted the town, heading for the river. The town slept beside the river and along the highway. Some grain elevators stood tall and spare against the sword of Orion. He walked over the bridge and saw a truck stand ahead. He waited until a truck pulled in; then he followed the trucker inside and sat at the counter. "Hot beef," he ordered. "Coffee and berry pie."

The waitress yawned and took the trucker's order too.

"This state got anything besides tornadoes and heat?" the trucker asked as the waitress served their coffee.

"Cold. We've got cold in the winter," Asher said.

"That I know, friend. Mean cold and wind." The trucker wiped his forehead and drank his coffee.

"Paper says rain," the waitress said, and laid their plates on the counter.

"Well, so did the tree frogs yesterday. Or was it still today?" Asher licked the gravy off his fork and took a stab at the pie.

The waitress stood in front of him. "That's ninety-five cents," she said, staring at him.

"I've got it." Asher handed her a dollar bill. "Keep the change."

She said, "Aw, I wanted to make sure you had the money. More coffee?"

"No. No, thanks." He drank the last of the coffee and wiped his mouth. He went out of the truck stand, hearing their chuckling. "Tree frogs," the waitress said.

He had gone a few yards down the highway when the trucker called, "Hey, you, want a lift?"

Asher went back, nodding his head.

"You going anywhere special, or will Denver do?" The trucker pointed at the large semi that dwarfed him.

"Colorado?" Asher asked.

"That's right. Unless there's a Denver in some other state."

"Fine. Thanks." Asher watched the trucker swing up into the truck cab. Then he went to the other side and climbed the ladder. He sat in the cab and jiggled his feet as the trucker made the diesel engine snarl and howl beneath them.

"You in any hurry, or will it be all right if we get there sometime around noon?"

"No. No hurry." Asher settled back and watched the truck make its way through the night. He stared out the window and thought, Siiri, you'd never think of this, that I'm going out and away in plain sight. With red and yellow lights to catch your attention. And enough noise to rattle your teeth. He smothered a laugh behind his hand and watched Nebraska surge by.

"Where you going, Harmless?" the trucker yelled.

"Colorado. Mountains," Asher yelled back. The trucker said something Asher couldn't hear, so he yelled, "I'm running away from my wife."

The trucker looked at him and slapped his knee. "Harmless, you are a screw! Let me know if you get away with it." He added, seriously, "No kids left behind?"

"No. No kids. She never wanted any. She didn't like carrying on like that."

The trucker grunted understanding. Then he yelled, "What was it you said about tree frogs and rain?"

"Oh. Well, tree frogs call for rain. And sometimes it rains. They sing *whee-ee-ee*, and if they sing long enough, it rains for them."

"Where'd you learn that?"

"Books. Stories. Locusts can tell weather too. They know it'll freeze in six weeks."

The trucker shook his head and made silent laughter. He kept Asher talking until the sun had come to ten o'clock in the sky. The trucker said, "Now, Harmless, do you really want to go on to Denver? Or don't you think it would be better if I let you off somewhere on the road? You *can* work, can't you?"

"Oh, yeah. I work good and hard. You have a fine idea about letting me off before Denver. I couldn't work in a town. Where d'you think I should get out?"

"There's a dirt road somewhere up ahead," the trucker said. "It goes off to some burgs. But mostly it's ranch and farm country here. You want to take the chance of just finding work?"

"I never had to look for it before. It always came to hand natural. Seems like it was always following me around."

"See, here's the road I mean. Now, I come this way once a month. I don't mean to give advice, but if things don't work out, you come sit here and wait for me."

Asher nodded, trying to think of some good thing to say. But the words had gone dry in his mouth. So he only nodded again.

"Not that you need any help. Hell, Harmless, I act like you weren't a man. Here's a card with my name and address. You know how to write?"

Asher nodded and took the card.

"Well, you send me a postcard sometime. Let me know how you make out." He stuck out his hand, and Asher seized it. "Good luck."

Asher opened the cab door and climbed down. He stood back from the truck and waved. The trucker throttled the motor furiously and moved down the highway, blaring the horn in farewell.

How had it been with him, to make him run? He had been born and raised in a Swedish settlement in the Sandhills of Nebraska. He had been a slow baby to walk and talk. He had grown into a strong-bodied boy with wheat-colored eyes and pale, no-color hair; and he helped his father around the farm, but he was missing something inside. Not brains, for he learned how to read and write. Slowly. He learned everything slowly. And he had to be reminded of what to do next, even urged. In school he did all right if you kept at him. "Dodo," the other children called him; and he didn't resent it, if he even noticed it, for he was always that pale husk of a child who lingered at the edge of your attention.

No, it wasn't that he was short on brains, they said. There's a saying that goes: When it came time to hand out the brains, you stood behind the door and didn't get any. Well, Asher had got his share of brains. It was something else he had missed, standing behind that door when the others were out grabbing. His brain was good—look at the time he had remembered how to spell "Tyrannosaurus rex" in the science test. And he could talk, but the talk came like the spilling of grain from a sack, in bursts of fullness that were shut off in mid-sentence as if someone had closed the sack abruptly and there was more talk inside. So it wasn't brains Asher was missing. It was something else, and the lack made him a cripple.

He went through the eighth grade in that way, then quit school to stay home and work the farm with his father. He spent the next years working the fields, coming home at night to milk the cows and eat supper, listening to his father talk, reading the books his mother kept in the glass-doored cabinet: Indian lore, a book about nature with colored pictures, Greek mythology, and a book about the stars and how to tell fortunes by them. Asher's mother had been a schoolteacher before she married, and she had kept her favorite books. She was Finnish and, according to the Swedes, a little weird, for she could tell fortunes, even the weather, by the stars and with cards. She died when Asher was fifteen, but she had left so much of herself in the books that Asher didn't feel the loss.

The Davidson farm was across the road from Asher's. They had made their farm grow and spread by means that Asher's father envied. Old Man Davidson had three sons and a daughter, Siiri, and all of them worked like demons on the acres of corn, winter wheat, and sorghum. Asher's father would watch from his farm as the combines went over the tilting hills across the road; he envied the Davidsons, and yet there was something that made him tighten his fence lines.

"That's a big farm," he would say to Asher. "Gonna be the biggest in the state."

His tone made Asher come to attention for once. "Isn't it good to have a big farm, Pa?"

"Well, if you ask it like that. Yeah."

Asher waited.

"Who owns that place?" Asher's father asked.

"They all do. Don't they, Pa?"

"That's how it looks on paper. I mean, who really owns it? Never hear about the boys except as Davidson's boys. And they're all married." Seeing Asher's blank face he went on. "I mean, that's a big place. You listen to me now, boy. No place is big enough if you ain't your own man. When I go, you start to think for yourself." He meant to go on, but Asher was lost again, so he put it off until another day.

When Asher was eighteen his father died, and he was left with the mortgage-hounded farm. The crops fell off because Asher would start the day's work and then subside in the rhythm of the heat waves on a hill, he would plow late and the crop would freeze before it ripened. The farm lost money until Asher awakened to himself. He had one good year. That year he plowed early and got the crops in on time. Summer went well, and he would make back some of what he had lost.

Siiri Davidson was five years older than Asher. She would come to borrow Asher's Angus bull when a cow was in season, and she came to borrow mower blades. One night she came for no reason that Asher could see, perhaps just to visit. They went out to look at the tasseling corn, and the locusts sang their green and silver song. Asher could see the locust's vibrating bodies, the silver strutted wings that trembled with the sound. Siiri wore a dress that night, and her hair was short and soft like dandelions that have dried. She leaned on him; she was soft and full in front. She leaned on him, and it made him ache and hot. He said,

"You're too nice, Siiri." But she leaned harder, and there was an open space between her legs that smelled strong and good. She kissed him, and her tongue was like a kitten's, soft and rough, tasting of milk. She let him kiss her, and she put her tongue deeper into his mouth, let him touch her breasts. She said, "Marry me." And he said, "Yes." Then she put him inside her like you put money into a purse.

They were married the next week. Because Asher was still a minor, Mr. Davidson let him sign the mortgage over to the Davidson name; it was to protect Asher from losing the farm, he said. Asher went to live with Siiri at her father's house. Living at the Davidsons' was different from his own home. They all sat down to table, but only after the Old Man had sat down first, and they got up at his signal. That was what Asher noticed first: the Old Man gave little signals. And life ran according to those little signals: a knife laid across his plate meant that they could leave the table; the Old Man's coughing in the morning meant that they could come down for breakfast. He would talk to them at supper, and you knew when he wanted you to listen, for he would lean in your direction, not looking at you, merely leaning his head and eating through his words.

But those were the small things. There were things that Asher missed: his books, time to read them, and time just to— Asher didn't know what he wanted to do with his time, for now there was no time to spare; it was all used up. Time with Siiri was scarce, and it was only at night. They shared a room and a bed, nothing else, for she turned away from him and shamed him when he would press against her body. "No, please," she said, her back straight like a board across the bed. Once he had come against her buttocks and made her nightgown wet. She had been sick all night, even though she changed into a clean gown. And she hated it so that he couldn't get any feeling for her again. They hadn't spoken of it between themselves or to anyone else; there was only the look Siiri gave him, cold and passionless.

When he worked in the fields someone would appear on the hill to watch him. Some days it would be Siiri, and she would watch, never waving or calling to him, just watching him with her cold eyes, then going back to the house. It was that way in the barn, too; he would look up from milking and find one of them at his elbow, never speaking. And they traded looks about him with one another, shutting him out of the circle of their family and their talk. He mooned to himself more and more, unable to find a chink in the Davidsons for himself; never alone, yet lonely.

The supper table, cleared of the dishes, was the Davidsons' gathering place. Old Man Davidson would sit down at the head of the table, and one by one the rest of the family would take their places. The Old Man would outline in his dragging, heavy and light Swedish accent the long-range plans for the Davidsons. These plans were simply, Be something. Even Siiri was part of it. Be something. The farm was what they would be, and it had to be a bigger farm so they could be more and more something. "Men need to be something in our family," the Old Man said. "You work hard and put more into the farm, that's the way."

Once Siiri said, "I want to be something, too, Pa."

The Old Man leaned toward her. "Ah, now. You're a woman. Women ain't got no place in it, except to help."

"I could be something on my own, though," Siiri said. "When I was little—" She hesitated.

"Eh. Yeah, we know when you were little. That's done now, and I ain't going to hear about it anymore."

Siiri looked so worn down, sitting there with all the family covering their mouths at her, that Asher stuck his hand out to touch her. But she moved away from him and frowned.

When Siiri had been a young girl she had heard, or thought she heard, voices in the silent fields. She had gone out many days to bring the cows home; and several times in the cottonwood grove she had heard the trees echo the stillness, or were they voices? Once she had fainted in the heat; it had been a dark space in the blue day. It had been something from God, she was sure; but she told no one, keeping it as her private ecstasy. Then, when she was fourteen, she had found traces of blood where there had never been blood before. Now confident that she was chosen by God, she had gone to her parents. "I'm a child of God," she said, breathless and almost out of her senses.

"Oh. Now," her mother said.

"I am. I know. I heard voices in the fields, and now God gave me a sign." She told them where the blood was, expecting them to be awed, and that they would agree with her.

"Nay. You talk to her, Mama," said the Old Man. "The lilleh flicka is thinking wrong. You set her right." He went outside, frowning and embarrassed.

"Siiri, that blood. That's a sign, all right, but not what you think. It's only a sign that you're a woman now. You can have babies now."

"No, I don't want babies. I want to be special for God."

"Well, we all want to be special. But you ain't. Not that way. You be a good farmwife. That's good enough."

"But Pa wants me to be something. Like he wants the boys."

"Ah, Siiri. That's just for the boys. Women can't be that. You do best to marry someone who has a good farm."

Siiri looked stubborn, but her mother refused to listen to her. From then on they watched her and talked to her. "We all work the farm and make it grow, that's the best way to be something." She listened, of course, for it was said often. And she gradually believed them. But within herself she waited for that sign, and made her life a preparation for the sign. She married Asher because it was her father's wish, and she did it to please him, knowing that the marriage didn't mar her or her preparation.

Siiri had no feelings for Asher, unless they were mild scorn, for how could any real man let his farm be taken from him so easily? And he needed to be watched or he would moon away the day over a rabbit's nest instead of plowing. She had tried to pray with him, but he disappointed her by humming in the middle of a prayer, or by talking to her. Once he had pushed himself on her in a carnal way, and it disgusted her; but that's what men were, animals.

Asher had lived at the Davidsons' for over five years; they were good to him in some ways, like they bought his clothes in town and brought them home to him. But it was the watching on the hill and the grinding down on him that made him think of running away. He might have stayed, even with the grinding, but that spring the Old Man had taken over the farm next to Asher's and had pulled the fence down to make one long rich cornfield where Asher's father had always grown sorghum. And the Old Man hadn't asked Asher what he thought about the

fence. It was merely torn down. Asher had said, "How can anyone tell that's my farm?"

The Old Man answered, "Was your farm. Ain't now. *Our* farm.
Who d'you think paid the taxes this year? You?"

Asher subsided, for he had forgotten the taxes. For that matter,
he had forgotten the mortgage too. The farm was no longer his.
When you looked at it that way, nothing was his anymore. He
ran off the next morning.

Asher walked along the gravel, admiring the pole fence that
edged it, and walked to the open gate. He stopped to look around
and to wait for the ranch dogs that came yiping, plume-tailed, to
meet him. He held out his open hands to let them come close
and sniff at him; when they were sure of him, they relented their
assumed ferocity.

The house stood some fifty yards back from the road, and now
a woman came out of the doorway to stand on the porch, shading
her eyes with one hand to see who had stirred the dogs so. She
yelled something Asher couldn't understand, and he went nearer.
"Ma'am," he called.

But she was only calling the dogs by name. "Tobe, Sam, you
quit that!"

"Oh, they don't mean any harm, ma'am. Dogs just like to
come up and visit, like folks, sometimes."

"I guess they do." She laughed. "Come along there, you looking
for somebody?"

"I was wondering if you had any work I could do?"

She smiled cautiously. "You hungry?"

"No, ma'am. Not yet, anyway. I'm looking for a steady job.
Farm work."

"Oh. Well, you'd have to talk to my husband. He'll be coming
for lunch pretty soon. Sit down on the porch."

Asher sat down on the top step, inside the overhanging eaves.
"Nice cool porch you have."

"My husband built the house. He did a good job. Farm work,
you say. Let me see your hands."

Asher held out his hands, palms up, and questioned her with
his eyes.

"Well, I see you've done some hard work in your life. I always look at a man's hands," she explained. "You'd be surprised at how many young boys come here for farm work, saying they'd done it before. I look at their hands, and they're soft. No, a farming man has hard hands. Callouses and old scars."

From somewhere behind the house came the jingling and creaking of harness and horses' hooves thudding.

"Well, there he is now. You come in and wash."

Asher had washed his face and hands, smoothed back his hair, and sat down at the table when her husband came in.

"He's here to find work, Jamey," the woman said.

"Ah. You saw the ad in the newspaper?"

"No." Asher stood, and they shook hands. "Name's Asher," he said.

"Waller. Jamey Waller." Waller motioned Asher to sit down again, and they served themselves from the dishes Mrs. Waller brought to the table. "You good at farm work?"

"I was raised on a farm. Done it all my life."

"You intend to stay on permanent?"

"Yeah," Asher smiled. "I like farming."

"You ride?"

Asher was confused for a moment. Did he mean ride here from Nebraska, or ride horses? "I can ride. Not so good, maybe, but I can ride."

"I need someone who can ride good enough to help me with the stock. They're up in the summer pasture now. Come fall we'll have to bring them down. Not so many to herd, but they'll be a little woolly when we go up to get them."

Asher looked at Waller.

"I mean beef cattle, not sheep," Waller explained.

"Oh, yeah. I never worked sheep, that's all."

Waller glanced at his wife, and something passed between them. Asher could see the question and the understanding that came and went in their eyes. Waller looked at Asher. "How much do you want for pay?"

"I don't know. Never worked for money before." Asher turned hot and red at the disbelief in Waller's eyes.

"Well, you'd get your meals here. We got room upstairs or in the tack house, whichever you wanted."

Asher grinned. "I'd like the tack house."

"Well, a man's got to have some time to himself, I always say. And you wouldn't be under our feet that way." Waller grunted and drank some more coffee. "Saturday nights off. You don't drink much, do you?"

"No. Not much."

"That's good. Last man we had out here drank like prohibition was coming back. I drink some. All I want is that you don't make an ass out of yourself and can't work. Let me pay you seventy-five a month until fall. Then we'll settle it for good."

"That's fine."

Waller finished eating and sat back with a cigarette. "You come from Nebraska?"

Asher nodded, unwilling to say anything about Siiri or the farm.

"You got a family there?"

Asher shut his mouth in a determined line, not looking at Waller. There was a short silence.

"Ah-hum," Waller cleared his throat. "You aren't in any trouble that I should worry about?"

"No. You don't have to worry about me." Asher met Waller's eyes and then looked at the floor.

So Asher was set to work, that first afternoon, doing small chores around the barnyard. Waller went back to the field with the team of horses.

That night, after supper, Asher settled himself into the tack house. The Wallers had provided sheets and blankets and a change of clothes for him. He made the iron bed up and went to lie down early. He turned the light out and left the door open so he could see outside and watch the road. "Siiri, you won't come this far looking, will you?" he asked softly. But he watched the road until he fell asleep.

Waller took Asher out with him the next day to the hayfields, and they finished the mowing. Then they raked the hay and hauled it to the various hay barns. They did the milking and other chores, clearing up the barnyard, making ready for the winter ahead. And Waller would leave Asher to do chores alone without coming to watch him work.

Saturday nights they went into town together for some drinking; and, as Waller said, he did drink some. A few times Asher would have to load Waller into the box of the truck and carry him home, holding his head under the barn pump while Mrs. Waller stood by with black coffee and aspirin. Then Waller would go into the house and fall asleep.

Sunday mornings were quiet. Asher would do the milking alone while Waller slowly recuperated from the trip to town. At second breakfast, Waller would come downstairs, mumbling about his head, "My God, my eyes feel like red-hot coals. And they're burning chunks out of my skull. I got up so I wouldn't set the bed on fire."

"You need a sauna. A good hot sauna on Saturday night before you go into town, and you won't be sick the next day," Asher said.

"Sauna?"

"Yeah, like the Finns have. A steam bath. Makes your blood go better. Carries the poison out of you faster," Asher explained.

"I don't know. Just the three of us. Would it cost much?"

"No. I could build it myself from old lumber. Pa built one, and I helped him. When it's done you could have friends over. Missus could visit with them, and we go to town later."

Waller and his wife made their eyes talk again, then both smiled at Asher. "Damned good idea. You could build it?"

"Yeah. Not much money. I'll do all the work."

Sunday mornings Waller and his wife would go to church, leaving Asher alone on the ranch. These were the best times for Asher. Time of his own; and he used it to please himself by reading, or lying down in the grass and listening to the chickens as they sang in their dust baths, or he could just listen to his own blood running in and out of his heart.

This Sunday Mrs. Waller brought a small box home from the church. After dinner she opened it and showed Asher the Apache tears. "Aren't they pretty?" she asked, taking a silver chain from the box. The dusky, dark, clear stones were suspended from the chain; they were oval, tear-shaped, and reflected the light softly. "I love holding them," Mrs. Waller said.

"What are they?" Asher hung back from touching them, they had such a fragile look.

"Apache tears, they're called. They're stones." Mrs. Waller laid them on Asher's palm. "They said that these are the tears shed by the Apache maidens for their dead warriors."

Asher held the stones gently, turning his head from side to side. Something, he thought, so good. He lost all his words, even in his head, and only looked at the stones.

Mrs. Waller went on, smiling at him. "They're found in the mountains. My uncle polished them and made them into this bracelet." She took the chain and laid it next to her skin. "Don't they make my skin pretty?" The stones fell along her arm, bringing out the candle color of her flesh.

Waller grumbled at them, not cross, but reminding them of his presence. "Taking on like kids over that bracelet, you two. You going to build us a sauna, Asher?"

"Yeah, if you want. It wouldn't take long, working nights at it. I'll start the foundation tomorrow."

They decided where they wanted the bathhouse, and by working evenings, they finished it just before the fall frosts started. The first Saturday night after it was finished they had a small party for themselves. Asher heated the sauna during the day, building the heat slowly in the cast-iron stove, so that the rocks over the stove would be evenly heated. He carried water into the steam room to heat in a large steel barrel, and he brought cold water for the rinsing. The steam room was small, with benches that went up the wall like bleachers of a ball field.

Waller and his wife went in first, undressing in the outer room and going into the steam room. Mrs. Waller sat on the wooden bench gingerly, for the wood was hot. Waller mixed a bucket of hot and cold water for her; he threw cold water on the stones and made copious amounts of steam. They sat and perspired like horses, washing themselves and finally rinsing with cold water.

When they came out, dressed, Asher asked them how they liked it.

"Fine. Damn fine, Asher," Waller said, clapping him on the shoulder. "You go in next."

Waller and his wife could hear Asher singing in the sauna as they sat on the front porch of the house. "Man's a good worker," Waller said, "even if he is on the dumb side."

"You shouldn't talk like that. He's done a lot for us."

"Well, I know. And I don't hold it against him." Waller took out a bottle of Old Crow and set it on the floor beside him.

"Going to have a snort right now. See if that sauna works."

"I wonder about him sometimes. He never said anything about his home."

"I know how he got here. Came on a truck."

"How'd you find out? He didn't tell you."

"Hah, a trucker told me last week. He picked him up in Nebraska and gave him a lift here. Called him 'Harmless.' Said he'd run away from his wife."

"Oh." Mrs. Waller was shocked. Now she worried. "Was he in trouble?"

"Guess not. Trucker said no one had posted any bills."

"What kind of man would run away from his wife?"

"What kind of wife would make a man run away, I want to know." Waller took a second snort.

"He must've loved her sometime," Mrs. Waller said.

"Women." Waller sighed. "I figured it out. Loving's a lot like dying; you know you're bound to do it, but that don't mean you're going to like it. No. Nor even enjoy it." They sat quietly for some minutes, chewing that like a cud.

Mrs. Waller said, "You know, I got him a present. I thought I should because of the sauna and all. Now I wonder if I should give it to him."

"That's a daft thing to do. Give a hired hand a present. And because he did some extra work. You start that, and they'll all expect presents. Not to mention money." Waller wiped his mouth. "What difference does it make if he ran away from his wife? You can still give him the present. What'd you get?"

"Well, after what you told me, it doesn't seem right."

"Oh, hell. Takes a woman to think of right and wrong." Waller sat still. "Listen to those locusts yell. Damn few left anymore, what with the frost we had last night." He turned his head. "Hey, Asher!" he called.

"Yeah?" Asher answered.

"You in there for the night?"

"No, I'm coming right now." And Asher came out to join them on the porch.

"Damned good sauna you built." Waller offered him the bottle.

Asher took a small drink. "That's strong. I better not drink much."

"How will we find out if the sauna works? Can't tell if I'm not good and soused. Come on, keep up with me."

Asher took another drink and returned the bottle to Waller.

"Oh, Asher. I got something for you." Mrs. Waller handed a small white box to him.

Waller took another swig of the Old Crow and grinned in the dark.

Asher made his eyes open wider; he was sleepy, and the liquor had made his upper lip numb. He opened the box slowly, feeling hot and miserable. "I didn't need any present."

Mrs. Waller smiled and kneaded her hands together. "They aren't put on a chain or anything. I didn't know what you'd use them for, but I saw how you liked my Apache tears."

Asher stared at the five small stones and then at Mrs. Waller.

"You get the notions, don't you?" Waller asked. "What'll he do with them?"

"Oh, no. I like them fine, Mrs. Waller. Fine." Asher spoke hastily. "I thank you very much. You both been so fine to me."

Waller shoved the bottle at him. "Have a drink, Asher. That's something a man can always use."

Asher took a large drink this time and sat down on the porch step to look at the stones, turning them under the dark sky to see how they held even this dim light. He wouldn't do anything with the stones, he thought, only let them be like they were.

Waller was beginning to feel good. He let a long draft of the liquor pour down his gullet, then said, "Here, Harmless. Have another."

Asher ducked his head, then looked hard at Waller.

"Oh, don't get riled up. I met that trucker that gave you a ride. Nice guy. Said to say hello to you."

Asher put the stones into their box and tucked the box into his shirt pocket. He took a long pull at the bottle to start his blood going. Would he have to run again?

Waller said, "I don't much care, you see, but it sounds funny for a man to run out on his wife."

Asher scrambled off the porch. It wasn't far enough, he thought; if Waller knows, then she'll find me. He looked up at the night sky; this was a such a good place here, he thought. "I won't go back."

"Who said you had to go back? I didn't."

"You talked to Siiri?"

"No. I don't know any Siiri. That your wife?"

"Yes."

"Not much of a man if you can't handle your wife."

"Your wife, maybe," Asher said resentfully. "You go out in the field. Where's your wife? In the house. She never comes to see if you're plowing right."

"Hell, no. She doesn't know that much about plowing."

"Her father doesn't have the title to your place. He doesn't keep track of your money and your time."

"No. By God, I'd kick him off the place if he tried." Waller was astonished. "How'd he get title to your farm?"

"When we got married, I was underage. He took it over to keep it from going to the bank."

"You never got it back?"

"No. And Siiri, she didn't want me the way your wife does you." Asher paused. "You know. She prayed a lot."

"She was your wife, wasn't she? You should have done it anyway."

Asher sighed. "Well, she hated me so much I lost the feeling."

"Huh. Sounds like she was crazy."

"Her pa made her that way. He wanted to own a lot of land. He had his sons to help farm it, and their wives. And kids all over. The Old Man let them live how they wanted as long as they were on the farm."

"What was he? A Communist?"

"I don't know what church they went to. They never went to any. Only Siiri, and she had a look in her eye sometimes—" Asher let the sentence trail off.

"You sure were dumb, getting tied up that way."

"Yeah. I know I'm dumb about things."

"So you ran away."

Asher nodded.

"Well, be easy about it. I won't talk. Want another drink?"

"No. Thanks. I guess I've had enough."

"Well, I don't feel up to any more, either."

Yawning, Mrs. Waller murmured, "Good night," and went into the house.

The two men sat on the porch together, without talking. Waller shook his head and pondered the dumbness of his hired hand. Asher took the Apache tears and rubbed them with his handkerchief. After a while Waller hoisted himself up and went to bed, slamming the screen door softly against the night air. He went upstairs and crawled into the warm bed. His wife moved to make room for him, and he ran a hand under her nightgown. Her skin bunched into goose bumps, but she came to him under the blankets. Then she prodded him with her elbow.

"What was that you said out there?" she asked.

"Huh? What'd I say?" Waller weaseled himself closer; now the two of them were bound within the nightgown.

"You said you didn't enjoy love," she accused mildly, but she wasn't responding to him.

"Oh, honeybunch," Waller said, and pressed himself to her.

"No, you quit that leeching around until you tell me what you meant. You don't enjoy love, you can just quit being miserable in my bed." She stuck both elbows in his chest and knotted her knees hard against him.

Waller cursed himself and said, "Oh, I said loving's like dying. Bound to happen, but it's no guarantee you're going to enjoy it. I didn't mean you and me. I was thinking about old Asher down there. He never enjoyed any loving."

She was appeased. "You didn't mean me?"

"No. You're the best in the world." Waller settled himself on his back.

They lay snug and warm in bed for a few minutes; then Mrs. Waller said, "Well, aren't you coming over here?"

"Mhm. I kinda got out of the mood."

She whispered, "You come over here, and I'll get you in the mood."

Waller jounced over to her side of the bed, yelling, "Whoopee! I'm coming!"

Out on the porch, Asher sat and looked at his Apache tears until the chickens began their early-morning crooning. He had heard Waller whoop once, and smiled to himself. This is a nice place to be, he thought.

Winter came. The mountains at the west let snow and more snow fall until they were entirely covered, and the snow crept even to the ranch. Waller and Asher went up after the stock, returning in a few days with the bunched cattle.

Mrs. Waller came out to meet them at the feed yards. "Much snow up there?" she called.

"Enough. It was time we got there. The lakes are frozen good, even the one on our near forty. Had to chop holes to water the cattle. Won't hold any weight, though."

Asher limped over to them, leading his horse.

"What happened to your foot?"

"He fell off Blackie. Wasn't watching where he was going and got knocked off." Waller grumbled, "That wasn't enough, Blackie had to walk on him. You want to tie it up? I think a bone's broken in there."

"It don't hurt so much, only when I walk on it." Asher grinned at her, but his face was set in new lines.

"I'll tie it up. Heals faster that way." Mrs. Waller walked to the house with him and made him sit on a chair in the kitchen.

Asher pulled off his boot and held out the foot. "It smells bad, I think," he apologized.

"No matter. Waller smells like a dead skunk some nights." She washed his foot in the enamel basin and tied a white cloth around it up to the ankle. "There, if it doesn't feel better in a few days, you go into town for the doctor."

"Mrs. Waller, you're so nice."

"Oh." She laughed nervously. "You go on. You don't talk that way to married women." She blushed and emptied the basin. "Now, you sit there and eat some supper."

The next day came bright and cold. It was dead winter now, and the stream of their breath froze in crystals that hung in mid-air. Waller did most of the chores, allowing Asher only to feed the chickens and to putter in the barn. Asher's foot pained him badly, and by noon he was faint.

Waller and Asher went back to the house for lunch, pulling their boots off on the porch, and Waller opened the door to let Asher go inside first.

As Asher came into the kitchen he saw a stranger sitting at the table. Not a stranger, he thought. "Siiri," he said, and knew he hadn't run far enough.

"I'll be go to hell," whispered Waller, and stuck his arm under Asher's elbow.

"She came to get Asher," Mrs. Waller said, not certain how she felt about it. "She wants him to come home with her."

Siiri sat at the table; she wore a man's black jacket and a pair of heavy denim pants. She was pale, slender, with very short, ash-colored hair. She wore no makeup; her face was clean and barren of expression. She looked only at Asher, holding him almost by the force of her eyes. "You hurt your foot," she said. Her voice was surprisingly soft but flat.

"He had a fall," Waller said, shortly.

"I prayed for you, Asher," Siiri said, ignoring Waller.

Waller snorted and came to stand between them.

"Never mind," Mrs. Waller said. "We'll let them talk alone." She prodded Waller out of the kitchen and up the stairs.

"You don't know what she's like," Waller crabbed. "And he's so damned dumb she'll tie him up again. Praying!"

"She can't be so bad. She started to pray when we came out of the kitchen. She seems to be a real good woman."

Waller threw up his hands and sat down on the top step. He thought, No, if he's been easy here, this is where he should stay. I don't give a damn if he polishes those stones all day long.

In the kitchen, Siiri had finished praying. "You have to come home now. It isn't right to leave your wife. That's one of God's laws."

Asher was silent; he had no words, no thoughts even, only the emptiness. "How did you find me?" he managed to ask.

"It was God's will. And the girl at the truck stand remembered you. Tree frogs." Siiri smiled. "God's will," she repeated.

"I don't hear God telling me to go back."

"You'll have to come back. Pa and Arn are coming to get you."

She had spoken so calmly, as if it were all beyond his changing, that Asher felt his blood drain away and panic splintered his chest. He sat warily and watched her as she resumed praying. Then he stood up and tiptoed out of the kitchen; she'd not notice him for the time she was lost in her own distance. He went out of the house and off the front porch. He saw a car coming down the

road. He ran around the corner of the house to the barn; no time
now even to pick up his boots, so he ran sock-footed. His foot
pained him sharply, and he knew it wouldn't carry his weight
long. Hiding here at the Wallers' was futile; or anywhere along the
road, for they'd find him. If he hid anywhere away from shelter,
he would freeze before morning. Where could he go? His mind
blurred with the agony from his foot and the panic in his chest.
Nowhere was far enough.

He hobbled across the barnyard and over the fence to the
pasture. The cottonwood tree stood at one edge of the clearing,
not far from the frozen lake. He sat down under the cottonwood
tree, stretching out his crippled foot. I'll sit here and rest a minute,
he thought. He took out the Apache tears and started polishing
them.

Siiri was still praying, eyes closed, at the kitchen table when
Waller burst through the door.

"Where's Asher?" he demanded.

Siiri opened her eyes. "Why, I don't know. I suppose he went to
get his things. He's going back with me." She spoke soothingly.

"Did he say he was going back?"

"No. I didn't see him go out. But he'll come back with me."

"Well, I say he ain't going back." Waller snarled, "You just go
back without him."

"How foolish you are. He belongs to us."

"The hell he does. He stays here. Or anyplace he wants to be."
Waller glanced out the window. "That your car in my yard?"

"I suppose so. Pa and Arn came to help me."

"The hell they did." Rage filled Waller as he ran out the door,
shoving against the two men who stood on the porch.

"Where're you going?" Mrs. Waller called.

"The tack house. I got to find Asher and tell him he can stay
here." Waller ran to the tack house, but Asher wasn't there and
hadn't been there. Waller ran to the barn and searched through the
stalls, mangers, and the haymow. He ran out of the barn and
was met by Mrs. Waller and the three Davidsons. "Get out of my
way," he snarled at Siiri, and ran to the sauna.

"Not in here," he yelled, sweating hard. He looked at the Davidsons. "See this? He built it for us." He looked around the farm-

yard as if to conjure Asher up out of the air. He swore and ran to the pasture fence. The others followed at his heels, running over the pasture, calling and stopping to listen.

"Shut up a minute," Waller commanded, and they were all silent. "Look for tracks. No, stay still and let me look." He went before them, crossing and recrossing the snow cover. Then he held up a hand and followed the pattern of Asher's footprints. He stopped under the cottonwood. "He came here," he said.

"Well, where is he?" Old Man Davidson asked.

Waller grunted and moved off ahead of them; the footprints made a dark blurring to the lake. Waller stood at the edge of the lake, staring out toward the center. The tracks went on, straight out. Damn fool, Waller thought, you can't make it on that ice. He said, "He's out there."

PHILIP ROTH, short story writer and novelist, has been published in *Harper's*, *The New Yorker*, *Epoch*, *Commentary* and
others. He was represented in *Prize Stories 1960: O. Henry Awards*
and *Best American Short Stories* of 1956. He was the recipient
of the Aga Khan prize for fiction in 1958, was a Guggenheim
fellow in 1959–60 and won the National Book Award in 1960
for *Goodbye, Columbus*. His novel, *Letting Go*, was published
in 1962 by Random House.

Novotny's Pain

In the early months of the Korean War, a young man who had
been studying to be a television cameraman in a night school
just west of the Loop in Chicago was drafted into the Army and
almost immediately fell ill. He awoke one morning with a pain on
the right side of his body, directly above the buttock. When he
rolled over, it was as though whatever bones came together inside
him there were not meeting as they should. The pain, however,
was not what had awakened him; his eyes always opened themselves five minutes before the appearance in the barracks of the
Charge of Quarters. Though there was much of Army life that he
had to grit his teeth to endure, he did not have to work at getting
up on time; it simply happened to him. When it was necessary to
grit his teeth, he gritted them and did what he was told. In that
way, he was like a good many young men who suffered military
life alongside him or had suffered it before him. His sense of
shame was strong, as was his sense of necessity; the two made him
dutiful.

Also, he was of foreign extraction, and though his hard-working
family had not as yet grown fat off the fat of the land, it was
nevertheless in their grain to feel indebted to this country. Perhaps if they had been a little fatter they would have felt less indebted. As it was, Novotny believed in fighting for freedom, but

because what he himself wanted most from any government was that it should let him alone to live his life. His patriotism, then—his commitment to wearing this republic's uniform and carrying this republic's gun—was seriously qualified by his feeling of confinement and his feeling of loss, both of which were profound.

When the C.Q. got around to Novotny's bed that morning, he did not shine his flashlight into the soldier's eyes; he simply put a hand to his arm and said, "You better get yourself up, young trooper." Novotny was appreciative of this gentleness, and though, as he stepped from his bunk, the pain across his back was momentarily quite sharp, he met the day with his usual decision. Some mornings, making the decision required that he swallow hard and close his eyes, but he never failed to make it: *I am willing*. He did not know if any of those around him had equivalent decisions to make, because he did not ask. He did not mull much over motive. People were honest or dishonest, good or bad, himself included.

After dressing, he moved off with four others to the mess hall, where it was their turn to work for the day. It was still dark, and in the barracks the other recruits slept on. The previous day, the entire company had marched fifteen miserable miles with full packs, and then, when it was dark, they had dropped down on their stomachs and fired at pinpoints of light that flickered five hundred yards away and were supposed to be the gunfire of the enemy. Before they had climbed into trucks at midnight, they were ordered to attention and told in a high, whiny voice by their captain, a National Guardsman recently and unhappily called back to duty, that only one out of every fifty rounds they had fired had hit the targets. This news had had a strong effect upon the weary recruits, and the trucks had been silent all the way to the barracks, where it had been necessary for them to clean their rifles and scrape the mud from their boots before they flung themselves onto the springs of their bunks for a few hours' rest.

At the mess hall, the K.P.s were each served two large spoonfuls of Army eggs and a portion of potatoes. The potatoes had not been cooked long enough, and the taste they left on the palate was especially disheartening at such an early hour, with no light outdoors and a cold wind blowing. But Novotny did not complain. For one thing, he was occupied with finding a comfortable position in which to sit and eat—he had the pain only when he twisted the wrong way. Besides, the food was on his tray to give him strength, not pleasure. Novotny did not skip meals, no matter how ill-prepared they were, for he did not want to lose weight and be unequal to the tasks assigned him.

Before entering the Army, Novotny had worked for several years as an apprentice printer with a company that manufactured telephone books in Chicago. It had turned out to be dull work, and because he considered himself a bright and ambitious young man, he had looked around for a night school where he might learn a job with a future. He had settled on television, and for over a year he had been attending classes two evenings a week. He had a girl friend and a mother, to both of whom he had a strong attachment; his girl friend he loved, his mother he took care of. Novotny did not want to cause any trouble. On the other hand, he did not want to be killed. With his girl friend, he had been a man of passion; he dreamed of her often. He was thrifty, and had four hundred dollars in a savings account in the First Continental Bank on LaSalle Street in Chicago. He knew for a fact that he had been more adept at his work than anyone else in his television course. He hated the Army because nothing he did there was for himself.

The labors of the K.P.s began at dawn, and at midnight—light having come and gone—they were still at it. The cooks had ordered the men around all day until five in the afternoon, when the Negro mess sergeant showed up. He hung his Eisenhower jacket on a hook, rolled up the sleeves of his shirt, and said, "As there is a regimental inspection tomorrow morning, we will now get ourselves down to the fine points of housecleaning, gentlemens." The K.P.s had then proceeded to scrub the mess hall from floor to ceiling, inside and out.

A little after midnight, while Novotny was working away at the inside of a potato bin with a stiff brush and a bucket of hot, soapy water, the man working beside him began to cry. He said the sergeant was never going to let them go to sleep. The sergeant would be court-martialled for keeping them up like this. They would all get weak and sick. All Novotny knew of the fellow beside him was that his name was Reynolds and that he had been to college. Apparently, the mess sergeant only knew half that much, but that was enough; he came into the storeroom and saw Reynolds weeping into the empty potato bins. "College boy," he said, "wait'll they get you over in Korea." The sergeant delivered his words standing over them, looking down, and for the moment Novotny stopped feeling sorry for himself.

When the scrubbing was finished, Novotny and Reynolds had to carry back the potatoes, which were in garbage cans, and dump them into the bins. Reynolds began to explain to Novotny that he had a girl friend whom he was supposed to have called at ten-thirty. For some reason, Reynolds said, his not having been able to get to a phone had made him lose control. Novotny had, till then, been feeling superior to Reynolds. For all his resenting of the stupidity that had made them scrub out bins one minute so as to dump dirty potatoes back into them the next, he had been feeling somewhat in league with the sergeant. Now Reynolds' words broke through to his own unhappiness, and he was about to say a kind word to his companion when the fellow suddenly started crying again. Reynolds threw his hand up to cover his wet cheeks and dropped his end of the can. Novotny's body stiffened; with a great effort he yanked up on the can so that it wouldn't come down on Reynolds' toes. Pain cut deep across the base of Novotny's spine.

Later, he limped back to the barracks. He got into bed and counted up the number of hours he had spent scrubbing out what hadn't even needed to be scrubbed. At a dollar and a quarter an hour, he would have made over twenty dollars. Nineteen hours was as much night-school time as he had been able to squeeze into three weeks. He had known Rose Anne, his girl, for almost a year, but never had he spent nineteen consecutive hours in her company. Though once they had had twelve hours. . . . He had driven in his Hudson down to Champaign, where she was a freshman at the University of Illinois, and they had stayed together, in the motel room he had rented, from noon to midnight, not even going out for meals. He had driven her back to her dormitory, his shoelaces untied and wearing no socks. Never in his life had he been so excited.

The following week, he had been drafted.

After completing his eight weeks of basic training, Novotny was given a week's leave. His first evening home, his mother prepared a large meal and then sat down opposite him at the table and watched him eat it. After dinner, he stood under the hot shower for twenty minutes, letting the water roll over him. In his bedroom, he carefully removed the pins from a new white-on-white shirt and laid it out on the bedspread, along with a pair of Argyles, a silver tie clasp, cufflinks, and his blue suit. He polished his shoes—not for the captain's pleasure, but for his own—and chose a tie. Then he dressed for his date as he had learned to dress for a date from an article he had read in a Sunday picture magazine, while in high school, that he kept taped to the inside of his closet door. He had always collected articles having to do with how to act at parties, or dances, or on the job; his mother had never had any reason not to be proud of Novotny's behavior. She kissed him when he left the house, told him how handsome he looked, and then tears moved over her eyes as she thanked him for the government checks—for always having been a good son.

Novotny went to a movie with Rose Anne, and afterward he drove to the forest preserve where they remained until 2 A.M. In bed, later, he cursed the Army. He awoke the following morning to find that the pain, which had not troubled him for some weeks, had returned. It came and went through the next day and the following night, when once again he saw Rose Anne. Two days later, he visited the family doctor, who said Novotny had strained a muscle, and gave him a diathermy treatment. On their last night together, Rose Anne said that if writing would help, she would write not just twice a day, as was her habit, but three times a day, even four. In the dark of the forest preserve, she told Novotny that she dreamed about his body; in the dark, he told her that he dreamed of hers.

He left her weeping into a Kleenex in her dim front hallway, and drove home in a mood darker than any he had ever known. He would be killed in Korea and never see Rose Anne again, or his mother. And how unfair—for he *had* been a good son. Following his father's death, he had worked every day after school, plus Wednesday nights and Saturdays. When he had been drafted, he had vowed he would do whatever they told him to do, no matter how much he might resent it. He had kept his mouth shut and become proficient at soldiering. The better he was at soldiering, the better chance he had of coming out alive and in one piece. But that night when he left Rose Anne, he felt he had no chance at all. He would leave some part of his body on the battlefield, or come home to Rose Anne in a box. Good as he had been—industrious, devoted, stern, sacrificing—he would never have the pleasure of being a husband, or a television cameraman, or a comfort to his mother in her old age.

Five days after his return to the post—where he was to receive eight weeks of advanced infantry training, preparatory to being shipped out—he went on sick call. He sat on a long bench in the barren waiting room, and while two sullen prisoners from the stockade mopped the floor around his feet, he had his temperature taken. There were thirteen men on sick call, and they all watched the floor being washed and held thermometers under their tongues. When Novotny got to see the medic, who sat outside the doctor's office, he told him that every time he twisted or turned or stepped down on his right foot, he felt a sharp pain just above the buttock on the right side of his body. Novotny was sent back to duty with three inches of tape across his back, and a packet of APC pills.

At mail call the following morning, Novotny received a letter from Rose Anne unlike any he had ever received from her before. It was not only that her hand was larger and less controlled than usual; it was what she said. She had written down, for his very eyes to see, all those things she dreamed about when she dreamed about his body. He saw, suddenly, scenes of passion that he and she were yet to enact, moments that would not merely repeat the past but would be even deeper, even more thrilling. Oh Rose Anne—how had he found her?

Novotny's company spent the afternoon charging around with fixed bayonets—crawling, jumping up, racing ahead, through fences, over housetops, down into trenches—screaming murderously all the while. At one point, leaping from a high wall, Novotny almost took his eye out with his own bayonet; he had been dreaming of his beautiful future.

The next morning, he walked stiffly to sick call and asked to see the doctor. When, in response to a question, he said it was his back that hurt him, the medic who was interviewing him replied sourly, "Everybody's back hurts." The medic told Novotny to take off his shirt so that he could lay on a few more inches of tape. Novotny asked if he could please see the doctor for just a minute. He was informed that the doctor was only seeing men with temperatures of a hundred or more. Novotny had no temperature, and he returned to his unit, as directed.

On the seventh weekend, with only one more week of training left, Novotny was given a seventy-two-hour pass. He caught a plane to Chicago and a bus to Champaign, carrying with him only a small ditty bag and Rose Anne's impassioned letter. Most of Friday, most of Saturday, and all day Sunday, Rose Anne wept, until Novotny was more miserable than he had ever imagined a man could be. On Sunday night, she held him in her arms and he proceeded to tell her at last of how he had been mistreated by the medic; till then he had not wanted to cause her more grief than she already felt. She stroked his hair while he told how he had not even been allowed to see a doctor. Rose Anne wept and said the medic should be shot. They had no right to send Novotny to Korea if they wouldn't even look after his health here at home. What would happen to him if his back started to act up in the middle of a battle? How could he take care of himself? She raised many questions—rational ones, irrational ones, but none that Novotny had not already considered himself.

Novotny travelled all night by train so as to be back at the base by reveille. He spent most of the next day firing a Browning automatic, and the following morning, when he was to go on K.P., he could not even lift himself from his bed, so cruel was the pain in his back.

In the hospital, the fellow opposite Novotny had been in a wheelchair for two years with osteomyelitis. Every few months, they shortened his legs; nevertheless, the disease continued its slow ascent. The man on Novotny's right had dropped a hand grenade in basic training and blown bits of both his feet off. Down at the end of Novotny's aisle lay a man who had had a crate full of ammunition tip off a truck onto him, and the rest of the men in the ward, many of whom were in the hospital to learn to use prosthetic devices, had been in Korea.

The day after Novotny was assigned to the ward, the man the
crate had fallen on was wheeled away to be given a myelogram. He
came back to the ward holding his head in his hands. As soon as
Novotny was able to leave his bed, he made his way over to this fellow's bed, and because he had heard that the man's condition had
been diagnosed as a back injury, he asked him how he was feeling.
He got around to asking what a myelogram was, and why he had
come back to the ward holding his head. The fellow was talkative
enough, and told him that they had injected a white fluid directly
into his spine and then X-rayed him as the fluid moved down
along the vertebrae, so as to see if the spinal discs were damaged.
He told Novotny that apparently it was the stuff injected into him
that had given him the headache, but then he added that, lousy
as he had felt, he considered himself pretty lucky. He had heard
of cases, he said, where the needle had slipped. Novotny had
himself heard of instances where doctors had left towels and
sponges inside patients, so he could believe it. The man said that
all the needle had to do was go off by a hairbreadth and it would
wind up in the tangle of nerves leading into the spine. Two days
later, two damaged discs were cut out of the man with the injured back, and three of his vertebrae were fused together. All
through the following week he lay motionless in his bed.

One evening earlier, while Novotny was still restricted to bed,
he had been visited by Reynolds. Reynolds had come around to
say goodbye; the entire outfit was to be flown out the next
day. Since Reynolds and Novotny hardly knew each other, they
had been silent after Reynolds spoke of what was to happen to
him and the others the following day. Then Reynolds had said
that Novotny was lucky to have developed back trouble when he
did; he wouldn't have minded a touch of it himself. Then he
left.

When Novotny was out of bed and walking around, X-rays
were taken of his back, and the doctors told him they showed
no sign of injury or disease; there was a slight narrowing of the
intervertebral space between what they referred to on the pictures
as L-1 and L-2, but nothing to suggest damage to the disc—which
was what Novotny had worked up courage to ask them about.
The doctors took him into the examination room and bent him
forward and backward. They ran a pin along his thigh and calf

and asked if he felt any sensation. They laid him down on a table and, while they slowly raised his leg, asked if he felt any pain. When his leg was almost at a ninety-degree angle with his body, Novotny thought that he did feel his pain, and remembered the misery of no one's taking it seriously but himself. Then he thought of all the men around him who hobbled on artificial limbs during the day and moaned in their beds at night, and he said nothing. Consequently, they sent him back to duty.

He was shunted into an infantry company that was in its seventh week of advanced training. Two days before the company was to be shipped out, he awoke in the morning to discover that the pain had returned. He was able to limp to sick call, where he found on duty the unsympathetic medic, who, almost immediately upon seeing Novotny, began to unwind a roll of three-inch tape. Novotny raised an objection, and an argument ensued, which was settled when the doctor emerged from behind his door. He ordered Novotny into his office and had him strip. He told him to bend forward and touch his toes. Novotny tried, but could come only to within a few inches of them. The doctor looked over Novotny's medical record and then asked if he expected the Army to stand on its head because one soldier couldn't touch his toes. He asked him what he expected the Army to do for him. The doctor said there were plenty of G.I.s with sore backs in Korea. And with worse. Plenty worse.

Though the pain diminished somewhat during the day, it returned the next morning with increased severity. Novotny could by this time visualize his own insides—he saw the bone as white, and the spot where the pain was located as black. At breakfast, he changed his mind three times over, then went off to the first sergeant to ask permission to go on sick call. He had decided finally that if he did not go and have the condition taken care of within the next few days it would simply get worse and worse; surely there would be no time for medical attention, no proper facilities, while they were in transit to Korea. And, once in Korea, those in charge would surely be even more deaf to his complaints than they were here; there they would be deafened by the roar of cannons. The first sergeant asked Novotny what the matter was this time, and he answered that his back hurt. The first sergeant said what the medic had said the first day: "Everybody's back hurts." But he let him go.

At sick call, the doctor sat Novotny down and asked him what *he* thought was wrong with him. What the suffering soldier had begun to think was that perhaps he had cancer or leukemia. It was really in an effort to minimize his complaint that he said that maybe he had a slipped disc. The doctor said that if Novotny had slipped a disc he wouldn't even be able to walk around. Novotny suddenly found it difficult to breathe. What had he done in life to deserve this? What had he done, from the day he had grown out of short pants, but everything that was asked of him? He told the doctor that all he knew was that he had a pain. He tried to explain that taping it up didn't seem to work; the pain wasn't on the surface but deep inside his back. The doctor said it was deep inside his head. When the doctor told him to go back to duty like a man, Novotny refused.

Novotny was taken to the hospital, and to the office of the colonel in charge of orthopedics. He was a bald man with weighty circles under his eyes and a very erect carriage, who looked to have lived through a good deal. The colonel asked Novotny to sit down and tell him about the pain. Novotny, responding to a long-suffering quality in the man that seemed to him to demand respect, told him the truth: he had rolled over one morning during his basic training, and there it had been, deep and sharp. The colonel asked Novotny if he could think of anything at all that might have caused the pain. Novotny recounted what had happened on K.P. with Reynolds. The doctor asked if that had occurred before the morning he had awakened with the pain, or after it. Novotny admitted that it was after. But surely, he added, that must have aggravated the pain. The doctor said that that did not clear up the problem of where the pain had come from in the first place. He reminded Novotny that the X-rays showed nothing. He ordered Novotny to take off his hospital blues and stretch out on the examination table. By this time, of course, Novotny knew all the tests by heart; once, in fact, he anticipated what he was about to be asked to do, and the colonel gave him a strange look.

When the doctor was finished, he told Novotny that he had a lumbosacral strain with some accompanying muscle spasm. Nothing more. It was what they used to call a touch of lumbago. Novotny stood up to leave, and the colonel informed him that when he was released from the hospital he would have to appear at a summary court-martial for having refused to obey the doctor's order to return to duty. Novotny felt weak enough to faint. He was suddenly sorry he had ever opened his mouth. He was ashamed. He heard himself explaining to the colonel that he had refused to obey only because he had felt too sick to go back to duty. The colonel said it was for a trained doctor to decide how sick or well Novotny was. But, answered Novotny—hearing the gates to the stockade slamming shut behind him, imagining prison scenes so nasty even he couldn't endure them—but the doctor had made a mistake. As the colonel said, he *did* have a lumbosacral strain, and muscle spasm, too. In a steely voice, the colonel told him that there were men in Korea who had much worse. That was the statement to which Novotny had no answer; it was the statement that everyone finally made to him.

When they put him in traction, he had further premonitions of his court-martial and his subsequent internment in the stockade. He, Novotny, who had never broken a law in his life. What was happening? Each morning, he awoke at the foot of the bed, pulled there by the weights tied to his ankles and hanging to the floor. His limbs and joints ached day in and day out from being stretched. More than once, he had the illusion of being tortured for a crime he had not committed, although he knew that the traction was therapeutic. At the end of a week, the weights were removed and he was sent to the physical-therapy clinic, where he received heat treatments and was given a series of exercises to perform. Some days, the pain lessened almost to the point of disappearing. Other days, it was as severe as it had ever been. Then he believed that they would have to cut him open, and it would be the doctor at sick call who would be court-martialled instead of himself. When the pain was at its worst, he felt vindicated; but then, too, when it was at its worst he was most miserable.

He was only alone when he was in the bathroom, and it was there that he would try to bend over and touch his toes. He repeated and repeated this, as though it were a key to something. One day, thinking himself alone, he had begun to strain toward his toes when he was turned around by the voice of the osteomyelitis victim, who was sitting in the doorway in his wheelchair. "How's your backache, buddy?" he said, and wheeled sharply away. Everybody in the ward somehow knew bits of Novotny's history; nobody, nobody knew the whole story.

Nobody he didn't know liked him; and he stopped liking those he did know. His mother appeared at the hospital two weeks after his admittance. She treated him like a hero, leaving with him a shoebox full of baked goods and a Polish sausage. He could not bring himself to tell her about his court-martial; he could not disappoint her—and that made him angry. He was even glad to see her go, lonely as he was. Then, the following weekend, Rose Anne arrived. Everybody whistled when she walked down the ward. And he was furious at her—but for what? For being so desirable? So perfect? They argued, and Rose Anne went back to Champaign, bewildered. That night, the Negro fellow next to Novotny, who had lost his right leg in the battle of Seoul, leaned over the side of his bed and said to him, with a note in his voice more dreamy than malicious, "Hey, man, you got it made."

The next day, very early, Novotny went to the hospital library and searched the shelves until he found a medical encyclopedia. He looked up "slipped disc." Just as he had suspected, many of his own symptoms were recorded there. His heart beat wildly as he read of the difficulties of diagnosing a slipped disc, even with X-rays. Ah yes, only the myelogram was certain. He read on and on, over and over, symptoms, treatments, and drugs. One symptom he read of was a tingling sensation that ran down the back of the leg and into the foot, caused by pressure of the herniated disc on a nerve. The following morning, he awoke with a tingling sensation that ran down the back of his right leg and into his foot. Only momentarily was he elated; then it hurt.

On his weekly ward rounds, the colonel, followed by the nurse and the resident, walked up to each bed and talked to the patient; everyone waited his turn silently, as in formation. The colonel examined stumps, incisions, casts, prosthetic devices, and then asked each man how he felt. When he reached Novotny, he asked him to step out of bed and into the aisle, and there he had him reach down and touch his toes. Novotny tried, bending and bending. Someone in the ward called out, "Come on, Daddy, you can do it." Another voice called, "Push, Polack, *push*"—and then it seemed to him that all the patients in the ward were shouting and laughing, and the colonel was doing nothing to restrain them. "Ah, wait'll they get you in Korea"—and then suddenly the ward was silent, for Novotny was straightening up, his face a brilliant red. "I can't do it, sir," he said. "Does your back feel better?" the colonel asked. "Yes, sir." "Do you think we should send you back to duty?" "I've had a tingling sensation down the back of my right leg," Novotny said. "So?" the colonel asked. The ward was silent; Novotny decided not to answer.

In the afternoon, Novotny was called to the colonel's office. He walked there without too much difficulty—but then it was not unusual for the pain to come and go and come back again, with varying degrees of severity. Sometimes the cycle took hours, sometimes days, sometimes only minutes. It was enough to drive a man crazy.

In the colonel's office, Novotny was told that he was going to get another chance. Novotny was too young, the colonel said, not to be extended a little forgiveness for his self-concern. If he went back to duty, the charges against him would be dismissed and there would be no court-martial. The colonel said that with a war on there was nothing to be gained by putting a good soldier behind bars. The colonel let Novotny know that he was impressed by his marksmanship record, which he had taken the trouble to look up in the company files.

When it was Novotny's turn to speak, he could only think to ask if the colonel believed the tingling sensation in his leg meant nothing at all. The colonel, making it obvious that it was patience he was displaying, asked Novotny what *he* thought it meant. Novotny said he understood it to be a sympton of a slipped disc. The colonel asked him how he knew that, and Novotny—hesitating only a moment, then going on with the truth, on and on with it—said that he had read it in a book. The colonel, his mouth turning down in disgust, asked Novotny if he was that afraid of going to Korea. Novotny did not know what to answer; he truly had not thought of it that way before. The colonel then asked him if he ever broke out in a cold sweat at night. Novotny said no—the only new symptom he had was the tingling in the leg. The colonel brought a fist down on his desk and told Novotny

that the following day he was sending him over to see the psychiatrist. He could sit out the rest of the war in the nuthouse.

What to do? Novotny did not know. It was not a cold but a hot
sweat that he was in all through dinner. In the evening, he walked
to the Coke machine in the hospital basement, as lonely as he had
ever been. A nurse passed him in the hall and smiled. She thought
he was sick. He drank his Coke, but when he saw two wheelchairs
headed his way he turned and moved up the stairs to the hospital
library. He began to perspire again, and then he set about looking
through the shelves for a book on psychology. Since he knew as
little about psychology as he did about medicine, he had to look
for a very long time. He did not want to ask for the help of the
librarian, even though she was a civilian. At last he was able to
pick out two books, and he sat down on the floor between the
stacks, where nobody could see him.

Much of what he read he did not completely follow, but once
in a while he came upon an anecdote, and in his frustration with
the rest of the book, he would read that feverishly. He read of a
woman in a European country who had imagined that she was
pregnant. She had swelled up, and then, after nine months, she
had had labor pains—but no baby. Because it had all been in her
imagination. *Her imagination had made her swell up!* Novotny
read this over several times. He was respectful of facts, and believed what he found in books. He did not believe that a man
would take the time to sit down and write a book so as to tell
other people lies.

When he walked back to the ward, his back seemed engulfed
in flames. It was then that he became absorbed in the fantasy of
reaching inside himself and cutting out of his body the offending
circle of pain. He saw himself standing over his own naked back
and twisting down on an instrument that resembled the little
utensil that is sold in dime stores to remove the core of a grape-
fruit. In his bed, he could not find a position in which the pain
could be forgotten or ignored. He got up and went to the phone
booth, where he called long distance to Rose Anne. He could
barely prevent himself from begging her to get on a plane and
fly down to him that very night. And yet—the darkness, his fright,
his fatigue were taking their toll—if it wasn't his back that was

causing the pain, was it Rose Anne? Was he being punished for
being so happy with her? Were they being punished for all that
sex? Unlike his mother, he was not the kind of Catholic who
believed in Hell; he was not the kind who was afraid of sex.
All he wanted was his chance at life. That was all.

In the washroom, before he returned to bed, he tried to touch
his toes. He forced himself down and down and down until his
eyes were cloudy from pain and his fingers had moved to within
an inch of the floor. But he could not keep his brain from working, and he did not know what to think. If a woman could imagine
herself to be in labor, then for him, too, anything was possible.
He leaned over the sink and looked into the mirror. With the
aid of every truthful cell in his pained body, he admitted to his
own face that he was—yes, he was—frightened of going to Korea.
Terribly frightened. But wasn't everybody? He wondered if nothing could be wrong with him. He wondered if nothing he knew
was so.

The next day, the psychiatrist asked Novotny if he felt nervous.
He said he didn't. The psychiatrist asked if he had felt nervous
before he had come into the Army. Novotny said no, that he had
been happy. He asked if Novotny was afraid of high places, and
if he minded being in crowds; he asked if he had any brothers
and sisters, and which he liked better, his mother or his father.
Novotny answered that his father was dead. He asked which
Novotny had liked better before his father died. Novotny did not
really care to talk about this subject, particularly to someone he
didn't even know, but he had decided to be as frank and truthful with the psychiatrist as it was still possible for him to be—at
least, he meant to tell him what he *thought* was the truth.
Novotny answered that his father had been lazy and incompetent,
and the family was finally better off with him gone. The psychiatrist then asked Novotny about Rose Anne. Novotny was frank.
He asked Novotny if his back hurt when he was being intimate
with Rose Anne. Novotny answered that sometimes it did and
sometimes it didn't. He asked Novotny if, when it did hurt, they
ceased being intimate. Novotny dropped his head. It was with a
searing sense that some secret had been uncovered, something he
himself had not even known, that he admitted that they did not.
He simply could not bring himself, however, to tell the psychiatrist

what exactly they did do when Novotny's back was at its worst.
He said quickly that he planned to marry Rose Anne—that he
had always known he would marry her. The psychiatrist asked
where the couple would live, and Novotny said with his mother.
When he asked Novotny why, Novotny said because he had to
take care of her, too.

The psychiatrist made Novotny stand up, close his eyes, and
try to touch the tips of his index fingers together. While Novotny's
eyes were closed, the psychiatrist leaned forward and, in a whisper, asked if Novotny was afraid of dying. The weight of all that
he had been put through in the past weeks came down upon
the shoulders of the young soldier. He broke down and admitted
to a fear of death. He began to weep and to say that he didn't
want to die. The psychiatrist asked him if he hated the Army, and
he admitted that he did.

The psychiatrist's office was across the street from the main hospital, in the building the colonel had called the nuthouse. Novotny, full of shame, was led out of the building by an attendant
with a large ring of keys hooked to his belt; he had to unlock
three doors before Novotny got out to the street. He went out
the rear door, just in sight of a volleyball game that was being
played within a wire enclosure at the back of the building. To
pull himself together before returning to the hostile cripples in
the ward, Novotny watched the teams bat the ball back and forth
over the net, and then he realized that they were patients who
spent their days and nights inside the building from which he
had just emerged. It occurred to him that the doctors were going
to put him into the psychiatric hospital. Not because he was making believe he had a pain in his back—which, he had come to
think, was really why they had been going to put him in the stockade—but precisely because he was *not* making believe. He was
feeling a pain for which there was no cause. He had a terrible
vision of Rose Anne having to come here to visit him. She was
only a young girl, and he knew that it would frighten her so
much to be led through three locked doors that he would lose
her. He was about to begin to lose things.

He pulled himself straight up—he had been stooping—and
clenched his teeth and told himself that in a certain number of

seconds the pain would be gone for good. He counted to thirty, and then took a step. He came down upon his right foot with only half his weight, but the pain was still there, so sharp that it made his eyes water. The volleyball smashed against the fence through which he was peering, and, trying to walk as he remembered himself walking when he was a perfectly healthy young man, a man with nothing to fear—a man, he thought, who had not even begun to know of all the confusion growing up inside him —he walked away.

The colonel had Novotny called to his office the following day. The night before, Novotny had got little sleep, but by dawn he had reached a decision. Now, though he feared the worst, he marched to the colonel's office with a plan of action held firmly in mind. When Novotny entered, the colonel asked him to sit down, and proceeded to tell him of his own experiences in the Second World War. He had flown with an airborne division at a time when he was only a little more that Novotny's age. He had jumped from a plane over Normandy and broken both his legs, and then been shot in the chest by a French farmer for a reason he still did not understand. The colonel said that he had returned from Korea only a week before Novotny had entered the hospital. He wished that Novotny could see what the men there were going through—he wished Novotny could be witness to the bravery and the courage and the comradery, and, too, to the misery and suffering. The misery of our soldiers and of those poor Koreans! He was not angry with Novotny personally; he was only trying to tell him something for his own good. Novotny was too young to make a decision that might disgrace him for the rest of his life. He told the young soldier that if he walked around with that back of his for a few weeks, if he just stopped *thinking* about it all the time, it would be as good as new. That, in actual fact, it was almost as good as new right now. He said that Novotny's trouble was that he was a passive-aggressive.

Novotny's voice was very thin when he asked the colonel what he meant. The colonel read to him what the psychiatrist had written. It was mostly the answers that Novotny had given to the psychiatrist's questions; some of it had to do with the way Novotny had sat, and the tone of his voice, and certain words he had apparently used. In the end, the report said that Novotny was a passive-aggressive and recommended he be given an administrative separation from the Army, and the appropriate discharge. Novotny asked what that meant. The colonel replied that the appropriate discharge as far as he was concerned was "plain and simple"; he took down a book of regulations from a shelf behind him, and after flipping past several pages read to Novotny in a loud voice. " 'An undesirable discharge is an administrative separation from the service under conditions other than honorable. It is issued for unfitness, misconduct, or security reasons.' " He looked up, got no response, and, fiery-eyed, read further. " 'It is recognized that all enlisted personnel with behavior problems cannot be rehabilitated by proper leadership and/or psychiatric assistance. It is inevitable that a certain percentage of individuals entering the service subsequently will demonstrate defective moral habits, irresponsibility, inability to profit by experience—' " He paused to read the last phrase again, and then went on—" 'untrustworthiness, lack of regard for the rights of others, and inability to put off pleasures and impulses of the moment.' " He engaged Novotny's eye. " 'Often,' " he said, returning to the regulation, " 'these individuals show poor performance despite intelligence, superficial charm, and a readiness to promise improvement. The effective leader is able to rehabilitate only the percentage of persons with behavior problems who are amenable to leadership.' " He stopped. "You can say that again," he mumbled, and pushed the book forward on his desk so that it faced Novotny. "Unfitness, soldier," he said, tapping his finger on the page. "It's what we use to get the crackpots out—bed-wetters, homos, petty thieves, malingerers, and so on." He waited for Novotny to take in the page's contents, and while he did, the colonel made it clear that such a discharge followed a man through life. Novotny, raising his head slightly, asked again what a passive-aggressive was. The colonel looked into his eyes and said, "Just another kind of coward."

What Novotny had decided in bed the night before was to request a myelogram. Of course, there lived still in his imagination the man who had said that all the needle had to do was be off by a hairbreadth; he was convinced, in fact, that something like that was just what would happen to him, given the way things had begun to go in his life. But though such a prospect frightened him, he did not see that he had any choice. The truth had to be known, one way or the other. But when the colonel finished and waited for him to speak, he remained silent.

"What do you have against the Army, Novotny?" the colonel asked. "What makes you so special?"

Novotny did not mention the myelogram. Why *should* he? Why should he have to take so much from people when he had an honest-to-God pain in his back? He was not imagining it, he was not making it up. He had practically ruptured himself when Reynolds had dropped the end of the can of potatoes. Maybe he had only awakened with a simple strain that first morning, but trying to keep the can from dropping on Reynolds' toes, he had done something serious to his back. That all the doctors were unable to give a satisfactory diagnosis did not make his pain any less real.

"You are a God-damned passive-aggressive, young man, what do you think of that?" the colonel said.

Novotny did not speak.

"You know how many people in America have low back pain?" the colonel demanded. "Something like fifteen per cent of the adult population of this country has low back pain—and what do you think they do, quit? Lay down on the job? What do you think a man does who has a family and responsibilities—stop supporting them? You know what your trouble is, my friend? You think life owes you something. You think something's coming to you. I spotted you right off, Novotny. You're going to get your way in this world. Everybody else can go to hell, just so long as you have your way. Imagine if all those men in Korea, if they all give in to every little ache and pain. Imagine if that was what our troops had done at Valley Forge, or Okinawa. Then where would we all be? Haven't you ever heard of self-sacrifice? The average man, if you threatened him with this kind of discharge, would do just about anything he could to avoid it. But not you. Even if you have pain, haven't you got the guts to go ahead and serve like everybody else? Well, answer me, yes or no?"

But Novotny would not answer. All he had done was answer people and tell them the truth, and what had it got him? What good was it, being good? What good was it, especially if at bottom you were bad anyway? What good was it, acting strong, if at bottom you were weak and couldn't *be* strong if you wanted to? With the colonel glaring across at him, the only solace Novotny had was to think that nobody knew any more about him than he himself did. Whatever anybody chose to call him didn't really mean a thing.

"Ah, get out of my sight," the colonel said. "People like you make me sick. Go ahead, join the bed-wetters and the queers. Get the hell out of here."

Within six days, the Army had rid itself of Novotny. It took Novotny, however, a good deal more than six days to rid himself of infirmity, if he can be said ever to have rid himself of infirmity —or, at least, the threat of infirmity. During the next year, he missed days of work and evenings of night school, and spent numerous weekends on a mattress supported by a bed board, where he rested and nursed away his pain. He went to one doctor who prescribed a set of exercises, and another who prescribed a steel brace, which Novotny bought but found so uncomfortable that he finally had to stick it away in the attic, though it had cost forty-five dollars. Another doctor, who had been recommended to him, listened to his story, then simply shrugged his shoulders; and still another told Novotny what the colonel had— that many Americans had low back ailments, that they were frequently of unknown origin, and that he would have to learn to live with it.

That, finally, was what he tried to do. Gradually, over the years, the pain diminished in severity and frequency, though even today he has an occasional bad week, and gets a twinge if he bends the wrong way or picks up something he shouldn't. He is married to Rose Anne and is employed as a television cameraman by a educational channel in Chicago. His mother lives with him and his wife in Park Forest. For the most part, he leads a quiet, ordinary sort of life, though his attachment to Rose Anne is still marked by an unusual passion. When the other men in Park Forest go bowling on Friday nights, Novotny stays home, for he tries not to put strains upon his body to which he has decided it is not equal. In a way, all the awfulness of those Army days has boiled down to that—no bowling. There are nights, of course, when Novotny awakens from a dead sleep to worry in the dark about the future. What will happen to him? What won't? But surely those are questions he shares with all men, sufferers of low back pain and non-sufferers alike. Nobody has ever yet asked to see his discharge papers, so about that the colonel was wrong.

WALLACE STEGNER has been a professor of English at Stanford University since 1945 and is the author of numerous books, some of the most recent being *Beyond the Hundreth Meridian, The City of the Living,* and *A Shooting Star.* He is a frequent contributor to magazines and was the first prize winner of the O. Henry Short Story Awards in 1950.

Carrion Spring

The moment she came to the door she could smell it, not really rotten and not coming from any particular direction, but sweetish, faintly sickening, sourceless, filling the whole air the way a river's water can taste of weeds—the carrion smell of a whole country breathing out in the first warmth across hundreds of square miles.

Three days of chinook had uncovered everything that had been under snow since November. The yard lay discolored and ugly, grey ash pile, rusted cans, spilled lignite, bones. The clinkers that had given them winter footing to the privy and stable lay in raised grey wavers across the mud; the strung lariats they had used for lifelines in blizzardy weather had dried out and sagged to the ground. Muck was knee-deep down in the corrals by the sod-roofed stable, the whitewashed logs were yellowed at the corners from dogs lifting their legs against them. Sunken drifts around the hay yard were a reminder of how many times the boys had had to shovel out there to keep the calves from walking into the stacks across the top of the snow. Across the wan and disheveled yard the willows were bare, and beyond them the floodplain hill was brown. The sky was roiled with grey cloud.

Matted, filthy, lifeless, littered, the place of her winter imprisonment was exposed, ugly enough to put gooseflesh up her backbone, and with the carrion smell over all of it. It was like a bad and disgusting wound, infected wire cut, or proud flesh, or the gangrene of frostbite, with the bandage off. With her

From *Wolf Willow* by Wallace Stegner. Copyright © 1962 by Wallace Stegner. Reprinted by permission of The Viking Press, Inc. Originally published in *Esquire.*

packed trunk and her telescope bag and two loaded grain sacks
behind her, she stood in the door waiting for Ray to come with
the buckboard, and she was sick to be gone.

Yet when he did come, with the boys all slopping through
the mud behind him, and they threw her trunk and telescope
and bags into the buckboard and tied the tarp down and there
was nothing left to do but go, she faced them with a sudden
desolating desire to cry. She laughed, and caught her lower lip
under her teeth and bit down hard on its trembling and went
around to shake one hooflike hand after the other, staring into
each face in turn and seeing in each something that made it
all the harder to say something easy. Good-by. Red-bearded, black-
bearded, grey-bristled, clean-shaven (for her?), two of them with
puckered sunken scars on the cheekbones, all of them seedy, mat-
haired, weathered and cracked as old lumber left out for years,
they looked sheepish, or sober, or cheerful, and said things like,
"Well, Molly, have you a nice trip, now," or "See you in Malta
maybe." They had been her family. She had looked after them,
fed them, patched their clothes, unraveled old socks to knit them
new ones, cut their hair, lanced their boils, tended their wounds.
Now it was like the gathered-in family parting at the graveside
after someone's funeral.

She had begun to cry quite openly. She pulled her cheeks
down, opened her mouth, dabbed at her eyes with her knuckles,
laughed. "Now you all take care," she said. "And come see us,
you hear? Jesse? Rusty? Slip? Ed? Buck, when you come I'll
sure fix you a better patch on your pants than that one. Good-
by, Panguingue, you were the best man I had on the coal scuttle.
Don't you forget me. Little Horn, I'm *sorry* we ran out of pie
fixings. When you come to Malta I'll make you a peach pie a
yard across."

She could not have helped speaking their names, as if to name
them were to insure their permanence. But she knew that though
she might see them, or most of them, when Ray brought the
drive in to Malta in July, these were friends lost for good.
They had already got the word: sweep the range and sell everything—steers, bulls, calves, cows—for whatever it would bring. Put
a For Sale sign on the ranch, or simply abandon it. The country
had rubbed its lesson in. Like half the outfits between the Milk

and the CPR, the T-Down was quitting. As for her, she was
quitting first.

She saw Ray slumping, glooming down from the buckboard
seat with the reins wrapped around one gloved hand. Dude and
Dinger were hipshot in the harness. As Rusty and Little Horn
gave Molly a hand up to climb the wheel, Dude raised his tail
and dropped a bundle of dung on the singletree, but she did not
even bother to make a face or say something provoked and joking.
She was watching Ray, looking right into his grey eyes and his
somber dark face and seeing all at once what the winter of disaster
had done to him. His cheek, like Ed's and Rusty's, was puckered
with frost scars; frost had nibbled at the lobes of his ears; she
could see the strain of bone-cracking labor, the bitterness of failure, in the lines from his nose to the corners of his mouth. Making
room for her, he did not smile. With her back momentarily to
the others, speaking only for him, she said through her tight
teeth, "Let's git!"

Promptly—he was always prompt and ready—he plucked whip
from whipsocket. The tip snapped on Dinger's haunch, the lurch
of the buggy threw her so that she could cling and not have to
turn to reveal her face. "Good-by!" she cried, more into the collar
of her mackinaw than to them, throwing the words over her
shoulder like a flower or a coin, and tossed her left hand in the
air and shook it. The single burst of their voices chopped off into
silence. She heard only the grate of the tires in gravel; beside
her the wheel poured yellow drip. She concentrated on it, fighting
her lips that wanted to blubber.

"This could be bad for a minute," Ray said. She looked up.
Obediently she clamped thumb and finger over her nose. To
their right, filling half of Frying Pan Flat, was the boneyard,
two acres of carcasses scattered where the boys had dragged them
after skinning them out when they found them dead in the brush.
It did not seem that off there they could smell, for the chinook
was blowing out in light airs from the west. But when she let
go her nose she smelled it rich and rotten, as if it rolled upwind
the way water runs upstream in an eddy.

Beside her, Ray was silent. The horses were trotting now in the
soft sand of the patrol trail. On both sides the willows were
gnawed down to stubs, broken and mouthed and gummed off by

starving cattle. There was floodwater in the low spots, and the sound of running water under the drifts of every side coulee.

Once Ray said, "Harry Willis says a railroad survey's coming right up the Whitemud Valley this summer. S'pose that'll mean homesteaders in here, maybe a town."

"I s'pose."

"Make it a little easier when you run out of prunes, if there was a store at Eastend."

"Well," she said, "we won't be here to run out," and then immediately, as she caught a whiff that gagged her, "Pee-you! Hurry up!"

Ray did not touch up the team. "What for?" he said. "To get to the next one quicker?"

She appraised the surliness of his voice, and judged that some of it was general disgust and some of it was aimed at her. But what did he want? Every time she made a suggestion of some outfit around Malta or Chinook where he might get a job he humped his back and looked as impenetrable as a rock. What *did* he want? To come back here and take another licking? When there wasn't even a cattle outfit left, except maybe the little ones like the Z-X and the Lazy-S? And where one winter could kill you, as it had just killed the T-Down? She felt like yelling at him, "It isn't *me!* I could stand it. Maybe I wouldn't like it, but I could stand it. But it just makes me sick to see you work yourself to death for nothing. Look at your face. Look at your hands—you can't open them even halfway, for calluses. For what? Maybe three thousand cattle left out of ten thousand, and them skin and bone. Why wouldn't I be glad to get out? Who *cares* if there's a store in Eastend? You're just like an old bulldog with his teeth clinched in somebody's behind, and it'll take a pry bar to make you unclinch!" But she said nothing; she made herself breathe the tainted air evenly.

Floodwater forced them out of the bottoms and up onto the second floodplain. Below them Molly saw the water astonishingly wide, pushing across willow bars and pressing deep into the cutbank bends. She could hear it, when the wheels went quietly—a hushed roar like wind. Cattle were balloonily afloat in the bush where they had died. She saw a brindle longhorn waltz around the deep water of a bend with his legs in the air, and farther on a whiteface that stranded momentarily among flooded rose bushes, and rotated free, and stranded again.

Their bench was cut by a side coulee, and they tipped and rocked down, the rumps of the horses back against the dashboard, Ray's hand on the brake, the shoe screeching mud from the tires. There was brush in the bottom, and stained drifts still unmelted. Their wheels sank in slush, she hung to the seat rail, they righted, the lines cracked across the muscling rumps as the team dug in and lifted them out of the cold, snowbank breath of the draw. Then abruptly, in a hollow on the right, dead eyeballs stared at her from between spraddled legs, horns and tails and legs were tangled in a starved mass of bone and hide not yet, in that cold bottom, puffing with the gases of decay. They must have been three deep—piled on one another, she supposed, while drifting before some one of the winter's blizzards.

A little later, accosted by a stench so overpowering that she breathed it in deeply as if to sample the worst, she looked to the left and saw a longhorn, its belly blown up ready to pop, hanging by neck and horns from a tight clump of alder and black birch where the snow had left him. She saw the wind make cat's-paws in the heavy winter hair.

"Jesus," Ray said, "when you find 'em in *trees!*"

His boots, worn and whitened by many wettings, were braced against the dash. From the corner of her eye Molly could see his glove, its wrist lace open. His wrist looked as wide as a doubletree, the sleeve of his Levi jacket was tight with forearm. The very sight of his strength made her hate the tone of defeat and outrage in his voice. Yet she appraised the tone cunningly, for she did not want him somehow butting his bullheaded way back into it. There were better things they could do than break their backs and hearts in a hopeless country a hundred miles from anywhere.

With narrowed eyes, caught in an instant vision, she saw the lilac bushes by the front porch of her father's house, heard the screen door bang behind her brother Charley (screen doors!), saw people passing, women in dresses, maybe all going to a picnic or a ball game down in the park by the river. She passed the front of McCabe's General store and through the window saw the counters and shelves: dried apples, dried peaches, prunes, tapioca, Karo Syrup, everything they had done without for six weeks; and new white-stitched overalls, yellow horsehide gloves, varnished ax handles, barrels of flour and bags of sugar, shiny boots and work shoes, counters full of calico and flowered voile and crepe de chine and curtain net, whole stacks of flypaper stuck sheet to sheet, jars of peppermints and striped candy and horehound. . . . She giggled.

"What?" Ray's neck and shoulders were so stiff with muscle that he all but creaked when he turned his head.

"I was just thinking. Remember the night I used our last sugar to make that batch of divinity, and dragged the boys in after bedtime to eat it?"

"Kind of saved the day," Ray said. "Took the edge off ever'-body."

"Kind of left us starving for sugar, though. But I can see them picking up those little bitty dabs of fluff with their fingers like tongs, and stuffing them in among their whiskers and making faces, yum, yum, and wondering what on earth had got into me."

"Nothing got into you. You was just fed up. We all was."

"Remember when Slip picked up that pincushion I was tatting a cover for, and I got sort of hysterical and asked him if he knew what it was? Remember what he said? 'It's a doll piller, ain't it, Molly?' I thought I'd die."

She shook her head angrily and a tear splashed on the dash. Ray was looking sideways at her in alarm. She turned her face away and stared down across the water that spread nearly a half mile wide in the bottoms. Dirty foam and brush circled in the eddies. She saw a slab cave from an almost drowned cutbank and sink, bubbling. From where they drove, between the water and the outer slope that rolled up to the high prairie, the Cypress Hills made a snow-patched, tree-darkened dome across the west. The wind came off them mild as milk. *Poisoned!* she told herself, and dragged it deep into her lungs.

She was aware again of Ray's grey eye. "Hard on you," he said. For some reason he made her mad, as if he was accusing her of bellyaching. She felt how all the time they bumped and rolled along the shoulder of the river valley they had this antagonism between them like a snarl of barbed wire. You couldn't reach out anywhere without running into it. Did he blame her for going home, or what? What did he expect her to do, come along with a whole bunch of men on that roundup, spend six or eight weeks in pants out among the carcasses? And then what?

A high, sharp whicker came downwind. The team chuckled and surged into their collars. Looking ahead, she saw a horse —picketed, probably, or hobbled—and a man who leaned on something—rifle?—watching them. "Young Schulz," Ray said, and then there came the dogs, four big, bony hounds. The team began to dance. Ray held them in tight and whistled the buggy whip in the air when the hounds got too close.

Young Schulz, Molly saw as they got closer, was leaning on a shovel, not a rifle. He had dug a trench two or three feet deep and ten or twelve long. He dragged a bare forearm, across his forehead under a muskrat cap: a sullen-faced boy with eyes like dirty ice. She supposed he had been living all alone since his father had disappeared late in the winter. Somehow he made her want to turn her lips inside out. A wild man, worse than an Indian. She had not liked his father and she did not like him.

The hounds below her were sniffing at the wheels and testing the air up in her direction, wagging slow tails.

"What've you got, wolves?" Ray asked.

"Coyotes."

"Old ones down there?"

"One, anyway. Chased her in."

"Find any escape holes?"

"One. Plugged it."

"You get 'em the hard way," Ray said. "How've you been doing on wolves?"

The boy said a hard, four-letter word, slanted his eyes sideward at Molly in something less than apology—acknowledgment, maybe. "The dogs ain't worth a damn without Puma to kill for 'em. Since he got killed they just catch up with a wolf and run alongside him. I dug out a couple dens."

With his thumb and finger he worked at a pimple under his jaw. The soft wind blew over them, the taint of carrion only a suspicion, perhaps imaginary. The roily sky had begun to break up in patches of blue. Molly felt the solid bump of Ray's shoulder as he twisted to cast a weather eye upward. "Going to be a real

spring day," he said. To young Schulz he said, "How far in that
burrow go, d'you s'pose?"

"Wouldn't ordinarily go more'n twenty feet or so."

"Need any help diggin'?"

The Schulz boy spat.

"Ray . . ." Molly said. But she stopped when she saw his face.

"Been a long time since I helped dig out a coyote," he said.
He watched her as if waiting for a reaction. "Been a long time
since I did anything for *fun*."

"Oh, go ahead!" she said. "Long as we don't miss that train."

"I guess we can make Maple Creek by noon tomorrow. And
you ain't in such a hurry you have to be there sooner, are you?"

She had never heard so much edge in his voice. He looked at
her as if he hated her. She turned so as to keep the Schulz boy
from seeing her face, and for just a second she and Ray were all
alone up there, eye to eye. She laid a hand on his knee. "I don't
know what it is," she said. "Honestly I don't. But you better
work it off."

Young Schulz went back to his digging while Ray unhitched
and looped the tugs and tied the horses to the wheels. Then
Ray took the shovel and began to fill the air with clods. He moved
more dirt than the Fresno scrapers she had seen grading the
railroad back home; he worked as if exercising his muscles after
a long layoff, as if spring had fired him up and set him to running.
The soil was sandy and came out in clean brown shovelfuls. The
hounds lay back out of range and watched. Ray did not look
toward Molly, or say anything to Schulz; he just moved dirt as
if dirt was his worst enemy. After a few minutes Molly pulled
the buffalo robe out of the buckboard and spread it on the drying
prairie. By that time it was getting close to noon. The sun was
full out, warm on her face and hands.

The coyote hole ran along about three feet underground. From
where she sat she could look right up the trench and see the
black opening at the bottom when the shovel broke into it. She
could imagine the coyotes, crammed back at the end of their
burrow, hearing the noises and seeing the growing light as their
death dug toward them, and no way out, nothing to do but wait.

Young Schulz took the shovel and Ray stood out of the trench,
blowing. The violent work seemed to have made him more cheer-

ful. He said to Schulz, when the boy stooped and reached a gloved hand up the hole, "She comes out of there in a hurry, she'll run right up your sleeve."

Schulz grunted and resumed his digging. The untroubled sun went over, hanging almost overhead, and an untroubled wind stirred the old grass. Where the terrace of the floodplain rolled up to the prairie the first gopher of the season sat up and looked them over. A dog moved, and he disappeared with a flirt of his tail. Ray was rolling up his sleeves, whistling loosely between his teeth. His forearms were white, his hands blackened and cracked, as the charred end of sticks. His eyes touched her—speculatively, she thought. She smiled, making a forgiving, kissing motion of her mouth, but all he did in reply was work his eyebrows, and she could not tell what he was thinking.

Young Schulz was poking up the hole with the shovel handle. Crouching in the trench in his muskrat cap, he looked like some digging animal; she half expected him to put his nose into the hole and sniff and then start throwing dirt out between his hind legs.

Then in a single convulsion of movement Schulz rolled sideward. A naked-gummed thing of teeth and grey fur shot into sight, scrambled at the edge, and disappeared in a pinwheel of dogs. Molly leaped to the heads of the horses, rearing and wall-eyed and yanking the light buckboard sideways, and with a hand in each bridle steadied them down. Schulz, she saw, was circling the dogs with the shotgun, but it was clear that the dogs had already done it for him. The roaring and snapping tailed off. Schulz kicked the dogs away and with one quick flash and circle and rip tore the scalp and ears off the coyote. It lay there wet, mauled, bloody, with its pink skull bare—a little dog brutally murdered. One of the dogs came up, sniffed with its neck stretched out, sank its teeth in the coyote's shoulder, dragged it a foot or two.

"Ray . . ." Molly said.

He did not hear her; he was blocking the burrow with the shovel blade while Schulz went over to his horse. The boy came back with a red-willow stick seven or eight feet long, forked like a small slingshot at the end. Ray pulled away the shovel and Schulz probed in the hole with the forked end of the stick. A hard grunt came out of him, and he backed up, pulling the stick from the hole. At the last moment he yanked hard, and a squirm of grey broke free and rolled and was pounced on by the hounds.

This time Ray kicked them aside. He picked up the pup by the tail, and it hung down, blood on its fur, and kicked its hind legs a little. Schulz was down again, probing the burrow, twisting, probing again, twisting hard.

Again he backed up, working the entangled pup out carefully until it was in the open, and then landing it over his head like a sucker from the river. The pup landed within three feet of the buckboard wheel, and floundered, stunned. In an instant Molly dropped down and smothered it in clothes, hands, arms. There was snarling in her very ear, she was bumped hard, she heard Ray yelling, and then he had her on her feet. From his face, she thought he was going to hit her. Against her middle, held by the scruff and grappled with the other arm, the pup snapped and slavered with needle teeth. She felt the sting of bites on her hands and wrists. The dogs ringed her, kept off by Ray's kicking boot.

"God A'mighty," Ray said, "you want to get yourself killed?"

"I didn't want the dogs to get him."

"No. So maybe they get you. What are you going to do with him now, anyway? We'll just have to knock him in the head."

"I'm going to keep him."

"In Malta?"

"Why not?"

He let go his clutch on her arm. "He'll be a cute pup for a month and then he'll be a chicken thief and then somebody'll shoot him."

"At least he'll have a little bit of a life. Get *away*, you dirty, murdering . . ." She cradled the thudding little body along one arm under her mackinaw, keeping her hold in the scruff with her right hand, and turned herself away from the crowding hounds. "I'm going to tame him," she said. "I don't care what you say."

"Scalp's worth three dollars," Schulz said from the edge of the ditch.

Ray kicked the dogs back. His eyes, ordinarily so cool and grey, looked hot. The digging and the excitement did not seem to have taken the edge off whatever was eating him. He said, "Look, maybe you have to go back home to your folks, but you don't have to take a menagerie along. What are you going to do with him on the train?"

Now it was out. He did blame her. "You think I'm running out on you," she said.

"I just said you can't take a menagerie back to town."

"You said *maybe* I had to go home. Where else would I go? You're going to be on roundup till July. The ranch is going to be sold. Where on earth *would* I go but home?"

"You don't have to stay. You don't have to make me go back to ridin' for some outfit for twenty a month and found."

His dark, battered, scarred face told her to be quiet. Dipping far down in the tight pocket of his Levis he brought up his snap purse and took from it three silver dollars. Young Schulz, who had been probing the den to see if anything else was there, climbed out of the ditch and took the money in his dirty, chapped hand. He gave Molly one infuriatingly cool and knowing look with his dirty-ice eyes, scalped the dead pup, picked up shotgun and twisting stick and shovel, tied them behind the saddle, mounted, whistled at the dogs, and with barely a nod rode off toward the northeastern flank of the hills. The hounds fanned out ahead of him, running loose and easy. In the silence their departure left behind, a clod broke and rolled into the ditch. A gopher piped somewhere. The wind moved quiet as breathing in the grass.

Molly drew a breath that caught a little—a sigh for their quarreling, for whatever bothered him so deeply that he gloomed and grumped and asked something impossible of her—but when she spoke she spoke around it. "No thanks for your digging."

"He don't know much about living with people."

"He's like everything else in this country, wild and dirty and thankless."

In a minute she would really start feeling sorry for herself. But why not? Did it ever occur to him that since November she had seen exactly one woman, for one day and a night? Did he have any idea how she had felt, a bride of ten days, when he went out with the boys and was gone two weeks, through three different blizzards, while she stayed home and didn't know whether he was dead or alive?

"If you mean me," Ray said, "I may be wild and I'm probably dirty, but I ain't thankless, honey."

Shamed, she opened her mouth to reply, but he was already turning away to rummage up a strap and a piece of whang leather to make a collar and leash for her pup.

"Are you hungry?" she said to his shoulders.

"Any time."

"I put up some sandwiches."

"Okay."

"Oh, Ray," she said, "let's not crab at each other. Sure I'm glad we're getting out. Is that so awful? I hate to see you killing yourself bucking this *hopeless* country. But does that mean we have to fight? I thought maybe we could have a picnic like we had coming in, back on that slough where the ducks kept landing on the ice and skidding end over end. I don't know, it doesn't hardly seem we've laughed since."

"Well," he said, "it ain't been much of a laughing winter, for a fact."

He had cut down a cheek strap and tied a rawhide thong to it. Carefully she brought out the pup and he buckled the collar around its neck, but when she set it on the ground it backed up to the end of the thong, cringing and showing its naked gums, so that she picked it up again and let it dig along her arm, hunting darkness under her mackinaw.

"Shall we eat here?" Ray said. "Kind of a lot of chewed-up coyote around."

"Let's go up on the bench."

"Want to tie the pup in the buckboard?"

"I'll take him. I want to get him used to me."

"Okay," he said. "You go on. I'll tie a nose bag on these nags and bring the robe and the lunch box."

She walked slowly, not to scare the pup, until she was up the little bench and onto the prairie. From up there she could see not only the Cypress Hills across the west, but the valley of the Whitemud breaking out of them, and a big slough, spread by flood-water, and watercourses going both ways out of it, marked by thin willows. Just where the Whitemud emerged from the hills were three white dots—the Mountie post, probably, or the Lazy-S, or both. The sun was surprisingly warm, until she counted up and found that it was May 8. It *ought* to be warm.

Ray brought the buffalo robe and spread it, and she sat down. One-handed because she had the thong of the leash wrapped around her palm, she doled out sandwiches and boiled eggs. Ray popped a whole egg in his mouth, and chewing, pointed. "There goes the South Fork of the Swift Current, out of the slough. The one this side, that little scraggle of willows you can see, empties into the Whitemud. That slough sits right on the divide and runs both ways. You don't see that very often."

She appraised his tone. He was feeling better. For that matter, so was she. It had turned out a beautiful day, with big fair-weather clouds coasting over. She saw the flooded river bottoms below them, on the left, darken to winter and then sweep bright back to spring again while she could have counted no more than ten. As she moved, the coyote pup clawed and scrambled against her side, and she said, wrinkling her nose in her frecklefaced smile, "If he started eating me, I wonder if I could keep from yelling? Did you ever read that story about the boy that hid the fox under his clothes and the fox started eating a hole in him and the boy never batted an eye, just let himself be chewed?"

"No, I never heard that one," Ray said. "Don't seem very likely, does it?" He lay back and turned his face, shut-eyed, into the sun. Now and then his hand rose to feed bites of sandwich into his mouth.

"The pup's quieter," Molly said. "I wonder if he'd eat a piece of sandwich?"

"Leave him be for a while. I would."

"I guess."

His hand reached over blindly and she put another sandwich into its pincer claws. Chewing, he came up on one elbow, his eyes opened. He stared a long time down into the flooded bottoms and then across toward the slough and the hills. "Soon as the sun comes out, she don't look like the same country, does she?"

Molly said nothing. She watched his nostrils fan in and out as he sniffed.

"No smell up here, do you think?" he said.

But she heard the direction he was groping in, the regret that could lead, if they did not watch out, to some renewed and futile hope, and she said tartly, "I can smell it, all right."

He sighed. He lay back and closed his eyes. After about three minutes he said, "Boy, what a day, though. I won't get through on the patrol trail going back. The ice'll be breaking up before tonight, at this rate. Did you hear it crackin' and poppin' a minute ago?"

"I didn't hear it."

"Listen."

They were still. She heard the soft wind move in the prairie wool, and beyond it, filling the background, the hushed and hollow noise of the floodwater, sigh of drowned willows, suck of whirlpools, splash and guggle as cutbanks caved, and the steady push and swash and ripple of moving water. Into the soft rush of sound came a muffled report like a tree cracking, or a shot a long way off. "Is that it?" she said. "Is that the ice letting loose?"

"Stick around till tomorrow and you'll see that whole channel full of cakes."

Another shadow from one of the big flat-bottomed clouds chilled across them and passed. Ray said into the air, "Harry Willis said this railroad survey will go right through to Medicine Hat. Open up this whole country." Now in fear she sat very still, stroking the soft bulge of the pup through the cloth. "Probably mean a town of Eastend."

"You told me."

"With a store that close we couldn't get quite so snowed in as we did this winter."

Molly said nothing, because she dared not. They were a couple that—like the slough spread out northwest of them—flowed two ways, he to this wild range, she back to town and friends and family. And yet in the thaw of one bright day, their last together up here north of the line, she felt the potential weakening of her resolution. She herself teetered on a divide. She feared the softening that could start her draining toward his side of their never fully articulated argument.

"Molly," Ray said, and made her look at him. She saw him as the country and the winter had left him, weathered and scarred. His eyes were grey and steady, marksman's eyes.

She made a wordless sound that in her own ears seemed almost a groan. "You want awful bad to stay, somehow," she said.

His fingers plucked a strand of grass, he bit it between his teeth, his head went slowly up and down.

"But how?" she said. "Do you want to strike the Z-X for a job, or the Lazy-S, or somebody? Do you want to open a store in Eastend for when the railroad comes through, or what?"

"Haven't you figured that out yet?" he said. "I thought you'd see it in a minute. I want to buy the T-Down."

"You *what*?"

"I want us to buy the T-Down and make her go."

She felt that she went all to pieces. She laughed. She threw her hands around so that the pup scrambled and clawed at her side. "Ray Henry," she said, "you're crazy as a bedbug. Where'd we get the money?"

"Borrow it."

"Go in debt to stay up *here*?"

"Molly," he said, and she heard the slow gather of determination in his voice, "when else could we pick up cattle for twenty dollars a head with sucking calves thrown in? When else could we get a whole ranch layout for a few hundred bucks? That Goodnight herd we were running was the best herd in Canada. This spring roundup we could take our pick of what's left, including bulls, and burn our brand on 'em and turn 'em into summer range and drive everything else to Malta. We wouldn't want more than three, four hundred head. We can swing that much, and we can cut enough hay to bring that many through even a winter like this last one."

She watched him; her eyes groped and slipped.

He said, "We're never going to have another chance like this as long as we live. This country's going to change. There'll be homesteaders in here soon as the railroad comes. Towns, stores, what you've been missing. Womenfolks. We can sit out here on the Whitemud with good hay land and good range and just make this God-darned country holler uncle."

"How long?" she said. "How long have you been thinking this way?"

"Since we got John's letter."

"You never said anything."

"I kept waiting for you to get the idea yourself. But you were hell bent to get out."

She escaped his eyes, looked down, shifted carefully to accommodate the wild thing snuggled in darkness at her waist, and as she moved her foot scuffed up the scalloped felt edge of the buffalo robe. By her toe was a half-crushed crocus, palely lavender, a thing so tender and unbelievable in the waste of brown grass under the great pour of sky that she cried out, "Why, good land, look at that!"—taking advantage of it both as discovery and as diversion.

"Crocus?" Ray said, bending. "Don't take long, once the snow goes."

It lay in her palm, a thing lucky as a four-leaf clover, and as if it had had some effect in clearing her sight, Molly looked down the south-facing slope and saw it tinged with faintest green. She put the crocus to her nose, but smelled only a mild freshness, an odor no more showy than that of grass. But maybe enough to cover the scent of carrion.

Her eyes came up and found Ray's watching her steadily. "You think we could do it?" she asked.

"I know we could."

"It's a funny time to start talking that way, when I'm on my way out."

"You don't have to stay out."

Sniffing the crocus, she put her right hand under the mackinaw until her fingers touched fur. The pup stiffened, but did not turn or snap. She moved her fingers softly along his back, willing him tame. For some reason she felt as if she might bust out crying.

"Haven't you got any ambition to be the first white woman in five hundred miles?" Ray said.

Past and below him, three or four miles off, she saw the great slough darken under a driving cloud shadow and then brighten to a blue that flickered with little wind-whipped waves. She wondered what happened to the ice in a slough like that, whether it went on down the little flooded creeks to add to the jams in the Whitemud and Swift Current, or whether it just rose to the surface and gradually melted there. She didn't suppose it would be spectacular like the breakup in the river.

"Mamma and Dad would think we'd lost our minds," she said. "How much would we have to borrow?"

"Maybe six or eight thousand."

"Oh Lord!" She contemplated the sum, a burden of debt heavy enough to pin them down for life. She remembered the winter, six months of unremitting slavery and imprisonment. She lifted the crocus and laid it against Ray's dark scarred cheek.

"You should never wear lavender," she said, and giggled at the very idea, and let her eyes come up to his and stared at him, sick and scared. "All right," she heard herself say. "If it's what you want."

MAGAZINES CONSULTED

THE ANTIOCH REVIEW—212 Xenia Avenue, Yellow Springs, Ohio.

THE ARIZONA QUARTERLY—University of Arizona, Tucson, Arizona.

ARTESIAN—2223 S. Main Road, Ann Arbor, Michigan.

THE ATLANTIC MONTHLY—8 Arlington Street, Boston 16, Massachusetts.

AUDIENCE—140 Mt. Auburn Street, Cambridge 38, Massachusetts.

AUDIT—Box 92, Hayes Hall, University of Buffalo, Buffalo 14, New York.

BETWEEN WORLDS—Inter American University, San Germán, Puerto Rico.

CARLETON MISCELLANY—Carleton College, Northfield, Minnesota.

THE CAROLINA QUARTERLY—Box 1117, Chapel Hill, North Carolina.

CHELSEA REVIEW—Box 247, Old Chelsea Station, New York 11, New York.

CHICAGO REVIEW—University of Chicago, Chicago 37, Illinois.

COASTLINES—471 Sycamore Road, Santa Monica, California.

THE COLORADO QUARTERLY—Hellums 118, University of Colorado, Boulder, Colorado.

COMMENTARY—165 East 56th Street, New York 22, New York.

CONTACT—Box 755, Sausalito, California.

COSMOPOLITAN—57 Street and Eighth Avenue, New York 19, New York.

THE CRITIC—210 West Madison Street, Chicago 6, Illinois.

ENCOUNTER—25 Haymarket, London, S. W. 1, England.

EPOCH—159 Goldwin Smith Hall, Cornell University, Ithaca, New York.

ESQUIRE—488 Madison Avenue, New York 22, New York.

EVERGREEN REVIEW—64 University Place, New York 3, New York.

FANTASY AND SCIENCE FICTION—580 Fifth Avenue, New York 36, New York.

THE FAT ABBOT—278 Central Avenue, Needham, Massachusetts.

FOCUS MIDWEST—P. O. Box 3086, St. Louis 30, Missouri.

FOUR QUARTERS—La Salle College, Philadelphia 41, Pennsylvania.

GENESIS WEST—711 Concord Way, Burlingame, California.

GQ (GENTLEMEN'S QUARTERLY)—488 Madison Avenue, New York 22, New York.

THE GEORGIA REVIEW—University of Georgia, Athens, Georgia.

HARPER'S BAZAAR—572 Madison Avenue, New York 22, New York.

HARPER'S MAGAZINE—49 East 33rd Street, New York 16, New York.

THE HUDSON REVIEW—65 East 55th Street, New York 22, New York.

IDENTITY—Box 773, Boston 2, Massachusetts.

THE KENYON REVIEW—Kenyon College, Gambier, Ohio.

LADIES' HOME JOURNAL—1270 Sixth Avenue, New York 20, New York.

THE LITERARY REVIEW—Fairleigh Dickinson University, Teaneck, New Jersey.

MCCALL'S—230 Park Avenue, New York 17, New York.

MADEMOISELLE—575 Madison Avenue, New York 22, New York.

MAINSTREAM—832 Broadway, New York 3, New York.

THE MASSACHUSETTS REVIEW—University of Massachusetts, Amherst, Massachusetts.

MIDSTREAM—515 Park Avenue, New York 22, New York.

MINNESOTA REVIEW—Box 4068, University Station, Minneapolis, Minnesota.

MSS—702 Madrone, Chico, California.

MUTINY—Box 278, Northport, New York.

NEW MEXICO QUARTERLY—University of New Mexico Press, Marron Hall, Albuquerque, New Mexico.

NEW WORLD WRITING—c/o J. B. Lippincott Company, 521 Fifth Avenue, New York 17, New York.

THE NEW YORKER—25 West 43rd Street, New York 36, New York.

THE NOBLE SAVAGE—Meridian Books, 119 West 57th Street, New York 19, New York.

NORTHWEST REVIEW—Erb Memorial Student Union, University of Oregon, Eugene, Oregon.

THE OUTSIDER—618 Rue Ursulines, New Orleans 16, Louisiana.

THE PARIS REVIEW—45-39 171 Place, Flushing 58, New York.

PARTISAN REVIEW—22 East 17 Street, New York 3, New York.

PERSPECTIVE—Washington University Post Office, St. Louis 5, Missouri.

PLAYBOY—232 East Ohio Street, Chicago 11, Illinois.

PRAIRIE SCHOONER—Andrews Hall, University of Nebraska, Lincoln 8, Nebraska.

QUARTERLY REVIEW OF LITERATURE—Box 287, Bard College, Annandale-on-Hudson, New York.

RAMPARTS—1182 Chestnut Street, Menlo Park, California.

REDBOOK—Published by McCall Corp., 230 Park Avenue, New York 17, New York.

THE REPORTER—660 Madison Avenue, New York 21, New York.

SAN FRANCISCO REVIEW—Box 671, San Francisco, California.

THE SATURDAY EVENING POST—666 Fifth Avenue, New York 19, New York.

SEQUOIA—Box 2167, Stanford University, Stanford, California.

THE SEWANEE REVIEW—University of the South, Sewanee, Tennessee.

SHENANDOAH—Box 722, Lexington, Virginia.

SILO—Bennington College, Bennington, Vermont.

SOUTHWEST REVIEW—Southern Methodist University Press, Dallas 22, Texas.

STORY—135 Central Park West, New York 23, New York.

TEXAS QUARTERLY—Box 7527, University of Texas, Austin 12, Texas.

THE TRANSATLANTIC REVIEW—821 Second Avenue, New York 17, New York.

THE UNIVERSITY OF KANSAS CITY REVIEW—University of Kansas City, 51st and Rockhill Road, Kansas City, Missouri.

THE VIRGINIA QUARTERLY REVIEW—University of Virginia, 1 West Range, Charlottesville, Virginia.

VOGUE—420 Lexington Avenue, New York 17, New York.

WESTERN HUMANITIES REVIEW—Bldg. 41, University of Utah, Salt Lake City 12, Utah.

WOMAN'S DAY—67 West 44 Street, New York 36, New York.

THE YALE REVIEW—28 Hillhouse Avenue, New Haven, Connecticut.